MW00462205

MURDER AT THE MAJESTIC HOTEL

Books by Clara McKenna

MURDER AT MORRINGTON HALL

MURDER AT BLACKWATER BEND

MURDER AT KEYHAVEN CASTLE

MURDER AT THE MAJESTIC HOTEL

Published by Kensington Publishing Corp.

A Stella and Lyndy Mystery

MURDER AT THE MAJESTIC HOTEL

CLARA McKENNA

KENSINGTON
PUBLISHING CORP.

www.kensingtonbooks.com

KENSINGTON BOOKS are published by

Kensington Publishing Corp.
119 West 40th Street
New York, NY 10018

All Kensington titles, imprints and distributed lines are available at special quantity discounts for bulk purchases for sales promotion, premiums, fund-raising, educational or institutional use. Special book excerpts or customized printings can also be created to fit specific needs. For details, write or phone the office of the Kensington Special Sales Manager: Kensington Publishing Corp., 119 West 40th Street, New York, NY, 10018. Attn. Special Sales Department. Phone: 1-800-221-2647.

The K with book logo Reg. U.S. Pat. & TM Off.

Library of Congress Control Number: 2022939870

ISBN: 978-1-4967-3818-9

First Kensington Hardcover Edition: November 2022

ISBN: 978-1-4967-3819-6 (e-book)

10 9 8 7 6 5 4 3 2 1

Printed in the United States of America

To a wee lass who feels more like family than friend

CHAPTER 1

Late September 1905
Yorkshire, England

Horace cursed as his ankle twitched, and he nearly missed the step. The doorman reflectively reached for his arm, but Horace waved him off. He regained his balance and tottered through the open door. Sharply sucking in his breath, Horace lurched to a halt. He hadn't prepared himself properly for the flood of memories: of a newlywed couple eager to start their new life together, of countless family holidays with Agnes and Morgan, of somber visits to the nearby churchyard. With tears blurring his vision, his lips relaxed into a bittersweet smile. He'd made the right choice to come.

This was where it all began.

Though filled with strangers, the lobby was the same as greeted him forty years ago. Granted, the crystal chandelier and the myriad of sconces lining the whitewashed walls were electrified now, but the black and white marble tiles still reflected the bottom of his shoes. The fireplace, tall enough for a child of ten to stand in, glowed as usual with a crackling warmth, while the shiny black grand piano sat silent in the corner. Horace imagined the gentle strains of Liszt's *Liebesträume* or some other sweet melody drifting across the room. Clusters of inviting sofas and chairs beckoned him to rest his weary, old bones. He envied the young man in the herringbone cap taking advantage of the seat near the fire to read his paper. Horace inhaled deeply. Even the lush bouquets of roses placed here and there about the lobby evoked a time long past.

Gratefully, without being asked, a porter, a young towheaded fellow, slipped past to collect his luggage outside, where the hansom cab driver had left it; Horace's hands weren't much use these days. With his hand visible shaking, Horace was fortunate not to drop the green and gold chocolate box he carried. *Just in case.* A handsome couple, dressed for a night on the town, skirted around him. He tipped his top hat at their indulgence (he was blocking their way, after all) and gathered his strength before approaching the long mahogany desk on the far end of the lobby. The strapping clerk, his back turned, busily sorted the day's last post into the pigeonholes that lined the wall. Horace, already tiring, cleared his throat to get the clerk's attention. He couldn't afford for this to take too long.

"I would like the Honeymoon Suite for the night, young man."

The clerk, in his black coat and tie, reminded Horace of himself thirty years ago, fit with a full head of dark ginger curls. The clerk said nothing but stared, unblinking, sizing him up. In a few seconds, he'd studied Horace's expensive, well-tailored suit, his closely trimmed white beard, the piercing green stare that challenged him to find fault. Horace would've almost enjoyed the battle of wills had he been a few years younger, but now he just wanted his bed.

Having met with approval, the clerk asked respectfully, "And you are, sir?"

"Horace Wingrove."

The clerk flipped the registration book open. "I beg your

apologies, Mr. Wingrove," the clerk said, after flipping back and forth in consternation several times, "but it seems that suite has been reserved for the next fortnight. In someone else's name, sir. Can I get you another suite, perhaps?"

"No. I'm intent on sleeping in the Honeymoon Suite tonight, young man."

The clerk's glance darted around the room before lowering his voice. "I wish there was summat I could do for you, sir." The clerk licked his lips.

Horace knew the type. This was a man willing to break the rules, for a price, and he'd come prepared.

He first set his top hat and then the chocolate box, its gold ribbon slightly worse for wear, down on the shiny surface of the desk. He could see his withered face in it as he leaned forward. "I'll be needing it for the one night."

"Ah, but this reservation was made far in advance." The insincere regret marked the clerk as one who'd done this before. "A young viscount and his new bride are expected any moment."

"I stayed in that suite on my honeymoon night, forty years ago," Horace said, reaching into his breast pocket. "Would it make a difference if I told you my dear wife, Marie, passed on to the next world only two months ago?"

"I sympathize, Mr. Wingrove, I truly do, but if I let you have that suite, what am I going to tell Lord Lyndhurst when he arrives?"

"Don't you have another where you can put His Lordship? It would only be one night, mind."

"I am sorry, sir, but rules are rules."

Horace pinched the envelope twice before he was confident he wouldn't drop it. The clerk licked his lips again when Horace produced the plain white envelope and tucked it beneath the bow on the chocolate box, obscuring the picture and brand name.

"Here." Horace slid the box a few inches toward the clerk.

"Accept this small token of my gratitude for allowing this old man one last night in your fine establishment. Your sweetheart will thank you."

Horace followed the clerk's furtive glance behind him. He caught sight of someone ducking behind one of the massive pillars that punctuated the lobby. *Was he seeing things?* No one knew where he was, surely. Then why did he think he'd seen Lily? It couldn't be her. He'd left her in Wolverhampton. Was he no longer able to trust his sense either? What was going to go next? Horace didn't want to find out.

He turned back as the clerk slid the box toward him. The clerk gingerly pulled the envelope out, revealing the box's cover—an illustrated portrait of a lovely young woman with porcelain skin and a genial smile on her rosy lips. "WINGROVE'S CREAM MILK" was written in large letters below the picture.

Horace chuckled at the flash of recognition, the clerk's eyes darting from him to the box and back to him again. He never tired of people's reactions when making the connection. The clerk peeked inside at the hundred-pound note. Then the envelope was gone, tucked away somewhere beneath the desk. The clerk, transformed by his broadening grin, reached toward the row of dangling keys. He snatched up the one hanging beneath the label "Honeymoon Suite," and handed it to Horace.

He tapped the bell on the desk, and over the high-pitched ring, called, "Max!" The towheaded porter reappeared, a suitcase in his hand.

"Bring Mr. Wingrove's case to the Honeymoon Suite, won't you, and see that he's got everything he needs."

"Aye, Mr. Coombs," the young man answered. "If you'll follow me, sir." The porter raised Horace's case with an ease Horace couldn't ever remember having and indicated with his arm the lift across the lobby.

"Thank you again, young man," Horace said to the clerk,

sliding his top hat off the desk and slapping it on his head. "And do apologize to the young couple I've displaced. Though if I remember right, they won't care if they're given a linen cupboard to stay in as long as it's private." His face brightened, recalling memories, as fresh today as forty years ago, and the hope of unsullied young love.

"Enjoy your stay at the Majestic Hotel, Mr. Wingrove."

"And you enjoy your chocolates, Mr. Coombs."

Horace winked at the clerk, pleased he'd read the man right. Horace glimpsed back at the pillars as he hobbled after the porter with his case. But was he right about the others? If Horace couldn't trust his senses, could he no longer trust his instincts? He prayed it hadn't come to that. All his plans depended upon it.

Felix Middleton hadn't given the old fellow a second thought. After an early dinner and a pint or two or three at the nearest pub, Felix had settled in to read the latest news by the fire. The longer he lingered here, the less time he had to spend in that dim-lit, top-floor room. What was he, a servant? But it was the best view he could afford. As he sat there, guests came and went. Wealthy couples, in their baubles and glitter, heading out for the opera, businessmen hoping to loosen their ties after a long day on the train, groups of giggling country girls with their dowdy chaperones in tow here to do some shopping. What use did Felix have for any of them? The old fellow was no different. That is until he'd heard the porter mention "Their Royal Highnesses."

Felix lifted the broadsheet to cover his face as the porter paused near his spot, waiting for the old fellow, shuffling along as slow as golden treacle, to catch up.

"You're not going to the statue unveiling?" the porter said.

Felix couldn't avoid the headline inches from his face: MEMORIAL STATUE UNVEILING OF LATE QUEEN VIC-

TORIA. He'd just finished reading the article. Felix had heard about little else since the day he arrived. Princess Beatrice, Queen Victoria's youngest, and the princess's daughter, Princess Victoria Eugenie, "Ena," were to visit York to unveil a statue of the deceased monarch. From what Felix could gather, everybody who was anybody would be there. Felix wouldn't miss it for his grannie's funeral. He rubbed his hand over the stubble shadowing his chin, curious as to the old fella's answer.

"No, son, I have no intention of attending the royal event." The pair moved off a bit to wait for the lift to arrive.

Felix shook the newspaper straight as he turned the crinkled page, frustrated. Something didn't settle right about the old fella's tone. He tried to pay them no mind, but with the temporary hush falling over the lobby, Felix couldn't block their conversation out.

"Why ever not?" the porter asked.

"I have more momentous things to attend to."

"What could be more important than seeing Their Royal Highnesses? Ah, I get it." The porter set down the old fella's case as if he couldn't think and hold it at the same time. "You're one of those, ain't ya?"

"One of those?"

Felix peered over the edge of the paper, careful not to get caught earwigging. The porter was pointing to the painting of York Minster hung across from the lift, the massive Gothic cathedral dominating the skyline of the city. Even with the hotel being outside the city walls, any vantage point above the first floor offered an impressive view. That included Felix's room.

"The sort who come to York just to visit the Minster," the porter said disparagingly. "And miss everything else."

Felix, his muscles taut with anticipation, studied the old gent. He was posh and proud, but he twitched now and again, his fingers or the side of his face, as if he were waging an inner battle. Had Felix seen him before? *Was he one of us?* As if sensing Felix's scrutiny, the old fella's gaze swept over the lobby. When he spotted Felix, he hesitantly dipped his head in greeting. Felix pinched the brim of his cap in response. The old fella quietly chuckled, almost in relief, before turning his attention to the arriving lift.

The porter pulled back the lift door with its wrought-iron fretwork. Inside, the attendant waited patiently for instructions.

"The proper term for *that sort*," the old man explained, "is *cathedral enthusiasts.*"

Hearing those words, Felix bolted from his chair, casting aside the paper. As the old fella hobbled into the lift, the rest of what he said was muffled. Felix had to know more. He dashed toward the lift as the porter stepped in.

"Oi. 'old up!" Felix shouted.

The attendant, gripping the door handle, waited. Felix slipped into the crowded lift, the old fella's labored breath hot on his neck as he shuffled to make room. The overpowering scent of bay rum made Felix cough.

"Floor?" the attendant asked.

"Fourth," was the porter's reply.

"Same," Felix said. Near to bursting, he could hardly wait to chat the old fella up as the lift attendant slid the door shut with a *clang*.

Stella lifted her head from Lyndy's shoulder as the hansom cab halted beneath the stone-columned porte cochere. They were finally here. After spending their wedding night in London, they'd spent hours traveling by train. The sky had opened up as they passed through Peterborough, the strong wind lashing the rain against their private, first-class carriage's windows, obscuring any hint of the passing countryside. Not that she had minded, lying cradled in Lyndy's arms, far from Morrington

Hall, far from the trauma and confusion of the past few days (*First Daddy's death and then to see Mama!*), far from any concerns of their future together. She had Lyndy all to herself. She'd never been so happy.

Lyndy kissed her temple. "Shall we?" he whispered.

The dark had drawn around them, and the rain hadn't let up. Though they'd raced from the train station to the cab, the rain had dampened their clothes, gloves, hats, and hair. Stella peered through the rain-splattered window at the hotel's bright, sparkling electric light welcoming them. Soon she'd be in a dry bed snuggled against Lyndy's warm body. Her heart quickened in anticipation.

How had she ever slept alone?

The hotel doorman skittered down the steps and hurriedly opened the door, flooding the cab with earthy-scented cool air. Stella shivered. Lyndy alighted and offered her his hand. Clutching her soggy hat (the green velvet ribbons now ruined), she allowed him to help her down. With the rain held at bay under their sheltered spot, she lingered a moment to take it all in.

With its crenellated six-story wings of yellow and brown brick, the hotel spanned away on either side of the drive. Despite being in the city, it was surrounded by extensive parkland punctuated by halo-encircled lampposts. Stella could scarcely remember Brown's Hotel, where they'd spent last night. Overwhelmed with anxiety and passion, she could've spent the night in a horse stall for all that she noticed her surroundings. The Majestic Hotel, claiming to be the finest in York, was aptly named. It resembled a dazzling, modern castle.

Castle. Stella shivered again, and not from the cold. Would she always be reminded of that tragedy at Keyhaven? How could she not? But that didn't mean she'd let it spoil a minute of her honeymoon. This was York, after all, a city of ancient history and wonder. After a good night's sleep, she was determined to explore every inch.

Explore every inch. Heat crept up Stella's neck and into her face as she recalled Lyndy's whispered desire last night. She'd been so nervous. What woman, particularly one raised by a man who showed her no genuine affection, wouldn't be? But Lyndy surprised her. She'd had no idea how tender and gentle a man could be. And he was all hers.

With a quick kiss, Stella pecked his cheek, uncharacteristically bristly with unshaven whiskers, as he paid the cab driver. Startled, he swiftly recovered, allowing a thin, knowing smile to spread across his lips, desire smoldering in his dark brown eyes.

"Let's go in," Stella said, grabbing hold of his hand as the cab with Ethel, Finn, and their luggage arrived.

They passed two bellhops in their brightly colored caps, descending the stairs to help the servants as Stella eagerly pulled Lyndy up them.

"How satisfying it is to have a wife as eager to be alone with you as you are with her," he quipped.

Not denying it, Stella giggled as they entered the bright hotel. Stark with its vaulted ceiling, white marble columns, white walls, and fine-cut crystal chandeliers, the warmth of the lobby resonated from the details: plush, green velvet-covered couches, pink rose bouquets, lush ferns, its roaring fire. In her burgundy-trimmed green traveling suit with a white-lace-fronted shirtwaist, Stella matched the decor. They followed the colorful Persian runner to the registration desk, where Lyndy announced himself.

"Good evening, Lord and Lady Lyndhurst. We've been expecting you," the square-faced man behind the desk gushed.

Lady Lyndhurst. The sound of it thrilled Stella. She, a girl from Kentucky who'd spent most of her life surrounded by straw and horses, was a viscountess now. She still couldn't believe it.

"Welcome to the Majestic. I'm Mr. Herman Haigh, hotel manager, and I am delighted to be at your service day or night for whatever your needs may be."

"Thank you, Haigh," Lyndy said. "Right now, all we require is our key."

Stella wrapped her arms around one of Lyndy's and smiled sheepishly at the manager. "It's been a very long journey," she said. "You'll see that our servants get settled in?"

"Very good, my lady." Mr. Haigh lowered the spectacles resting on his high forehead to read the registration book laid out before him. "Ah, yes, two top-floor rooms for your staff and the Honeymoon Suite."

The manager tapped the book twice appreciatively before turning to the bank of keys dangling behind him. Stella noticed the Honeymoon Suite hook was empty. Mr. Haigh involuntarily winced under Lyndy's impatient scrutiny before again referring to the registration book.

"I do apologize, my lord. If you'll wait one moment." He forced a nervous smile as he shoved his spectacles back onto his forehead. As he turned away, his lips thinned into a grim, straight line. He disappeared into the door to the left of the desk. "Charlie!" he barked.

"What the devil is going on?" Lyndy muttered, his jaw clenched as he restrained his building frustration.

Mr. Haigh reappeared, empty handed. He slammed on the desk bell.

"Charlie," he called, more restrained for having witnesses. He reluctantly faced the waiting couple. "I am terribly sorry for the inconvenience, my lord, but the key to your suite appears to have gone missing. There you are." This was directed at a burly clerk with two perfect waves of reddish-brown hair on either side of his part. "Charlie. Lord and Lady Lyndhurst are most patiently waiting to be taken to their room. Where is the key to the Honeymoon Suite?"

"There must be some mistake. Mr. Wingrove is staying there tonight." The clerk purposely dodged Lyndy's piercing stare, keeping his attention on his boss.

"But I arranged for those rooms in advance," Lyndy said.

A little over two weeks ago, they'd attended the races in Doncaster. Seeing how much Stella had enjoyed the area, Lyndy had suggested exploring more of Yorkshire and honeymooning at the Majestic Hotel in York. She had wholeheartedly agreed.

"How could this have happened?" Mr. Haigh demanded.

"I haven't the foggiest idea."

"You're the desk clerk, Charlie. How can you not know?" The manager sputtered, trying his best to contain his fury.

The clerk shrugged as if as baffled by the mix-up as anyone. "Bright side, Mr. Haigh. It's only for tonight."

"Bright side? Only for . . . ?" The manager struggled to re-gain his composure. Mimicking a restrained smile, he spoke through his teeth. "Where then do you propose His Lord and Ladyship spend the night?"

"The Royal Suite's available."

The manager waved Charlie off. "Go help with the luggage. Forgive me, my lord, my lady," Mr. Haigh said as Charlie saun-tered way. "This is most irregular, but rest assured, I will see you're well situated. We have many well-appointed rooms."

He slid his spectacles down again, referred to the registration book briefly, grabbed a key, and held it out to Lyndy. The brass key and fob glinted in the harsh electric light.

"The Royal Suite. It is identical in almost every way to the one you reserved. A night free of charge, of course. I will see to it that complimentary champagne is sent up as well." Mr. Haigh peered over the rim of his fogged-up spectacles. "Would that suit Your Lordship?"

Lyndy grumbled, about to say something to the contrary, when Stella leaned in and whispered in his ear. "The sooner we get our key, the sooner we can get out of these wet clothes."

"Right you are." Lyndy snatched the key from the relieved manager, and the couple eagerly headed toward the elevator.

CHAPTER 2

Despite his eagerness to be alone with Stella, Lyndy's ardor had been severely dampened, not by the miserable weather (he'd quite enjoyed having to keep each other warm), but by the affront of being denied his suite. They were on their honeymoon, were they not? Then why were they not staying in that said suite, which was hailed as the finest guest accommodation in the city? Lyndy had wanted nothing but the best for his new bride.

"The audacity of them to give our rooms away."

Stella playfully shook his arm she held tightly, a mischievous grin on her bow-shaped lips. "What difference does it make? As long as it has a bed, a fire, and you."

My God, how I love this woman.

She was right. Why should Lyndy care what the suite was called as long as they were alone? Not waiting for the porter, Lyndy unlocked the door. It opened onto a good-sized room, much about the size of the drawing-room at Morrington Hall, with a scattering of plush sofas, rosewood armchairs, and an intimate dining area. The ceiling-to-floor windows, streaked with rain, promised bright light and a view of the towers of York Minster, providing the skies cleared by morning. Unlit coals sat ready in the carved stone fireplace. To the right was the bedroom, equipped purportedly with an adjacent bath and dressing room. Off to the left was a small sitting room with a secretary desk and a second fireplace. Yes, the rooms were quite suitable but for the rich purple accents throughout. The drapery, the chair cushions, the table linen, all were in varying shades of purple. Threads the color of aubergine were woven into the thick Persian carpets. The four-poster bed's counterpane was the color of spring lilacs. Even the bouquets of pink roses on the side tables were accented with spikes of lavender.

Royal, indeed. Despite its association, Lyndy had never been fond of the color. Mother adored it.

With no such repulsion, Stella threw her overcoat over the nearest chair and hurried to the fireplace. Not waiting for the servants or porter to do it, Stella, as proficient as a housemaid, located the matches from the coal scuttle, stuck one against the box, and cupping her hand to prevent the draft from extinguishing the flame, lit the prebuilt fire. Red and yellow flame licked the wood beneath the coals, and soon tendrils of gray smoke from the burning coal ascended the chimney.

"Care to join me?" she said, slipping gracefully to the carpeted floor. An adorable smudge of ash dotted her nose where she'd touched it.

Instantly dismissing his misgivings, Lyndy strode eagerly toward her, sloughing off his overcoat, jacket, and tie. He never made it. Without warning, a small brown winged creature darted from the chimney and shot into the room.

"Augh!" Stella squealed, flapping her hands about her head and face, as the tiny pipistrelle bat, barely the size of her hand, swooped back and forth above their heads.

Lyndy couldn't help but chuckle as the woman he loved, who could tussle with a thousand-pound racehorse and win, leaped to her feet and ran scurrying from the room. From the safety of the hall, she demanded he do something.

"What would you have me do?"

"I don't know. Open a window and shoo it out!"

This wasn't the moment to enlighten her about Morrington Hall—bats that frequently roosted in its chimneys were much larger than this tiny pipistrelle. He was surprised she hadn't encountered one there yet. He turned the wrought-iron latch and shoved the windows open. A chilly breeze swept in, ruffling his open collar. He doubted the bat would choose to fly back out into such weather but didn't say so.

"There's a bat in our suite," Stella told the distinctive young porter arriving with the luggage; his hair was so light, it looked almost white.

"Can I help, m'lord?"

"Yes." Lyndy pointed to the brown spot perched almost imperceptibly above the bedroom door frame. "It's just there. Remove it if you would."

"But don't kill it," Stella directed as the porter took to his task.

"It's only a bat," Lyndy teased, but he instantly regretted it.

He'd found her fright amusing at first, but to see the tips of her ears flaming red in distress, the bulk of her silky light-brown bun flopping to one side, her hand pressed against her mouth as she hugged her arms against her chest, chastened him. She'd been petrified.

This isn't how I envisioned this at all.

Someday he'd get her to tell him why (he imagined her father at the root of it), but for now, all Lyndy could do was pace, which is what he was doing when the porter reappeared.

"I've managed to get it out the window, Your Lordship," he said. "Is there owt you need assistance with?"

"No, that will be all."

"Thank you." Stella rewarded the porter with a brilliant, appreciative smile.

With the porter retreating toward the lift, a lopsided grin plastered on his face, Stella flung her arms around Lyndy in relief. He returned the embrace, wrapping his arms about her waist, but catching sight of the brass plate on the door opposite rekindled the grievance he had with the Honeymoon Suite's present occupant. Who was this usurper, Wingrove, anyway? Wasn't he the cause of all this fuss? Lyndy gently extricated himself from Stella's arms and strode across the hall.

"Where are you going?"

"Perhaps this Wingrove chap can be persuaded to switch."

"Like you said, it's just a bat."

"You shouldn't have had to suffer that."

"But now it's gone. We can go back in."

Despite Stella's objections, he knocked. No answer. He knocked again, more insistently. He'd lifted his fist to pound when a slow shuffling inside preceded the door creaking open.

"Yes?"

Lyndy immediately regretted his impulsiveness. The man before him was old, feeble, and in visible pain. He gripped the edge of the door frame as if in need of support.

"Mr. Wingrove?"

"Yes?"

"May I introduce myself. I am Viscount Lyndhurst, and this is my wife, Lady Lyndhurst." He indicated Stella, who had joined him and, now standing behind, rested her chin on his shoulder.

"I see." Amusement flickered across the older man's face. "The honeymooning couple. How lovely."

Did he know of us? Lyndy had assumed otherwise.

"Yes, well, it seems there's been a mistake. We reserved these rooms"—Lyndy pointed over Mr. Wingrove's shoulder—"for the fortnight. For some reason, which has yet to be satisfactorily explained, you were given the key instead. I propose that we switch suites and no harm done."

"I do apologize, young man, with you being on your honeymoon with such an exquisite creature as Lady Lyndhurst"—here he returned Stella's unabashed smile with a warm but weary grin—"but I must refuse."

Had he heard the commotion about the bat?

"Surely you haven't settled in so that you can't move across the hall?"

"Ah, but across the hall wouldn't be as desirable, or you wouldn't fancy switching."

Taken aback by Wingrove's audacity, Lyndy clenched his jaw. Noticing, Stella pecked him on the cheek.

"Besides, young man, it's only for one night."

True, but his admonishing tone was more than Lyndy could take.

"Quite but—"

"Why is this suite so important to you, Mr. Wingrove?" Stella asked, cutting off Lyndy's retort. "Mr. Haigh said it was the same as the Royal Suite."

Yet without the bats or the offending color.

From what Lyndy could see beyond the old chap, this suite was tastefully decorated with gold, green, and deep hues of blue.

"Not exactly." Mr. Wingrove's vacant stare drifted past them as if witnessing something only he could see.

"Marie and I honeymooned here over forty years ago," Wingrove said in a singsong voice. "My dear wife loved this suite, this hotel, this city. With her now gone, I vowed I'd enjoy it in her stead, even if for one more time." His eyes snapped to Lyndy's, his tone turning sharp. "Although I do appreciate your request, my lord, I am unable to accommodate you."

Unable or unwilling?

Wingrove held up his hand as Lyndy began to object. It twitched twice. "Nothing you can say will change my mind."

Lyndy, frustrated at being thwarted, though not unsympathetic, tugged on his shirtsleeve. It was still damp.

"Ah, but there is something I can do for you," Mr. Wingrove added, pointing a thin, shaky finger at them.

He hobbled back into the suite. Stella leaned against Lyndy's back, her breath warm against his neck, standing on her tiptoes, straining to see what the old chap was up to. Mr. Wingrove had made his way to a fine leather suitcase laying open on the stand. It was empty but for four green cardboard boxes tied with gold ribbon. Another reason Wingrove didn't want to be put out. He'd already unpacked. Wingrove brought one of the boxes to the door and handed it to Lyndy.

"Here." It was a box of chocolates. "Enjoy these and think of how you've let an old man rest in peace."

"Thank you," Stella said, eagerly reaching around Lyndy and accepting the box for him. "We will."

"Good night, young ones," the old man said pleasantly. "Cherish each other." Without waiting for their reply, he closed the door in their face.

"I say," Lyndy protested at the abrupt dismissal.

Stella slipped off the ribbon, lifted the lid, and selected a square piece of chocolate. Lyndy only then caught the company's name blazoned across the top, "Wingrove's."

"Here. Have one." She offered to feed it to him. Lyndy parted his lips, and she slipped the luscious bite into his mouth. Its sweet richness started to melt the moment it met his tongue. He had to hand it to the old man. The chocolate was exquisite.

"Now, what were we doing before that bat disturbed us?" Stella said meaningfully, an impish glint in her eye. "Getting out of our wet clothes, weren't we?"

In an instant, Lyndy forgot his dislike of purple, his annoyance at the chocolatier, forgot even the splendid taste of chocolate from a moment ago. "Yes. Yes, we were."

In one swift motion, he swept her into his arms, the chocolates threatening to spill out as Stella wrapped her arms around his neck. She squealed with delight.

"My lord! You surprise me."

"I surprise myself," he admitted. Before Stella, he'd never done anything so flirtatious, so spontaneous. And in public too. "Shall we proceed?" he teased, nuzzling her neck and covering it with kisses.

"By all means."

With that, he carried her, both laughing, across the hall, and finding the room empty of any bothersome bats, kicked the door closed with his foot.

Stella rested her cheek against the pillow as Lyndy traced the length of her neck with hot, gentle kisses. She shifted to capture his lips with her own, wrapping her arms around his shoulders and pulling him to her. She couldn't get close enough.

"Bugger off the pair of ya!" A door slammed, and someone began pounding on it from outside in the hall.

The hostility jolted Stella upright. Flashes of her father's temper flooded her with emotions she hadn't had to face in days—grief, guilt, fear. But Lyndy's warmth as he wrapped his arm around her bare shoulders, pulling her protectively to him, eased it all away.

"Horace, please," a woman's voice pleaded. "We need to speak with you."

"Confound it, Uncle, what's going on?" a man's voice demanded. The pounding continued.

"Bloody hell," Lyndy whispered as he flung the bedclothes off.

For a moment, the sight of his skin, the well-formed muscles in his back glistening with sweat in the glow of the fire, made her forget there was an altercation taking place a few feet from their door. Then curiosity overcame her, and she followed Lyndy in slipping off the bed, wrapping her silk dressing gown around her. Wanting to see how the argument would play out, she laid a hand on Lyndy's shoulder as he, poised to storm into the hall demanding he and his bride be left in peace, reached for the doorknob. He hesitated, preparing to object, but she put her finger to her lips and, reaching past him, turned the brass knob. It was pleasantly cool against her clammy palm.

What compelled her to eavesdrop on Mr. Wingrove's argument, she couldn't say. Was it memories of her father? Did she need to know why someone was disturbing the older man's peace in order to restore her own? She should either ignore the clash in the hall or let Lyndy put a stop to it. She did neither. Instead, with Lyndy peering over her shoulder, Stella peeked out through the tiny crack she'd opened in the door. Though he'd never admit it, Lyndy was as curious about what was going on as she was.

Across the hall, a tall woman, smartly dressed in a brown, tailored traveling suit, the same coffee color as her expensively coiffed hair, not a strand of it out of place beneath her cream, felt toque, continued to bang on the Honeymoon Suite door. A bare-headed man, with a full sandy-blond mustache and prominent square chin, stood off to the side behind her, disheveling his hair more and more as he combed his hands through it in frustration. His dark gray pant legs were wrinkled, presumably by sitting uneasily for too long. He was in his mid to late twenties, she slightly older, by five, perhaps even ten years. Stella would never have assumed they'd make a couple. Yet, here they were, alone together at this time of night, demanding entrance to Mr. Wingrove's room. But then again, she wasn't the best judge. Who would've bet she and Lyndy would make such a good pair?

"Oh, all right," Mr. Wingrove said before he swung open his door. "Stop that infernal pounding."

The old man was in his dressing gown, but with his hair neat and his expression wary, he hadn't the look of someone recently woken. He clutched the doorknob and leaned on the door's edge. His face was flush as he scanned the hall beyond his intruders. Stella cringed, despite knowing full well that from that distance, he couldn't tell their door was cracked open, let alone that they were spying on him.

"This is a respectable hotel, not some fire station. You'll wake everyone."

"Uncle, won't you let us in?" the young man asked.

"So, Lily, it wasn't my imagination after all," Mr. Wingrove said, meaningfully dressing down the woman with his frosty glare. The woman shouldered past him into the room.

"I don't know what you're going on about, Horace."

"I thought I left you in Wolverhampton," the old man grumbled. "I should've known you would follow me here. You might as well come in too, Morgan."

"We didn't come to be a bother."

Mr. Wingrove dismissed him with a wave as he shuffled back into the suite. The nephew disappeared inside, closing the door behind him.

"What was that all about?" Stella said, turning to face Lyndy.

"As long as they are done disturbing us, I couldn't care less." Lyndy slipped his hand under her loose, cascading hair, resting it on the nape of her neck. He leaned into her, guiding her against the door, which closed with a faint click. "Now, my love, where were we?"

His lips met hers softly at first, then pressed more firmly as he sought to move past the interruption. With questions swirling in her head, Stella couldn't dismiss it as easily. Who was that couple? What were they doing here after midnight? Why was Mr. Wingrove so upset about seeing them? But as Lyndy's other hand slipped beneath her dressing gown, finding its way to the small of her back, her mind emptied, and she could think of nothing but his touch. She returned his kiss with a hunger that surprised her.

A startling bang of a door resounded from the hall.

"That's it! I've had enough."

Lyndy broke away in frustration and anger, ready to yank

the door open and demand an apology. But voices, on the other side, stilled him yet again. It was the disruptive couple walking past. Through the door, Stella caught snippets.

"Not well."

"Difficult to reason with."

"He's getting worse."

"Something must be done."

Stella assumed they were referring to Mr. Wingrove. But what did they mean?

Lyndy, determined to say his piece, eased Stella aside. But when he flung open the door, still tying the belt around his dressing gown, the pair was gone.

CHAPTER 3

Felix took one last swig from the bottle and laid it sideways on the ground. He tapped it with his foot, with the idea of dribbling it down the path. In his primary school days, he'd once fancied himself rather good at football, but it was no good. The glass was too slick, and his foot slipped before he gained control. The bottle rumbled swiftly across the paving stones beyond his reach, and he ran to catch up. Unsteady on his feet, the next kick caught the bottle with the tip of his boot, sending it careening toward the river.

"Goal!" he cried at the satisfying but unintended splash.

He must be getting on. Yet he lingered a moment, appreciating the widening ripples on the glass-like surface before climbing the stairs to the Lendal Bridge. A lone narrowboat chugged down the channel toward him. Felix paused on the bridge as it slid beneath and out of sight. Lit by a few widely spaced lamps, the bridge, like the stretch of road as far up as York Minster, was free of traffic. Felix had timed his journey well.

Turning his back to the narrowboat, he stepped out of a pool of light and crossed. Downriver, a stone's throw away, was the

Guildhall, a dirty, yellow-colored, stone, medieval building fronting the river where the royals planned to host the statue unveiling. Felix leaned over the stone railing of the bridge and spat into the river. He tapped the box under his arm before continuing on.

Within a few moments of chatting up the old fella, Felix had realized his mistake. Mr. Wingrove had not been who Felix hoped he'd be. But he was nothing if not generous, and seeing Felix's disappointment, the old bloke had produced this lovely consolation gift. The box of sweets was what put this idea into Felix's head. It was brilliant if Felix did say so himself.

Won't Mr. Wingrove be surprised!

Felix stepped off the curb and into the road.

"Oi!" the driver of a hansom cab shouted.

The dark stillness had lulled Felix into a false sense of security. He leaped back as the visible puffs of the horse's breath came within inches of his face. His heel caught the curb, and he stumbled backward, fumbling the box. The cab rumbled past. With both feet planted, Felix doubled over, panting. He set the box on the ground, his heart thumping in his chest.

Bloody 'ell! How could he be so daft? He needed to be more careful.

As the night enveloped him in silence again, Felix cautiously picked up the box and made for the end of the bridge. To calm his nerves, he decided on a more circuitous route than he'd planned. He aimed for York Minster, its hulking presence inescapable even cloaked in dark shadow. When the night watchman, his lantern swinging at his hip, rounded the corner, Felix turned right onto High Petergate. From Low Petergate, he cut down a narrow lane toward St. Sampson's Square and then circled back to Mansion House, where he slipped through the arch. Virtually invisible in the unlit passage, he leaned against the stone wall of the adjacent building and let out a long sigh. Somewhere in the distance, a dog barked.

All in all, it had taken him three times as long to get here, but he was more clearheaded, and this way, there was little chance of anyone knowing what he was about. Hugging the box to his chest, Felix smiled. It was all going according to plan.

"I didn't have you down as a sneak, Private."

Felix froze. The figure beside him was but a shadow in the darkness of the alley, but he knew who it was. Where'd he come from? Felix had been so careful.

"I don't know what you mean, Sergeant." Felix sucked in his breath at the glint of steel in the fella's hand. His chest tightened so he could hardly breathe.

"But you did slink out all quiet-like, an hour early. Why'd you do that, Private, eh? Not up to owt, are you?"

Even sloshed, Felix knew it was better to deny everything. Trying to sound nonchalant, he said, "No, no. Just fancied me some extra time to make sure I ain't followed."

"Good. What's with the chocolate box?"

Felix raised the box up for the sergeant to see. He relieved Felix of his burden, lowering the gun to lift the lid. He studied its contents. "At least, that's summat."

Felix let out a breath, but his relief was short-lived with the cold, steel barrel of the gun unexpectedly pressed against his forehead. Felix shuttered his eyes in fear.

"What you play at, Private? I saw how keen you were to ride up with the old fella. Who's he to us?"

"Nobody. Thought he was, but he ain't."

"Did you blabber to him?"

With the gun preventing him from shaking his head, Felix croaked out a whisper. "I never. I swear, I ain't told 'im nothin'."

"Then why the chocolates?"

"Seein' 'im gave me an idea, that's all." The sergeant drew back the gun. Felix's body sagged in relief. "Everything's all right, then, yeah?"

"Don't be daft."

The whack from the butt of the gun sent Felix staggering. Pain shot through his head. His shoulder smashed against the nearby wall. He stumbled, caught his boot on the uneven cobblestones, and careened forward. The sergeant stepped aside and let Felix crash to the ground, his knees connecting with the slick, hard stone. The sole of a shoe on his back shoved him onto his belly. Cold, wet blood dripped down his cheek. Dirt and moss stuck to his lips. Felix groaned.

"You aren't paid to get ideas, Private. You follow orders. Understand?" Felix groaned in reply. The sergeant leaned down close to Felix's face, his breath smelling of ale and onions. "And let's hope you're right about the old fella. If you lied to me, you're a dead man."

Dr. Bertram Bell couldn't sleep, yet again. Tonight, he'd forgone his sleeping draught, opting instead to rely on the calming effects of fresh air and exercise. After a late dinner, he'd taken to the streets of York. Though the rain had ceased, the storm had left a damp chill to the air. With his tie loosened and his overcoat collar pulled up, he'd wandered through the Museum Gardens, the Minster Gardens, and couldn't recall how long he'd stood staring up at the magnificent edifice of the cathedral itself. He'd strolled along the entire length of the city walls (well over two miles) that encircled the greater part of the town. His guidebook claimed the Romans built sections of it. The elevated stone walk, connected by several tower-like gateways, or "bars," as the locals call them, afforded him brilliant views. It hadn't been enough.

Bertram stepped into his room, took one glance at the fastidiously made bed, and retreated to the hall. It was useless. He'd never be able to nod off yet.

Where to now?

He didn't want to go back outside and inconvenience the

poor night porter again. The youth had stumbled from a back room, rubbing the sleep from his eyes when Bertram knocked to be let in. He'd returned so late they'd locked the lobby doors. He'd heard tell of a lounge on the fourth floor. Not fancying taking the lift up one level, Bertram decided on the service stairs. The plain, whitewashed stairwell was almost too dark to navigate, with but one mounted electric lightbulb on the first-floor landing, but he made it without incident.

When he pushed open the solid, heavy service door, he expected to find a similar narrow passage as those below. Instead, it opened into a long, wide hall. He passed two doors on his way to the lounge, opposite each other. On each was a brass placard, a glint from the overhead gas chandelier reflecting off the words "Honeymoon Suite" and "Royal Suite" etched on them. He passed the lift before coming to the lounge he sought, a large sunroom, populated with white wicker chairs and settees, thriving ferns, and a plush Persian carpet, flanked on one side by French doors that opened onto a balcony, and a bank of leaded glass windows on the other.

What a brilliant hideaway. No one but those privileged few staying in the suites would even know this splendid sanctuary was here. Promising himself to come back during the day, Bertram found a seat in a wicker rocker and, pushing himself back and forth slowly with his foot, let his mind drift.

Had he fallen asleep? He couldn't be sure, but the ding of the lift doors opening caught him unaware. A porter (Max, if Bertram recalled his name correctly) stood waiting to push a food trolley into the lift. The trolley was piled high with trays of dirty dishes, glasses, partially eaten food. The porter, whistling "Sing a Song of Sixpence," seemed unaware of Bertram, sitting in the shadows. When the lift doors closed behind the porter, Bertram shuddered. The peace he'd sought alluded him, the effort leaving him drained and exhausted. But he couldn't stay here. As he chatted himself up, attempting to convince his body to rise, he spied someone approaching from the same way he'd come. About Bertram's age, maybe a few years younger, the man wore a pair of striped pajamas, had disheveled flaxen hair, and walked barefoot. He padded down the hall without a sound.

"Can't sleep either?" Bertram called in greeting, one insomniac to another. The man ignored Bertram and said nothing. Instead, he pivoted abruptly and plodded back the way he came. "I say, are you all right?"

Nothing. If anything, the man shuffled his feet faster, as if by putting more distance between them, he could pretend he'd never heard. He passed the lift, passed the suites, and disappeared into the shadow at the end of the long hall. The faint clink of a door closing marked his departure.

How odd.

A sudden heaviness crept over him. He was thirty-two, but as Bertram lugged his body out of the rocker, he felt twice his age. He hadn't been this despondent in years. Despite his exhaustion, his nerves were on edge. He had something in his physician's bag that would help him sleep, but Bertram knew, after years of caring for others, there was no remedy against what afflicted him.

Lyndy folded his arms under his head. It was still dark, but he'd heard the clock chime and knew dawn wasn't far off. He'd awoken, never feeling so rested, so relaxed in his life. Perhaps he'd have to reevaluate his distaste for lavender and lilac. At this moment, he did feel like royalty.

Stella curled onto her side beside him, murmuring something indecipherable under her breath. Lyndy reached over, tracing the lines of her face, marveling at her flawless, alabaster skin. He'd longed for this, being alone with her, having her share his bed. He'd imagined how deeply satisfying it would be. He hadn't counted on how completely safe he would feel, how loved and accepted. With no one else about, no Mother or Papa, to press opinions, judgments, or expectations upon him, this time alone with Stella was as close to heaven as Lyndy could imagine. If only they never had to go back.

He leaned over and kissed her pale, bare shoulder poking above the bedsheet. No need to cover her up. The room was pleasantly comfortable. Although the embers in the grate had long grown cold, they were merely for extra warmth; the radiator hissed with heat.

Morrington Hall needs radiators. That was the type of improvement Stella's inheritance would allow. One that Stella would be most keen to have done. Although she'd never complained, Lyndy had seen her shivering or wearing unbecoming heavy cloaks inside the drafty old manor house he called home. In America, she'd been used to more modern conveniences— radiating heat, electricity, hot running water throughout. This hotel, updated with the latest comforts, made him realize how antiquated his ancestral home was. *Not for long.*

Stella stirred, shifting away from him. He nestled against her back, matching the curve of her body, and wrapped his arms around her. He should resist the urge to wake her and be content with being this close, but instead, he nibbled on the soft lobe of her ear. She sighed contentedly, rolled in his arms to face him, and smiled. How he loved that smile.

"Good morning, husband," she whispered.

Lyndy never dreamt a word, that word in particular, would send such a thrill through his body. He'd resigned himself long ago to his duty, to marry for money, to save Morrington Hall and his family from destitution, never imagining what a delight his duty could be.

"Good morning, my love," he said before tenderly caressing her lips with a kiss. "Sleep well?"

"Mm-hmm. You?"

He smiled against her lips. "Never better." He pulled her

against him so that not a wisp of air could slip between them and pressed his lips more fervently against hers. She responded in kind, and a wave of heat, having nothing to do with the hissing radiators, surged through him.

"Help! Please!" The frantic scream emanated from outside their door. "Someone, help!"

Good God! How many times were they to be interrupted?

Lyndy swiftly swept aside his instinctive annoyance as Stella rolled away from him. This time, something was truly wrong. As one, they flung the bedclothes off and scrambled to find their discarded dressing gowns laying in heaps on the floor. Stella's long tresses cascaded loose halfway down her back, unruly from tumbling about in bed. Despite his trepidation in not knowing what awaited them on the other side of the door, Lyndy couldn't help but remark how beautiful his bride was. The chambermaid, on the other hand, looked a fright. Her white cap had fallen askew on her head, tears ran down her freckled, ruddy cheeks, every aspect about her wild with fear. When she saw Lyndy and Stella emerge from their room, she dashed to them, seizing Stella's arm.

Stella, ignoring the impropriety of it, asked, "What's wrong?"

"In here, m'lady!" The maid dragged Stella toward the closed door of the suite opposite.

Stella wrapped a reassuring arm around the maid's shoulders while Lyndy tried the door. It was unlocked. He pushed it slowly open. "Mr. Wingrove? It's Lord and Lady Lyndhurst. May we come in?"

No answer. Though stale and smelling faintly of something overheating, the living room was empty with only the pale gleam of the rising sun casting any light. Lyndy felt along the smooth, plastered wall for the light switch and pushed it. Nothing seemed amiss. He glanced over his shoulder at the maid lingering in the hall. She'd pulled her apron up and was using it to wipe her face.

"I don't see—" he began.

"He's in there." The maid pointed to the room beyond.

Lyndy swung open the bedroom door and coughed, the distinct taste of smoke in his throat. Yet nothing but cold ash lay in the grate. Mr. Wingrove lay undisturbed in the middle of the bed, his arms resting naturally on top of the white linen bedsheet, his head peacefully settled into his pillow. But the man's skin and lips, seen up close, disturbingly matched his exotic red silk pajamas.

"Is he all right?" Stella asked, throwing opening the drapes and unlatching a window, allowing in cool, fresh air. Several pigeons roosting on the ledge flapped and fluttered away in startled haste. The maid was nowhere to be seen.

"I think not." Lyndy would've preferred to shield her from any ugliness but had long learned she'd have none of it. Besides, she was made of sterner stuff than most. He shouted into the old chocolatier's ear. "Mr. Wingrove!"

When that didn't work, Lyndy tried shaking him, his elbow accidentally knocking the gilded frame of a woman's portrait on the nightstand. It clattered to the floor. "Sir. Wake up!"

It was no use. The man wouldn't stir. Was he even breathing?

Stella, her features etched with worry, approached and gingerly placed her fingers on the man's red, wrinkled neck, as they'd seen Inspector Brown do too many times.

"Well?" Lyndy stared at her, anticipating her answer.

In response, she stepped back, clutching her hands beneath her chin, and dropped her gaze to the ground. Mr. Wingrove was dead.

CHAPTER 4

"The poor sod." Mr. Haigh, the hotel manager, muttered beside Stella.

"It's terrible," she agreed.

Stella, Lyndy, and the manager hovered around Mr. Wingrove's bedside. Stella had sent the maid to fetch Mr. Haigh, who'd brought with him a doctor, a square-faced man with a thick brown mustache and compassionate brown eyes who'd introduced himself as Dr. Bertram Bell, a fellow guest at the hotel.

"He was quite elderly, though," the manager mused. "At least he breathed his last in the suite he was so keen to stay in."

"Indeed," Lyndy agreed. "Though I'm still not certain how he came to stay here." Mr. Haigh winced at Lyndy's reminder of the mix-up.

"Please," Dr. Bell, sitting on the edge of the bed, said with a weary sigh. He'd spent the last few minutes checking for a pulse, first with his fingers, then with a stethoscope. He'd then examined Mr. Wingrove's hands and feet, lifted the bedsheet, glancing at the dead man's body, and was now scrutinizing his face, which looked like it had been stained by cherry juice or burned by fire. Stella had never seen anything like it.

What could've caused that? Stella knew better than to ask. At least not yet.

Dr. Bell peeled the older man's eyelids apart. Mr. Wingrove stared unseeing at the intricate plaster scrollwork lacing across the ceiling high above. Stella had to look away. His blank expression reminded her too much of the last she'd seen on her father's face.

"Well, Dr. Bell?" The manager asked, anxiously pulling on his earlobe. Stella sympathized. A death in his establishment wouldn't be good for business. "Natural causes, was it?"

No one would argue that Mr. Wingrove wasn't elderly. But it was wishful thinking on Mr. Haigh's part to believe he'd died of natural causes. Besides the strange discoloration of Mr. Wingrove's skin, they'd had to open all the suite's windows to dispel the stuffy, smoke-tinted air.

"An accident, I regret to say."

"An accident?" the manager said, taking his spectacles from his head, fogging them with his breath, and wiping them rapidly with a handkerchief. "How do you mean?"

"It's my opinion this man died of carbon monoxide poisoning."

Goose bumps raced up Stella's arms. This suite was supposed to be theirs. If not for chance, if not for Mr. Wingrove's sentimentality, it would've been them lying there dead with a group of strangers standing over them. She hugged herself to ward off a sudden chill. Lyndy, his posture stiff and visibly shaken by the news, wrapped a reassuring arm around her shoulders.

"No," Mr. Haigh declared. "That can't be. We don't have gas in the rooms anymore. That was all done away with when we converted to electric lighting last year. Only the hall chandeliers still use gas. The radiators are steam, and this floor's suites aren't anywhere near the boiler flues." His voice rose to a fevered pitch. "How could Mr. Wingrove have possibly been poisoned by gas?"

"That I can't tell you," Dr. Bell said, packing up his well-worn leather doctor's bag. "I'm terribly sorry. Shall I arrange for someone to take the body?"

"I prefer the police to do that."

The police? Not again. Stella massaged her forehead with her fingertips; she had a headache coming on.

"If you think that necessary," Dr. Bell was saying.

"I do," Mr. Haigh said, firmly settling his spectacles back on his head. He winced, having jabbed the top of his head too hard. "This hotel's reputation depends upon finding the truth. Perhaps, with a medical examiner's more thorough examination, you'll be proven wrong, Dr. Bell. The old man was suffering from something."

"Perhaps, but I wouldn't get your hopes up. This was clearly an accident."

"Is Mr. Wingrove's nephew staying here?" Stella said. "He'll need to be told about this."

The manager's face paled. "He is a guest. Mr. Morgan Amesbury-Jones, room twenty-seven. But I . . . I couldn't possibly . . ." he stammered, rubbing the back of his neck. "Won't the police . . . ?"

"It shouldn't be left to the police," Dr. Bell said, not unkindly.

"But I . . . I wouldn't know the first thing about breaking such tragic news."

Dr. Bell put a reassuring hand on the distressed man's shoulder. "Regrettably, it is a task with which I am well accustomed. While you're telephoning the police, I will inform Mr. Amesbury-Jones."

The manager wobbled, clasping his hands in relief. "Thank you, Dr. Bell."

"If you'll excuse me, Lady Lyndhurst."

Stella stepped aside as Dr. Bell, intent on his sad errand, took his leave. Mr. Haigh held the door for them.

"I do apologize again, Your Lord and Ladyship. To be witness to such . . . sad business. I can't possibly imagine how much distress this has caused you."

"Needless to say, we won't be switching suites as we intended today," Lyndy said.

"No, no, of course not. And, please, if there is anything I can do to make your stay more pleasant, do not hesitate to ask. A pot of tea, perhaps?"

Stella marveled how a cup of tea here in England was the salve for anything. Daddy would be asking for a bourbon about now. She inwardly flinched at the thought of him.

"With plenty of milk and sugar," Lyndy added, knowing how Stella liked her tea. Not having the heart to smile, Stella reached for Lyndy's hand and squeezed it. "And some buttered toast?"

"Of course, my lord. The dining room isn't open yet, but I'll see to it."

Before Mr. Haigh closed and locked the suite's door, Stella caught a last glimpse of the dead man in what was, forty years ago, his honeymoon bed, which was meant to be theirs the previous night. Her stomach churned; she wouldn't be eating or drinking anything for a while.

The knock came as Lyndy kissed the nape of his wife's neck while fastening the clasp on her collar. She swiveled around and kissed him back before slipping past.

"I'll get the door," she said.

After their grim discovery, they'd returned to their suite, ill at ease and distracted. There was nothing to do but await their tea and dress. It being too early to summon the servants, Lyndy could do for himself, having done so while attending Eton, but

Stella couldn't tighten her corset or fasten the line of buttons that ran down her back. That task had fallen to Lyndy. He never imagined dressing Stella would be almost as intimate as undressing her.

He admired his handwork as she crossed the room in the lacy shirtwaist and burgundy and rose striped skirt that matched the blush on her cheeks. She looked a picture, except for her hair. She'd twisted it up into a bun and proceeded to thrust dozens of pins into it. It wasn't perfect, but it was the best they could do until Stella's lady's maid arrived.

The knock grew insistent. Why would a porter bringing their tea be in a hurry?

"Lord and Lady Lyndhurst?"

"Yes?" Stella said.

It wasn't the porter at the door. Instead, there stood the woman they'd seen arguing with Mr. Wingrove last night. What did she want? Lyndy was quick to join Stella at the door.

"You're the ones who found Horace, aren't you?" the woman rather impertinently demanded. She smelled of camphor oil.

"I don't believe we've been introduced," Lyndy said.

The woman spared him a glance, dismissed him in a moment's notice, and replied to Stella. "Miss Lily Evans, Horace Wingrove's secretary."

That explains some things. Miss Evans and the nephew did seem the odd couple. Wearing a high-collared shirtwaist and brown wool skirt, she had more semblance of the part this morning.

"Were you or weren't you the first people to find him?"

Before Lyndy could admonish the secretary for her brash tone, she raised the handkerchief she'd been clutching and sneezed three times, loud enough to be heard in the lobby four floors down.

"No," Stella said, as the woman wiped her nose, "that would've been Eliza, the unfortunate chambermaid, who'd come to light Mr. Wingrove's fire this morning."

Eliza? Why was he so surprised? Lyndy struggled to recall the names of anyone not family or an intimate friend, and yet Stella learned and remembered the name of every person she'd ever met, be they a humble stable hand, a shopgirl, or a duchess.

"But Lord Lyndhurst and I were the first to come to her aid," Stella continued.

"Did he say anything?"

"No, he—"

"Are you certain?"

"Lady Lyndhurst has kindly answered your question, Miss Evans," Lyndy said, plucking a strand of Stella's hair from his shoulder.

"Did he say anything to Dr. Bell?"

"Sadly, he was dead long before Dr. Bell examined him," Stella said. "I checked for a pulse myself."

As if hearing his name mentioned, Dr. Bell strolled into view behind Miss Evans. Accompanying him was Mr. Wingrove's nephew, tugging ruthlessly at his earlobe. Ignoring their approach, the secretary continued. "And you're a qualified physician, are you?"

"No," Stella said calmly, but her patience was beginning to waver. "But I have encountered more than my share of dead bodies, Miss Evans."

"Have you now?"

"Must we do this here?" the nephew said, glancing about him, appearing a bit dazed.

"Shall we sit while we wait for the police, then?" the doctor said, guiding the nephew toward the sunroom lounge at the other end of the hall.

"I'm not done here," Miss Evans said as if she was owed something. "I've got more to ask His Lord and Ladyship."

"Do you mind?" Dr. Bell said, gesturing for Lyndy and Stella to join them.

Lyndy would've told the secretary what she could do with her questions, but he knew his wife. Having some of her own, Stella didn't hesitate.

"I do apologize for this," Dr. Bell said, dropping his voice once the secretary and the nephew had preceded them down the hall. "Miss Evans was with Mr. Amesbury-Jones when I informed him of the death of his uncle. I made the mistake of explaining how Mr. Wingrove was found. I never imagined she'd disturb you like this."

"She's grieving," Stella said graciously. "Everyone reacts differently."

"Yes, but to be so . . ." As the doctor sought a diplomatic word for *churlish*, Lyndy saved him the trouble.

"Think nothing of it," Lyndy said, feeling less magnanimous than he sounded. "Besides, the police may want to speak to us." *Regrettably.*

"Do you believe, Dr. Bell, that if Mr. Wingrove hadn't been so frail, he might've survived?" Stella asked.

Lyndy knew what she was thinking. Would they have survived if they'd been sleeping in that bed? The notion of their suffering Mr. Wingrove's fate, although ultimately adverted, haunted them both.

"I couldn't be certain," Dr. Bell said.

"But it's possible?" Stella pressed.

"Perhaps."

Clinging to the belief that they might've survived the ordeal, Lyndy shared a relieved glance with his wife.

"We are so sorry about your uncle, Mr. Amesbury-Jones," Stella said when they'd reached the sitting room and settled into one of the white wicker settees.

"Thank you," the nephew said solemnly. A man of average stature, he seemed to shrink before Lyndy's eyes. Mr. Amesbury-Jones slumped against the back of his wicker chair. A flourishing potted fern, its stand set too close, brushed against his arm. He didn't seem to notice.

"The hotel manager refuses to let us see Horace's body," Miss Evans, who'd remained standing with her arms tightly folded across her chest, said. "Therefore, we must rely on you." She took Lyndy, Stella, and the doctor in with her steely glare. "We've heard what Dr. Bell had to tell us. What can you?"

With a patience Lyndy didn't have, Stella answered, "What do you want to know?"

"Why, everything."

Stella recounted their morning: the maid's scream, the condition and smell of the suite, the state Mr. Wingrove was in. She described the arrival of Mr. Haigh and Dr. Bell, who confirmed Mr. Wingrove's accidental death. When Stella finished, the secretary had the decency to thank her before throwing accusations at Dr. Bell.

"I heard nothing from Lady Lyndhurst's account that warrants involving the police."

"As I explained before," the doctor said patiently, "if it were up to me, I'd not involve them either, but Mr. Haigh was dissatisfied with my conclusions and wished to have the police and a medical examiner involved in the case."

"Couldn't you have said he died in his sleep and saved us all the trouble?" Miss Evans said.

"Thankfully, he did die in his sleep," Dr. Bell said, "but not from natural causes." Sorrow flickered over his features. "The color of his skin indicated that. I'm sure you can appreciate how I'm obligated to give an honest, professional opinion."

"Horace wasn't a well man, Doctor," Miss Evans scoffed. A sudden attack of trumpeting sneezes overtook her again. When she'd finished, she added, "And we certainly didn't need to consult a physician to tell us that."

"She's right," the nephew said. "I've suspected he's been ill for quite some time. Yet he soldiered on, kept everything going." With a catch in his voice, he added, "And now he's gone."

He rose, laced his fingers together behind his head, and wandered over to the bank of leaded windows. The dawn had come and gone. From the sun streaming through, the morning, at least, promised to be pleasant and dry. Lyndy longed to leave this ugly business behind and tour the city. He'd never been to York before.

"This has all come as a shock," Dr. Bell said. "You're exhausted, sir. Why not have a lie down when this police business is through?"

"Absolutely not," Miss Evans declared. "Morgan is head of the company now, and there's too much to be done. Everything must be put in order. We must inform"—she began ticking off names on her gloved fingers—"Mr. Corcoran, the company's solicitor, Mr. Quiney, Horace's solicitor, everyone back at the factory, the London newspapers—"

"The Peggs," the nephew added while still gazing out the windows at the city's skyline, dominated by the massive York Minster. Lyndy could see the tops of the towers even from where he sat.

"Yes, right. The Peggs. We'll need to . . ." The secretary abruptly turned her scowl on Stella and Lyndy. "You didn't remove anything, did you? Paperwork, ledgers, that sort of thing?"

"I say!" Lyndy had had quite enough. He stood, tugging at his morning jacket. "Who do you think we are?" Stella laid a calming hand on Lyndy's arm, encouraging him to sit back down.

"Except for the windows, which had to be opened, we left the suite exactly as we found it. Mr. Wingrove was nice enough to give us a box of chocolates, but that was before he died."

"That's Uncle Horace," the nephew said as if speaking to himself. "He was such a sweet man." He laughed mirthlessly at his unintended pun.

"Horace is always doing that," the secretary said, rolling her eyes. "Carries a box or two with him everywhere. 'Just in case,' he says. Whatever that means." Miss Evans caught herself, a hint of regret in her voice. She shifted in her seat, smoothing her skirt across her lap. Perhaps she was human, after all. "I mean, he used to, that is."

"This has all been quite unsettling," Dr. Bell said. "From one insomniac to another, may I reassert my recommendation for some much-needed rest? Any business matters can undoubtedly wait." He reached for his medical bag set on the floor. "I'll prepare you a draught to help if you'd like."

As he began rummaging through, searching for something, Miss Evans said, "What are you talking about? I'm not an insomniac."

"I was speaking to Mr. Amesbury-Jones."

"I'm not an insomniac either, Dr. Bell," the nephew insisted, dropping his arms and turning toward them. "What gave you that idea?"

The nephew's face was drawn, his expression slack. To be fair to Dr. Bell, even to Lyndy's untrained eye, the man appeared exhausted.

"But then why . . . ?"

Miss Evans's expression hardened, daring him to say another word. Dr. Bell held his tongue and snapped his bag shut. "Yes, well." He pulled out his pocket watch, a nicely etched, highly polished silver piece. "What's taking the police so long, do you suspect?"

Mr. Amesbury-Jones pressed the heels of his hands against his forehead. Miss Evans picked at a thread on her sleeve. Lyndy's and Stella's eyes met as the group fell into an uneasy silence, an unspoken question passing between them.

What was that about?

CHAPTER 5

Something was nagging at Stella.

She and Lyndy had returned to their rooms when Mr. Haigh, with a very tall, burly policeman in a brown sack suit and matching fedora in tow, unlocked the suite across the hall, and the others had accompanied them inside. She sat at the mahogany dressing table, fiddling with the tassels on the lace runner, as her maid styled her hair. After finding the *Sporting Times* had arrived with the newspapers, Lyndy was reading in the outer room.

Stella lifted the stopper on the crystal perfume bottle, releasing a waft of her favorite fragrance, a scent Lyndy described as the New Forest in springtime, and then dropped it again with a *clink*. She should feel relieved the morning's ordeal was over. Yet something didn't seem right.

"Is something bothering you, my lady?" Ethel said, skillfully pinning a few loose strands in place.

"Why do you ask?" News of Mr. Wingrove's death hadn't been made public yet.

"Because you won't sit still."

Stella regarded Ethel's reflection in the mirror, the maid biting her lip in concentration, and smiled. "I'm sorry." Stella slipped her hands under her thighs, hoping that would help.

She usually enjoyed Ethel's calming ministrations of combing and styling her hair. It often made her head tingle. But she was too distracted this morning to enjoy it.

"You're right, but I can't put my finger on it." Even as the words left her mouth, she caught sight in the mirror of the bed recently made.

That's it!

She'd confirmed that the Honeymoon Suite was almost identical to this one, as Mr. Haigh had claimed. Yet it wasn't until Miss Evans accused them of removing things that it occurred to Stella something in the other suite was missing. The pillows! She and Lyndy had more pillows than they knew what to do with, stacked on the bed, in the corner of the couches, set into the backs of chairs. In the Honeymoon Suite, the only pillow she'd seen lay beneath Mr. Wingrove's head. Where were all the extras? Definitely not littering the floor as they'd been in here last night.

"Are you finished?"

Her lady's maid hastily adjusted a pin as Stella, without warning, rose from the dressing table bench.

"Thank you, Ethel. I'll ring your room when I need you again. Make sure to enjoy the hotel breakfast. I hear it's as good as anything Mrs. Cole can cook up."

Ethel, shocked by the comparison, laughed nervously. "Thank you, my lady." With that, the maid was gone.

"I need to get into the other suite," Stella said, quickening her pace as she passed through the living room.

Lyndy tossed the pink-colored racing newspaper down and rose. "I think they're all still over there. I haven't heard anyone leave."

Before he reached the door, Stella stepped in front of him and slipped her arms around his neck. He smelled of aftershave, a crisp, sweet mix of lemon, lime, lavender, musk, and pine. While her lady's maid was fixing Stella's hair, Lyndy's valet must've given him a shave.

"I thought you wanted to go across the hall?" he teased.

In response, she kissed him. "I do, but that's for not asking why."

Lyndy laughed. "I've long learned not to question you, my love."

"And why is that?"

"Because I don't always want to know the answer."

An amused smile still clung to the corners of Stella's mouth as they approached the opposite suite, but disappeared abruptly when the door flew open.

"Excuse me," Mr. Amesbury-Jones muttered, knocking shoulders with Stella as he darted past.

Miss Evans gave chase. "Morgan, please wait!"

Stella watched the pair disappear into the elevator before taking advantage of the open door. She stepped tentatively inside while Lyndy closed the door behind them. A deep quiet permeated the suite. Stella's gaze traveled over the outer room. There were a few smaller pillows scattered among the couches and chairs. But what about those on the bed?

Mr. Haigh, standing in the bedroom doorway, turned at the sound of their approach. "My lord, my lady," Mr. Haigh said with a slight bow, his face pale and haggard. He seemed to have aged in the last few minutes. Yet, he never forgot his courtesy.

Perhaps he needed to ask Dr. Bell for something to help him sleep.

The manager stepped aside to allow them to pass. Poor Mr. Wingrove lay as they'd left him. If his face hadn't had that odd cherry color, she'd swear he was sleeping. Without a doubt, he was the most peaceful-looking corpse she'd ever seen. Dr. Bell, whom Stella expected to see, wasn't there, only the detective, his back partially turned, scribbling with his left hand into a palm-sized notebook as he stood over the dead man's bed.

Mama's left-handed.

Mixed emotions about Katherine Kendrick Smith swept through Stella's mind. After thinking her dead for years, her mother had startlingly reappeared in her life. Had it only been two days ago? How long had they to talk, to get to know one another again—a few hours? Not long enough. *Not by a long shot.* With the excitement of the wedding and the honeymoon, the idea of her mother's resurrection still seemed unreal. Almost as unbelievable as being in the room with yet another dead man. Stella brushed the thoughts of her mother aside. Right now, she needed to find the other pillows.

"Who are you?" the detective demanded, fixing them with a critical stare. With one eyelid slightly drooping, the policeman seemed to have a perpetual wink. But he wasn't joking.

"Lady Lyndhurst." Despite the sad circumstances, an unintentional spark of joy lit her face as she said it. Would introducing herself as Lady Lyndhurst ever get old? She doubted it.

"How's that?" The detective squinted at her, closing his drooping eyelid completely. "You're an American, aren't you?"

Stella flinched, attempting to ignore his bold scrutiny.

"What if she is?" Lyndy said, a flicker of annoyance crossing his face.

"And who might you be?"

"The lady's husband, Viscount Lyndhurst." Lyndy jutted his nose upward as Stella had seen his mother do so many times. "And I'd appreciate it if you spoke to my wife with the deference she deserves."

"My apologies, Your Lordship," the detective said, overly polite. "I meant no disrespect."

Stella sighed. Was it too much to hope for a fresh start? Now that she and Lyndy were married, she'd hoped her past was just that, past. But judging by the detective's reaction, she realized she'd been naive. To some, she'd always be the "American interloper."

"I presume you're the detective assigned to Mr. Wingrove's case?" Lyndy said.

"It's Detective Sergeant Thomas Glenshaw, m'lord, and if you pardon my saying, you're not supposed to be in here. This isn't a garden party." He pointed to the bed with his pencil. "If you haven't noticed, there's a dead man in the bed." The detective's steely gaze revealed where he placed the blame for the oversight. "You were meant to be guarding the door, Mr. Haigh."

"Forgive me, Your Lordship," Mr. Haigh said. "I forgot to inform the detective sergeant you and your wife were the first to find poor Mr. Wingrove."

"After the poor chambermaid," Stella said.

She'd never forget the poor maid's fright. Stella had been in the maid's shoes, stumbling on a dead body, more than once. Each time she'd been devastated. This time had been different. Seeing Mr. Wingrove had saddened her, yes, but nothing more. Maybe it was because he was old and had died peacefully in his sleep, or because she'd been alerted by the chambermaid and hadn't found the body herself, or maybe, heaven forbid, she was growing used to seeing such things? Nothing more, that is until she'd discovered that she and Lyndy could've been the victims instead. Stella's legs weakened at the thought.

"If it suits, I'll speak to you both after I'm finished here," the detective sergeant said.

"I needed to ask you something first," Stella said, "to set my mind at rest."

"Yes?" Detective Sergeant Glenshaw grumbled, already turning back to his task of examining the body.

"Did you find the extra pillows?"

His head lifted; his thick brown eyebrows pinched together. "Pillows?" he spat out the word derisively. "What pillows?"

"Exactly. What happened to them all?"

"What happened to what?"

Stella should've known he hadn't noticed. She dropped to the floor, and crouching on all fours, lifted the dust ruffle. The floor beneath the bed was swept clean and clear of anything but Mr. Wingrove's fur-lined bedroom slippers.

"Oi! M'lady! You can't do that."

Stella stood, smoothing out her skirt. "Then you'll look?"

"For what?"

"For all the extra pillows." Stella turned to the hotel manager. "There should be several more, right?"

The hotel manager skimmed the carpet around his feet as if expecting the missing pillows to appear. "Yes. Yes, indeed. Six standard, four decorative, and two bolster."

"Then where are they?" Stella cast a sweeping glance around the room. Mr. Wingrove had kept it tidy. Nothing out of place but last night's clothes draped neatly across the dark green wingback chair by the window.

The detective sergeant, disgruntled, shrugged. "Who knows? Who cares?"

"But aren't you investigating Mr. Wingrove's death?"

"I believe I was clear that I was."

"Mind your tone, Glenshaw," Lyndy said.

"Then you'll want to know what happened to the pillows," Stella said.

The detective offered them a fleeting, tight-lipped smile. "Why, may I ask, Your Ladyship, should I care about missing pillows?"

"Because it's something unexplained, and as you know, that's never a good thing when you're investigating a death."

The detective sergeant sputtered curses under his breath. Stella ignored him and crossed over to the wardrobe. Mr. Wingrove's suitcase was closed and stored on the bottom next to his shoes. His overcoat, a fresh suit, and white shirt hung inside. His top hat lay on the high shelf. There were no pillows.

"I'm baffled as to what could've happened to them. Perhaps they're in the bathroom?" the manager suggested, eager to appear helpful. Mr. Haigh scampered into the bathroom; his frustrated sigh heard echoing against the tile.

Why they'd be there, Stella couldn't fathom. But why not? They weren't where they were supposed to be.

Mr. Haigh reappeared, carrying a broom. "No pillows, just this the chambermaid left behind the door."

The detective threw up his hands in frustration. A long, raised scar crisscrossed his left palm.

"All right, enough of this nonsense. If everyone would please clear the room." Seeing Lyndy about to object, he added, "That would be you too, m'lord. I need to make quick work of this. So, if you please." He gestured toward the door.

"But you will be thorough?" Mr. Haigh asked, voicing the doubts that Stella had.

Detective Sergeant Glenshaw wasn't interested in finding out why the pillows were gone. It probably didn't mean anything, but Inspector Brown would've followed up on it, just to be sure.

"It seems pretty well sorted."

"But—"

When Mr. Haigh didn't follow Stella and Lyndy's lead, the detective loomed over the short-statured manager backing him through the bedroom door into the outer room. The manager knocked into a side table, toppling a crystal dessert wineglass and upsetting a half-empty bottle of port. The contents of the bottle puddled across the surface, the embroidered white table linen absorbing the wine like a bandage soaking up blood.

"Apologies, Mr. Haigh," the detective said, attempting to smile but failing.

The manager, red-faced, ignored the detective and scrambled to mop up the port with his handkerchief. Stella retrieved a towel from the bathroom, which Mr. Haigh accepted graciously while purposely avoiding her sympathetic gaze.

"It's just that Dr. Bell thinks this man's death was an accident when more likely it was simply his time," Mr. Haigh said, clutching the wad of crimson-colored cloth in his hands. "The hotel can't be held accountable for an act of God."

"I'll make certain the medical examiner does an autopsy," Detective Sergeant Glenshaw said, "but I'm afraid, Mr. Haigh, God had nowt to do with this."

"Pillows?" Detective Sergeant Glenshaw stared down at the dead man whose head was cradled in the crevice of a very thick pillow. "Who needs more than one anyway? You didn't."

Leave it to the feminine mind to concern itself with fripperies and frivolities when real work needed doing.

Which I hope to get to directly.

Glenshaw should've been down at the Guildhall with the lads securing the building for tomorrow's unveiling. But then the founder of England's largest chocolate manufacturer died on his patch, so his superiors had other ideas. Instead of ensuring the safety of Their Royal Highnesses, they'd saddled him with this nonsense. There was nothing suspicious about Mr. Wingrove's death. Glenshaw had seen the likes of it before. Yet that bothersome manager insisted he poke about, and with the hotel's owner being a mate of the chief constable, the sooner Glenshaw did his bit, the sooner he could get back to the Guildhall.

"Shall we get on with it then?"

Not expecting an answer, Glenshaw turned his back on the body and did a cursory search of the room. As he expected, nothing seemed amiss. A single framed photo, a pair of reading spectacles, and a plain, solid gold pocket watch engraved on the back, *To my sweetie, love Marie*, lay on the night table. The drawer was empty. Searching through trouser and jacket pockets revealed nothing but a silk handkerchief and a loose guinea. He left both where he'd found them.

The dressing table was bare but for a vase of roses and a scattering of fallen pink petals. Ashes, still in the grate, confirmed a fire had been lit last night. Glenshaw rummaged his pockets for a matchbox, grabbed a fist full, and struck the matches against the brick fireplace. Before the flame burned his fingers, he crooked his neck to peer up the chimney. Black with soot, it reeked of recent smoke. Nothing he could see was blocking it. It could be faulty farther up.

"Oi, What's this?" He snatched something clinging to the inside brick. A bird feather. He should've known.

Tucking the feather into his breast pocket, he blew the flame out and tossed the matches into the grate. He wiped his hands on the soft bedsheet next to the body, leaving a small black smudge. No matter. Mr. Wingrove was well beyond caring how clean his linens were.

Glenshaw strolled through the outer room, glancing about. Only the suitcase was of any interest. Surprisingly left unlocked, it opened with a satisfying snap. Lifting the lid, he discovered why. All the case contained was a box of chocolates, not unusual considering whom it belonged to, and a kit containing a heap of pill bottles and tinctures. Glenshaw picked up one and read: *Strychnos nux-vomica*. It meant nowt to him. He scribbled the name in his notebook before tossing the bottle back in.

He finished his survey in the lavatory, which was spotless, except for a slightly crumpled hand towel left on the edge of the sink. The toothbrush was dry, and the comb held a few gray strands. The waste bin contained an invitation to tomorrow's royal reception.

"Oi!" Glenshaw exclaimed, retrieving the gold, embossed card. Why would anyone toss this?

He smoothed out the small corner crease and left the invitation squarely in the center of the small secretary desk. With that done, he quit the suite, catching the manager, still hovering about, biting a hangnail off his little finger. The bothersome American lady was nowhere to be seen.

"Well?" the manager said.

"The coroner will have the last word, but I'm putting in my report that Mr. Wingrove died of accidental gas poisoning."

"But how?" The manager slid his spectacles from his forehead to his nose, then fumbled through a jingling ring of keys before finding the right one and locking the door.

"Fumes from the fire. Most likely, a bird's nest blocking the chimney. You'd be surprised how common that is."

"That can't be," the manager pleaded, catching up with Glenshaw as he strode toward the lift. "The chimney sweep was here but two weeks ago. I must insist you rethink this. Such a claim would be most deleterious to the hotel's reputation."

"Then I suggest you not advertise it." Glenshaw called for the lift.

"But—"

"I'll inform the nephew. Mr. Jones, was it?"

"Amesbury-Jones, room twenty-seven, but—"

"And I'll send some of my lads to remove the body. With the imminent arrival of Their Royal Highnesses, it may take longer than usual." Preempting the manager's protest, he held up a hand and added, "Don't worry. We'll get him out before he starts to smell."

"I never! Poor man. What I was going to say was—"

"Until then," Glenshaw continued, eager to get away, "I expect that suite to stay locked. No maids, no gawkers." *No busybody American ladies searching for pillows.*

The lift doors opened, and Glenshaw stepped in, straightening his tie. Even if Their Royal Highnesses wouldn't be at the Guildhall yet, he meant to present his best.

"Ground floor," he informed the operator. "Good day, Mr. Haigh." He tipped his fedora as the lift doors slid closed, the first genuine smile of the day spreading across his lips.

CHAPTER 6

A fusion of fragrances from late-blooming roses and honey-suckle enveloped Stella as she and Lyndy ambled, arm in arm, through the hotel grounds, a garden oasis in a city built with stone. Colorful flower beds of asters, sedum, and salvias lined the lush, grassy path stretching straight toward a circular stone fountain. A train whistle blasted. Beyond the high hedges, the sea of gray tile slate roofs, smoke circling up from their chim-neys, the Gothic stone towers of York Minster jutting into the clear blue sky, offered an enticing glimpse of the bustling, an-cient city she was eager to explore. Taking a deep breath, Stella exhaled slowly. A bee whirred past, its orange and black body a blur. She'd been right to insist on a quick excursion for fresh air before breakfast. It was good to be outside.

She let go of Lyndy's arm and ran to the fountain, the spray misting and cooling her face. She plopped down to the fountain wall and splashed Lyndy when he approached.

"I say!" He leaped back, laughing. "Wasn't last night's drench-ing enough?"

"But look at all the fun we had drying out."

He dropped beside her, took her hands in his, and kissed the tips of her fingers. "You're all right, then?" He peered at her as if trying to read her mind.

She knew what he meant. Had seeing Mr. Wingrove brought back memories of her father? Oddly, her mother had been the one on her mind. She'd already grieved for Daddy as much as she was going to. *As much as he deserved.* The unbidden judgment pained her. Not for being heartless but for being true.

She smiled warmly at him. "I'm fine. You?"

"To be honest, I'm quite peckish. Despite the tea and toast."

"You should've said something."

Now that Lyndy mentioned it, she was starting to feel hungry too. She sprang to her feet, ignoring the dampened blotches ringing her skirt. She'd be changing after breakfast anyway.

"Let's go."

As they strolled back toward the hotel, a raised voice jarred with the tranquility of the garden. "What about the acquisition?"

A blaring set of sneezes followed.

Beneath an enormous oak tree, its golden leaves rustling in the cool morning breeze, sat Mr. Amesbury-Jones with Miss Evans standing beside him, stiffly patting him on the shoulder.

"Apparently, we're not the only ones needing some fresh air," Lyndy quipped.

Stella, drawn to them, pulled Lyndy with her. Mr. Amesbury-Jones was still mumbling something about "the acquisition" when they approached. Up close, in the bright daylight, Stella detected a caked-on layer of powder across the secretary's nose, fading but not hiding the freckles that dotted her face. Her lips, too, seemed brighter red. Had Miss Evans applied makeup since she'd last seen her? If so, it did little to soften the harsh angles of her unhappy face.

"Again, I'm so sorry about Mr. Wingrove."

The man took a moment or two before realizing Stella had

been speaking to him. She remembered that feeling when she'd been in his shoes. She repeated herself.

"What? Oh, right. Thank you."

With eyes bright from blinking back tears, his unreadable expression was unlike any she'd ever seen on a man. Was it grief, shock, or fear? Without thinking, she slipped down into the space next to him on the hard stone bench and placed a gentle hand on his back.

"Lady Lyndhurst," the secretary hissed under her breath in disapproval.

Miss Evans shot a sideways glance at Lyndy, who stood before them, tugging on the lapels of his morning coat. He didn't like it any more than Miss Evans did.

Stella ignored them both as Mr. Wingrove's nephew dropped his head into his hands and sobbed. This is what he needed, to cry, to mourn. Why couldn't the others see that? After a moment or two, he sat back, sniffling. Miss Evans retrieved a handkerchief from an assortment of several in her white beaded handbag and offered it to him.

"Thank you for your kindness, Lady Lyndhurst," Mr. Amesbury-Jones said, sounding much more like himself, after wiping his nose. "What you must think of me."

"I know grief when I see it. You obviously loved your uncle very much."

"I did, you see. But here's the rub. The last time I saw him, we argued. How am I to live with that?"

"You will take over where he left off and make him proud," Miss Evans stated pragmatically.

"And complete the acquisition. Yes, yes." A flash of new distress streaked across his face. "Maisie!" Yet, something beyond grief, lighter but distant, colored Mr. Amesbury-Jones's voice at the mention of the woman's name.

To Stella, it sounded like hope.

"The Peggs. They must be told about Uncle Horace."

"The Peggs?" Stella asked.

"They own the second-largest confectionery company in England," Miss Evans explained. "Rountree's, here in York."

"Rountree's?" Lyndy blurted.

That was Sir Owen's surname, Lyndy's roguish Yorkshire cousin who'd attended their wedding. (Though she should be thinking of him simply as Owen as he was her cousin now too.) Owen meant well, even if he was too cavalier when it came to women's affections. Lyndy had been like that when he and Stella met too. So, there was hope for Owen yet.

"What a coincidence."

Lyndy laughed as if the idea of Owen owning a confectionery company was absurd. He had a point. Stella couldn't imagine Lyndy's cousin doing anything as "ungentlemanly" as own a factory—except, of course, to run off with a commoner's daughter and some of his best New Forest ponies.

"Coincidence?" Miss Evans puckered her lips in annoyance. "What are you talking about?"

Here was a woman who held no awe for Lyndy's title, or Stella's for that matter. Stella had to admire her for it. Though, oh, how Miss Evans reminded her of her new mother-in-law.

"It's nothing," Stella assured them. "What were you saying about the Peggs?"

"Being in the same business," Mr. Amesbury-Jones said, "we've known the family for years, even socializing with them in London during the Season. Supposedly John Pegg had, in the end, decided to sell his factory to Uncle Horace. That's why we're in York."

Stella didn't mention overhearing Mr. Wingrove riled up when the pair appeared on his doorstep. If they were in York together to conduct business, why the hostility? Had he wanted to do the deal on his own? Was there something about the acquisition he didn't want his nephew or secretary to know about?

She swept away the crumbled fallen oak leaves beside her on the bench, their aromatic, earthy scent filling her nostrils. She was getting ahead of herself. She didn't even know anything improper was going on. Then why were little things starting to add up?

When Mr. Amesbury-Jones sprang from the bench, Stella rose too, with Lyndy unhesitatingly at her side. The nephew pulled his tie straight, ran his fingers through his hair, and tugged his jacket into place. Stella smiled inwardly at the last gesture, so like what Lyndy was prone to do when frustrated, what he'd been doing for the past few minutes. But Mr. Amesbury-Jones wasn't frustrated. He appeared almost excited. As if having a plan of action, something to focus on besides his uncle's death, energized him. Stella could relate to that too.

"I must telephone the Peggs at once," he declared. He turned on his heel and strode purposely across the shortly mowed lawn toward the hotel.

"I'll meet you in the dining room for breakfast," Miss Evans called after him.

He acknowledged her with an affirming wave as he mounted the steps two at a time before disappearing inside. Before heading in for breakfast herself, Stella flicked away a shriveled leaf clinging to the folds of her skirt. Miss Evans considered her as if reevaluating what she saw.

Stella, more than used to the scrutiny of strangers, straightened the brim of her hat and said, "Can't go in looking like I've been rolling around in the leaves. Honeymoon or not."

Caught off guard by her innuendo, Lyndy snorted with laughter. Miss Evans's lips never moved.

"You certainly aren't like any noble lady I've ever met," she said. Whether it was intended kindly or not, Stella took it as a compliment.

"I hope not." Stella smiled disarmingly. "Just don't tell my mother-in-law."

*   *   *

"Lady Lyndhurst?"

Lyndy, escorting Stella toward the breakfast room, glanced in the direction of the call. The hotel clerk, his stare fixed on Stella's back, tapped an envelope repeatedly on the smooth surface of the registration desk.

They'd returned to the hotel in a playful mood, the garden having done wonders, but ill-timed their return. A few minutes longer, and they'd been spared seeing the black glass-sided hearse carrying Mr. Wingrove's coffin approach from behind the hotel, the *clip-clop* of the horse's shoes echoing off the walled-in service drive. Stella had paused, her face unreadable. To lighten the mood, Lyndy had remarked upon the striking black Friesians, dressed in plumes and silver funeral harnesses that caught the sun. With no enthusiasm, his bride had absent-mindedly agreed. Such magnificent horses normally would've captivated her.

Lyndy began to fret. Had the chocolatier's death shaken her more than she'd made on? Or could that man's death have opened wounds not yet healed? Bloody Kendrick! Will her father ever stop plaguing her?

"Lady Lyndhurst!" the clerk shouted.

Lyndy suspected whatever emotions surfaced at seeing the hearse continued to preoccupy her mind. Or could it be her title was so new she hadn't come to recognize it yet? Lyndy presumed it was a bit of both.

"My love, he's talking to you," Lyndy whispered.

"He is?" She cupped her cheek with her hand. "Will I ever get used to being called that?"

Lyndy certainly hoped so. She may have been born a Kendrick, but she belonged to him now. Pride swelled in his chest, but he resisted the sudden urge to kiss her. It would never do. With breakfast being served, the lobby was growing crowded with an odd jumble of high society types, their modestly dressed servants, and foreign families on holiday. (Was that Spanish he'd heard?) Instead, he followed as Stella gravitated toward the desk to see what the desk clerk was going on about.

"Yes?" Stella said.

The clerk held out the envelope. "This arrived by post."

"Thank you, Mr. Coombs." Stella, accepting the envelope, shared with Lyndy a look of concern. It had no return address. Not waiting to find a letter opener, she ripped open the envelope with her finger.

Who could've sent it? Few people knew where they were. Lyndy had made sure of it. He hadn't even told his family, entrusting the information instead to Gates, Morrington Hall's stablemaster, with strict instructions not to reveal their location except in the case of an emergency. Stella had only told . . .

"It's from my mother," she said, rapidly reading the contents. Fearing bad news, Lyndy watched her face for clues. She glanced up at him, beaming.

"She, Aunt Ivy, Gertie, and Sammy are still in London," she said, as Lyndy guided her toward a velvet, green, cushioned Eastlake settee near the fire, crackling low and pleasantly warm.

Several of Stella's relations had traveled to England to attend their wedding: her mother, Mrs. Eugene Smith (that one was a bit of surprise); her maternal aunt, Miss Ivy Mitchell; her father's brother, Jedidiah Kendrick; and his young children, Gertie and Sammy. After the brief reunion, they were to return to America, all except Jedidiah Kendrick, who awaited trial in the Lyndhurst jail. With their father in custody, the care of the children was uncertain until Stella's Aunt Ivy, having no children of her own, had happily agreed to take them on. Stella's old Aunt Rachel, who'd accompanied Stella to England last spring, had refused to return with the other Americans, citing her advanced years. Who could blame her? It wasn't a journey to be entered into lightly for such an elderly woman. Not even Lyndy's

mother could find a reason to object. So, they'd agreed. Miss
Luckett would remain in residence at Pilley Manor, the family's
dowager house.

Stella eased herself down while still reading the letter. "They
couldn't get passage on a ship to New York sooner than next
week, so they decided to do some sightseeing while they
waited. She sends her love."

She laid the letter down in her lap with a flourish and smiled
at Lyndy meaningfully. *Oh, no.* He knew that look. Some impulsive idea had taken hold, and he knew he wasn't going to be
able to refuse her.

"What would you say to the idea of inviting them to visit us
here before they go back?"

Lyndy took his wife's hands in his. "I know how much
you'd like to spend time with your family"—a concept as foreign to him as a bridle would be to brown bear—"but my love,
we are on our honeymoon."

He tried to say it kindly, but it came out mirroring too
closely the way he felt. He had no intention of sharing Stella
with a throng of her relatives on their honeymoon. Yet he
wasn't unsympathetic to her needs either, she so newly re-
united with her mother.

"Perhaps just your mother could come?" he suggested.
Stella's face lit up like fireworks on Guy Fawkes Day. "For a
day or two," he promptly added, afraid he'd opened the flood-
gates.

"Oh, Lyndy. You don't mind?"

Lyndy loved to see her like this. He envied her too. When
had he ever anticipated seeing his mother with a fraction of
Stella's exuberance? To keep that joy on her face, he shook his
head.

"Then that's perfect. Aunt Ivy can easily keep the children
busy in London while Mama's here. And with the train ride
here and back, Mama wouldn't have much more time to visit

than that before her ship leaves anyway. Besides, no matter how much I want to see her"—she raised her hand to his cheek—"I'd hate to give up too much of the little time we have alone together."

Gratified that they agreed, he kissed the inside of her hand. Then an alarming concern crossed his mind. "Your mother wouldn't stay here, would she?"

"Are you kidding? As you said, we are on our honeymoon. I want to see Mama but not at breakfast."

As if on cue, the irresistible aroma of bacon and fried potatoes wafted in from the dining room. "Then, by all means, go invite Mrs. Smith before I pass out from hunger." His stomach rumbled loudly.

Taking his face in her hands, Stella planted an exuberant kiss on his lips. Her doing so unabashed, in the presence of a lobby of strangers, thrilled him to the core.

"Bloody hell," he blurted, his pulse racing. "If I wasn't so hungry, I might be inclined to order room service instead."

Stella swatted him playfully before bounding off to wire her mother the invitation.

CHAPTER 7

Stella stepped into a cacophony of voices, talking and laughing, silverware clinking on porcelain, and the clattering of plates and crystal as serving staff cleared the tables of dirty dishes. With breakfast in full swing, the dining room, its round tables covered in starched white linen and adorned with large blooms of fresh yellow dahlias, was teeming with fellow tourists and hotel guests—a stark contrast to the solemn quiet of Mr. Wingrove's bedroom or even the gardens outside. The vibrant energy was invigorating, not to mention the delicious aromas of bacon and freshly baked bread permeating the room.

"Lord and Lady Lyndhurst! Come join us," Dr. Bell called from a table by a bank of windows with a commanding view of the hotel's gardens. With him was a slight young man with dark, deep-set eyes Stella had never seen before.

Stella gauged Lyndy's feelings about sharing the doctor's table. There were a few empty tables staggered throughout (they could be alone if they chose), but Stella wanted to be social for some reason. Lyndy shrugged as if he didn't care, so they crossed the room to join the others. As they did, Stella noticed neither Miss Evans nor Mr. Amesbury-Jones had made it to breakfast yet.

"Good of you to join us," the doctor said as she sat across from him in the chair Lyndy pulled out for her. Lyndy seated himself beside her.

"We didn't get an opportunity to speak properly this morning," the doctor continued after a waiter took Lyndy's and Stella's order for coffee and tea. "This is Mr. Felix Middleton." Dr. Bell indicated the other man at the table with a tilt of his head. Mr. Middleton, who, unlike Dr. Bell, hadn't risen at Stella's approach, crammed a forkful of egg in his mouth and wiped his thin black mustache before saying hello. "Felix and I have made fast friends over our mutual fascination with York Minster."

"Touring on your own then?" Lyndy asked.

Stella marveled at Lyndy's question. He'd never been one for small talk but, here he was, asking strangers about themselves. Perhaps it was his mother's presence that had suppressed his natural curiosity? Too bad Lady Atherly was waiting for them back at Morrington Hall.

"Unfortunately, yes," Dr. Bell said. "I'm a widower with nothing more exciting to do on my holiday than to visit the grand cathedrals. What about you, Felix?"

"'ad a chance to visit, so I did, didn't I?" Mr. Middleton said, cutting up his kippers.

It wasn't much of an answer, so Dr. Bell added laughingly, "We are but two solitary men in search of inspiration."

"It's a remarkable edifice," Lyndy said. "I've promised my wife a visit while we're here."

"Completed in 1427, it's the second-largest Gothic cathedral in the Northern Hemisphere," Dr. Bell said proudly, as if he'd had a hand in its construction. "And the six-hundred-year-old Great East Window is the largest expanse of medieval stained glass in the country."

"Why are you in York?" Mr. Middleton asked as if Dr. Bell hadn't spoken, in an accent Stella wasn't used to hearing and couldn't place.

She reached for Lyndy's hand and clasped it. "We're on our honeymoon."

"Cheers, mate!" Mr. Middleton raised his teacup, the delicate floral-patterned porcelain appearing small in his hands. He took a sip before asking, "But why York? Ain't there more posh places, like London or Paris?"

"Those places don't have the first-ever racing grandstand," Stella said. She knew York was the perfect place to start their new life together when she'd learned of that. "And did you know that people have raced horses here since Roman times? How many places can boast a seventeen-hundred-year tradition?"

"Or stay in a hotel that has the custom of allowing local horse trainers to make their jockeys run up and down the hotel's hundred-yard-long corridor to lose weight while the trainers retire to the comfort of the bar for drinks?"

"Yes, well," Dr. Bell sighed. "Congratulations on your recent nuptials. Such a shame it had to be interrupted unhappily this morning."

"Bertram, here, has been tellin' me about 'ow you two found the old man," Mr. Middleton said, stabbing a sausage with his fork. "Shame, that."

"Yes, well . . ." Lyndy said. "Shall we see what's on offer, Lady Lyndhurst, or take our chances at the buffet?" He perused his menu, in hopes, no doubt, of changing the subject, but Stella wasn't ready to move on yet. She left her menu on the table.

"Speaking of," she said, "I wanted to ask you, Dr. Bell . . ."

At that moment, Mr. Amesbury-Jones appeared in the wide doorway of the dining room. He took in each table as if searching for someone. Miss Evans, presumably, but he headed directly for them when he spied their table. His hair was even more disheveled, despite or maybe because of his habit of running his fingers through it.

"I do apologize for interrupting, but I promised Miss Evans I'd meet her here for breakfast. Have you seen her?"

"Sorry, no," was the consensus.

"You are more than welcome to join us, Mr. Amesbury-Jones," Dr. Bell said, indicating the two empty seats at the table.

"Thank you. That's kind." He dropped into the one with its back to the windows, facing the door. "And please, after all we've been through this morning, do call me Morgan."

After Dr. Bell introduced Morgan to Mr. Middleton, and the waiter took Morgan's order for tea, Stella asked, "Did you reach the family you were going to telephone?"

"That's just it. No." Morgan regarded Stella with a worried expression. "Supposedly, the Peggs are in the Dales visiting cousins at their country estate, but from what the Peggs' butler told me, Hubberholme Park doesn't have a telephone. However, I did get ahold of Uncle Horace's solicitor. He insists on coming down tomorrow. Something concerning Uncle Horace's will that can't wait."

"Did you say Hubberholme Park?" Lyndy asked.

Morgan nodded. "That's the name of the cousin's estate."

"You could wire them. Even the Dales aren't too remote for that," Dr. Bell suggested lightly.

"But I can't see my way to sending a telegram with such news. It's too shocking. Besides, why are they in the Dales? Weren't they supposed to be in York for the acquisition? I was hoping Miss Evans might know more." His gaze anxiously swept the room again—still no Miss Evans.

"You could deliver the news in person," Stella suggested, encouraged by Lyndy's bemused expression. "And get the answers you need."

Morgan adamantly shook his head. "But I can't arrive unannounced on a stranger's doorstep."

"Then we shall take you," Lyndy offered.

"You, Lord Lyndhurst? Why would you do that?"

"To help you," Stella answered. "Besides, in addition to a tour of York Minster and the York Racecourse, Lord Lyndhurst promised me a ride on the Dales. I know for a fact that Hubberholme Park stables some excellent horses." Stella smiled guiltily at Lyndy. He never promised any such thing, but she knew he'd never deny her a ride across the Yorkshire countryside.

Morgan seemed overwhelmed but skeptical by the offer. He sought silent support from the two other, more clearheaded men at the table. When neither the doctor nor Mr. Middleton spoke up, he said, "I appreciate the gesture, Lady Lyndhurst, Lord Lyndhurst. I truly do. But surely even lords and ladies can't impose on strangers uninvited."

A peal of laughter from a boisterous group across the room rose above the background din of chatter and clinking plates.

"Ah, but you see, we wouldn't be strangers," Lyndy said, enjoying himself. Confusion, doubt, and hope flashed across Morgan's face.

"What are you saying, Lord Lyndhurst. You know these people?" Dr. Bell laughed incredulously.

Lyndy, holding them all in rapt attention, took a sip of his tea and set the cup down on its saucer before replying, "Indeed. Hubberholme Park is home to my mother's sister. Sir Owen Rountree, lord of the manor, will be delighted by a visit."

Ethel Eakins paused at the window, a white silk nightdress draped over her arm. From here, she could overlook the ancient, crenellated wall snaking its way past. She'd never been to York before. She had left the New Forest once, for a seaside holiday at Weymouth with her mum and sisters when she was twelve. To accompany Her Ladyship (though she'd always be *Miss* in her mind) on her honeymoon was a delight. And to stay at the Majestic Hotel! On the top floor with the other servants and working class, Ethel's room had an even better view of the city than this and was nowhere near the electric bell boards that rang day and night summoning porters or chambermaids. The radiators in her room sizzled with heat, she had her own water closet, and in the shared bath two doors down, she only had to turn a tap to draw the water. Yesterday, Ethel couldn't have imagined such luxuries.

Still, the journey had been a challenge. The train ride, through a harrowing storm, had been taxing and long, and after the first two hours, Ethel had tired of having nothing to do but stare out the rain-streaked window. Next time, if there were a next time, she'd bring her darning along or something to preoccupy her hands. When she and Harry Finn, Lord Lyndhurst's valet, had at last arrived, per his lordship's instruction, they'd been dismissed for the night. If that hadn't been enough, she'd come this morning to find both Lord and Lady Lyndhurst had gone and dressed themselves. What had Her Ladyship been thinking, pinning her own hair? *What would the other ladies' maids say?* The shame of it would've forced Ethel to hide in her room.

Ethel had long accepted that Her Ladyship, with her odd American ways, did things a bit different. But what's a lady's maid to do if her mistress didn't make use of her? Even Harry was a bit put out. Thankfully, Ethel was able to restyle Her Ladyship's hair before breakfast. Lady Lyndhurst had been restless but had said nothing. Ethel had learned the reason for it at breakfast.

A widow, clad all in black crepe, pushed a pram on the top of the medieval wall, an older child skillfully rolling a hoop before her, both unaware of Ethel's scrutiny. Ethel shuddered.

After arranging for Her Ladyship's mother's visit with the desk clerk (by chance, Mr. Coombs had a widowed friend who ran a respectable inn nearby), Ethel had overindulged at breakfast. Having never seen such a varied buffet, she'd loaded her plate with lamb chops, fried mushrooms, omelet, two buttered crumpets, and a whole sliced pear. She'd found an empty seat but was soon joined by a talkative, young chit of a maid who'd spoken of nothing but Mr. Wingrove, the sweets man: how he'd been found dead in the Honeymoon Suite in the early morning hours, how his face resembled an overripe tomato, how frightful it must've been for the chambermaid who found him, how marvelous his chocolates were, how she tried to emulate the model on the chocolate box, how irregular it was that Lord and Lady Lyndhurst came to the poor maid's rescue.

As the young maid moved on to admiring a ruddy-faced young man giving her the eye, Ethel had pushed back her half-eaten plate. Little wonder Lady Lyndhurst had been abrupt. Had that been why they'd done for themselves? She hadn't wanted to disturb Ethel or Harry so early? Wasn't that just like Her Ladyship? Her mistress had found another dead body, and still, she'd concerned herself with her servants' welfare.

Watching the widow and her children disappear from view, replaced by an animated couple gesturing excitedly to points below, Ethel tsked at the memory of her disloyalty. How unkind she'd been to be vexed by Her Ladyship's behavior. Ethel should've known better. Perhaps the long journey had put her more out of sorts than she'd realized.

It won't happen again.

Ethel returned to unpacking Her Ladyship's luggage: carefully unwrapping her clothes from the tissue paper and hanging them in the wardrobe, laying her undergarments in the lavender-scented chest of drawers, setting out Her Ladyship's slippers, shoes, and boots, placing the hatboxes on the shelves in the suite's dressing room. Once her task was done, she'd been given the remainder of the day off. It wasn't even a Sunday. Ethel, having thumbed through a copy of *Baedeker's* someone had left on the train, plotted her day in her head: visit York Minster, the Antiquities Museum with its Roman curiosities; ending with a stroll along the river and a spot to eat. Maybe Harry had other ideas. She couldn't go alone, so they'd agreed he'd accompany her. She hoped he'd fancy letting her decide.

With her mind full of the grand day ahead, she locked up Her Ladyship's suite and headed for the lift. Ethel scarcely noticed the woman stepping off, except for her lovely dark blue kid gloves.

Maybe I'll buy myself a new pair of gloves. Ethel had found another loose thread last night. How long they'd be respectable to wear, she couldn't say.

When the woman purposefully marched toward Her Ladyship's room, Ethel hesitated. She ignored the attendant's "On or off, miss?" and the lift doors closed with a *clang*. Was the woman seeking Lord or Lady Lyndhurst? Ethel waited to see, but the woman didn't stop in front of the Royal Suite. She approached the suite across the hall—where the dead man had been. Earlier, as she'd laid out Lady Lyndhurst's morning attire, Ethel had heard the undertakers barking orders and had peeked out as they wheeled the coffin past, never imagining Her Ladyship had seen the body first.

Ethel watched the woman try the door. It was locked. She jiggled it again as if in frustration.

"The guest from that suite was found dead this morning," Ethel called helpfully.

The woman jumped as if caught doing something she oughtn't.

"It's most certainly the wrong one then," the woman said, self-consciously touching her blue toque hat covered in large, white ostrich feathers.

The lift chimed, and the door opened again, and this time Ethel eagerly stepped in, anticipating her sightseeing adventure. She never gave the woman a second thought.

CHAPTER 8

Steaming westward through the Yorkshire countryside, Stella was struck by the picturesque beauty of the open landscape. From the rushing rivers carving their way through the expansive, rolling valleys, to the vast, treeless moors, vibrant in hues of golden bracken and faded purple heather, to the stark, craggy, windswept peaks, she'd never seen anything like it. Miles and miles of dry stone walls lined every field, every carriage road, like uneven stitching on a patchwork quilt. White-faced wooly sheep dotted the verdant pastures like spilled pearls on a plush green carpet. When the train clattered along high on the top of the ridge, the vista appeared endless. It was breathtaking.

She'd regretted having to leave the Daimler back at Morrington Hall to collect dust (no one else knew how to drive), but it had been impractical, too compact to hold both their luggage and the servants. Besides, she suspected Lyndy's pride may have suffered had she driven them from Rosehurst to York. Or worse yet, demand he do it without knowing how. But this was ideal. The train had a speed superior to her car without the need to navigate the harrowingly narrow, stone-wall-lined lanes. She could sit back, listening to the rhythmic *clickity-clack* of the train on the rails, and enjoy the view.

Her travel companions didn't seem to agree. Lyndy fidgeted, shifting in his seat, adjusting his waistcoat, brushing soot and dust from his sleeves and the crushed-velvet upholstery of the first-class carriage bench seats. Stella took his hand, hoping to ease his impatience but, after a brief moment, he was back picking at invisible lint again. Across from them, Morgan sat sullen and silent, staring down at the box of Wingrove chocolates in his lap.

The chocolates Mr. Wingrove had given them were the best she'd ever had. She licked her lips, the memory of them still lingering on her tongue.

"Are you bringing the chocolates to Miss Pegg?" Stella said, hazarding a guess.

Morgan bobbed his head absentmindedly, as if he wasn't listening.

"The chocolates are delicious," she said, hoping to draw Morgan out. "We've already eaten almost half of the box your uncle gave us."

"He stole our suite," Lyndy grumbled.

"Makes sense. Uncle Horace believed his chocolate was the answer to everything. Used to call it his 'secret weapon.' What else could be equally employed to persuade, apologize, or express affection? This"—Morgan tapped his box—"was his way of apologizing for the argument we had last night."

"I thought you said you didn't see him again after you argued?" Stella said.

"I didn't. The box was on the doorstep of my hotel room when Dr. Bell arrived to tell me the news."

"I admire your constraint," Lyndy said. "As my wife said, they are jolly good. I would've opened the box."

"It's kind of you to say so. We pride ourselves on producing the finest. But to be honest, I don't have much of a stomach for anything, not even the chocolates. I'm hoping Maisie—Miss Pegg," he corrected, "will appreciate them more."

Stella heard the same hint of hope and affection she'd detected before. She waited for him to say more, but he fell silent again as they rumbled across an iron bridge. Stella gazed out the window at the sparkles dancing on the water as the swiftly flowing river captured the morning sun.

"If you don't mind my asking, what was the argument about?"

Lyndy raised an eyebrow at her intrusive question but stopped trying to pull a loose string from the lacy edge of the handkerchief in his breast pocket to hear the answer. Morgan, lulled by the beauty of the passing landscape, didn't hesitate.

"I'm not quite sure. Miss Evans and I came to York to help with the Peggs' company's acquisition—Uncle Horace rarely met suppliers or competitors on his own. I thought it routine. Yet he was rather upset, furious really, when we arrived. As if we had no right to intrude on his business." These last words were tinted with the hurt that flashed across Morgan's face. "Not a week before, he was expounding on my need to be involved in every aspect of the business. I needed educating in 'all things Wingrove' to steer the company into the future. His words, not mine. Yet, when I attempted to help him with the most important company decisions in a decade, he slams the door in my face."

"How odd," Lyndy said.

"Indeed. I chalk it up to his illness. Because of it, Uncle Horace's behavior has been more and more erratic."

"What did he have?" Stella asked.

Lyndy flinched. Was this like money or age? A question never to be asked in polite society? Still. Given the man had died, who wouldn't want to know?

Morgan shrugged. "He was never one to talk about it."

"Quite," Lyndy agreed. "Few men want to admit their health is failing."

Lyndy was thinking of his father. Lord Atherly had collapsed with heart troubles when his precious fossils had been stolen. He always seemed a rigorously healthy man. As he hadn't said anything to anyone, it had come as a shock. Happily, Stella's father-in-law had recovered well enough to walk her down the aisle.

"I could've pressed him on it," Morgan was saying. "But never truly had cause to. When it came to the business, he was rather forthcoming. As I said, he intended for me to take over someday. Then this acquisition pops up, and he doesn't even inform me of it. I only learned about it yesterday. It's so strange."

"Buckbotton Station, ladies and gentlemen," the train conductor, a long-faced man with a drooping white mustache, called, lurching his way past their carriage. "Arriving at Buckbotton Station."

"This is us," Lyndy announced.

As the whistle screeched and the train crawled to a halt, Stella peered out at the cluster of stone buildings that made up the village of Buckbotton, its squat church's steeple barely jutting higher than the houses. An enormous curly-haired bull lumbered down the middle of the main street led by a farmer in knee-high boots. Beyond the village, treeless, walled-in pastures stretched for miles. Hubberholme Park was nowhere in sight.

"Can we walk?" Stella asked, eager to get outside and explore.

She stifled her enthusiasm when Morgan, his eyes wide with apprehension, tunneled his fingers deep along his scalp.

Lyndy must've noticed it too. "No, we'll hire a carriage. Hubberholme Park's a few miles from here. And not to worry, Morgan. They're expecting us."

Hubberholme Park hadn't changed since Lyndy saw it last. Owen enjoyed describing his ancestral home as an immense pile of rocks. He wasn't far off. The large, three-story block of a manor was built entirely of the local stone with little embellishments. Only the brightly painted red door gave any sign re-markable people lived within.

Lyndy had regretted leaving York the moment they left the railway station. They'd chosen York to visit; the cathedral, the museums, the ancient walls, the crooked narrow streets, the quaint, old houses with overhanging upper stories, the race-course with the world's first grandstand. What were they doing leaving the city before they'd had a chance to explore it? Now once committed, how frustrating to have Stella beside him, in a private compartment, feeling her warmth where their thighs and shoulders touched, but unable to pull her to him. He ad-mitted he had become more emboldened in showing her affec-tion in public of late, but how could he, in all good conscience, embrace his wife with Morgan Amesbury-Jones mournfully staring at them from across the way?

A sheep bleated as Lyndy alighted the carriage. He filled his lungs with the fresh, country air, recalling why he'd agreed to come.

Lyndy had spent some of his happiest days here, countless summer holidays traipsing across the rugged landscape, far from his mother's disparaging tongue. Now he could share it with Stella even if they did have a somber stranger in tow.

"I say, old chap," Owen said, stroking his beard, a twinkle in his eye. "What's the meaning of this?"

Lyndy's cousin, dressed in tweeds and knee-high boots as if about to go hunting, had been waiting in the drive when the carriage arrived. A mischievous smile spread across his face.

"I'm freshly back from Morrington, and already you're on my doorstep."

The gravel crunched behind Lyndy as Stella and Morgan alighted. Owen's smile widened. Without shifting his attention from Stella, Owen slapped Lyndy on the back. "At least you've brought your better half with you."

"You got our telegram then?"

"I did," he said, over his shoulder, "but I still don't quite understand to what I owe this pleasure." Owen approached Stella and, grasping her hand, lifted it to his lips. "For it is a pleasure. I'm delighted to see you, my dear, Lady Lyndhurst. I do hope my cousin is treating you well." He winked at her.

"Oh, Owen," Stella said playfully, pulling her hand away. "We're family now. Call me Stella."

"If you insist, Stella."

Lyndy rolled his eyes at his cousin's antics. "This is Mr. Morgan Amesbury-Jones," he said, indicating the third member of their party.

"Welcome to Hubberholme Park, Mr. Amesbury-Jones," Owen said, clearly enjoying playing the host. "Since you did give us rather a bit of warning, Lyndy, Mummy has delayed luncheon. I hope you like poached salmon, Mr. Amesbury-Jones."

Morgan, with a noncommittal mutter, followed Owen into the house.

"Come meet my aunt," Lyndy said, looping Stella's arm through his. She clenched her teeth together in a nervous grimace. He patted her hand. "Don't worry. She'll adore you."

How can she not?

The drawing-room was as Lyndy remembered it, an eclectic mix of formal rosewood furniture draped in exotic embroidered silks and colorful Ottoman horse blankets. Dour ancestral portraits hung beside whimsical paintings of foreign landscapes and monuments. Bric-a-brac, hand-carved wooden animals, woven bowls with geometric patterns, ceramic statues of half-naked figures filled every surface. A prodigious bouquet of purple Michaelmas daisies filled a four-foot-tall painted porcelain vase set against the opposite wall. The smell of the place, which pulled him back to his childhood, was the pungent aroma of incense mingled with the fainter scent of cat.

Aunt Winnie, dressed in an odd, multicolored, loose-fitting

silk dress covered in embroidered flowers and sporting long, oversized sleeves that draped off her arms as she raised them out in greeting, didn't rise when Stella and Lyndy entered the drawing-room. Boulder, the Rountree family's sleek, gray-colored Persian cat, lounged on her lap. Stella crinkled her nose.

"She's your mother's sister?" Stella whispered.

"Indeed." An amused smile tugged at the corner of his mouth. "In many ways, her complete opposite, I'm happy to say."

Except for the familial patrician nose, strong chin, and love of flowers, his mother's younger sister was nothing like the Countess of Atherly. Although some said the sisters shared the same shape and color of eyes, Mother's never sparkled with delight or mischief. Mother was the epitome of a proper countess. Aunt Winnie, unapologetically unconventional, had married "beneath her," wedding Sir John Rountree, a kind, adventure-seeking baronet who worshipped her, and together they had traveled extensively until Uncle John died of influenza three years ago. Aunt Winnie had been devastated. Theirs was a marriage Lyndy hoped to emulate.

"Lyndy, my dear boy." Aunt Winnie smiled. "What unexpected pleasure. But aren't you on your honeymoon?"

Before her on the low table was a tea service unlike any he'd ever seen. The domed, long-handled, engraved copper pot was accompanied by undersized, unadorned white porcelain cups nestled in carved copper cradles attached to the copper saucer. Wherever did she get that?

Aunt Winnie waved them over to her. Each time her long sleeves swished past, Boulder swatted at them with his claws. Aunt Winnie reached out to clasp Stella's hands, briefly causing Boulder, his front claws snagged on silk threads, to dangle over her lap. "And you most certainly must be my new niece."

"I am." Stella beamed, delighted, no doubt, to find herself more welcome here than she had at Morrington Hall. "And I'm so happy to meet you, Lady Rountree. And you too."

Stella leaned forward to scratch Boulder between the ears. Lyndy, who'd always been a favorite of the cat's, noted he never purred like that for him.

"Boulder has good taste," he quipped.

"I've always said he was an excellent judge of character. And, Stella, my dear, it's Aunt Winnie, please. I think *lady this* and *lady that* among family grows old, don't you?"

"I wouldn't have it any other way," Stella said enthusiastically.

Aunt Winnie urged Lyndy closer and then tapped her cheek with her finger. Lyndy gave her a peck before gliding his hand down the length of Boulder's back. The cat languidly wrapped its tail around Lyndy's arm, prompting him to do it again.

"She seems rather too good for you, my boy," Aunt Winnie said playfully, stealing glimpses of Stella's bemused smile. "I suppose, though, you aren't without your charms." She winked at him, as she used to when he was a boy.

"Are the Peggs here?" Morgan asked.

With more gray curls than Lyndy remembered, Aunt Winnie cocked her head to the side and frowned as Lyndy stepped aside. "And who might you be, my dear?"

"I do apologize. Mr. Morgan Amesbury-Jones, may I introduce my aunt, Lady Winifred Rountree?"

"I beg your pardon, Lady Rountree. You must think me an awful brute." Morgan slipped the hat from his head but never changed his focus away from the doorway.

"You're forgiven as I believe I have you to thank for bringing my nephew and his lovely new bride to Hubberholme Park in this most unexpected but delightful visit. Here, have a cup of Turkish coffee."

She reached for the strange copper pot, pouring a thick, dark liquid into the small cups. She handed one to each of them. With a robust coffee scent, the drink was thick like black treacle. Lyndy took a cautious sip but needn't have. It was delicious. Stella crinkled her nose as she tried hers. Her face brightened in surprise, and she took a second, more eager sip. Morgan set the cup down without sampling his coffee.

"I do apologize, my dears, for not attending your wedding," Aunt Winnie continued. "As you can see, I'm still relegated to my chair. I twisted my ankle dismounting Sundara and am on strict orders from the doctor to stay off my horse and my feet."

"We did miss you," Lyndy said, "but as Owen most certainly told you, it wasn't without its difficulties."

If one can call murder a difficulty.

"My, I do forget myself," Aunt Winnie said, raising her palms to her cheeks. "My most sincere condolences for your loss, Stella, my dear."

"Thank you, Aunt Winnie," Stella said, with the briefest of pauses.

Lyndy studied Stella's face, trying to gauge how she was holding up. Was she still grieving her brute of a father? From all outward appearances, she'd moved on. She rarely spoke of it, and he was loath to bring it up, if doing so caused her additional pain. Knowing Stella, she would talk of it if and when she was ready.

"To answer your question, Mr. Amesbury-Jones, John and Maisie are here. Distant cousins of John's, here for a visit," she added as an explanation for Lyndy and Stella. "There they are now."

The pair emerged from a French window that hadn't been there during Lyndy's last visit. Behind them, Lyndy spotted a newly added conservatory bursting to the ceiling with palms, exotic fruit trees, and a vine with gigantic red blossoms. The young, rather attractive, light-brown-haired woman wore a lacy blue tea dress that complemented her large, blue eyes. She had a distinctive beauty mark on her upper lip. In many ways, she reminded him of Stella. Yet without the spark or the charm that his wife exuded without realizing it. More than twice her senior, the older man had little hair on his head but an impressively bushy gray mustache. Both were at least a head shorter than Lyndy.

"Maisie, John, this is my favorite nephew, Lyndy, and his new bride, Stella." As an afterthought, she added, "She's an American. And this young man is—"

"Morgan, what are you doing here?" Miss Pegg said gleefully.

Owen, still holding his Turkish coffee cup, frowned, his countenance clouded in confusion. "Maisie, you two know each other?"

"Oh, yes!"

Prompted by the young woman's enthusiasm, Owen shot daggers at Lyndy and then downed his coffee in so many gulps as if it were whiskey.

"I say, what's that for?" Lyndy said.

Owen shook his head vigorously as if warding off any further comment.

"We are well acquainted with Mr. Amesbury-Jones, Sir Owen," Mr. Pegg said. Turning to Morgan, he added, "Son, to what do we owe the pleasure?"

"Maisie, John, it's—"

"Please, everyone, sit," Aunt Winnie directed.

Morgan, Lyndy noticed, dragged a chair close to where Miss Pegg had lowered herself on the sofa.

"What is it, Morgan?" Miss Pegg said, biting her lip.

"How do I say this?" Morgan squared his shoulders and addressed the Peggs. "Well . . . Uncle Horace is dead."

"Oh, Morgan, no."

Miss Pegg reached across the sofa's scrolled armrest to grasp Morgan's hand. Owen squinted at the pair's intertwined fingers, a disapproving pinch to his lips. It was a display more suited to Lyndy's mother than Owen.

What's put a bee in his bonnet?

"How did it happen, son?" Mr. Pegg asked, in a low, sonorous voice.

"We believe fumes from a faulty chimney might've overcome him."

"How terrible. Poor Horace. He was such a lovely man," Miss Pegg said. Letting go of Morgan, she snapped open her silver beaded reticule bag and retrieved a snow-white, scalloped-edged handkerchief.

"What bad luck," Owen quipped offhandedly, sounding too much like he was the one put out.

Miss Pegg narrowed her eyes at him before returning her attention to Morgan.

"How are you holding up?" she asked, forcing the handkerchief into Morgan's hand, who forced a half smile of thanks but, not in need of it, tucked it under his leg.

"As good as can be expected." Morgan glanced at Lyndy and Stella sheepishly, knowing they'd seen him at his worst. "I brought these for you." He presented Miss Pegg with the box of chocolates.

"Oh, Morgan, how kind," she said, her voice syrupy. "Thinking of me at a time like this?" She leaned toward him, and while taking the box, tenderly brushed strands of hair from his forehead. "Thank you."

Lyndy noted Owen's uncharacteristic sour glare aimed at the pair. Granted, the two were more familiar than Morgan led them to believe, but why should Owen care?

"We appreciate you coming all this way to tell us, son," Mr. Pegg said. He coughed into his fist. "But you could've telephoned us the news."

"I telephoned you from the hotel, but your housekeeper said you'd come here."

"Hotel? Where are you staying?"

"We're all staying at the Majestic."

"In York?" Miss Pegg asked. "Morgan, why didn't you tell us you were coming?"

"Did Uncle Horace tell you I wasn't?"

"Horace didn't tell us anything."

"But you were planning to sign the papers today, weren't you, John?"

"What papers are you talking about, son?"

"The papers to acquire Rountree Confectionery, of course."

Aunt Winnie exchanged a worried look with Mr. Pegg. Miss Pegg twisted the silken cord of her reticule around her fingers.

"Maisie, John? What are you not telling me?"

"I have no idea what you're talking about, son," Mr. Pegg said.

"The acquisition, of course!" Morgan leaped to his feet, frustrated, startling Boulder. The cat launched off Aunt Winnie's lap, crouched as if preparing to pounce, and hissed his displeasure. Morgan took a cautious step back.

"What was that about Boulder being a good judge of character?" Owen chuckled as he snatched Boulder from the floor. He returned the cat to his mother's lap, who tried soothing him with quiet coos.

"Son, did Horace tell you he was buying us out?" Mr. Pegg said, carefully articulating his words.

"Yes, I mean no. Gosh, John, it's all rather peculiar." Morgan raked his hands through his hair again.

"Sit down, my dear," Aunt Winnie said placatingly.

With Miss Pegg's grip on his arm, Morgan collapsed into his chair. With his head tipped back, he stared up at the ceiling, a mural of floating cherubs in an idyllic sky with bits of peeling blue plaster threatening to plummet to the carpet.

"Are you saying, John, you weren't planning to sell Rountree's to Uncle Horace?"

As Mr. Pegg shook his head, Lyndy caught apprehension flash momentarily across Stella's face. "I'm afraid this is the first I've heard of it, son."

CHAPTER 9

The wind lashed at Stella's face, whipping her hat, hair, and skirt around like a flag planted in the soil, claiming the land for her own. She and Lyndy had left Hubberholme Park far behind.

After Mr. Pegg's revelation, Newsham, the butler, had arrived announcing luncheon was served. Stella had been relieved. Questions swirled in her head enough already about Mr. Wingrove and his secrets. Why she couldn't figure out, but she knew she needed to let them go, had to relish getting to know her new husband's extended family, and not focusing on a stranger's lies. Aunt Winnie had tried her best to help, being nothing if not a good hostess and doing her sister proud. She steered the conversation toward the wedding, pressing for details she insisted her son had neglected, which according to her, were many. She expounded on the sightseeing virtues of York, drawing the Peggs into a debate over which were better: the Museum Gardens or the Deanery Gardens. And the food she served! Dish after exotic dish, like the one Aunt Winnie called "ball curry," a meat course with hints of cloves and cinnamon and other fragrant flavors Stella had never dreamed of. Its aroma filled the dining room long after the footmen had taken the plates away. Yet Morgan's confusion, the specter of the dead Mr. Wingrove, and the unspoken questions surrounding his purpose in being in York dampened what could've been a delightful meal.

It was a relief to be outside, and just the two of them, again.

After a long hike up the hill, through a rare patch of forest, they scrambled over an old wooden stile, the only way over a six-foot stone wall, where her skirt caught on a splinter in one of the boards. Confident Ethel could fix the rip, Stella yanked it free and clambered on. Behind the wall, a purple and gold moor stretched across the hilltop like a hidden treasure. It had started to sprinkle halfway up the hillside, and despite the damp, the two had silently agreed to keep going. Rooted at the highest point, with a ray of sun breaking through the steel-colored sky, like a spotlight shining on the distant valley, Stella felt small, and at the same time, a part of everything. It was exhilarating.

Lyndy stood behind her, his arms wrapped around her waist, his dimpled chin resting on her shoulder. "I used to love it here."

She snuggled against him closer, noting something wistful in his voice. Without being told, she understood how these rugged hills had meant freedom to him: from his duty, his boredom, his overbearing mother. It was something they shared. If she had had a Yorkshire hillside to escape to as a child, she would've, every chance she got. Instead, her escape was her father's stables. Shying away from thoughts lurking at the edges of her mind, of an unloving father and a mother that should've been there, Stella purposely drew on happier memories of her childhood spent with stable hands and horses and pictured the friend she could always rely on.

"I wonder how Tully is doing?"

"No doubt being spoiled rotten with apples and peppermint

by Gates and the rest of the stable staff." Lyndy was right. Stella had left her beloved horse in good hands. *But oh, to be able to ride her across this landscape.*

They stayed in each other's arms, admiring the view in silence, for a long time, enjoying being quiet and alone.

"Next time, let's take Owen up on his offer," she said.

When announcing their intention to hike after luncheon, Owen had offered them horses to ride instead. But without the proper attire and the limited time, they'd agreed a hike would be less complicated.

"Yes, let's."

"Speaking of Owen. What's the matter with him? He seemed happy to see us and then—"

"It was like he'd gotten his nose bent all of a sudden. You noticed that too?"

Of course, she did. If anything, she was surprised that Lyndy had. Then again, he was surprising her every day. *Wasn't it wonderful?*

Surprises. The word triggered thoughts of the one Morgan got earlier. Suddenly, like the opening of the starting gate, her mind was racing with questions she couldn't suppress.

"Why did Mr. Wingrove lie about the acquisition? Could it have anything to do with his death?"

Lyndy pulled her closer and rested his warm cheek against hers as the sun finally reached their lofty spot. "Why even concern ourselves with the death of this stranger? He was an old man, an unwell old man, at that, and his death was the result of an accident."

Stella turned in his arms, draping hers casually around his neck. Movement in the brush caught her eye. Three or four yards away, a plump, round, reddish-brown grouse pecked at the vegetation. She pointed the bird out to Lyndy.

"Either it was an accident," she whispered in his ear, not wanting to disturb the bird, "and we should've been the victims, or considering no one knows why he was in York in the first place—" She paused, hesitating to say it out loud.

"Now, now, my love," Lyndy said. He kissed the tip of her nose. "Don't let your concerns cloud your judgment. Simply because strange circumstances surround the man's purpose in being in York—"

"About which he lied," Stella interjected.

"Yes," Lyndy said indulgently. "Or because he happened to displace us from the rooms we reserved on the same night the chimney proved faulty or the fact that the man's beneficiary argued with him hours before his death . . ." Lyndy hesitated as it dawned on him that he was building a case for something other than a straightforward accident.

"Don't forget the missing pillows," Stella added.

Lyndy sighed. "Doesn't mean the man was murdered." Even he didn't sound convinced.

"No, you're right," Stella said, returning the kiss to his nose. "How could I have ever gotten such a crazy idea?"

Herman Haigh raised the simple, gold-rimmed porcelain teacup to his lips. The rim struck the edge of his tooth. It clattered in the saucer as he set it down. Leaving the tea, he nibbled at the last bit of shortbread biscuit. Brushing crumbs from his waistcoat, he stood. Rounding his small, oak desk, he fetched the duster he always kept on hand and swished the feathers over the desk and then across the shelf displaying his collection of royal coronation mugs. Admiring the portraits of His and Her Majesties hung above the shelf, the black frames setting off well against the whitewashed walls, he straightened the Royal Doulton cup before returning to his desk. He lowered himself into his chair, took a deep breath, and lifted the teacup again. The black tea, laden with too much sugar, was tepid on his tongue by the time he finished it, but it had done its job. Herman had summoned the fortitude necessary for what he must do next.

He unlocked the middle drawer and reverently slid it open. There lay his reward beside the hotel master key—a gold, embossed invitation to Their Royal Highnesses' private reception. Herman never imagined the likes of him would bask in the presence of royalty. But it had been dearly won, and Herman lifted it out with reverence, hugging it to his chest like his firstborn.

Even Mr. Wingrove's unfortunate demise won't spoil this.

By the time Herman informed the Majestic's owner (whose current location was best described as "somewhere in the wilds of South America") that the maker of England's finest chocolates died in York's finest suite, it would be too late. The reception was the day after tomorrow, and Sir Peter would be none the wiser that Herman had attended in his stead.

To represent the Majestic, of course.

Wasn't it Herman and not Sir Peter who upheld the superior standards the Majestic was renowned for? Wasn't it Herman who faced an ice field when the boiler broke last winter and flooded the gardens? Wasn't it Herman who calmed a mutinous chef when a guest's pet monkey broke free and wreaked havoc in the kitchens? Wasn't it Herman who confronted both the doctor and the detective to ensure that Mr. Wingrove's ill-fated visit didn't tarnish the Majestic's sterling reputation?

With the invitation propped up against the obligatory framed photograph of his wife, he seized a sheet of stationery imprinted with the hotel's name and closed the drawer. He would have to choose his words carefully. He selected his favorite fountain pen from the brass tray and, licking the nib, began: *Dear Sir Peter . . .*

He paused, his mind seeking the best way to describe the latest developments, when a flicker of movement drew his attention. Had someone passed his door, left open to allow the heat out? (The radiator was far too efficient for this small room.) But Herman's office, his refuge from the chaos without, was at the far end of the hall. Unless otherwise invited, no one was welcome. Today, of all days, and specifically at teatime, no one had call to be here but him.

"Who's there?"

When no answer came, he pushed back from his desk. In three strides, he was at the threshold, peeking his head into the hall. "How odd. I could've sworn I saw—"

His words caught in his throat, replaced by a garbled cry, as a precisely placed blow to his head sent Herman sprawling. He heard a sickening crunch of his spectacles, knocked loose from his face, as a figure stepped over him, like a fallen limb blocking the lane, and into his office.

My invitation!

Herman, recalling how he'd carelessly left it out for the taking, struggled in protest, raising himself but an inch before slumping to the cool wooden floor, unconscious.

No one noticed Stella lingering at the threshold of the drawing-room, waiting as Lyndy directed Newsham to send for the carriage.

Aunt Winnie, facing away from the door, petted the cat. With hooded eyes, appearing to study the leaves he swirled around in his teacup, Owen watched Miss Pegg as she nibbled on a thick slice of parkin, a moist, oat-based Yorkshire gingerbread. Stella could smell the ginger from here. Stella had tried some parkin at breakfast. She liked it better than Aunt Rachel's Christmas crunchy gingerbread men. But it wasn't the parkin Owen hungered for; Miss Pegg was a beautiful woman with a heart-shaped face and a ready smile. Yet she was obviously attached to Morgan, and after what had happened with Penny Swenson, Stella would've hoped Owen had learned his lesson. His longing gaze told a different story.

"Isn't Marie buried in York?" Mr. Pegg was saying.

Being mother, Aunt Winnie poured him a cup of tea from a bright red teapot encircled by a hand-painted golden dragon. The Turkish coffee set had been taken away.

"She is," Morgan said solemnly. "Along with their daughter."

Miss Pegg, seated beside him, patted his knee. Owen crossed his arms against his chest and glanced away. Stella followed his gaze as he feigned interest in a dreary painting of a crumbling medieval abbey done by an amateur's hand. It looked out of place beside the masterful depiction of the Taj Mahal.

"Perhaps he fancied a visit to his wife's grave in peace?" Miss Pegg concluded.

"Then why not simply tell me?" Morgan said, frowning. "I would've understood."

Stella scrutinized Morgan, viewing him in a whole new light. On their hike back, she and Lyndy had discussed the "coincidences" surrounding Horace Wingrove in more depth and from every angle. One name kept cropping up, Morgan Amesbury-Jones. Morgan claimed Mr. Wingrove was in York to acquire the Peggs' factory, but that was untrue. He'd argued with his uncle hours before his death, and if anyone profited from Mr. Wingrove's demise, Morgan was the most likely candidate. Granted, he seemed to be genuinely grieving, but Stella had been fooled before.

"The carriage will be ready in a few minutes," Lyndy whispered, joining her. Stella looped her arms through his and stepped into the room. "Well, that's us off, Aunt Winnie," he said as they strolled toward Lyndy's aunt.

Aunt Winnie patted the space on the couch beside her. "My, you two wet dears. You must dry out before you leave." There was room enough for one.

Stella begrudgingly obliged. Having shed her wet hat and jacket, she was perfectly dry. Lyndy smoothed the front of his waistcoat before taking the nearest chair. Aunt Winnie called for the dying fire to be stoked and for the servants to bring more tea. Stella didn't want tea. She was eager to get back to York. She'd enjoyed meeting his aunt and exploring the countryside, but they hadn't even walked the city walls yet.

"But then why use us as an excuse?" Mr. Pegg, acknowledging their arrival with a nod, argued with his daughter.

Aunt Winnie leaned toward Stella conspiratorially, stroking the sleeping cat on her lap. Set before her on the low, mahogany table were plates that matched the exotic red teapot. Only two cucumber sandwiches and a miniature apple tart remained. Another plate contained molasses-colored crumbs.

"We're speculating as to what actually brought poor Mr. Wingrove to York and his untimely date with death," she whispered.

"Horace knew full well I'd never sell," Mr. Pegg continued, waving his empty teacup in the air. "He also had no cause to be surprised when Morgan arrived." Morgan must've described his uncle's reaction. Had he admitted they argued as well? "Horace was well aware that announcing a trip to York to do business with me would precipitate Morgan's desire to join him."

"Oh?" Aunt Winnie said with an air of mock innocence. "And why would that be?"

Owen's focus darted from Miss Pegg, who smiled daintily, her eyes dropping to a distant point on the carpet, to Morgan, who shifted and straightened and shifted again in his chair. Not liking what he read in their reactions, Lyndy's cousin tossed back what remained of his tea, stood, and began pacing the room. Sitting on the edge of his chair, Lyndy seemed poised to spring up and join him.

"That's beside the point," Morgan said as if the reason was best left unsaid. "What matters is that Uncle Horace never told me about the acquisition."

"And why would that be?" Owen snipped, his words echoing his mother's. Miss Pegg's mouth fattened into a humorless smile. Owen leaned against the mantel and crossed his arms in response, deflecting her silent rebuke. "Well, old chap?" Owen pressed, his glare defiant.

Morgan's cheeks colored, with embarrassment or anger, Stella couldn't tell. He said nothing as he raked his fingers through his hair.

"If you must know, Horace had been struggling of late," Miss Pegg answered for him, delicately tiptoeing around the old man's apparent frailties. "Perhaps he was visiting a doctor in York? A specialist, perhaps?" She looked to Morgan for confirmation.

"Do you know what your poor uncle suffered from?" Aunt Winnie said, conscientiously adjusting her injured ankle on the pillow.

"I don't," Morgan admitted, "but it's been coming on for a while." The Peggs, as one, nodded in agreement. "I'd noticed his hands tremble; his gait was awkward, and he often lost his balance."

"That could simply be a sign of old age, my dear," Aunt Winnie retorted.

"No disrespect, Lady Rountree, but Uncle Horace also had difficulty concentrating. On several occasions, I'd caught him hesitating over business papers as if he couldn't make out what was before him. Sadly, I've had to recheck his figures more than once."

"But if that were the case," Owen wondered, his tone less combative, as he stroked his beard, "he wouldn't go to York. Surely he'd go up to London where he'd be guaranteed the best medical care the country has to offer?"

Owen had a point.

"Perhaps we'll never know, and perhaps it's best we don't," Aunt Winnie declared matter-of-factly, putting to rest any further speculation. She picked up a plate from the table and offered it to Stella. "Apple tart, my dear?"

CHAPTER 10

After the long train ride, the lure of a hot bath was more than appealing, but Stella wanted to check something first. Aunt Winnie may not have wanted to know, but Stella couldn't help herself. When Lyndy returned to the room, Stella headed for the front desk. The ever-present Mr. Coombs was behind it, a well-worn map of the city laid out before him. She waited while he gave detailed walking directions to Mansion House, the Lord Mayor's residence, to a gentleman in a gray top hat and matching overcoat.

"Do you have a copy of the York city directory?" she asked the moment the gentleman stepped aside.

"We may." He folded the map and tucked it away below the desk. "It may take me quite some time to fetch it." He paused to regard his cuticles. "For a little something extra . . ."

"I'll wait."

His lips tightening into a frown, the desk clerk lifted a stack of letters to demonstrate he had more important tasks. "Won't sort themselves, will they?"

"Please?" Stella flashed him a smile.

In response, Mr. Coombs deliberately set the stack down, bared his teeth in a mocking smile, and disappeared into a back room. Stella leaned her back against the desk to wait. Across the lobby, a woman in a gray dress and white apron absent-mindedly pushed a baby carriage back and forth, her attention on her open book, *The Woman with the Fan*. In the chair beside her, a girl about five years old, wearing a light green pinafore over her dress and large matching bow, plucked petals from one of the hotel's bouquets. Pink petals danced and scattered when the girl swung her legs exuberantly several inches from the floor. When their eyes met, Stella and the child shared a mischievous grin.

Without warning, something dropped to the floor behind her with a thud. Startled, Stella smacked her back against the raised edge of the desk, the boning of her corset digging into her skin. The little girl flinched, and the unseen infant wailed from inside the baby carriage. The woman glanced up from her book, her eyes narrowed in annoyance.

"The directory you requested, Your Ladyship," Charlie said insolently.

Stella whirled around to see him shove a thick, red book across the polished surface toward her. It read *Kelly's Directory of the City of York* and smelled of sweet, decomposing paper. She caught it as it threatened to slip off the edge. Dust and dirt from the book's cover soiled her gloves. After a lifetime of her father's ridicule and being well-accustomed to such rudeness, Stella could ignore the clerk's self-satisfied sneer. But why had she provoked such disdain? The clerk had been cordial to the gentleman needing directions. Was it that he hated Americans or women or both? It wouldn't be the first time Stella encountered such prejudice. Without another word, the clerk returned to his mail sorting.

It was just as well, she thought, swiping her gloves together. She didn't want anyone to see what she was looking up.

Stella slid the book to the far end of the desk, quickly found what she was searching for in the table of contents, and flipped to the appropriate subject heading—*PHYSICIANS*. There were dozens listed. After a glance, she closed the heavy book with a thump. What was she thinking? Even if Mr. Wingrove had visited a local doctor, she'd never have time to find out which one.

At least not without ruining my honeymoon.

Leaving the directory on the desk, she made her way toward the elevator but stopped when she heard a familiar voice ask, "Any post for me?" Seizing the chance to question the doctor about Mr. Wingrove's possible illness, Stella reversed course.

"Yes, Dr. Bell. This just arrived." Mr. Coombs, an affable smile on his face, handed the doctor a letter. Dr. Bell slipped the man a coin.

Dr. Bell glanced at the envelope, and his congenial smile faded from his lips. He was staring at the envelope in his hand as if pondering whether to open it or not when Stella inquired, "Bad news, Dr. Bell?"

He refocused his attention as Stella cautiously approached, forcing himself to smile. "Good evening, Lady Lyndhurst."

The sadness enveloping him belied his attempt to appear cheery. He slipped the envelope into the pocket of his jacket, but Stella briefly caught sight of the distinctive sprawling scrawl of the sender. It was nearly illegible.

"Nothing unexpected," he said in the way of explanation.

"I wonder if I could ask you something in a professional capacity?"

"I'm flattered, Lady Lyndhurst, truly, but I think it best you consult your personal physician if you have any complaints."

"You misunderstand me. I wanted to ask you about Mr. Wingrove."

"Indeed?" He indicated that they should move away from the registration desk. Stella followed him to a quiet corner near the fire. The warmth reminded her of the hot bath and the man currently soaking in the tub who awaited her. One quick question, and she'd be happy to join Lyndy upstairs.

"I can't think of anything I'd be able to tell you that you don't already know," Dr. Bell said.

"Mr. Wingrove's nephew believes his uncle was ill before his death but could never confirm what he suffered from. I was hoping if I gave you a list of his symptoms, you might be able to hazard a guess."

"You want me to give you a diagnosis of a dead man's prior illness? Whatever for?"

Did she tell him about all the inconsistencies surrounding Mr. Wingrove's visit to York? Did she confide in him her suspicions that Mr. Wingrove's death was more than an accident? That she wasn't reassured that Detective Sergeant Glenshaw was up to the task?

No. Viscountesses didn't say such things to new acquaintances. At least that's what she imagined her mother-in-law would advise.

"I've often been accused of being curious to a fault, Doctor," she said. "And for some reason, I feel a connection to Mr. Wingrove," both of which were true. "Maybe it's because he serendipitously took the rooms that we had reserved. I can't help feeling that my husband and I might've died if Mr. Wingrove hadn't interceded the way he did."

"I never thought of it that way."

"So obviously, I'm curious to learn more about the man who inadvertently gave his life for mine."

"Very well, Lady Lyndhurst." He indicated the closest settee for her while taking the chair set across from it. "Describe to me the symptoms."

She related the detailed list: hand tremors, awkward gait, loss of balance, difficulty concentrating, calculation mistakes, increased melancholy, and irritability. "Do those indicate anything to you?"

Dr. Bell stayed quiet for some time. "You must understand

that Mr. Wingrove was never my patient, nor have I ever run any laboratory tests to verify what I'm about to say."

"I understand completely."

"But from what you described, I would presume that he suffered from . . ." Again, he hesitated as if deciding to proceed or regret what he was about to say. "It sounds to me like it could be chorea, first described by your compatriot, Dr. George Huntington."

Stella had never heard of chorea, but it was a cruel disease if the doctor's expression was any indication. Pity welled up in her, and she wondered if Mr. Wingrove's premature death wasn't a mercy.

"Could Mr. Wingrove have visited a specialist for chorea here in York?"

"I suppose, but you'll never discover one way or another. If you visit every surgery in the city, no one will tell you anything. We physicians are funny like that. Why do you ask?"

"We discovered Mr. Wingrove wasn't in York to acquire the Peggs' confectionery company, as his nephew believed. Some in his party speculated it could've been for his health."

Dr. Bell tipped back his head and laughed. It was good to hear after such a day she'd had. "That's certainly possible, but there are plenty of other reasons to visit York, you'll recall. The royal reception is going to be quite the event, I hear. The city walls are splendid, and of course, York Minster is a wonder to behold. Someone even told me the York Racecourse's grandstand is worth a visit."

Stella chuckled. "That's true."

Stella had never considered that Mr. Wingrove could've wanted a vacation. Away from his business, his health concerns, his family? That he was visiting York for the same reasons she was. To relax and start afresh. It would explain his anger in seeing Morgan.

"And speaking of York Minster," the doctor continued, "I've arranged a deacon from the church to give Felix and I a private tour in the morning before any other sightseers are allowed inside. We'll practically have the place to ourselves. You and Lord Lyndhurst would be most welcome if you'd care to join us."

Stella smiled broadly, grateful for the change in subject and the marvelous opportunity. "Thank you, Dr. Bell. We'd love to join you."

"Maid service," a chambermaid called before trying the doorknob.

Stella tossed her hat onto the nearest armchair. Having just returned to their rooms, she still wore her overcoat. Before she could respond, the door creaked open a few inches, revealing the chambermaid in the hall, her outstretched arms piled with several freshly laundered white towels, her foot poised to push the door fully open. She was the same freckle-faced maid that had awakened them with her screams early this morning.

Was it just this morning they found Mr. Wingrove? It felt like days ago.

Stella, dead on her feet, couldn't imagine how the girl, who was not yet out of her teens, could still be working.

"You requested more towels, m'lady?"

Stella opened the door wider to let the maid in, saying, "You can put them on the couch. Lord Lyndhurst is in the bath."

Dragging her feet, a sign she was more tired than she appeared, the maid set down the towels and turned to leave.

"May I ask you something, Eliza?"

The maid stopped, her shoulders drooping, her focus averted to her feet. "M'lady?"

"How are you?" Stella would never forget her first encounter with a dead body. She'd accidentally stumbled across it. She'd come across others several times since, too many times, but she didn't think she'd ever get used to it. "You had a horrible shock this morning. Didn't Mr. Haigh give you the day off?"

The chambermaid snuck a glance at Stella as if trying to

determine if she was in earnest. "I'm well, m'lady. Thank you. Mr. Haigh was kind enough to offer me the afternoon and evening off, but I prefer to work. Keep busy if you get my meaning."

"Yes, I can understand that."

"Is that all, m'lady?" Her weary tone had an edge to it. The chambermaid was impatient to leave.

"No, actually, I wondered if you could tell me if there are supposed to be as many pillows in the Honeymoon Suite as we have in here?"

The maid, to her credit, didn't blink at the strange question. "Yes, m'lady."

Stella inwardly cheered. Finally, an answer to one of her questions. "Are you the only chambermaid that services these suites?"

"I am."

"You didn't remove any pillows from Mr. Wingrove's room, did you?"

This time the maid squinted a bit at the accusation. "No, m'lady. Why would I do that?"

Exactly. Why would she? Why would anyone?

"Is someone saying I stole some pillows?" the maid asked, suddenly defensive. "I can assure you—"

"No, no." Stella reassuringly touched the maid's arm. "But a bunch are missing, and I'm curious what's happened to them."

The maid nodded tentatively, eyeing Stella's hand suspiciously, as if suspecting she'd still be to blame. Stella dropped her hand and tucked a loose tendril of hair behind her ear.

"You must have keys to both suites. Could you let me into the Honeymoon Suite?"

A frown spread across the chambermaid's face. "I beg your pardon, m'lady, but I couldn't do that. Mr. Haigh insists it stay locked until tomorrow when Mr. Wingrove's relatives can collect all his things. He won't even let me go in to clean."

Knowing the room hadn't even been touched by the maid made Stella want to see it all the more. "I wouldn't touch a thing. I just want to have a peek around."

"I'm awfully sorry. You've been kind to me, but I can't risk getting sacked."

"We could pay you," Lyndy said, entering the room in his dressing gown and toweling off his hair. A light spray of water splashed Stella's cheek when he got closer. He smelled strikingly of hyacinth and sandalwood soap.

How handsome he was, all tousled and relaxed. If the chambermaid wasn't there, Stella would've kissed him.

"My wife only fancies a look around. Surely Mr. Haigh wouldn't object to that?"

All signs of her weariness gone, the chambermaid's face hardened, her hands clenched into fists at her sides. "I'm not Charlie Coombs, m'lord. I'm an honest, hardworking girl. You can't buy me!" With an indignant flip of her head, she turned on her heel and stomped out of the room.

CHAPTER 11

Morgan dropped back into bed, staring blankly at the canopy above. He'd never felt so exhausted, so thoroughly drained in his life. Yet he couldn't sleep. Lady Rountree had kindly offered for him to stay the night, and he'd said his good nights what seemed like hours ago. The moon, its brilliance unmarred by passing clouds, had crossed the sky to shine through one window into the next. In the silence of the night, the *tick-tick-tick* of the clock on the mantel drove him to distraction. He threw off the bedclothes and placed his bare feet on the carpet.

What am I going to do now?

Uncle Horace was gone. Everyone was gone but Maisie. Lovely, lovely Maisie. What a comfort she'd been to him. Surely Uncle Horace's death wouldn't change anything between them? And, presumably, the company was his to run. Uncle Horace had always implied he wanted Morgan to take over when he stepped down. The responsibility would do wonders in grounding him. But what if his uncle, with his increasingly erratic behavior, had changed his mind? Hadn't he kept the trip to York secret? Hadn't he lied about his purpose for going? Hadn't he been outraged when Morgan arrived to assist him? Uncle Horace, who had raised him like a son, had shut Morgan out.

Morgan threw himself back against the bed. "Oh, Uncle Horace. I don't know what to think."

Morgan bolted upright at the knocking on his door. How long had they been at it? From the insistency, it had been rather a long time.

"Mr. Amesbury-Jones, sir?"

Morgan slipped out of bed, wrapped the dressing gown around him, and padded across the carpet. Sir Owen's butler, Newsham, an oil lamp in his hand, stood in the doorway.

"My sincerest apologizes for disturbing you, sir, but there is a gentleman downstairs who insists on speaking with you."

"At this time of night?"

"He says it's urgent."

After donning his slippers, Morgan followed the butler down to the library, the lamp casting eerie shadows against the walls of the portrait-lined staircase. He was astonished to find Mr. Quiney, Uncle Horace's solicitor, black bowler hat in hand, pacing the large but cozy room. Much like the drawing-room, it smelled faintly of freshly burned incense and was packed with comfortable, overstuffed armchairs draped with colorful, exotic blankets and shawls. Books lined every wall but the one sporting the highly carved Italian marble mantel straddled by a mirrored pair of statues: jade creatures, part dog, part lion with menacing snarls carved onto their faces. A fire had been lit.

The moment the butler closed the door behind Morgan, the solicitor rushed to meet him, his balding head glistening in the dim light. An uncharacteristic grimace marred his sensible, clean-shaven face. "Morgan. Thank goodness."

"Quiney! What brings you here, and at such hour?"

"I did say over the telephone that I would be arriving."

"Yes, but I assumed you'd meant York. I never imagined you visiting me out here."

"It wasn't easy; I'll give you that."

"I plan to return to York in a day or two, the burial and all that. Surely whatever business we have can wait."

"I'm afraid not." Quiney began turning his hat in his hand. "When I arrived in York, Miss Evans told me you'd come here. With Hubberholme Park having no telephone, I had to come straightaway."

Morgan didn't like the sound of that. He gestured for the solicitor to take a seat, which he reluctantly did, sitting on the edge as if poised to bounce back up at any moment. Morgan taking the chair opposite, shifted his weight under the intensity of Quiney's gaze.

"I see no need to prevaricate. You are Horace's sole beneficiary."

Morgan slumped back against the buttons sewn into diamond shapes in the leather. He lowered his head, letting the weight of it rest against his fingers. "Are you sure?" He'd always believed his uncle would be generous, but everything?

"There is no doubt. Horace had been rather industrious of late, getting his affairs in order. He updated his will as recently as three days ago." He set his hat on the small wooden side table, retrieved a handkerchief from his breast pocket, and wiped his forehead. "No, the paperwork is thorough and complete. You needn't worry of anyone else contesting it."

"I never dreamt anyone would. But, Quiney, not that I'm ungrateful to you for going to such trouble in bringing me this . . ." What should he call it? Life-changing, unexpected, overwhelming? "News. But I do have to wonder. If everything is in order, why was it urgently necessary to tell me tonight?"

"For the very reason, everything is in order."

Morgan sat up and sighed. He dragged his fingers through his hair. "It's rather late, and it's been a dreadful day, but I have to admit, you're not making any sense."

"It's precisely because all the paperwork is thorough and

complete that I'm concerned. I'm not sure how to say this, Morgan, but . . ."

Quiney stared down at his shoes, his left one splattered with newly dried mud. He reached down and wiped it away with his damp handkerchief. When he raised his gaze again, Morgan didn't like what he saw. The solicitor was afraid.

"The formula for Cream Milk was not among your uncle's papers."

Morgan scoffed. "How could that be? That formula is the lifeblood of the company."

"Yes, I know. That's why I'm here."

"You've searched everywhere?" Morgan unbuttoned the collar of his pajamas, the air suddenly hot and stifling.

"I've scoured his offices, at the factory and at home. Your uncle thoughtfully left me with the combinations and copies of the keys for his desk, cabinets, safes, including his private safe and the one at his home that holds the silver, everything. Morgan, the formula isn't anywhere."

When Uncle Horace introduced Cream Milk to the British public a decade ago, the company was on the verge of bankruptcy. Now Wingrove's was the top confectionery company in the country. Cream Milk was still the company's signature chocolate, and its formula a well-kept secret. Uncle Horace, having formulated it, had no need of a written formula. Yet, a few years ago, he decided to write it down and lock it away. About the time, Morgan realized, when symptoms of Uncle Horace's illness began to manifest themselves.

Good God! Had Uncle Horace inadvertently lost or destroyed it? No, it couldn't be true. Uncle Horace guarded that secret with his life. Even Morgan had never seen it.

"You're telling me the formula is missing?"

"Missing?" Quiney vigorously shook his head. "No, Horace was too fastidious for that. More likely, it's been stolen."

* * *

Owen set the empty glass on the side table, the burn of the whiskey still in his throat, and stared into the dying embers of the fire.

"Damn," he quietly swore to himself.

He considered pouring himself another but decided against it. Everyone else had gone to bed hours ago. The solicitor, who'd arrived to speak to Amesbury-Jones (God knows why at this late hour), had come and gone. Only Owen and the mice scurrying in the wall of Owen's study, or his "bolt-hole," as his mother called it, were still awake. A small cupboard of a room, it held a secretary desk that Owen never used. Two rather comfortably worn leather chairs, one bearing the imprint of his backside he used it so much, faced the fire. Besides him sat a side table, well-stocked with crystal decanters of various means to get sozzled. It might've served as a gun room in his grandpapa's day but was converted into a private study when his father became master of Hubberholme Park. Whatever for, Owen could only guess. He had no memory of his father ever using it. A single framed map of the world, a relic from his father's days, hung on the wall.

Sharing a wall with the library, Owen had heard Amesbury-Jones and his solicitor talking. Frustratingly, he couldn't make out a word. He'd been tempted to put a glass to the wall, but his better nature kept him in his chair. With their conversation concluded, Owen had heard the two men exchange strained farewells in the hall. That was well over two hours ago. Wallowing in self-pity, Owen hadn't the common sense to go to bed. Instead, he'd gone over every minute of the last two days in his head. Every laugh, every smile, every shared glance. Owen sighed, laying his head against the back of the chair.

How could he have misjudged Maisie's regard for him so wrongly?

Despite his misery, Owen's lips grudgingly lifted as he recalled the sight of Stella and Lyndy appearing on his doorstep. What a charming pair they were. He'd always been fond of his cousin, but who knew he'd adore Stella as well. Yet wasn't his predicament almost entirely their fault? His smile faded, recollecting their travel companion. Why did they have to bring him? Yet that wasn't the half of it. Owen had always been one to treat his dalliances as just that, flirtations, a bit of fun, nothing more. Most of the ladies were jolly good sports about it. Granted, he'd found himself in a bit of a scrape now and then—that recent escapade with Miss Swenson, the American beauty, landed him in jail—but all in all, he'd had no regrets. That is until he'd seen Lyndy ridiculously, deliriously happy with Stella. Owen had never envied anyone; now, he coveted what Lyndy had.

And look where that got him. Owen groaned.

When the clock on the mantel struck two, Owen hoisted himself out of the chair.

"Damn," he swore again. He'd felt truly smitten, and yet the woman's affections lay elsewhere. Was it simply bad luck, poor timing, or what his mother called "karma"? Was he paying for his past?

He tottered into the darkened hall, grateful Newsham had left one wall lamp lit, knowing his master's penchant for staying up to all hours. Owen stumbled up the stairs cursing having ever laid eyes on Morgan Amesbury-Jones. To his chagrin and astonishment, at the top of the stairs, there stood the very rascal, in wrinkled striped pajamas, steps from Maisie's door.

"The bloody cheek," Owen mumbled to himself. Granted, the chap had tragically lost his uncle yesterday, but whatever comfort he craved should be done during daylight hours. "I say," Owen called out, "have you no shame?"

Owen almost laughed as the words spilled from his lips. Who was he to talk? Yet, his indignation was righteous and sincere. No harm, in body or reputation, would come to Maisie Pegg as long as she was a guest under his roof, even if she had chosen this cad, Morgan, over him.

In response, the chap said nothing, refusing even to acknowledge Owen had spoken to him. Like a thief in the night, he slunk away, disappearing down the hall, toward his guest bedchamber.

Just wait until morning. Owen vowed to give the scoundrel a right and proper upbraiding.

The thought of it cheered Owen immensely. As did the anticipation of Maisie's regret of the late-night assignation come morning. He knew it to happen more often than not. Perhaps there was hope for him yet.

Owen confidently swaggered down the hall toward his own bed, allowing a brief grin to play on his lips. Only once did he bump a hall table, nearly toppling Mummy's favorite Egyptian vase.

CHAPTER 12

"I'll be right back," Stella said, patting her lips with her napkin before slipping from behind the table and dropping the napkin on her chair.

Breakfast had been delicious. Stella had woken ravenous and had particularly enjoyed the grilled tomato and black pudding. She'd taken her last bite of her crumpet slathered with orange marmalade when she'd seen Charlie Coombs pass by the open dining room door.

"Where are you—?" Lyndy asked, reaching for his cup of tea.

Without waiting for him to finish, Stella hurried across the room, scooting out of the way of a waiter carrying a huge, hefty tureen full of steaming hot porridge, and waved to Miss Evans, seated alone close to the door. The secretary glanced over her shoulder as if believing Stella was greeting someone behind her.

The porter who'd rescued Stella from the bat, unforgettable with his almost white, blond hair, was at the desk. "Good morning, m'lady," the cheerful fellow said as she approached.

"Good morning. I never did get your name."

The young man straightened his tie, his lips broadening into a toothy smile. "It's Max Telford, Your Ladyship. Is there something I can do for you?"

"Well, Max, I'd like to speak to Mr. Haigh if he's around."

The grin faded from the clerk's face. "I'm sorry, but Mr. Haigh is in hospital."

"That's terrible. What happened?"

"He's recovering from a blow to the head. Seems he slipped after the floors were waxed last night."

How awful. First, Mr. Wingrove's sudden death, and then Mr. Haigh falls and hurts himself? What a horrible day the poor man had. "But he'll be okay?"

"So far as I've been told."

"Thank goodness."

"Charlie, I mean, Mr. Coombs is acting manager if you need to speak to someone."

Stella hesitated. She'd hoped to ask Mr. Haigh about Mr. Coombs in light of Eliza's remark. It had been an impulsive decision. Did she really need to know? What was it to her what Eliza meant? Except that the chambermaid's comment needled her as if Stella had picked up on something in Mr. Coombs that didn't sit right. She couldn't shake the feeling he knew more about Mr. Wingrove than he was saying. But was it worth asking Charlie Coombs himself? Before she could resolve her dilemma, Mr. Coombs emerged from the back room.

"Lady Lyndhurst," he said, a hint of irony in his voice.

"I'm sorry to hear about poor Mr. Haigh."

"Yeah. Poor Herman." Not a flicker of sympathy crossed his face. "Is there summat I can do for you?"

"May we speak in private, Mr. Coombs?" Stella said, glancing around at several potential eavesdropping guests lingering about.

"Yes, of course." He indicated the door he'd emerged from and waited for her to proceed him through.

The simple, whitewashed room smelled of stale tobacco and

vinegar. Tall, built-in, wooden cabinets lined one wall, each one labeled with a staff member's name for them to store their belongings while on duty. The one labeled "Coombs" had a brass padlock on it. A small sink and a stove with an iron kettle set on the front burner sat opposite. A long table covered in out-of-date magazines ran down its middle. It was a good-sized room, but it seemed to shrink when Mr. Coombs closed the door behind him and stood with his back to the door.

Maybe this wasn't a good idea.

He rubbed his palms together. "How can I help you, m'lady?"

An eagerness in his eyes mirrored his sudden accommodating tone. It was unnerving. Whatever he was expecting, Stella couldn't guess, but she was sure it hadn't been the first time he'd stepped in here for a "private word." Either way, she was about to disappoint him.

"Last night, when I asked if she would let me in to see Mr. Wingrove's room, Eliza said, 'I'm not Charlie. You can't buy me.' What did she mean by that?"

Stella braced herself, not knowing what to expect, but a congenial chuckle hadn't been it. "Is that what she said, the silly girl?"

"So, there's nothing to it?"

"Well . . ." he hesitated.

A stained dishrag lay crumbled next to the leg of a nearby ladderback chair. Mr. Coombs bent down, snatched it up, and tossed it into the wastepaper basket. Before straightening, he glanced slyly over at Stella's skirt as if imagining her legs beneath. She took a step back.

Choosing his words carefully, he continued, "I am known among our most discerning guests to be helpful in acquiring various bits and bobs. Or performing an extra service or two."

No wonder he agreed to speak in private. This is what the maid meant, and Stella had inadvertently initiated a conversation he'd been expecting. Charlie's profitable sideline couldn't be much of a secret. Who else knew? Mr. Haigh? Mr. Wingrove?

"For a small fee, of course."

"Of course," Stella said, acting the willing conspirator but inching casually toward the door.

"For example," he was saying, "I could arrange for you to have access to Mr. Wingrove's room if you still have a mind to. Cost you, say, fifty quid?"

"No, thank you, Mr. Coombs. I think I will pass for now. But I do wonder. Is that how the mistake with our reservation happened? Did you slip Mr. Wingrove the keys to the Honeymoon Suite for a small fee?"

The desk clerk shrugged, a self-satisfied smirk on his face. "Maybe I did. Maybe I didn't."

Stella knew what he wanted but wasn't about to fish through her handbag for coins; she had her answer.

"If that's all, m'lady," he said. "I was just going to have myself a cup of tea." He opened the door and stepped aside. "Now you know who to ask if you need owt."

"I do. Thank you."

As she gratefully scurried over the threshold into the safety of the public lobby, a thought crossed her mind. If the clerk was taking bribes, could he be stealing from the hotel as well? She turned back, and a shrewd smile touched the corners of his mouth.

"You forget summat, m'lady?"

"Did you take the extra pillows from Mr. Wingrove's room, Mr. Coombs?"

He narrowed his eyes at her, confusion and disappointment flashing across his face. Behind him, the kettle on the stove whistled. "Why would anyone do that?"

That was the trouble. Why Stella couldn't let it go. She had to know what happened to those pillows.

*   *   *

Stella couldn't move, transfixed by the vision before her. The morning sun streamed through an astonishing number of stained-glass windows, casting muted rainbows across the patterned marble floor and against the soaring stone columns. A hush filled the cavernous, vaulted space like the whisper of angels as everyone, even her irreverent husband, recognized they stood on sacred ground. She'd never seen anything like it, been anywhere like it.

Ever.

The small Norman church she and Lyndy had been married in was impressive, especially by American standards, having been built in the thirteenth century, four hundred years before George Washington was born. Yet, according to Dr. Bell, York Minster stood on the ruins of the Roman basilica where Constantine was declared emperor sixteen hundred years ago. When she'd gone to church back home in Kentucky, before Mama left, it had been to the Christ Church Episcopal, a large, redbrick cathedral with a central, square brick tower. As a child, she'd been intimidated by its size, by the overpowering message it sent. Yet beside York Minster, her childhood church looked like a dollhouse. Despite appreciating the grand presence this cathedral struck, its towering spires viewable from almost any vantage point in town, Stella hadn't been prepared for what awaited her when she stepped inside.

Built in the shape of a cross, the vast central space, or nave, was divided into three aisles that stretched hundreds of feet before her, a spectacle of stained glass and elaborately carved limestone, before reaching the space beneath the central tower and branching off into two separate wings, or transepts as Dr. Bell called them. Beyond lay a wall of intricately sculpted medieval figures capped by the massive brass pipes of the organ. Above it all, the vaulted ceiling soared well over a hundred feet. She'd read in a guidebook that that too was dwarfed by the dizzying height of the central tower's roof. Stella felt small and inconsequential, but so did her worries, her past. A lightness, a sense of belonging to the ages, stilled her tongue, but she reached for Lyndy's hand, beaming.

Deacon Lane, their arranged guide, met them as they admired the heart-shaped stained-glass window above the cathedral's entrance. He welcomed them, his hands clasped to his middle, with a paradoxical solemn lightness, a reverence underlying the energized delight he took in sharing this special place with others. He motioned for them to follow him, speaking of the wonders of the cathedral as he went, pointing out architectural details they might've missed, expounding on the building's ancient history, and impressing upon them the cathedral's significance to the city.

"The town is an extension of York Minster. There is no defining where the cathedral ends and the town begins," he said. "And I would say the same applies to England."

Stella, Lyndy, and Dr. Bell, who came with a whole slew of questions, consumed every detail with rapt attention. Started in 1220, York Minster took over 250 years to complete, was the second largest Gothic cathedral in Europe, and contained the finest collection of stained glass in the world. Yet when Deacon Lane had them stand beneath the central tower (Stella did get light-headed gazing up at it as the guidebook suggested she might), Mr. Middleton, who claimed to be a like-minded admirer, gave more attention to biting his cuticles than to the breathtaking view above him. He often glanced around furtively, not in admiration of his surroundings but as if someone was following him. But that was ridiculous. Besides the deacon and Stella's party, they'd seen one stooped, white-haired lady arranging flowers in a side chapel and a handful of praying worshippers scattered throughout the chairs set up in the central aisle. The enormous cathedral was practically empty.

The deacon moved ahead, leading them past a semi-enclosed alcove, pointing out a sanctuary for the tombs of past archbishops. A prayer kneeler had been set beside an elaborately carved tomb, complete with a fifteen-feet-tall stone canopy, a bank of flickering candles beside it. Stella had an urge to stop, kneel, and be mesmerized by the candle flames, but as she paused beneath the stone archway, Mr. Middleton was there, staring over her shoulder.

She'd noticed the bruises on his cheekbone and forehead, the limp he tried to hide when they first met up. She'd made a fuss, worrying over him, but as often happened when she got too personal with an Englishman, her concern was dismissed with an embarrassed wave of the hand. But Dr. Bell's hadn't been so easily ignored, and Mr. Middleton had been forced to explain.

"Had too much to drink and fell down the Lendal Bridge stairs," he'd said. Now he whispered, "Ain't we goin' get on with it?"

Get on with what? Touring the cathedral? Isn't that what they were doing?

She opened her mouth to ask, but his fierce expression as he scrutinized the alcove made her step out of his way and hurriedly join the others.

"This is the Rose Window," Deacon Lane was saying, as Stella approached a gloriously giant, round, stained-glass window decorated with white and red roses, set in the gables of the south transept. "Commissioned by Henry the Seventh to commemorate the end of the War of the Roses and the beginning of the Tudor Dynasty."

As everyone else gazed up at the wonder, admiring its beauty, its significance, Mr. Middleton, after rejoining them, examined his fingernails.

After answering one or two of Dr. Bell's inexhaustible questions, Deacon Lane escorted them back the way they came: Lyndy walking abreast with him, Stella lagging a bit behind, wanting to take everything in, Dr. Bell and Mr. Middleton bringing up the rear. The deacon led them through an archway in what he called the Kings' Screen, the stone wall containing the magnificent statues she'd seen before, and into an inner sanctum of richly stained, ornately carved, wooden choir stalls and pews. The dark, intimate space was a stark contrast to the rest of the massive cathedral. Mr. Middleton and Dr. Bell didn't follow them through, and behind her, Stella heard Mr. Middleton say something to his companion. Due to their hushed voices, Stella couldn't make out the words.

Lyndy plunked down on one of the pews and patted the space beside him. Stella joined him, wrapping her arm around his as they gazed upward at the breathtaking East Window, the largest expanse of medieval stained glass in Britain and the promised highlight of the tour. Peace washed over Stella as she sat basking in the cathedral's glory with her new husband beside her. They'd been right to come to York, no matter what had happened to the unfortunate Mr. Wingrove. This was the ideal spot for their honeymoon. She was almost loath to continue when Dr. Bell rejoined them, and Deacon Lane suggested they move on.

"Shouldn't we wait for Middleton?" Lyndy said politely.

"He promised to rejoin us, presently," Dr. Bell said. "Wanted more time to examine the Kings' sculptures. I'm sure he wouldn't mind if we pressed on. But before we do, Deacon Lane, I do have one question about—"

The simultaneous high-pitched wails that jolted Stella and Lyndy to their feet reverberated across the expansive church.

Stella was the first back through the archway, Lyndy, the doctor, and the deacon close on her heels. Footsteps echoed around her, and voices raised above the customary hush as others drawn by the screams rushed toward the spot. Two plainly dressed women, their faces contoured in wretchedness, clung to one another like shipwreck survivors in the vast expanse beyond the archway. One shielded her vision with splayed fingers, the other bit her knuckles. They both pointed adamantly behind her. Stella whirled around to face the fifteen nearly life-sized kings' statues, from William the Conqueror to Henry VI, looming above her.

"Bloody hell," Lyndy muttered at her side.

Bloody was right. Six of the seven kings on the left had red marks slashed across their legs, toes, or the hems of their robes as far as a man could reach. Why only six of the fifteen? Had the vandal been interrupted?

"Who would do such a thing?" Dr. Bell demanded.

Deacon Lane steepled his fingers and bowed his head over them. While the others, over a dozen or so who'd gathered, followed the deacon's example, hoping to find comfort and answers in prayer, Stella and Lyndy glanced around before sharing a knowing look.

Mr. Middleton was gone.

CHAPTER 13

Admittedly, Morgan had departed for the Majestic Hotel in a hurry. He'd packed the essentials he needed for a day or two at Hubberholme Park, leaving the better part of his luggage behind. But anyone who knew him knew Morgan to be the tidiest of men. Upon returning to the hotel, he expected to find his things all neatly where he'd left them. Never, not even in his frenzied, grief-driven rush, would he have left his room in this utter disarray.

Particularly if he knew Maisie would see it.

"What happened?" Maisie asked as she stepped into the room, followed by Sir Owen.

Maisie and her father had agreed to return to York a day early, to see that Morgan bucked up, insisting he stay with them until this business with his uncle was settled. Maisie had offered to accompany him to the Majestic to collect his and Uncle Horace's things. Morgan gratefully welcomed her company. Why Sir Owen Rountree insisted on accompanying them, he wasn't sure.

"I haven't the faintest idea," Morgan said.

He rushed to the writing desk, its drawers jutting out haphazardly, to straighten the company's ledgers he'd brought from Wolverhampton, essential for the acquisition. Some wide open, others flipped upside-down, they were scattered across the desk and the carpet.

"Someone was plainly seeking something," Sir Owen said, bending over to pick up a stray pillow and tossing it back onto the bed.

The bedclothes had been ripped off, down to the bare mattress, which was then moved too. Morgan's suitcase lay open and empty in the middle of it, the few contents he'd left inside piled on the floor. The drawers in the nightstand, the wardrobe doors, the entire chest of drawers were ajar, having been rifled through.

"What could you possibly have that someone would go to such lengths to find?" Maisie said, retrieving a pair of black wool stockings from the carpet.

Morgan, mortified, plucked the stockings from her hand, threw them in an open drawer, and shoved it closed with a hard bang. Only afterward did he notice he'd just put stockings in the nightstand.

Why was all this happening? Uncle Horace's unexpected death, the discovery of his inconceivable lies, Mr. Quiney's appearance at Hubberholme Park practically in the middle of the night, and now . . .

"The formula," Morgan said, finishing his thought out loud.

"You mean *the* formula?" Maisie asked, with an appropriate tint of awe in her voice.

"I say. What are you two blathering on about?" Sir Owen demanded, kicking one of Morgan's mislaid shoes beneath the bed skirt.

Maisie bit her lip, then explained, "Morgan's Uncle Horace went to chocolate factories in Belgium about ten years ago to learn what he could from the masters. When he returned, he developed the secret formula for Cream Milk."

"It's been our number-one seller ever since," Morgan said. "No other English confectionery company has anything like it."

"I prefer your father's chocolate, myself," Sir Owen said, flashing a smile at Maisie, but she'd turned too soon to notice. "So, what about this formula? Is that what you think whoever did this"—Sir Owen gestured to encompass the whole room—"was after?"

"Surely Horace would've kept it under lock and key?" Maisie said.

"That's the thing," Morgan said, rehanging a shirt that had slipped to the floor of the wardrobe. "Quiney, the company solicitor, came to visit me last night."

"At Hubberholme Park?" Maisie shot a questioning glance at Sir Owen, who shrugged. "Morgan, you never said."

"No. We'd all had a rather long day. And to be honest, I was hoping Quiney had overreacted. But he did say that while tidying up Uncle Horace's affairs, he's been unable to find the formula. He suspects someone might've stolen it."

Sir Owen plopped into the nearest armchair, putting his feet up onto the tapestry-covered ottoman. He pulled a packet of Rountree's Licorice from his waistcoat pocket and popped a pastille into his mouth. "Unquestionably, someone thought you had it."

"We have to search Horace's room." Maisie was already moving toward the door. Sir Owen, nearly choking on the sweet, jumped to his feet to join her. "If you don't have it and your solicitor couldn't find it anywhere in Wolverhampton, Horace must've brought it with him to York."

She sounded so certain, and she was probably right. But why? Why would Uncle Horace bring the company's most important asset with him here? Which brought Morgan back to the ever-nagging question. What was his uncle doing in York in the first place?

Morgan fretted over the remaining mess but, not wanting to

be left behind, folded the pajamas he was holding, dropped them in the chest of drawers, and pursued the other two to the lift doors. When the two men entered the open lift, Maisie abruptly volunteered to fetch a maid with a key and disappeared down the service stairwell. The operator closed the doors before either man could object. They reached the fourth floor and their objective, his uncle's suite, moments later. Morgan had never been alone with Sir Owen before, and as they lingered outside, waiting for Maisie to rejoin them, he was struck by the awkwardness of the silence between them. Sir Owen paced; Morgan stared at the intricate floral patterns of the carpet running down the center of the hall. Until yesterday, they'd been strangers. Their sole connection was Maisie.

Yet, he was blindsided when Sir Owen, the first to breach the silence, stopped pacing and said, "I saw you last night."

"Pardon me?"

"Don't play coy with me, old chap. I know all about midnight rendezvous."

"If you're referring to my meeting with the solicitor, I already explained that."

"That's not what I'm talking about, and you know it."

"I assure you, Sir Owen, I have no idea what . . ." Morgan could say nothing more in his defense, for at that moment, Maisie appeared from the stairwell, triumphantly holding up a key.

"Voilá!"

Sir Owen stepped a few paces back, letting Maisie pass as Morgan dragged his fingers through his hair. With a smile that lit up her face, she handed the key to Morgan. Her delightful enthusiasm vanished the moment Morgan swung open the door.

"Oh, no. Not here too?" Maisie bit her lip as she stepped over papers littering the carpet.

As if in slow motion, Morgan moved from one room to the next. It appeared much the same as in his room, the drawers partially open, their contents on the carpet, the wardrobe doors flung wide; even the bed his uncle had died in had been tipped, upturned, and slid halfway onto the floor. The upheaval in his room had been a transgression he could ignore. This, on the other hand, this disturbing of his deceased uncle's personal effects, was an inexcusable desecration.

Who would do such a thing?

"Sorry, old chap. Seems whoever searched your room had the same idea as Maisie," Sir Owen said, sounding none too sympathetic.

"The question is . . ." Maisie replied, retrieving a photograph of Aunt Marie from the floor. Uncle Horace never went anywhere without it. The villain had removed the back from the frame. "Did they find what they were searching for? Did they find the formula?"

"They must've," Morgan conceded, a heaviness rising in his chest. Was it despair or anger that fought to smother him? "Where else could it have been?"

"Where's Mr. Middleton?" Stella asked Dr. Bell in a strained whisper when Deacon Lane left to find a guard or police officer.

She didn't want to disturb the cluster of worshippers and priests sobbing and praying at the base of the defaced wall; word of the vandalism had spread. But Stella, her fists clenched, her eyes glued to the shocking red streaks on the statues, was angry. Someone had tainted this hallowed ground and shattered her hard-earned peace. She resented it.

Is this what Mr. Middleton had meant by "get on with it"?

"I have no idea," Dr. Bell, his fingers interlocked on top of his head, answered her question, both spoken and unspoken. "You think Felix has done this heinous thing?"

Stella nodded. Mr. Middleton had been twitchy and impatient from the moment they stepped into this peaceful haven.

He'd last been seen beside the kings' statues, and now he was nowhere to be found. And after his last cryptic comment, what else was Stella to think?

Lyndy jerked at the cuff of his morning jacket sleeve. "You knew him longer than we did—"

"Hardly," Dr. Bell interrupted as if to distance himself from the possible perpetrator. "And you'll recall I knew him as a fellow cathedral enthusiast." He waved toward the defaced statues. "Not someone capable of doing such sacrilege. It's unforgivable. I should've known something was off. He didn't ask a single question."

"Then you suspect him too?" Stella asked.

"I do. In hindsight, I should've realized Felix wasn't able to tell a nave from his navel."

"Why do you say that?" Lyndy asked.

"Did you not notice how he chewed his fingernails? How he seldom blinked at the wonder of the Rose Window? And when I pointed out how the builders used wood instead of stone for the ceiling in order to build at this unprecedented scale, he said, 'Fancy that?' Fancy that? It was brilliant! Vulnerable to fire, I'll grant you, but brilliant."

"Maybe it was a ruse, his saying he was a fellow enthusiast," Lyndy suggested. "A way to access the cathedral when few people were around?"

"If so, this is in part my fault," Dr. Bell said, gazing up at the marred statues, his expression full of pain.

Stella resisted laying a reassuring hand on Dr. Bell's shoulder and instead offered him a sympathetic smile before quietly creeping her way along the edge of the crowd. To get as close as possible, she squeezed by a man with an impressive paunch, his head bowed, his brown derby clutched in his hands clasped behind his back, his lips moving in silent prayer. On her tiptoes, she studied the streaks. *Blood or paint?* Paint, most likely; blood would've darkened by now.

She should know. She'd seen enough of it lately.

Where had it come from? Had Mr. Middleton brought it with him? Then she remembered his interest in the archbishop's tombs. Stella slipped past the crowd, ignoring the questioning creases on Lyndy's brow, and walked as quietly as she could to the south transept.

It was empty, every legitimate visitor compelled to see the damaged statues. She entered the alcove and moved among the silent sarcophagi, the plain rectangular ones, the one built like a tent, the one that bore a full-sized likeness of the archbishop buried beneath, his fingers steepled in prayer, his feet resting against the statue of a beloved dog. Staring down at the long-dead archbishop whose head rested on a pillow of marble, Stella couldn't dismiss the resemblance to Mr. Wingrove. She could even see a bit of her father in the peaceful, unmoving face. She pushed down the melancholy rising in her chest and continued to search.

"What are you looking for?" Lyndy asked. He and Dr. Bell stood under the vaulted archways.

She didn't pause to answer, glancing over and through the waist-high wrought-iron railings that separated the tombs. "I'm not sure."

Remembering back, something in Mr. Middleton's face when they'd peered inside earlier convinced Stella there were answers here. She just didn't know what. Then she found it. She had doubled back to the tomb of the medieval bishop holding his staff of office. It was labeled, "Walter de Gray, Archbishop 1215–1255." She'd circled the towering tented monument several times, combed every crevice of the tomb, every stone square of the floor, every inch of the entire area. Nothing. Then the flickering shadows of candles drew her to the nearby wrought-iron stand.

"I didn't take her as one to prostrate herself," Dr. Bell whispered jovially to Lyndy as she knelt and stretched her arm to touch the red drops splattered on the stone floor beneath the candle stand.

Lyndy chuckled. "She's found something."

A few rapid taps of their shoes across the stone floor, and Stella knew without looking up they were hovering over her.

"What is it?" Lyndy asked.

"This is where the culprit opened the can of paint." She lifted her finger to show the wet paint on her fingertip. "See, he spilled some."

"If it was Felix, he would've had to hide it under his jacket," Dr. Bell said. "His clothes should bear the telltale drops of paint."

"If he hasn't already disposed of them," Lyndy said. "But wouldn't we have noticed him hiding a can of paint?"

"Not when all of our focus was elsewhere, especially if it was a half-pint can," Stella said. She'd once snuck a half-pint jar of pickled peaches by her father on her way out to the stables when she was younger. He'd commented on the muck on the hem of her skirt but hadn't noticed the hidden jar stuffed under her shirt.

"Perhaps, but I'd be astonished if he'd take such strides to deface the statues with a half-pint of paint. Surely he must've known he couldn't do much damage."

"I beg your pardon, Lord Lyndhurst, but any damage is too much. The Kings' Screen is a masterpiece."

"I think Mr. Middleton wasn't trying for maximum damage," Stella said. "I think he was hoping to make a statement, and judging from the reaction of everyone, that didn't take much paint at all." Stella clambered to her feet and fluttered her skirt to remove any dirt. Thankfully Ethel had chosen a richly mauve-colored damask skirt for her to wear. It was pretty but durable and hid the dust well.

"What point was he trying to make?" Lyndy asked. "Middleton could've defaced anything—these tombs, the pulpit, one of the stained-glass windows. Why those statues? What's the significance of the Kings' Screen?"

"You're the expert on York Minster, Dr. Bell," Stella said expectantly. "What do you think?"

"Me?" Dr. Bell chuckled cheerlessly, stroking his mustache. "I couldn't possibly say."

CHAPTER 14

"Someone's in the Honeymoon Suite." Stella grabbed Lyndy's hand and dragged him along the hallway.

After telling the York Minster police what they knew (Who'd guess a cathedral had its own police force?), she and Lyndy had gratefully escaped, alone. They had lost themselves strolling the city's streets: broad thoroughfares, a legacy left by the Romans, and lanes so narrow the overhanging roofs of the timber-framed buildings almost touched. They passed abbey ruins with crumbling stone walls that reminded Stella too much of Keyhaven Castle, meandered arm in arm along the wide River Ouse, and rambled along a long stretch of the city walls. They'd finished their day with afternoon tea at the Windmill Hotel seated at a table with an unobstructed view of Micklegate Bar, half a block away.

Not a single drop of rain fell on their perfect afternoon.

The sight of the suite wide open yanked Stella out of her blissful reverie, rousing an unease that dampened her serenity like no amount of rain could've. Yet answers may lay beyond that door, and she didn't want to miss her chance.

Stella peeked in. The suite appeared empty and in disarray, but a woman's perfume lingered in the air, and the soft scratching sound of drawers opening was coming from somewhere inside.

"Hello?" she called cautiously from the safety of the hall.

"In here, Stella," Owen called from the bedroom.

"Owen?" Lyndy mouthed to Stella as they crossed the outer room. "What's he doing here?" he whispered. She shrugged, wondering the same thing.

In the same room they'd found Mr. Wingrove, Owen was lifting the dead man's mattress while Miss Pegg methodically pulled open every dresser drawer.

"What the devil's going on?" Lyndy said when Morgan, who'd been kneeling on the other side of the bed, popped his head up.

"Seems the Wingrove company's secret chocolate formula has disappeared," Owen said. He gestured with opened arms to encompass the whole room. "Mind, we didn't do this. Someone beat us to it. We're just confirming the formula isn't still here." Owen jabbed his thumb toward Morgan. "His room resembles this as well."

"You mean someone else was looking for it?" Stella said.

Morgan climbed off the floor, swatting at his pant legs. "Whoever it was must've searched the rooms while we were at Hubberholme Park. We can assume it was the formula they were after."

"Why on earth would the formula be here in the first place?" Lyndy asked. Maisie and Morgan exchanged meaningful glances.

"We've been asking ourselves the same question," Morgan admitted. "The company solicitor can't find it, so we presumed Uncle Horace brought it with him to York. And now this." His gaze swept the chaos.

"Want help looking?" Stella offered. She didn't expect to find the valuable formula; by the state of the rooms, whoever had searched the suite had been thorough. But this was the opportunity to poke around she'd been hoping for.

When Morgan gratefully accepted, Stella headed for the bathroom. It was in no better shape than the rest of the suite. Towels had been pulled from the racks and thrown into the tub. Mr. Wingrove's toiletries—a hairbrush, shaving kit and mug, toothbrush, and tube of dental cream—lay in a heap in the sink. Stella returned everything to the glass shelf above it before retrieving the small leather pouch tossed onto the floor tiles and lying against the wall. Inside were several medicine bottles labeled: *Zinc valerianate, Strychnos nux-vomica*, camphorated tincture of opium, among others. Except for chloral, a popular sleep draught, she had no clue what symptoms they treated, but knowing something about Mr. Wingrove's failing health, could hazard a guess. She'd have to check with Dr. Bell.

Having no luck in the bathroom, Stella returned to the main living room, where Lyndy was flipping open a suitcase. The luscious scent of chocolate filled the room.

"Bloody hell!" he exclaimed.

Inside, a Wingrove's chocolate box stuck to the upper lid, crushed into a thick layer of melted, smushed chocolate as if someone had emptied the chocolates into the suitcase and then stomped on them and the box. It was a smeared brown mess.

"Why would anyone do that?" Miss Pegg asked, peering between Stella and Lyndy down at the case on the floor.

Stella had no answer.

Lyndy kicked the suitcase shut and shoved it aside. It was caught by the excess fabric of the curtains that intentionally cascaded to the floor before it hit the wall.

"Morgan! Come see this," Miss Pegg excitedly called, having turned her attention elsewhere. She was picking a piece of paper from the floor. She eagerly held it out for Stella to inspect. The others clustered around, Owen wedging his way between Miss Pegg and Morgan in the pretext of wanting a better view.

It wasn't the missing formula, as Stella had hoped, but a personal invitation to the royal reception of Queen Victoria's statue unveiling tomorrow. Someone must've stepped on it; a partial shoe print stamped the righthand corner.

"I didn't know your Uncle Horace received a personal invitation," Miss Pegg said, slightly miffed. "Though I should've guessed. My father has been trying for months to get a royal warrant from Her Royal Highness to commemorate her visit to York, but she refused, insisting she and her daughter were partial to Wingrove's."

"Maisie, I had no idea," Morgan said, taking the invitation and gawking at it like it was a bar of solid gold.

"Could that be what brought your uncle to York?" Stella asked. "Maybe the princess was going to grant Wingrove's the royal warrant instead?"

"Perhaps," Morgan said skeptically, "although being invited would've been reason enough. It is an honor and a boon for the company. So much so, I should consider going in his stead, despite being in mourning."

"I guess whoever ransacked the room didn't think it such an honor," Stella said. Why else leave it on the floor?

As the others discussed the merits and disadvantages of Morgan attending tomorrow's royal event, Stella wandered over to the fireplace. She prodded the cold, gray ashes from Mr. Wingrove's last fire with the wrought-iron poker, hoping to find remnants of the formula or an explanatory letter half burned in the grate. No such luck. As she replaced the poker, she upset a tiny black goose feather that she hadn't noticed before, stuck to the fireplace's brick. She watched it float to the stone hearth.

Where did that come from?

She stepped closer, turned on the nearest wall sconce to see better, and combed each brick surface. Nothing. She peeked up into the chimney. She needed better light if she hoped to see beyond the first few feet up. Disappointed, she joined the others.

"What do you have in your hair?"

Stella broke into a smile as Lyndy gingerly plucked something off her head. The caring, intimate act seemed second nature to him. How untrue she knew that to be. She'd described him as arrogant, pretentious, and smug a few months ago. How far they'd come! A flush of affection for her new husband warmed her. He flicked away what he'd found from his fingertips. Two more goose feathers, caught in the rays of the setting sun like wisps of dust motes, drifted softly to the floor. Stella dashed over to the fireplace again.

"I say, that's going to be filthy," Owen exclaimed when Stella sunk to the hearth, pulled up her sleeve, and reached her hand as far up the chimney as she could, whipping up soot and smoke that clung to the inside walls.

She coughed but kept reaching.

"What on earth is she doing?" Miss Pegg exclaimed.

"Something extraordinary, no doubt," Lyndy answered.

After grasping at the falling debris she'd dislodged, Stella leaned back on her knees, the skin of her arm up to her elbow black with soot. With the front of her dress also covered in dark smudges, Stella silently apologized to Ethel, who'd have a heck of a time cleaning out the stains. But had it been worth it? Stella cautiously unclenched her fingers.

I knew it!

Lying in her soot-covered palm were several more feathers, all that was left of the Honeymoon Suite's missing pillows.

"What's going on in here?"

Lyndy cast a fleeting glance past his shoulder at Mr. Wingrove's churlish secretary standing in the doorway, her fists on her hips.

"Why is Mr. Wingrove's room in such disarray, Morgan?

And who are you?" This demand aimed at Owen, who was affronted.

"I say, I'm Sir Owen Rountree, if you must know, and who are you?"

She ignored him and continued: "And why is Lady Lyndhurst covered in soot?"

Lyndy's sides trembled with stifled laughter as Stella attempted to clean herself off once again. With tendrils of hair loose about her head, a small smudge of soot slashed across her cheek, a more prominent blotch of it across the bodice of her dress, and her arm up to her elbow blackened by rummaging about in the fireplace, his wife resembled a beautiful maiden playing chimney sweep. *By God was she charming!* Yet, he also understood the implication of the feathers clutched in her fists: Mr. Wingrove's death just became more complicated.

Lyndy had tried to persuade her that the missing pillows meant nothing. He should've known better than to discount her intuition. How many more times would it take for him to trust his new bride to know when something was amiss? But damn it all, why couldn't she have been wrong? Those tiny feathers, sweet as they clung to her hair, now meant more engagement with the police, more time discussing the death of a man they'd met but once. Why couldn't Mr. Wingrove have chosen another room, another hotel to die in?

It was a selfish wish, Lyndy admitted. But it was their honeymoon, after all. With everything that had happened of late, why must another suspicious death sully it?

"Lily, the formula has gone missing," Morgan explained.

"You must be joking," Miss Evans said.

Morgan picked up the photo of his aunt, gazing fondly at it. "Quiney visited me at Sir Owen's estate. It's not in Wolverhampton. Uncle Horace must've brought it with him to York."

"Surely, Horace had no business bringing it here. I mean, what did it have to do with acquiring Rountree's?"

"Nothing," Miss Pegg interjected, helping Stella tidy up the room. "That was a lie."

"What?"

"Uncle Horace wasn't here to acquire the Peggs' company," Morgan explained. He held up a palm to ward off further questions. "And before you ask, we don't yet know why he was here."

Miss Evans looked to Miss Pegg for confirmation, as if she didn't believe Morgan. Miss Pegg's grave countenance was answer enough.

"Morgan, this is disastrous. You must have some idea where the formula could be," Miss Evans insisted.

"It had to have been in this suite. And as you can see . . ." Morgan scrunched his shoulders toward his ears. "We've searched every nook and cranny, every crack and crevice, but it's gone."

"Gone? Where did it go?" Miss Evans demanded. "It didn't just walk away."

"Someone got here before we did," Owen said, staring down his nose at Miss Evans. "Whoever that was must have it."

Lyndy wasn't so sure.

"Then why was Morgan's room ransacked too?" Stella asked before Lyndy had the chance.

Stella couldn't read his mind, thank goodness for that, but her uncanny habit of voicing a question that he'd intended to ask never ceased to amaze him. Lyndy seldom bothered with questions until he'd met her, unless they served to annoy his mother. Now, he observed people, situations, life more as Stella did, and his curiosity, dare he say, his concern, had been stirred.

Receiving no reply, Stella added, "And who could've known Mr. Wingrove had it with him?"

"You must've, Morgan," Miss Evans accused.

Lyndy watched Morgan for a reaction. Lyndy would've sacked the woman on the spot. The disrespect was inexcusable.

Morgan hesitated. Why? Was there truth to what the secretary said? Did Morgan know more than he was admitting?

"If only I had," was Morgan's weary reply. "I would've made certain it was safe."

"May I speak to you in private?" Owen was beside Lyndy, gripping his shoulder, his face awash with concern, distracting Lyndy from Miss Evans's possible retort. In a licorice-scented whisper meant solely for Lyndy, Owen added, "Morgan can't be trusted."

Owen couldn't possibly know something about this formula business, could he? More likely, Owen's mistrust of Morgan arose from his fondness for Miss Pegg. Lyndy wasn't blind. Owen was smitten, again, with a woman who had made her choice—it wasn't Owen. Lyndy pitied his cousin. Though not too much. After all the hearts Owen had broken over the years, he was due his share of heartache.

With an exaggerated scrunch of his shoulders, Lyndy reassured Stella, her lovely brow crinkled in confusion, before following Owen into the hall. Owen strode past the lift into the sunroom, though the room seemed cold and unwelcoming with the darkness of evening settling in.

"What's all this about?" Lyndy asked.

"As I said, Morgan can't be trusted around Maisie."

Lyndy congratulated himself on guessing the source of Owen's misgivings. "And why would that be?"

Owen began to pace, pausing briefly when one of Miss Evans's sneezes resounded from down the hall. "I saw him, Lyndy, outside Maisie's door late last night."

Now that was surprising. Neither Morgan nor Miss Pegg seemed the clandestine type. Neither seemed bold enough to risk a midnight assignation. "Are you certain?"

Owen stopped abruptly, piercing Lyndy with a frosty glare.

"Most certainly I am." He rubbed his earlobe a moment before adding, a bit contritely, "Though I admit I didn't actually see him coming out of her door."

"He could've simply been passing by, then?"

Owen threw up his hands in exasperation. "Why in bloody hell would he do that?"

Clearly, Owen was thinking of what he would do. How, if the girl were willing, he'd not be able to resist the siren's call.

"Perhaps because Miss Pegg didn't invite him?" Lyndy suggested.

"Then why be outside her door?"

"Damned if I know what goes on in Morgan Amesbury-Jones's mind. I just met the man yesterday."

"True."

"But you've known Miss Pegg for years. Is she the type to—?"

"Absolutely not!" Owen's fervor in defending the woman's reputation confirmed Lyndy's suspicions. The poor sod thought himself besotted.

"Well then."

Owen strode to the window and stared out at the streetlights flickering warmly below like glowworms in June. He smoothed his beard, lost in thought. When he spoke, his voice sounded far away. "I accused Morgan of it before we found Wingrove's room ransacked."

"Here I was thinking you came to York to impose upon your favorite cousin on his honeymoon," Lyndy jested.

"He denied knowing anything about it."

"Then why assume the worst? Maybe the man needed to stretch his legs?"

"At that hour? No, old chap, Amesbury-Jones is not to be trusted. Why do you think I came to York? Someone needs to keep an eye on him."

Had Owen heard anything Lyndy said?

"Come now. Aren't you letting your feelings for Miss Pegg cloud your judgment?"

Owen pulled his focus away from the window to face Lyndy's accusation head-on. "It's not that. How bloody marvelous if it were." He returned to gazing out the window. "No, I'm afraid, old chap, no one gets up to anything good at that time of night." He chuckled. "I should know."

CHAPTER 15

Detective Sergeant Glenshaw wasn't happy. He shouldered past the doorman at the hotel entrance and yanked the door open for himself. What was he doing here again? He'd just ordered his second pint when his constable had tracked him down parroting "Chief Constable's orders." Served Glenshaw right for letting it slip that the Coach & Horses was his local. With the necessary paperwork filed and the routine inquest for Horace Wingrove's death set for a few days' time, the case was all sorted. Or so he thought.

This had better be quick. The unveiling of Her Majesty Queen Victoria's statue at the Guildhall tomorrow took precedence. Who would protect Their Royal Highnesses if he was here mucking about?

Glenshaw strode to the desk and demanded to speak to the manager. The young clerk disappeared through a side door. Glenshaw tapped his foot as he waited and waited. When some other fella besides Mr. Haigh at last appeared, it took everything he had not to bark at the blighter.

"I requested to speak to the manager," he said through clenched teeth.

"Sincerest apologies, Detective Sergeant Glenshaw," the fella said, not sounding sorry in the least. "I'm acting manager Mr. Charlie Coombs at your service. Mr. Haigh's in hospital."

That took Glenshaw slightly aback. "What happened to him?"

"Accident."

"Another one?"

Mr. Coombs shrugged, then began fiddling with his watch fob, a square piece of black onyx mounted in silver.

No love lost there.

"Did you request the follow-up regarding Mr. Wingrove's death then?"

A flicker of annoyance flashed across Mr. Coombs's face. "Not me. A guest."

Still tapping his foot, Glenshaw waited for the man to be more forthcoming. He wasn't. "Quit wasting my time, Coombs. Which guest and where can I find him?"

"Mr. Amesbury-Jones, Mr. Wingrove's nephew. He claims someone broke into his room and ransacked the suite where Mr. Wingrove died. Presumably, an extremely valuable company asset was stolen."

"Really?" Glenshaw relaxed his foot, crossed his arms, and cracked his neck with a quick snap. This sounded promising. Perhaps he was too quick to judge this case. "What asset was that?"

"According to the tittle-tattle of our chambermaids, it's the Wingrove secret formula for Cream Milk."

Cream Milk? Glenshaw loved Wingrove's creamy chocolates. They had a smooth taste that never left a bitterness in his mouth as other chocolates did. He could almost taste one now.

"Is Mr. Amesbury-Jones about?"

"You'll find him up in the Honeymoon Suite. Now, if you'll excuse me, my tea is getting cold." With no regard for possible follow-up questions, he turned his back on Glenshaw and retreated to whence he came.

Cheeky beggar!

Yet Mr. Coombs was true to his word. When Glenshaw stepped through the suite's open doorway, Mr. Amesbury-Jones bolted from his seat like a startled jackrabbit.

"Detective Sergeant Glenshaw, thank heaven," the nephew said.

He wasn't alone. The secretary Glenshaw had met before was with him, as were a posh couple Glenshaw hadn't seen before. Mr. Amesbury-Jones introduced the couple as Miss Maisie Pegg and Sir Owen Rountree. Glenshaw knew Miss Pegg by reputation. Hers was a prominent York family who owned Rountree Confectionery. Risking an appreciative glance, he could see why she was well-known in the society pages for her beauty, though a bit too petite for his taste. With his name being Rountree, Glenshaw could only assume the gentleman was likewise associated with the company. Cousins, perhaps?

"I appreciate you taking time to come back," Amesbury-Jones said.

"Yes, well, it's late, and I've got an early morning, what with the royal visit tomorrow. I can't stay long."

"We may not be royal, but this warrants your full attention, Detective Sergeant," the secretary chided, hands planted firmly on her narrow hips.

Glenshaw had known plenty of women like her. Despite being a mere secretary, they attempted to exert control over everyone and everything. Once a secretary at the station positioned her desk beside the storage closet. She wouldn't let a fella get ink for his pen without her permission. Glenshaw had paid her no mind. He chose to ignore this one too. Best way to deal with women like that.

"I was told this suite was ransacked." He glanced about him. "I see no sign of a search."

"That's because we tidied it," the secretary declared.

With Miss Pegg and Sir Owen concurring with silent nods, Glenshaw addressed his next comment to the nephew, presumably the new head of the company. "Mr. Coombs has explained to me that the secret formula for Cream Milk has been stolen."

"Yes, from among Uncle Horace's things in this room."

"And we think someone killed him to get it," a lilting, feminine voice from behind him said.

Glenshaw glanced over his shoulder to see the peculiar American lady and her aristocratic husband approaching from the suite across the way. She in light blue silk, him in a black coat and hat, they were dressed for dinner.

Murder? What was she talking about?

Glenshaw despised meddlesome women, even titled ones, and odds were against this one knowing anything he didn't. But could he risk missing the opportunity to bag a murderer? Glenshaw swallowed hard, pushing down his pride.

"If you'll excuse me one moment," Glenshaw said to the nephew, raising a finger for emphasis.

He backed out of the suite and indicated with a gracious sweep of his hand for Lady Lyndhurst to precede him to the sunroom, lit by sconces ringing the walls. Uninvited, her husband accompanying them. Glenshaw offered the lady a seat, but she refused. He crossed his arms against his chest and squinted at her.

"Ok, Lady Lyndhurst. You've got my attention. Care to explain what you meant?"

Stella held out the small mound of feathers and down she'd been holding in her fist. "Before you arrived, I found these."

"They came from the chimney," Lyndy said.

"I found one or two myself. No surprise there. Birds roost in chimneys."

So do bats. Stella shuddered involuntarily.

"Yes, but ducks and geese don't roost together." Lyndy pointed out the size difference.

Stella uncurled her other hand. "These came from a pillow in our suite."

To confirm her suspicions, they'd ripped open a pillow from their bedroom. Her nose still tickled from the sneezing it caused. They'd tried to contain the mess, but Stella didn't envy the chambermaid who'd have to contend with stray feathers for days. The contents in her outstretched palms were identical.

"And how do feathers indicate murder?" Glenshaw's toe began tapping incessantly.

"Don't you see? Pillows were used to kill Mr. Wingrove."

"May I remind you, Lady Lyndhurst, that Mr. Wingrove wasn't suffocated? The coroner is to testify at the inquest that Mr. Wingrove died of gas poisoning, as suggested by Dr. Bell."

"I know. I believe someone plugged up the chimney with pillows using the broom that we found earlier, blocking the airflow." Stella had been recreating how it could work in her head, over and over. She had to be right.

"With poor or no ventilation, a coal fire would produce deadly gas," Glenshaw said, musing it out to himself, not addressing anyone in particular. He regarded her with a strange expression, his drooping eyelid opened a mere slit. "And you thought up this on your own, did you, Lady Lyndhurst?"

Was that suspicion or respect in his voice? Stella couldn't tell.

Quick to defend her, Lyndy said, "Unfortunately, my wife and I have been involved in several murder investigations."

"Is that right?" The detective sounded skeptical.

"Together, we've helped our local constabulary apprehend several killers," Lyndy said, "including the one who murdered our vicar."

"As well as my father's killer," Stella said, unwanted images flooding her mind.

"My sympathies." Glenshaw regarded her as if seeing her for

the first time. "Your conclusions have merit, Lady Lyndhurst. When do you suppose this happened?"

"I'm guessing after Mr. Wingrove fell asleep," Stella said. "Chloral, a sleep aid, was one of the medicines he had with him. If the killer had been cautious, Mr. Wingrove wouldn't have woken up. I'm assuming they had a key and came back sometime later, confirmed Mr. Wingrove was dead, and then either burned or removed the pillows, making it look like an accident."

"Someone would've had to have known he'd taken that suite," Glenshaw argued. "Weren't the two of you supposed to stay there that night?"

Stella didn't like to be reminded. "Yes, but no one has a reason to kill us." *At least, I hope not.*

Stella exchanged a knowing look with Lyndy. They'd discussed this and weren't going to broach this subject unless they could speak to the detective alone. It was now or never.

"But you're right. The killer would've had to have known. Which narrows it down to hotel staff and anyone aware of Mr. Wingrove's travel plans like—"

A jarring pop cut off what Stella was going to say next. One of the electric lightbulbs in the brass sconces that ringed the room had burned out, leaving that corner in shadow.

"Like family, friends, or acquaintances of the deceased who might've visited him here," Glenshaw said, finishing Stella's sentence. "When searching the rooms, I never found Mr. Wingrove's key."

More evidence (including what Lyndy had told her about Owen's suspicions) pointed to Morgan or maybe Miss Evans. Neither made sense. They both had ready access to the secret formula, Morgan as presumptive heir to the company and Miss Evans as Wingrove's private secretary.

"If the Cream Milk formula was why he was killed, as we think, the list of suspects would have to be narrowed down further to those who knew Mr. Wingrove possessed it here in

York." Stella still couldn't imagine what had compelled him to bring it to York in the first place. "Which probably eliminates most, if not all, of the hotel staff."

"Ah, but that's where your reasoning breaks down, my lady." Glenshaw sounded pleased that she hadn't thought of everything. "If the killer returned to dispose of the pillows after Mr. Wingrove had succumbed to the fumes, why not take the formula then? Why was it necessary to ransack the room later in the day?"

He was right. *Why hadn't she thought of that?*

"Regardless," he added cheerfully, rubbing his hands together as if pleased at the latest turn of events, "I think there's enough suspicion here to investigate further." An odd smile curled the side of his mouth. "Now, if you'll excuse me, I have hotel staff to interview before it gets too late. I'm due at the Guildhall early tomorrow for the royal unveiling ceremony. You're attending, I presume?"

Without waiting for her answer, the detective clapped his hands together once and swiveled on his boot heels.

"Why the hotel staff?" Lyndy asked, watching the detective stomp resolutely toward the elevator. "It's clear he should be starting with Morgan and the secretary."

Stella thought the same thing. They were the most obvious suspects. But Detective Sergeant Glenshaw's odd strategy wasn't as concerning as the question he'd posed to her. If it wasn't to steal the formula, why *had* someone killed Mr. Wingrove?

Glenshaw stared at the crack, visible despite the excess of plaster used to fill it, streaking across the room toward the solitary window, a gaping dark rectangle in the stark, unadorned white wall. It was a prominent feature of the stark staff lounge, a room as bleak, with its harsh overhead lighting, as the interviews he'd conducted.

More sanitary, they say. He'd been grateful for its use, but

Glenshaw longed for the dark stained wood and worn green armchair of his sitting room.

He'd spoken to Charlie Coombs first, the arrogant chap of few words. As desk clerk and now acting manager, he had access to every key. Yet despite Glenshaw's best efforts, the fella revealed little, insisting he'd never met Wingrove before the chocolatier checked in, knew nothing of the stolen formula, and had no need to "poke about" the guest rooms. He sat across the table, flipping through a copy of last week's *Illustrated London News,* pausing but once when Glenshaw indicated that he was now investigating Mr. Wingrove's death as suspicious.

To that, he'd said, "That's got nowt to do with me."

Glenshaw got little out of him after that. The night of Wingrove's death, Coombs claimed to be at the desk all night. He merely shrugged in reply as to why Wingrove was in the Honeymoon Suite instead of the viscount and his bride. All the while flipping bloody pages. The dodgy blighter had the cheek to cut the interview short, sliding back in his chair and rising with Glenshaw in midsentence, insisting he needed to mind the desk. With no proof the man was involved, Glenshaw irritably waved him away. The moment the door closed, Glenshaw snatched up the pile of magazines and threw the lot in the bin.

Next had been the chambermaid who'd found the dead man. Despite her defiant stare, she'd twisted the string of her apron around and around her fingers. Thankfully, she'd been more informative, telling him of Lady Lyndhurst's request to get into the rooms where the old chocolatier had died. The maid had refused, but the incident served to remind Glenshaw how he needed to keep tabs on the meddling American viscountess. The maid had described how she'd fetched the spare key to the Honeymoon Suite that morning from behind the desk, as she did every day, and insisted she'd returned it. Before Glenshaw had set eyes on this dismal room, he'd checked the rack of keys. They were all accounted for.

Glenshaw took a sip of the tea Coombs had requested a waiter bring him. It was cold. There was nothing worse than cold tea. Having to postpone his interview with Mr. Haigh in hospital until the morning, Glenshaw had only the porter left.

At least then I can get to my bed.

"Ah, Mr. Maxwell Telford, is it?"

The young fella slid into the vacant seat across the table and shifted several times, attempting to get comfortable. A blush of red flared on his pale cheeks.

If ever I saw a guilty man . . .

"You were the one who assisted Mr. Wingrove with his bags the night of his death?"

"Aye."

"And since his death, you've been promoted to desk clerk. Isn't that right?"

"No. That was after Mr. Haigh had his accident."

"Had you ever seen Mr. Wingrove before?"

"No."

"Besides yourself and Mr. Coombs, who has access to the room keys?"

"I didn't have access to the keys that night." Glenshaw detected a hint of emphasis on the last two words. The porter was hedging the question. "I used Mr. Wingrove's key to help him settle in."

"Where is that key now, Mr. Telford?"

"I don't know."

"But you have access to the keys now." It wasn't a question.

"Aye."

"Someone ransacked the Honeymoon Suite. Summat rather valuable was stolen. How do you think they got in, Mr. Telford?"

The porter licked his lips and blinked several times in rapid succession. Glenshaw knew now was the time to press his point.

"Did you do it? Did you steal the formula, Mr. Telford?"

Vigorously shaking his head, the fella abruptly pressed his

palms against the tabletop and leaned forward. Glenshaw resisted the instinct to flinch.

"They said they needed to pack up the old man's things," the porter blurted. "Said they'd bring it right back. And they did. You can check. I hadn't the faintest idea that they'd . . ."

"Did they pay you to give them the key?"

"No." Slinking back into his chair, he rested his elbows on the table and dropped his head into his hands. With the light shining directly on the top of him, the fella's hair resembled the color of white Wensleydale cheese. "They seemed so nice, so friendly-like. I didn't think there was any harm in it."

"Is that what you thought when you let Mr. Wingrove take the Honeymoon Suite that night?"

"All I did was take up the old fella's bags."

"How much did these friendly folk pay you to slip them Wingrove's key, Mr. Telford? How much is a man's life worth these days?"

"What?" The porter's head shot up. "I know nowt about that."

"But you admit to offering to let strangers rummage around the dead man's things? Who were they, Lord and Lady Lyndhurst?"

"No, though if Her Ladyship had asked . . ." He wrapped his arms around himself and studied the tabletop. "I don't know who they were."

"How convenient." Glenshaw rose from his seat, engulfing the smaller man in his long shadow. "I don't think there were any strangers, Mr. Telford. I think you've made the whole thing up. You stole the formula, didn't you? Where is the formula, Mr. Telford?"

The porter scrambled to his feet, knocking into his chair. It tipped sideways and clattered to the floor. "I know nowt about any formula."

Glenshaw sidestepped the table and chair and cautiously approached the porter, backing him toward the wall. "Why'd you kill Mr. Wingrove, Max?"

The porter jumped like a frightened hare when his heel connected with the wall. "All I did was give out the key the day after. I didn't kill anybody!"

Before the porter could bolt, Glenshaw grabbed Max by the arm and slapped a handcuff on his wrist. "Maxwell Telford, I'm arresting you for theft. And if I have a mind, murder."

The porter shouted his innocence as if someone would bother to rescue him, but Glenshaw smiled. It was late, his head ached, and he was craving a nice spot of piping hot tea, but all in all, it had been a passable end to his day.

CHAPTER 16

"Lord and Lady Lyndhurst. Come join me."

Stella waved to the doctor who had called out to them. Today Dr. Bell was eating his breakfast alone. She set down her plate of poached egg, muffin, sautéed mushrooms, and black pudding at the place set beside him. She hadn't time to pick up her napkin before he leaned in conspiratorially.

"There are rumors that the police arrested a porter last night."

Taken by surprise, the questions spilled out of Stella's mouth without giving the doctor a chance to answer. "Already? Which one? Didn't Glenshaw talk to you? Was it for killing Mr. Wingrove or stealing the formula? Did the porter confess? How could Glenshaw know otherwise? Did he even question Morgan or Miss Evans? Did they—"

Almost spitting out his last bite, Dr. Bell held his palm up. "My lady! Slow down. Did you say someone killed Mr. Wingrove?"

Stella took a deep breath. "Yesterday, someone ransacked both Mr. Wingrove's and his nephew's rooms. In light of that, and some new evidence, Detective Sergeant Glenshaw now suspects foul play. And already you're saying a porter's been arrested?"

"That was efficient," Lyndy scoffed, cutting into his smoked haddock.

"Not efficient," Stella corrected, "steamrolled, more like it."

"Why do you say that?" Dr. Bell asked.

"His couldn't possibly have been a thorough investigation," Lyndy explained. "He hadn't even entertained the idea of murder ten hours ago. Has he spoken to you?"

The doctor shook his head, concern etched between his brows. "No. But I thought it was an accident. What made him change his mind?"

"My marvelous bride," Lyndy said before taking a sip of the tea the waiter had placed before him.

Dr. Bell turned toward Stella. "Lady Lyndhurst? How on earth did you convince the detective Mr. Wingrove died of anything but an accident?"

She held up a finger to allow time to chew and swallow the muffin in her mouth. "It all had to do with the missing pillows in Mr. Wingrove's suite." Stella explained finding the pillow feathers and down inside the chimney. "Since Mr. Haigh insists the chimney had been cleaned lately, the most likely explanation is that someone put them there."

"You think someone purposefully stoppered up the chimney?"

"And then disposed of the pillows," she said. "Yes."

"Why? Why would someone want to kill Mr. Wingrove?"

"Greed," Lyndy said. "Someone has stolen the formula for the Wingrove's Cream Milk."

The doctor was visibly shaken. Grappling for his napkin, he patted his lips for nonexistent crumbs. He glanced around the room and leaned in again. "This brings a whole new light to what I have to tell you. It's about Felix."

"What about him?" Stella asked.

"He's gone. I went to confront him in his room yesterday. When I received no answer, I inquired at the desk. According to Mr. Coombs, Felix packed up his things and checked out, two days earlier than he had reservations for."

"Now, why on earth would he ever do that?" Lyndy said.

Heedless of Lyndy's sarcasm, Dr. Bell replied, "It could be a coincidence, but according to Mr. Coombs, Felix had inquired about the presence of the police. It was that same informative fellow who told me about the porter being arrested."

"Which porter was it?" Lyndy asked.

"His name is Max Telford."

Max? That friendly, cheerful one who rid her of the bats? Stella couldn't believe it. "Mr. Coombs didn't say why?"

Dr. Bell scooped green peas onto his fork. "He's a bit dodgy, that one. I think he knows but implied anything more would cost me."

We'll see about that. Stella pushed back from the table and tossed her napkin down.

"Where are you going, my love?" Lyndy said with an uncertain uptick at the end.

"To persuade that 'informative fellow' to give me some answers." When Lyndy rose halfway out of his chair, intent on joining her, she added, "You keep eating. I'll be right back."

Mr. Coombs, scribbling something into a registration book, hardly acknowledged Stella when she approached.

"I've just learned Max was arrested last night."

"Yes, m'lady."

"Did Detective Sergeant Glenshaw tell you anything about it?"

"He might've, m'lady."

Stella slammed a sovereign down on the desk. That got Mr. Coombs's attention. He quickly covered it with his hand, slid it toward him, and pocketed the coin. A sly smile spread across his face.

"I knew I'd be of service to you eventually, m'lady."

"Why was Max arrested?" Stella asked, ignoring the clerk's self-satisfied smirk.

"For theft. There was also mention of a possible murder charge."

"Did they find the formula then?"

"Nowt that I know of."

"Did Max confess?"

"Only to giving strangers the key to Mr. Wingrove's room. The day after the old man died."

Stella didn't understand. Was that the basis for Max's arrest? Was Detective Sergeant Glenshaw running such a slipshod investigation he was willing to charge the first person to admit any wrongdoing?

"Did Detective Sergeant Glenshaw tell you anything else?"

"That's all of it." Mr. Coombs shrugged. "These came for you." He reached into the pigeonholes behind him and retrieved a telegram and an envelope with gold leaf around the edges. He weighed the letter in his palm to show how heavy it was before handing it over. "I've seen but one of these. Lucky you."

He smiled as he said it, but the edge to his tone belied his forced cheerfulness. Was he jealous or resentful? It read: *The Right Honble. The Viscount Lyndhurst and The Right Honble. The Viscountess Lyndhurst* scrawled across it in a highly stylized hand. A surge of emotion: joy, disbelief, gratitude, and awe swept through her on seeing her new title in writing. Her wedding, her new life with Lyndy, this honeymoon in York, this new beginning, was still like a dream. Would she ever wake up? Mr. Coombs then handed her the telegram. Her heart soared as if it weren't already full, every other thought swept away as she read a single typed line. It was from her mother. She'd agreed to come.

Without thanking Mr. Coombs, Stella dashed across the lobby, barely sidestepping a large family emerging from the breakfast room. The youngest, a little boy, holding his grandmother's hand, reached out and skimmed her skirt with his sticky fingers. Stella held up the telegram like a prize.

"She's coming in two days!" she announced breathlessly to a startled Dr. Bell and her bemused husband. Too excited to care about the stares, she pecked Lyndy on the cheek before slipping into her chair.

"That's jolly good," Lyndy said. Whether he meant her news or the kiss, she couldn't tell. Nor did she care. "Learn anything not related to your mother's visit?"

Stella relayed what Mr. Coombs had shared for a price.

"I fear we haven't heard the end of this," Dr. Bell said, placing his fork and knife diagonally across the top edges of his empty plate.

Stella agreed. They still didn't know why he was visiting York or if he was killed for the formula, or why he was so particular about staying in the Honeymoon Suite. Still, wouldn't it be nice, for a change, if she could enjoy the rest of her honeymoon without questions about a dead man plaguing her?

"So, what's this, then?" Lyndy pointed to the fancy envelope.

"In my excitement over my mother coming, I forgot to open it."

Though Dr. Bell squirmed in his seat, Lyndy laughed when Stella snatched up her unused table knife and sliced open the envelope. Inside was an invitation to the private reception being held before the unveiling of the Queen Victoria statue, signed personally by Princess Beatrice.

"By gosh, is that a personal invitation from Her Royal Highness?" Dr. Bell said, peering at it closer, all his embarrassment forgotten.

"It is," Lyndy said. "My ancestral home is in southwest Hampshire. As she's the governor of the Isle of Wight, my family is acquainted with Her Royal Highness. Someone, probably Mother, no doubt, must've made her aware we were honeymooning in York at the same time as her visit."

"Isn't that today?" Stella said.

"Indeed. Later this morning," Dr. Bell said. "I've had my suit already pressed. Though, of course, I wasn't invited to the private reception."

"We're not going, though, are we?" Stella asked of Lyndy, tucking the invitation under the edge of her plate and taking a bite of her black pudding.

"Ah, but we must," Lyndy said.

"But we've made plans to tour the racetrack today. They've made special arrangements for us." Not that she had minded the trip to Hubberholme Park and couldn't wait for her mother's visit—so much of their honeymoon had been spent in the company of others. Stella craved more time with Lyndy, alone. Not to mention, she'd been looking forward to seeing the world's first grandstand. "And we just got this." She indicated the invitation with her fork. "No one can expect us to drop everything at the last minute, can they?"

"Sorry, love, but one does not question or say no to Her Royal Highness."

Dr. Bell shook his head in agreement.

This was one part of British society Stella didn't think she'd ever get used to. She'd been shamed for doing her father's bidding. Yet to interrupt your plans because a distant royal says so, that was acceptable? She shrugged. She had vowed, "For better or worse." This was her life now, and she'd better get used to it.

"I better ring for Ethel then," she said, more brightly than she felt. "I hope she brought something appropriate to wear."

CHAPTER 17

"Are we late?" Stella asked.

They'd agreed to meet Owen and Aunt Winnie in the lobby and set off from there. Yet when Stella stepped off the elevator on Lyndy's arm, no one was there to greet them. Besides a be-spectacled clerk Stella had never seen before behind the registration desk, they were the only souls in the entire lobby.

"There you are." Owen strode confidently through the front doors. He wore a black cutaway coat and top hat identical to Lyndy's. Owen's roving attention inspected Stella's floral tulle dress of cream and dark rose with an embroidered burgundy silk panel accenting the bodice. "My, you look smashing, Stella."

Stella adjusted her hat with a matching burgundy bow and blushed.

"Now, now," Lyndy playfully chided, a proud, thin smile stretching his lips. "That's my wife you're talking to." He put his hand over Stella's and glanced around the empty lobby. "Where is anyone?"

"Making their way to the unveiling. Which is what we should

be doing, old chap." Owen led them toward the doors and down to several awaiting black coaches. "Your carriage awaits, my lady," he said with a laugh. "As does my lady mother and the rest of our party."

Owen wasn't kidding. Standing beside the second hired coach were Morgan, Miss Pegg, and her father, all dressed in their finest, patiently waiting. Aunt Winnie waved from the shadowy recesses of the first coach.

Stella understood why Aunt Winnie, who could barely put weight on her ankle, would need to ride, but why couldn't she, Lyndy, and the others walk? The Guildhall was a few blocks away. When she asked Lyndy, he mumbled something about needing to present their best. She acquiesced but only because she wanted time with the lead coach's matching pair of dappled grays; they reminded Stella of Tully. She hadn't realized how much she missed the mare. She tripped lightly down the steps ahead of Lyndy and Owen to say hello.

Sidestepping the coachman holding the carriage door, Stella approached the nearest horse to stroke its forehead. When the second horse neighed, in hopes of getting similar attention, Aunt Winnie, dressed in gold and white satin with blue and green peacocks embroidered on the bodice, poked her head out. The faux grape bunches and plumes of peacock feathers on her green toque bobbed as she nodded in appreciation of Stella.

"Aren't you lovely, my dear," Aunt Winnie said.

"Not as lovely as these two." Mindful not to get her hem dirty, Stella arranged herself before the horses so she could pet both at once.

"She's a credit to our family, Lyndy," Aunt Winnie added when Lyndy and Owen caught up. "I can't imagine how your mother managed such a perfect match."

Stella shot Lyndy a warning glance as he opened his mouth in what was sure to be a retort on the fact that his mother had done nothing to encourage the marriage and everything to sabotage it. Stella didn't think there was any call for such comments now. She was confident that she and Lady Atherly had come to an understanding. At least she hoped they had.

"When did you arrive, Aunt Winnie?" Stella asked.

"Little over a quarter an hour or so. The train ride was a bit tiresome, but I wasn't going to miss this for the world." She adjusted the hat's weight more evenly on her head. "Though I am a bit put out that the Peggs weren't invited to the private reception."

Owen explained that he and his mother had been invited to the private reception. The others planned to attend the public unveiling event.

"That's quite all right, Lady Rountree," Mr. Pegg said, in his deep baritone voice, his top hat in hand. "It's an honor just to be there. Besides, we wouldn't know nowt about what to say to royalty. Would we, Maisie?"

Miss Pegg bit her lip in anxious agreement, her flouncy royal blue gown swaying as she shook her head.

Thinking back on her one encounter with royalty, Stella told Miss Pegg not to be concerned. She'd met King Edward at Epsom on Derby Day. If Stella remembered right, all she'd managed to say was "Your Majesty," and the king had carried the conversation.

"Shall we?" Aunt Winnie hinted.

"Where's Miss Evans?" Stella asked Morgan when Mr. Pegg followed his daughter into the second coach, leaving him alone on the drive.

"She begged off with a headache," Morgan said. "Truthfully, I don't think Lily likes big crowds."

Stella sympathized. She could think of countless things she'd rather be doing than attending the reception: exploring York's gardens and museums, strolling the ancient walls, snuggling with Lyndy in front of the fire, or better yet, touring the York racetrack as they'd planned. She and Lyndy had that in common. Neither enjoyed the formal social gatherings they were forever expected to attend. Lyndy's insistence had surprised her. This wasn't a dinner party at Morrington Hall they could skip without repercussion, he'd explained. This was their duty as members of the aristocracy. If they'd snubbed a royal invitation, there'd be consequences that would affect the entire family.

Stella sighed. Of course, she'd do her duty as Lady Lyndhurst. *It didn't mean she had to like it.*

"Care to join us, Dr. Bell?" Stella called, spotting their new friend emerging from the hotel in a charcoal-gray morning suit and top hat. He looked quite dashing.

"Kind of you to offer, Lady Lyndhurst, but I prefer to walk."

"I don't blame you. It's a beautiful day. See you there then."

Stella took Lyndy's offered hand and joined Owen and his mother in the coach. It smelled of incense and oranges with orange peel littering the floor. The beautiful dapple grays high stepped in unison, and the carriage jolted forward. They rattled down the drive, past the parklike setting surrounding the hotel, past the train station, and under a span of the medieval wall. After crossing the river and the line of narrowboats moored along its banks, they took a sharp turn and pulled into a row of carriages waiting to approach the Guildhall. All in all, the trip had taken less than five minutes. Dr. Bell, already waiting for them, waved.

"Oh, my heavens," Aunt Winnie complained, shaking her finger at the dozen or so carriages ahead of them. "I'm not going to wait for this lot to move."

"What about your ankle?" Stella didn't want to sit in the carriage anymore than she had to but worried the older woman might reinjure herself.

Aunt Winnie waved off Stella's concern, pushing Owen's shoulder to prompt him to open the carriage door. "It's less than a block away. Even if we crawl, we'll be there before the others are."

Alighting from the carriage, Stella, Lyndy, and her aristocratic in-laws gradually weaved through the ever-growing crowd lining the street. Those who would see the unveiling later had come out to see the parade of nobility and dignitaries that flowed from the carriages: maids, housekeepers, and shopgirls in jaunty, elaborately adorned hats, merchants in tailor-made worsted suits, clerks, factory workers, field hands, and their wives in their Sunday best. As Stella passed, a young child on her father's shoulders tossed lilac-colored daisies into the street. Stella plucked one out of the air and put it up to her nose to smell the mild fragrance, sharing a friendly smile with the gleeful child.

Arm in arm, she and Lyndy followed Owen and his mother, hobbling courageously on the cobbled stones through an arch beneath an impressive red and white Georgian-style mansion. It led into a narrow, covered alley, or *snicket* as Owen called it, which then emptied into an enclosed courtyard fronting the Guildhall. Joining the others with private invitations as they streamed into the Guildhall to mingle with royalty, Lyndy quietly pointed out a duchess and a couple of earls' sons he knew by sight. Owen, not so subtly, explained the man Stella was gawking at in the bright red robe trimmed with fur and black velvet and wearing a heavy chain around his neck was the Lord Mayor of York. It was his Georgian-style mansion they'd passed under.

Though she knew she should be impressed by the company she kept, Stella was more captivated by the building they were entering. She'd seen women in richly colored taffeta and satin gowns more times than she cared to count. Men in top hats were a dime a dozen. Yet how often had she stepped into a medieval hall like this? Squat and plain on the outside, the gray stone building used since the fifteenth century as a meeting

place for the city's guilds, its city council, and on occasion its
courts, opened onto a long, lofty hall wide open but for the
twin rows of thick oak pillars supporting the vaulted ceiling, a
latticework of hand-hewn timbers. On one side of the room, a
long, lace-covered table held silver tea services, rows of royal
blue and gold bone china teacups, and more than a dozen three-
tiered trays laden with bite-sized cake. At the far end, beneath
an impressive stained-glass window (though nothing could
rival what Stella had seen in York Minster), was a bright white
sheet of linen covering what had to be the statue of Queen Victoria. Before it stood two women: one middle-aged, the other a
few years younger than Stella. As mother and daughter, they
had matching oval-shaped faces, patrician noses, and tired eyes.
They wore exquisite silk gowns: the elder in gray with a high
collar of white Battenberg lace, the younger in green with an
embroidered lace overlay. The pair greeted arrivals with the
somber demeanor of those who had done this too many times
before.

Had they chosen to wear such wide-brimmed hats to keep
people at bay? Stella had to wonder. They were twice as wide as
the one she wore; Stella hadn't seen the like of them before.

Finding a place in the reception line, Stella offered for Aunt
Winnie, as the elder among them, to go ahead of them. They'd
declined, leaving Lyndy the awkward task of explaining that, as
Owen is a baronet, she and Lyndy outranked them and should
go first. How strange this new life was. Stella, a Kentucky horse
breeder's daughter who'd spent more time in a stable yard than
a ballroom, now outranked native Englishmen who were born
to nobility. Stella offered them a conciliatory smile as she
stepped in front of them. As she did, she caught movement out
of the corner of her eye. It seemed out of place. The reception
line was orderly and defined to a particular part of the hall, but
someone was lurking around in the shadows.

Servants, maybe, trying to keep out of sight? Or the princesses' bodyguards trying to be inconspicuous? Stella looked ahead again as they were getting close to the royals. Despite her American upbringing, despite initially wanting to be elsewhere, she experienced a twinge of excitement in meeting them, nonetheless.

There it was again.

She turned her head sharply, hoping to catch a glimpse of who it was. She spotted a limping figure slip into a darkened alcove. Mr. Middleton? It couldn't be him, could it?

In the second before Stella could've heeded her impulse to drop out of line and follow the figure, someone, in a highly polished, articulate tone, said, "Ah, Lord Lyndhurst. How good of you to come."

Stella was stuck. Before her, anticipating a proper greeting, was Queen Victoria's youngest daughter, Princess Beatrice.

CHAPTER 18

Stella demurely dropped her gaze and tried not to sneak a peek at the spot where she'd lost sight of Mr. Middleton.

"Your Royal Highness. Your Highness." Lyndy bowed his head, first to the mother and then to her daughter, Princess Ena. "May I present my wife, Viscountess Lyndhurst."

Stella lowered herself into a perfect curtsy. Lyndy and his family had laughed at Stella's bow the day they'd met, but now, from the look of pride on Lyndy's face, she'd done well.

"Ah, yes. Your new American bride," Princess Beatrice said. "How lovely it is to meet you, my dear."

"Your Royal Highness," Stella said, having learned from her encounter with King Edward the princess didn't expect much of a reply.

She was surprised then when Princess Beatrice asked, "And how do you find your new home, Lady Lyndhurst?"

"It's wonderful," Stella said, thinking more of the New Forest countryside than Morrington Hall. She instinctually glanced at Lyndy and smiled. "It actually feels like home."

Princess Beatrice nodded her approval, and the conversation

shifted to something about the Isle of Wight. Stella let Lyndy do all the talking and purposefully blocked out their discussion. She'd almost drowned on the ferry to the Island and wasn't ready to revisit that frightening incident. Instead, Stella stole quick glances around to see if she could spot Mr. Middleton again. She didn't. Returning her focus to the princesses again, Stella offered a sympathetic smile to the younger one, Ena, who, after having been introduced, had remained silent. The teen princess looked miserable.

She doesn't like these events any more than I do.

Instead of responding in kind, Princess Ena glanced over her shoulder at the tribute table laden with brightly colored bouquets of fragrant roses, dahlias, and daisies, their stems tied together with silk ribbon, piled among dozens of velvet or cardboard gift boxes. The display reminded Stella of her wedding presents and her father's funeral flowers combined. Among the many tokens of people's affections was a large box of Wingrove's chocolates. Who had given those? The entire city, if not the country, had learned of the famous chocolate maker's death by now. Had it been presented in honor of his death, or had someone known they were a favorite of the princesses? Was that what Princess Ena was longingly peeking at? Was she craving chocolate? Stella hoped so. It made the princess seem less distant, more human.

The conversation ended before Stella could ask, and Lyndy led her away with his hand on her elbow. It was Aunt Winnie's and Owen's turn for a royal audience.

"Lyndy, I think I saw Fe . . ." Stella let Mr. Middleton's name fade on her lips. "Detective Sergeant Glenshaw," she called to the policeman strutting down the hall in a fashionable single-breasted, dark blue, worsted suit. "Any news?"

The detective, frowning at seeing them, hesitated before reluctantly making his way over. "Lord and Lady Lyndhurst," he said, with a slight bob of his head. "Guests of Their Royal Highnesses, I see."

Should Stella mention seeing Mr. Middleton? Had it even been him? For now, until she was sure, she'd keep it to herself. "We heard you arrested Max Telford."

"I did." He kept his focus constantly on the reception line.

"You've located the formula then?" Lyndy asked.

"He denies taking it. I had his locker at the hotel and his home searched. It wasn't in either place."

"Do you suspect he killed Mr. Wingrove?" Stella asked.

"Who else?"

That was a good question. Stella couldn't rectify the porter who'd rid her of the bat with the person who either murdered Mr. Wingrove or stole his most valuable possession. Or both.

"But why?" she asked. "If not for the formula, why would Max kill Mr. Wingrove? Did he say something that made you think he's the murderer? Did you find proof he put the pillows in the chimney? Besides having easy access to the room keys, I mean. Did you question Morgan or Miss Evans?"

Glenshaw turned to glare at Stella, his jaw slack in exasperation, his drooping eyelid lifted higher than she'd ever seen it, before returning his attention to the hall again.

"Don't you worry, Your Ladyship," he said, "Mr. Telford stole that formula. We just haven't found it yet. Now, if you'll excuse me."

He stepped away without a backward glance, skirting the reception line and rounding the statue. He reappeared on the other side by the tribute table. Stella watched him discreetly visually inspect every bunch of flowers and every gift, hands clasped behind his back.

If only he'd be as painstaking in his investigation of Mr. Wingrove's death.

What was he looking for? Was he satisfying his curiosity? Or was there a point to what he was doing? Stella doubted it. He hadn't spoken to Morgan, Miss Evans, or even Dr. Bell. Besides begrudging her involvement and arresting a porter who'd been loose with handing out the hotel keys, what had the detective done to find the formula or Mr. Wingrove's killer?

Disappointingly, very little.

Lyndy tugged on the bottom of his jacket, resisting the urge to pace. With his duty to Princess Beatrice done (Mother would be proud), he was restless to leave the boisterous crowd, swollen by opening the doors to the public. What did he care about seeing another statue of Her Royal Majesty, the late Queen Victoria? He'd had his fill of tea and cake. He'd enjoyed his spirited debate with Owen over the merits of breeding versus racing horses, but even that would've been better done over a private glass of port than jostled about by half of York. He'd practically had to shout to be heard. Lyndy slipped two fingers between his neck and tie and loosened it slightly. The hall was stifling hot. He could hardly breathe, yet the heat brought a charming blush to Stella's face.

With her attention drawn across the room, intently searching the hall for the others in their party, Lyndy studied her objectively as he would a masterpiece of art: the slight crease between her brows as she focused, her keen, blue eyes as she shifted her gaze, and the flash of recognition when she'd spotted Morgan and the others, the curve of her rosy lips as they widened into a smile. Each subtle fluctuation of the muscles, the eyes evoking the intelligence, the curiosity, the capacity for joy his new bride harbored beneath her exquisite visage. His chest swelled with a surge of emotion: pride, desire, tenderness, protectiveness.

How was it possible to love a woman so much?

He'd anticipated their wedding and honeymoon with the desperation of a losing punter wagering it all on the last race of the day. To have her entirely to himself, to enfold her with his arms, his legs, his whole body, to share his bed, to sleep peacefully beside her was utter bliss. But if he thought he'd be satiated by now, or ever, he'd be wrong. If he thought he'd stop craving her affection, her admiration, her mere presence beside him, he was wrong. He adored her and too often had to restrain himself from showing her how much. Undoubtedly, a public reception attended by servants, strangers, the royal guests of honor, and his mother's sister wasn't the time or the place.

Upon Dr. Bell's, Morgan's, and the Peggs' arrival, Lyndy endured their enthusiastic greetings and exclamations upon "witnessing such a grand event," mostly for Stella's sake, as she shared their delight. Or so he thought. Happily, the others swiftly continued on, joining Owen and Aunt Winnie, to a spot nearer to the statue than the one he and Stella had chosen by a small, rounded, wooden side door. At long last, alone with Stella, but not, he closed his eyes and took in the heady scent of her perfume, with hints of hyacinth and moss, and was startled when her warm breath tickled his ear.

"Let's get some fresh air."

Without hesitation, his hand on her back, he gently but steadily guided her through the crowd. Everyone else was filing forward, jockeying positions to get the best view. He had the only view he wanted, that of his wife. Ignoring the confused or disgruntled stares, they pushed their way through the doors and out into the brilliant sunshine, a brisk, cool, afternoon breeze whipping up around them. Stella grabbed his arm and pulled him into the nearest deserted alley. So narrow, the walls of the Guildhall left them in shadow. Lyndy shivered in the sudden chill.

"Lyndy, I think I saw—"

Lyndy couldn't resist pulling her to him, cradling her jaw with his hands and silencing her with a kiss. Her ardor matched his own, surprising him. When they pulled apart, she smiled against his lips.

"How long have you been wanting to do that?" she teased.

Lyndy responded by slipping his fingers into the hair at the nape of her neck and kissing her again, knocking her hat askew. She laughed when they jumped apart at the noise of something scraping the cobblestones as if they'd been caught out. Yet the sight of a stray mongrel, its ribs poking through its mangy fur, trotting by, quickly sobered them both. It resembled a starving vision of their new dog, Mack.

"You were saying something earlier, my love?"

"I was. I didn't want to say anything around the others, particularly Dr. Bell, but I think I saw . . ." Stella gripped Lyndy's arm and pointed down the alley the way they'd come. She mouthed in silence, "Felix Middleton."

Lyndy, following her gaze, saw a man limp hurriedly across the square, away from the Guildhall, but furtively casting glances over his shoulder in that direction. She was right. It was Middleton. Where was he going?

"I saw him earlier, inside," Stella said in a faint whisper. "Should we confront him?"

He knew what she meant. If he was the miscreant who had defaced the Kings' Screen in York Minster, he had some answering to do. But he was surprised she'd conferred with him before charging out on her own. From the tone of her voice, she was eager to do so. Yet why should they have to accost the blackguard? Wasn't Glenshaw conveniently on hand? Couldn't they make him aware of Middleton's whereabouts and leave it at that?

"Let's leave him to the proper authorities, shall we?" Lyndy suggested.

"Do you think we've done our duty here and can go soon?"

He hesitated, uncertain what she had in mind. With Stella, he never did quite know. "After the statue's been unveiled, I should think so."

"Good. We'll tell Glenshaw about Middleton, and then after the unveiling, we can hire a cab to the racetrack. We might still be able to catch the groundskeeper before he locks up for the day."

"Brilliant idea."

With the happier prospect of spending even part of the afternoon inspecting the York Racecourse, Lyndy strolled arm and arm with Stella back into the hall. Coming from the bright sunlight into the darker chamber, they stopped near the doorway to let their vision adjust. Lyndy could scarcely make out the bright white linen cloth as it was jerked from the statue. Thank goodness they'd arrived in time. As the fabric floated to the floor, a blinding flash of light exploded across his field of vision. A blast of deafening noise thundered in his ears, and the floor shifted beneath him. Stella was no longer at his side. As the brittle clattering of shattered glass crashed about them, Lyndy reached for her, grasping for a hold, any hold. Then something sharp struck his forehead, hurtling him to the hard, limestone floor.

CHAPTER 19

The hall erupted into pandemonium. Stone dust, paper fragments, pieces of white linen, and a rainbow of flower petals
fluttered and floated in the cloud of smoke the explosion left
behind. Through it, a multitude of panicking people stampeded,
staggered, or groped blindly toward the exit: high-society
women tripping over their silk skirts; mothers, with tears etched
on their grit-covered faces, clutching their children to their
breast; well-heeled men, as frightened as sheep being chased by
a wolf, brazenly shoving women aside. One dignitary's wife
limped along after losing a shoe, determined to get out as fast as
she could.

With her hands over her ears, Stella sat on the cold flagstones, collapsed against the hard wall, trying to stop the ringing. Splotches of light flashed across her vision. Wafting clouds
of pungent black smoke made her cough. Her legs stung and
her knee throbbed, having connected with the floor with
Lyndy's extra weight pressing down on it. But nothing worse
than being thrown from a horse. She'd be able to haul herself
up again soon.

Lyndy was another matter. She glanced over at him, slumped against the wall beside her. His head was back, his eyes shut, a thin line of blood running down the side of his face. When they'd crashed to the floor, he'd toppled on top of her. They'd laid still for a moment to see what would happen next. When the room had erupted with people racing for the door, Stella had roused him, and the pair had scrambled to all fours, crawling the few feet to the wall. She hadn't seen the blood until he'd propped himself up.

"Are you all right?" she asked him. Nothing. As if he hadn't heard her. "Lyndy. Lyndy?"

Please let him be all right. Please, God, let him be okay.

With her hands trembling, she reached for the spot on his neck to check his pulse, like she'd done days ago on Mr. Wingrove. The moment her fingers touched his skin, he reached up and grasped her hand. His eyes fluttered open, and turning to regard her, he blinked, his gaze unfocused and dazed. Then he bent his head and coughed into his fist.

"Are you all right?" he asked her, shouting.

"I'm fine, but you're bleeding."

"What? Can't hear you."

She pointed to the side of his face. He reached up to touch his temple, his fingers coming away with smears of blood.

"It's just a scratch."

It wasn't, but at the sound of his voice, understating his pain, she rested her head against his chest, listening to the reassuring thumping of his heart. He draped his arm over her shoulder, laying his chin against the crown of her head. They huddled together, out of the way, as the less mobile attendees, swaying unsteadily or clutching to one another for support, followed the initial crush to escape the building. She and Lyndy weren't going anywhere.

As the smoke cleared and Stella's vision improved, she expected to see the roof and walls lying in rubble. Yet the building, except for a few windows, appeared intact, as was the statue of Queen Victoria, and those weren't stones or piles of roofing tiles on the floor but people crouching or lying among the shattered glass. Groans and cries for help pierced the ringing in her ears, and already several figures moved purposefully about: several uniformed policemen, their distinctive brass buttons flashing when they stepped into a ray of sun, and Dr. Bell.

"Can you get up?"

When Lyndy didn't respond, she grasped his face in her hands and repeated herself, enunciating her words carefully and loudly. Lyndy nodded.

Pushing against the wall and leaning on one another, they thrust themselves off the floor. Hand in hand, they made their way past stragglers intent on the entrance doors, stepping over abandoned hats (Where was hers now that she thought of it?), canes, umbrellas, an errant shoe, discarded invitations, serving napkins, and a large splatter of something where someone had gotten sick. Everywhere, there were bits of flowers, petals, stems, leaves mingled with shards of glass glittering in the afternoon sunlight.

When they approached Dr. Bell, his face glistening with sweat but otherwise seeming unharmed, he was wrapping a young man's cut foot with what used to be part of the linen sheet covering the statue. His patient hobbled away, and relief flooded Dr. Bell's face when he saw them. But then he pressed his lips together, his brows drawing tight in concern. Something was wrong.

"What is it?" Stella demanded. "Is it Sir Owen or Lady Rountree?" Fearing the worst, she craned her head, twisting around, hoping for any sight of them. "Are they hurt?"

"That I don't know. I haven't seen them. I was admiring a carving on the far side before the blast. It's you I'm concerned with. You should be looked at."

Lyndy shook his head, dismissing the doctor's concerns.

"It's nothing," he said, unconsciously touching his temple and still speaking a bit too loud, "but my damn ears are ringing."

Dr. Bell inspected Lyndy's face anyway. "You're right. It's shallow, a flesh wound." Bell handed Lyndy a clean handkerchief. "And your hearing, my lord, that should improve with time." Stella silently rejoiced for Lyndy until she realized Dr. Bell was staring at her. "My lady, you too are injured."

"I am?" Stella dropped her gaze to her dress. Her skirt was dotted with blood. Without thinking, she raised it to reveal her legs. Tiny cuts slashed her silk stockings, riddling them with ladder-like tears and ruining them beyond repair. Her legs were caked with dried blood. She must've encountered broken glass when she crawled across the floor.

How had she not noticed? No wonder her legs stung so much.

She sheepishly dropped her skirt. "It's nothing," she echoed Lyndy, his eyes widened in alarm. At the sight of the blood or her bare legs in public, she wasn't sure.

Dr. Bell took her at her word. He glanced around at the bedlam surrounding them.

As if answering an unspoken question, he said, "So far, the most serious injuries I've encountered are temporary hearing loss, minor respiratory irritation, lacerations from the shattered glass, and a bone fracture caused by an elderly woman falling during the panic. It could've been much worse. Thank God someone didn't know what they were doing when they made that bomb."

Dr. Bell's words cut through her thoughts as the flash of brass buttons caught her eye. A policeman, posted where the royal princesses once stood, was pulling a notepad from inside his coat pocket. He licked his pencil before scribbling down notes on his pad.

This was intentional?

"Are you saying this wasn't an accident?" Lyndy asked, his voice still raised. "I suspected a faulty boiler or some such."

"No, no," Dr. Bell said, speaking loudly for Lyndy's sake. "According to a policeman I treated for minor lacerations, someone planted a bomb on the tribute table."

Unbidden, the image of Mr. Middleton dashing away from the Guildhall before the explosion popped into her mind. They'd wondered where he was going, so fast, so furtively. Was he getting clear of the Guildhall because he knew about the bomb? Had he set it? She was almost positive he'd been the one to desecrate the Kings' Screen at York Minster, but did that mean he was capable of bombing the Guildhall? Or why?

With the questions forming on her tongue, a child's cry pierced the room.

"I do apologize, but if you're well enough, I have others who need attending," Dr. Bell said.

Dr. Bell was right. Now wasn't the time for questions.

"He still needs to rest," she said, tilting her head in Lyndy's direction, "but I'm more than fit." She wiped the dust and dirt off her hands. "Tell me how I can help."

Stella moved around the damaged hall, working the stiffness out of her knee, offering comfort and aid to anyone willing to take it. A young woman, in a pretty high-necked apricot muslin dress smudged with the dirt from the bottoms of hundreds of pairs of shoes, crouched on all fours. She pleaded for help in getting to her feet. She appeared unhurt but paralyzed by the shock that any violence could've touched her life. She asked Stella repeatedly if Their Royal Highnesses were okay. Stella couldn't say. An elderly man, using the wall to keep himself upright, his face taut as he struggled to maintain his composure, gratefully accepted Stella's offer of a steady arm. As they plodded toward the door, he spotted his wife's trampled hat, a once handsome black toque with light green feather embellishments that now added to the debris. Stella presented both the husband and the hat to his grateful wife waiting anxiously in the square outside. A small boy, dirt under his fingernails but wearing well-mended short pants and jacket, needed reuniting with his family. Stella spotted him whimpering in the shadow of Queen Victoria's statue's emotionless stare. After a quick wipe of his running nose and a comforting hug, she lifted him into her arms and carried him around the hall until the boy boisterously cried out when he spied his father.

As more and more people roused and recovered from the shock, Stella was there to give a steady hand up, or on occasion, a shoulder to cry on. A few had endured minor injuries, but the unexpected, unexplained explosion had rattled everyone. Exhausted and at the limit of doing what she could, Stella found her way back to Lyndy, who'd joined his aunt and Owen at the far end of the hall. Aunt Winnie perched on a chair, procured from who knows where, cradled her arm tied in a makeshift sling, a strip of exquisite Battenberg lace tablecloth that covered the tea table.

"Aunt Winnie, what happened?" Without thinking, Stella knelt before Lyndy's aunt. A shock of pain shot up from her injured knee.

"As you can see, my dear, I'm now symmetrically challenged," she quipped, glancing briefly down at her immobile arm. Like her injured ankle, it was her right. "At least one side of me is still tip-top." She lifted her cane to demonstrate.

Aunt Winnie weakly chuckled as if to ward off any words of concern, but her pale face belied her brave facade. She was in obvious pain.

"Is there anything I can do?"

"No, no, Stella dear. But how kind you are to help the less fortunate." She patted Stella's cheek, her gaze drifting past Stella's shoulder to the hall at large. "A viscountess for a few days, and already you've found your head for charity."

"I think she'll do, don't you, Mummy?" Owen quipped, giving Stella a hand up. "No matter what Aunt Franny says." He winked.

Aunt Franny? Stella had never heard Lady Atherly called that before.

"If more of them are anything like Stella, perhaps we should find you an American bride," his mother said.

Owen's smile vanished.

"Come here, love." Lyndy, chuckling at his cousin's expense, opened his arms, and Stella gratefully snuggled against his chest. To her relief, he'd spoken in his usual, quiet voice.

"Has your hearing gotten better?"

"Still a bit of ringing, but it's much improved."

"What happened to your aunt?" she whispered, hoping he could still hear her.

"In the stampede that followed the blast, someone rammed into her, knocking her to the floor. Dr. Bell thinks she sprained her wrist trying to catch herself from the fall."

"And the others?" His aunt's offhanded remark suddenly brought Morgan and the Peggs to mind.

She twisted in his arms to see where he pointed. Not far beyond the dark recess of a hallway, Mr. Pegg, his back to Stella, hovered over a prone figure. The injured man's legs jutted out beyond Mr. Pegg, pink rose petals stuck to the bottom of his stone-dust-covered shoes. Stella slipped from Lyndy's embrace, interlacing her fingers into his, and led him to the distressed family.

Morgan lay prostrate on the floor, his head cradled in Miss Pegg's lap. His hair, more unruly than usual, sprang haphazardly out from around a bloodstained bandage, made from the linen that had covered Queen Victoria's statue, wrapped around his head.

"Is he okay?" Stella asked.

"Aye, thank goodness," Mr. Pegg said. "Dr. Bell says it looks worse than it is. Said cuts on the head bleed a great deal, but he didn't seem too concerned."

"What happened?" Stella asked. She was beginning to sound like a scratched phonograph record, repeating the same question over and over.

Miss Pegg, her bodice smeared with Morgan's blood, stared down at him, stroking his pale cheek with the back of her finger. "My poor fella scraped his forehead when he dodged for the ground."

By the looks of him, Morgan did more than scrape his skin.

Stella glanced at her "fella" standing hale and hearty beside her. Warmed by gratitude, she rose on her tiptoes and kissed Lyndy's temple. The blood from his head wound had reduced to a small dark spot just out of her lips' reach.

"We're waiting for the ambulance to take him to hospital," Miss Pegg said.

Morgan revived as if he'd been listening and stared straight up into her adoring face. She brushed hair from his bandaged brow. He opened his mouth to say something, but she placed a finger on his lips to shush him. Owen, supporting his mother on his arm, plodded over to join them.

"Where's Dr. Bell?" Stella asked. The hall was almost empty now.

"I'm here."

Dr. Bell emerged from a side room, wiping his hands clean with a plain white handkerchief. He'd stripped off his jacket and waistcoat and had rolled up his sleeves. His hat was gone. Dark splatters of dried blood stained his previously stark white shirt. He looked exhausted.

"This way," he called to four men bursting through the wide wooden front doors carrying stretchers. He directed two of them toward the room he'd left and the others to Morgan, who was lifted from Miss Pegg's lap and carried away. She scrambled to her feet to follow. Owen threw out an arm to stop her.

"Maisie! Where are you going?" Owen asked as if he had a right to know.

"Steady on, Owen," his mother chided. She wobbled, caught off balance by his sudden movement.

"With Morgan to hospital," Miss Pegg said, her adamance aimed at Owen, daring him to object.

Owen dropped his arm and kicked at a frayed piece of gold ribbon lying on the floor. Catching it on the toe of his shoe, he sent it fluttering into the air. It reminded Stella of something.

Wingrove's chocolate box.

"There's no need, Miss Pegg," Dr. Bell was saying, unrolling a sleeve. "I'm sending him to hospital as a precaution. They'll dress his wound more thoroughly than I could do here. Unless I'm wrong, they'll soon send him home."

"Home? You don't understand, Doctor," Miss Pegg said. "Morgan doesn't have a home anymore."

"What do you mean by that?" Owen asked.

"I think what Maisie means," Mr. Pegg said, "is that Morgan's uncle was the last in a long line. He lost his parents when he was small. Horace and Marie raised him. When he was off at boarding school, their newly married daughter died from a devastating disease. Poor lass was like a sister to him. And then he lost Marie a few months ago."

"He's utterly alone, Owen," Miss Pegg said, almost pleadingly.

"Poor chap," Owen muttered sincerely.

"Indeed," Dr. Bell said solemnly under his breath.

"Not entirely," Mr. Pegg said, a hint of optimism in his voice. "He has you now, Maisie."

"My dear, John, are you implying that there's an agreement between them?" Aunt Winnie asked.

Stella, wondering the same thing, inwardly cheered that someone in her new family was as curious as she was. Or at least willing to ask what Lady Atherly, her new mother-in-law, would call "a few meddlesome questions."

"Well," Mr. Pegg said sheepishly, "we were going to wait to announce it . . . considering Horace's unexpected death. But yes."

"Congratulations! What good news," Aunt Winnie gushed as Lyndy shoved his hand into Mr. Pegg's.

As the others congratulated the Peggs, Stella watched Owen's face fall, his shoulders sag.

"So, you can see why I need to be with him," Miss Pegg said.

"Certainly, my dear girl. Go, go," Aunt Winnie urged, waving her cane in the direction Morgan had been taken.

Promptly taking their leave, both Peggs hustled after the stretcher bearers.

"Blast!" Owen uttered, letting his pent-up disappointment sputter out.

Lyndy slapped his shoulder.

"Now, now, my dear," Aunt Winnie said, patting Owen's arm. "She's a charming girl, but her heart belongs to someone else. You need to respect that and move on."

"When has that stopped him before?" Lyndy quipped.

Owen chuckled; his spirits lifted. "True." He cocked his head in thought. "Shouldn't Mummy be going to hospital as well, Dr. Bell? See that her wrist is properly set?"

"Owen, you are hopeless," his mother mocked. "You're not fooling anyone. You are not going to bother the Peggs at hospital."

"What if Maisie needs a strong shoulder to lean on? Besides, Mummy, we do need to see that you're well cared for." He winked at Stella and then pecked his mother's cheek with a light kiss.

"It would be a good idea," Dr. Bell agreed, unrolling his second sleeve.

"Very well." Aunt Winnie sighed in defeat. "Do lead on then, my dear." She shuffled alongside her son with the gait of a woman twenty years her elder as the two headed toward the awaiting ambulance.

"You'll have to excuse me, my lord, my lady," Dr. Bell said, tipping his head to take their leave. "I have another patient to attend to."

"Wait," Stella said before he dashed away again. She'd been biding her time but couldn't hold her tongue any longer. She had to know. "You knew Mr. Middleton longer than any of us."

"That's not saying much."

"True, but either way. The bomb, Dr. Bell. Do you think he could've been involved?"

CHAPTER 20

What the bloody 'ell happened?

Felix had gotten himself to a safe distance, hiding in the darkest corner of the alley beneath Mansion House, his back to the wall. He should've scarpered the moment the bomb detonated. That would've been the clever thing to do. Instead, curiosity won out, and, to the distance din of panic, Felix limped into the mellowing afternoon sunlight. After the booming roar of the explosion, he half expected to see roofing tiles, timbers, and fallen brick littering the ground. Where was the smoke, the debris from the blast? He stepped gingerly, crunching a few glittering glass fragments beneath his boot as he crossed the courtyard. Then the Guildhall's thick wooden doors flew open, and he was overwhelmed by the chaotic parade of townspeople spilling out. This wasn't what he'd expected: children wailing, old fellas with shattered spectacles groping about them, posh ladies, dazed and frightened, stumbling on their skirts. How many had been hurt?

Felix could no longer deny the damage done. But what of the princesses? Of them, there was no sign.

"Were them Royal 'ighnesses injured?" Again and again, he asked.

Intent on getting themselves as far away as possible, none stopped. Few answered, the answer always the same. No one knew.

Panic struck Felix.

When a middle-aged bloke, clutching his brown bowler in both hands, staggered past close by, Felix hooked the man's arm, forcing him to lunge to a standstill.

"Were the royals 'urt in the blast? Was anyone killed?" Felix demanded.

"'ands off!" The man swatted at Felix's head with his hat, twisting his arm out of his hold. The bloke stumbled, dropping a hand to the cobbled stones to keep from falling before dashing back toward the safety of the surging crowd.

What if it hadn't all gone to plan? What would the sergeant do? It didn't bear thinking about. Instead, he began grasping at arms, demanding of each passerby, "Are them Royal 'ighnesses safe?" until he received the answer he dreaded.

"Aye, lad. They escaped unscathed, thank goodness."

Felix wheeled about, promptly bumping into a gentleman in a morning jacket that smelled like smoke. Head down, he tugged on the brim of his cap, yanked his coat collar up, and plunged across the courtyard, shoving his way toward the alleyway exit, knocking shoulders with others intent on doing the same. He didn't have a moment to lose.

If the princesses didn't die today, Felix feared he just might.

"Why do you say that?"

Stella explained to Dr. Bell how Mr. Middleton had been lurking around during the private event, which he wouldn't have had an invitation to, and his furtive manner when he'd run away from the Guildhall moments before the bomb exploded.

"We already suspect he defaced the Kings' Screen," she said.

"I see your point. Would you and Lord Lyndhurst care to

walk with me?" Dr. Bell lowered his voice. "I might know something."

Stella motioned for Lyndy to follow before falling into step beside the doctor. Lyndy, to his credit, didn't balk at having to trail behind her.

Dr. Bell led them through a low stone archway into a wide, squat hallway. Charred and blackened like nowhere else, the walls bore the scars of fire. The acrid scent of smoke clung to her tongue. A pile of gray ash and debris filled the central part of the corridor. There were no colorful petals to break the bleakness here—any flowers lay blackened in a heap. Ironically, after the heat in the main hall, cooler air drifting through the corridor raised goose bumps on Stella's skin; someone must've opened a nearby door or window.

"It's not official yet," Dr. Bell whispered, "but—"

A uniformed policeman emerged from a doorway, stopping short when he saw them. "This is not a place for ladies." He readjusted the strap that held his high-domed helmet to his head, purposefully avoiding Stella's determined stare.

"It's all right," Dr. Bell assured him. "Glenshaw and Lord and Lady Lyndhurst are well-acquainted."

Well-acquainted was stretching it, but if it got the policeman on his way quicker so Dr. Bell could finish what he was about to say, Stella was all for it. Or was it the aristocratic titles that moved the man's feet? Either way, the policeman tipped his head in deference. With disapproval evident in his squint, he marched away in silence.

Dr. Bell gestured for them to follow him, stopping by the door the policeman had just left. "As I was saying, I overheard a private discussion among some of the police officers. They believe anti-royal anarchists targeted Their Royal Highnesses."

Stella was mortified. Four years ago, an anarchist had assassinated President McKinley. She never understood why anyone would do such a thing. "Why?"

"Believe it or not," Lyndy said, "there are some in this country who call for the abolishment of the monarchy."

Anti-royalists? Abolishment of the monarchy? A granddaughter of Scottish immigrants who helped build the stone fences ubiquitous throughout Kentucky, Stella couldn't've imagined such foreign ideas. Her father often entertained the governor, and more than one congressman, who blatantly lobbied for his support. In the States, money, not birthright, gave a man power. Yet this was what her father wanted, what he used his money to buy. Stella was Viscountess Lyndhurst now, and the threat to life and limb because of a title was real.

"Did the police say where the bomb was?" Lyndy asked the doctor.

"They're highly certain it was planted among the tokens people brought to give Their Royal Highnesses."

"How could someone plant a bomb with so many policemen around?" Stella wondered out loud.

"It couldn't have been very big," Lyndy said.

An image of the box of Wingrove's chocolates she'd seen on the tribute table flashed in Stella's mind. Hadn't Morgan said his uncle called the chocolate boxes his "secret weapon"? *This* was definitely not what he meant.

"From what I heard," Dr. Bell said, "Detective Sergeant Glenshaw insisted the table with the tokens be moved before the unveiling. The bomb exploded here in this hallway after they relocated it. Otherwise, with the table so near Their Royal Highnesses' position by the statue, they might've been severely injured."

Or killed. Dr. Bell didn't say it. He didn't have to.

"I had many people ask if the princesses were all right," Stella said. "Were they hurt at all?"

"Thank heavens, no. Shaken, for certain, but they were shielded from the blast, and any flying debris, by the statue."

"Then where are they?"

"I asked Detective Sergeant Glenshaw. All he would tell me was 'somewhere safe.' Where I don't know."

"Strange. I never saw them leave."

"By the side entrance, I suspect."

And if you can slip the royals out the side door, who's to say the perpetrator didn't sneak in the same way?

The doctor pointed to the low, arched, wooden door with hammered wrought-iron hinges at the end of the corridor. Stella had seen it before, but from the other side, and knew where it led—the alleyway where she and Lyndy had stolen off to.

"If Their Royal Highnesses are uninjured, who's the patient you're attending to?" Lyndy asked.

"Didn't I tell you? It's Detective Sergeant Glenshaw. He had severe lacerations and burns to his hand. He needs to get to hospital."

A door swung open and the orderlies, not having waited for the doctor to arrive, marched past with the patient. Glenshaw's eyes were closed, his face slack with bits of drool clinging to the corner of his lip. One of his arms dangled over the side of the stretcher, his fingertips almost sweeping the floor.

"I thought you said only his hand was injured?" Stella said.

"The blighter demanded he be allowed to accompany Their Royal Highnesses. Much like Miss Pegg did with Mr. Amesbury-Jones. But Detective Sergeant Glenshaw wasn't fit, and he wouldn't let me treat his wounds. So, I had to sedate him."

As they carried the patient away, the detective's unbandaged arm flopped up and down.

Morgan may welcome having Miss Pegg at his bedside, but Stella pitied the person nearest Detective Sergeant Glenshaw when he woke up.

Lyndy shuddered in the shadow as they strolled through the archway of Monk Bar, the largest of the medieval wall gates, a small stone tower fortress in its own right.

That had been close. Too close.

Back at the Guildhall, he'd shrugged off Stella's concerns. He admitted to a bit of ringing in his ears, and by God, his palms and knees felt abused by the Guildhall's stone floor, but what clutched his heart, as the blast replayed in his head, was how unmoored he felt. Not by the explosion, as he lost his feet, but by the loss of Stella. For one brief moment, he couldn't see her, hear her, or touch her. As if she, and this life they were starting together, had been a dream all along. He didn't fancy the feeling one bit.

Lyndy had relished getting to stretch his legs. When he'd suggested hiring a cab, she'd insisted they walk as if she'd known he needed a bit of fresh air to clear his head. After their ordeal, he imagined they both did. They'd strolled at a brisk pace, saying little but enjoying the companionable silence, through the town center, past York Minster, and eventually out Monk Bar. Lyndy reached for Stella's hand when the York County Hospital came in sight, a long, impressive, three-story brick building seated in a pastoral parkland outside the city walls. Surprised by his public display of affection, she rewarded him with her brilliant smile and squeezed his fingers reassuringly.

Once inside the hospital, its stark white walls and worn linoleum flooring resembling faded Roman mosaic tiles, it didn't take long to find Owen pacing up and down the ground floor hall.

"How is Aunt Winnie?" Lyndy asked.

"Mummy's fine. She's just resting up a bit. The doctors said she'll be ready to leave soon."

"What a relief. And Morgan?" Stella asked.

Owen stopped his pacing and regarded Stella with a lopsided frown of annoyance. "You would have to bring him up."

"Owen, is he okay or not?" Stella insisted.

"All right. All right." Owen threw up his hands in supplication as if giving in to intense interrogation. "Maisie's been in with him the entire time. I popped in to check on her. Seems Amesbury-Jones will be free to go soon as well."

"That's good news, Owen," Stella reminded him gently. "The poor man has lost his uncle and his company's most valuable asset."

"I know."

"You've always been a good loser, old chap," Lyndy said. "Why is this any different?"

Owen's lips flattened into a humorless smile, then silently mouthed, "You tell me."

His gaze drifted to the side at Stella, obliviously fussing with trying to hide a tear in her skirt. Lyndy couldn't help but smirk. He understood the difference between a dalliance and love. Perhaps for the first time, God help him, Owen did too. Or at least now knew what he'd been missing.

"How long will it be before your mother can go?" Stella said, giving up on fiddling with her skirt. "Do I have time to track down Detective Sergeant Glenshaw?"

"Of course. Mummy won't be out that quick. Ask the duty nurse about Glenshaw. She'll know where they took him."

They left Owen to his pacing, and after Stella inquired at the desk, they followed the long corridor down to the room the nurse indicated. It was a large, austere, whitewashed room lined with rows of metal-framed beds and smelling strongly of carbolic soap and unemptied chamber pots. Lyndy reached for the handkerchief from his breast pocket to hold to his nose before remembering Stella had used it to staunch the blood on his face. A nurse, wearing a starched white uniform and the thickest spectacles Lyndy had ever seen, blocked their advance before they'd taken three steps inside. She pressed a clipboard into the crook of her hip.

"Visiting 'ours are over. Come back tomorrow."

Lyndy bristled at her sharp tone, but Stella laid a hand on his arm to silence him.

"We are hoping to find Detective Sergeant Glenshaw," Stella explained. "He was brought in during the past hour, with cuts and burns from the explosion at the Guildhall. The nurse at the desk suggested we inquire here."

The nurse shifted her weight to one hip, her demeanor softened. "Wasn't that summat? A bad 'un, that." The nurse glanced at her clipboard. "I'm sorry, m'love. I don't 'ave a patient with that name."

Stella thanked the nurse, which Lyndy thought more than the woman deserved, not having helped them in the least, and headed off down the hall, poking her nose at every window, pushing open every unlocked door. He dutifully followed, wondering if he shouldn't let her snoop about on her own, when she called, "I think I hear him talking," and disappeared up a stairwell.

The moment he lost sight of her, his chest tightened, flashes of the wreckage after the explosion coloring his view. He touched the blood-encrusted cut on his head and dashed after her.

CHAPTER 21

"What are you doing here?" a deep voice harshly demanded.

When Lyndy reached the second floor, Stella was confronting Detective Sergeant Glenshaw, his hand and left cheek sporting fresh bandages. He appeared posted outside one of the many nondescript whitewashed hospital doors. Not quite reaching his shoulder, Stella resembled David facing Goliath.

"Friends of ours were injured," Stella was explaining, "and I need to talk to you."

Lyndy loved how Stella undauntingly mingled with royalty and maids. Yet, she wasn't Miss Kendrick of Kentucky now. She was his wife, a viscountess, and she'd have to learn not to let commoners take liberties.

"I would be obliged if you were not to take that tone with my wife," Lyndy said, not bothering to hide his displeasure when he reached Stella's side. "I'll make allowances for your injuries, but you'd do well to remember who you're speaking to, Glenshaw."

Red blotches flared behind the detective's bandaged cheek. "I beg your pardon, m'lord, m'lady," Glenshaw said grudgingly.

"Apology accepted," Stella said kindheartedly, with a smile that would disarm anyone.

Detective Sergeant Glenshaw was no exception. His expression softened, and he relaxed his stance.

"I see you're back on your feet," Lyndy said.

"Aye. That Dr. Bell has some answering to do," the detective grumbled.

"Not loitering about, are you? Appears to me like you're still on duty."

The detective, who'd been monitoring the corridor with subtle sideways glances, jabbed the thumb of his good hand at the unblemished door behind him. It was without scuffs, scrapes, peeling, or cracks. Was that a hint of fresh paint Lyndy smelled?

"Their Royal Highnesses," Glenshaw whispered, his voice barely carrying over the sound of Lyndy's slightly labored breath.

So, the detective was still at his post despite his injures? Lyndy had to admire the man's fortitude and dedication.

"Are they okay?" Stella whispered from behind her hand.

The detective stiffened and stared straight over Stella's head. "You wanted to talk to me about summat, m'lady?"

Stella told him what Dr. Bell had overheard about what the police suspected happened. Glenshaw confirmed Dr. Bell had heard correctly.

"Is that all?" The man sounded exhausted. He'd given up on his stiff posture and was using the door frame to lean on.

"No, I wondered if you'd ever heard the name Felix Middleton before?" Stella asked.

"Should I have?"

"With all the lies he's told, that might not even be his real name."

"And why should I care about this man's lies?" With a cold

stare in Lyndy's direction, the detective added an overly emphasized, "M'lady."

Lyndy glared back.

Stella, ignoring the silent sparing between Lyndy and the detective, patiently explained all about Mr. Middleton: how he'd lied about his enthusiasm for cathedrals, about his suspected involvement in the defacing of the Kings' Screen in York Minster, and then his abrupt departure from the hotel. She finished with her spotting him lurking about during the private reception and his suspicious behavior outside the Guildhall as if he'd anticipated the explosion.

To his credit, the detective listened attentively, his face growing more and more interested. "Describe this character to me."

"Slight build, dark brown hair, dark, deep-set eyes, favors a herringbone cap."

When Stella was done, Lyndy added, "The chap strikes me as a Cockney, and he always has an unshaven chin, no matter the time of day."

"Well, well, well," Glenshaw said, a knowing smile spreading across his face. "If that doesn't sound like 'the Private.' Yes, must be. Ties in with the Kings' Screen too. Defacing four centuries' worth of English kings is an overt threat to the monarchy."

"The Private?" Stella asked.

"A squirrely little man, an anti-royalist, who has threatened members of the royal family before. He gets his code name from evidence he served in the army. We've been trying to nick him for years. I'll notify my station and get officers out scouring the city for him." Abruptly he hung his head. "This never should've happened. Ever since Her Highness, Princess Ena has been seen in the company of His Majesty King Alfonso of Spain, and most notably, now that there's talk of an impending engagement announcement, the anti-royalists have threatened to target her. How can we call ourselves Englishmen when we can't defend those greatest among us?"

Who would've suspected this crusty detective would be such a staunch royalist? Yet, the breadth of this man's knowledge of the royal gossip was impressive. Even Lyndy hadn't heard about a possible engagement. Then again, the two royals weren't horses, trainers, or jockeys, so why would he care?

"I should've stopped it." Glenshaw lifted his head slowly, pent-up anger and self-recrimination warring on his face as he tried to constrain himself. He glared at Stella. "If I weren't so busy investigating a murder that never happened, or the loss of some piece of paper, this might've never happened."

"I say, don't blame us for your failures," Lyndy retorted curtly.

"You did stop it," Stella snapped, glaring first at Glenshaw and then at Lyndy as if fed up with them both. "You had the tribute table moved. I can't imagine how many would've suffered, the princesses included, had you not had the foresight to do that."

"But—" Glenshaw growled.

Stella swiftly cut him off. She wasn't done. "Mr. Middleton might have gotten away, for now"—she jabbed her finger toward the closed door—"but the princesses are in there and not lying dead on the Guildhall floor. So, you did do right by them, Detective Sergeant Glenshaw, even putting yourself in harm's way. But you should also do right by Mr. Wingrove and Morgan Amesbury-Jones. Just because they aren't royalty doesn't mean they don't deserve your respect and attention."

Stella's rebuke of the detective hovered in the air, forcing him to ponder his scuffed shoes. Taken aback, Lyndy stifled a chuckle.

Time and again, he'd rushed to her defense: as an American, an outsider, a commoner, and now as his wife. How had he so soon forgotten the woman who had defied her brutish father, subdued his haughty mother, and more than once put him in his place? Wasn't her spirit, her earnestness, her pluck what had drawn him to her all those months ago?

Now she's my wife, by God!

Lyndy tilted his chin in pride, waiting for the detective's reply. Glenshaw shifted his weight and stifled a forced cough. He couldn't bring himself to rebuke Lyndy's righteous bride.

"Today has been terrible for all of us, Detective," Stella said more conciliatingly, "but you still have a chance to catch who did it and perhaps help Morgan as well."

Glenshaw conceded by slumping deeper against the door frame. "That may be, m'lady, but—"

With the *tap-tap-tap* of a woman's heels announcing her impending arrival, Glenshaw withheld any further reply. A stout, maternal nurse emerged from the stairwell and squinted suspiciously at them as she reached for the doorknob of a room several doors down.

"Didn't I order my men to keep this hall clear?" Glenshaw grumbled loudly to no one in particular. The nurse sniffed her disapproval at his remark before entering the far room.

"There was no one posted on the stairs we came up," Stella informed him.

Glenshaw nodded in acknowledgment and defeat. "As to helping Mr. Amesbury-Jones, I've arrested Max Telford; I still think he'll tell us where the formula is. But I don't think 'the Private' had owt to do with Mr. Wingrove's death."

"But we found an invitation to the royal reception in Mr. Wingrove's room," Stella insisted. "I'm sure you noticed the box of Wingrove's chocolates on the table where the bomb was left."

"Coincidences." Glenshaw dismissed the idea, pinching the bridge of his nose.

"I think there are enough coincidences to wonder if they really are coincidences."

"Isn't it possible that Mr. Wingrove learned about Middleton's plot and was killed for it?" Lyndy suggested.

"Then why do it in such a clandestine way?" Glenshaw

countered. "If we're right, the squirrely devil tried to blow up members of the royal family. If Wingrove was killed, this Middleton character wouldn't've made it look like an accident."

Glenshaw had a point.

"No, the Private, or Felix Middleton as he's calling himself, isn't one for nuance," Glenshaw continued. "If Wingrove was killed, and I'm not saying he was, then I'd bet my badge on it being someone else. Like the porter I've already arrested. Or that nervous nephew of his. Or—"

"You're going to keep investigating?" Stella asked.

"Weren't you the one to remind me of my duty, m'lady? I won't rest until either of these cases are closed. That means, of course, I may need additional statements from you, Lord and Lady Lyndhurst." His tone implied he hoped they'd beg off as Lyndy was inclined to do.

"Anything we can do to help," Stella said.

Lyndy inwardly groaned. Wanting nothing more than to go back to having a proper honeymoon, that was not what he wished to hear.

Stella lightly hobbled back down the stairs, clumsily leading with her left as her right knee had started to stiffen. Lyndy, following a pace off, rubbed the back of his neck. As agreed, they parted at the bottom of the stairwell. Lyndy hadn't liked the idea. After what had happened, he'd prefer never to let her out of his sight again. Yet she'd won the argument; Owen needed him more than she did. Besides, it didn't take both of them to visit Mr. Haigh.

She gave him a quick peck as he self-consciously glanced at the passing nurse, who was too absorbed in her thoughts to take note of a harmless kiss. Unlike the hall above, where Glenshaw kept watch, this one was congested with dazed nurses scuttling around and distressed visitors preoccupied with reading room numbers.

"Don't be long, love," Lyndy whispered, his cheek against hers but his focus beyond her shoulder. Down the long, stark hall, the white walls almost blindingly bright under the suspended electric lights, Owen was wearing a path in the linoleum floor.

"I'll be quick." Stella pecked his cheek a second time for good measure and turned away, not waiting to see what Lyndy did next.

Having already asked the duty nurse, she soon found the room she was seeking. Another long, vault expanse of whitewashed walls and rows of metal beds, it mirrored the one she'd seen before. Two young nurses bustled past, one pushing a medicine cart, the other a full bedpan. Stella twisted her head away at the repugnant smell.

Give me a stable anytime.

She'd spent most of her life around horses and in stables, even helping to clean the stalls. Perhaps she was biased, but no horse stall ever smelled so vile. Ignoring the stiffness in her knee, Stella stepped briskly down the aisle between the beds, but once in her nose, she couldn't shake the smell. The astringent scent of recently applied vinegar only made it worse. As she passed patient after patient, men groaned or called out for help. One had a sickly yellow complexion that reached his eyes, which followed her. Another patient lay prisoner with his leg wrapped like a mummy suspended above his bed in a sling. Yet another man, stretched out on his side, stared at her through drooping eyelids, his cracked lips as pale as his skin. Stella's nerves failed her, and she faltered. What was she even doing here? Why had she insisted on coming alone? Thoughts of Mr. Wingrove, Daddy, and the other dead bodies she'd seen crowded her vision. Too many of these men had that same vacant, pallid look of dead men but without the relief from suffering death brings.

"Help me," someone moaned, and like a spring released, Stella, her heart pounding, swiveled around and started walking as fast as she could back the way she came.

"Lady Lyndhurst?"

"There you are, Mr. Haigh." She'd walked right past the patient she'd come to see.

The Majestic Hotel's manager sat upright in his bed, propped up by several pillows, the blue stripes of his pajamas cutting across the starched white linens that surrounded him like a cloud. A newspaper lay spread out on his lap. Contrasting to those around him, he exuded a robustness Stella was relieved to see.

"My lady! What brings you here?" Mr. Haigh hastily folded the paper and pulled the spectacles from his face. He spit on his palm and slicked his hair across his forehead.

"Friends of mine were injured." Stella could read the headline of the paper he'd been reading even upside-down. ROYAL UNVEILING TODAY. Had he been told of the explosion? If not, he'd learn about it soon enough.

"I'm so sorry to hear that, my lady."

Stella struggled to smile, ashamed. How quick he was to offer her his sympathy. Wasn't he the one in a hospital bed, engulfed by stench and sickness?

"I also wanted to check up on you, Mr. Haigh. How are you?"

"How kind of you to think of me. How very kind indeed." He squared his shoulders, shifting around in his bed to sit up straighter as blood rose in his cheeks, adding a healthy blush to his face. "I am most well, thank you, and am due to be released tomorrow. I should be back at the Majestic to ensure that you and Lord Lyndhurst have a satisfactory conclusion to your stay."

"I'm glad to hear it." Stella's heart slowed as she concentrated on the man before her and her other reason for coming. Mr. Haigh had been attacked on the same day they'd found Mr.

Wingrove's dead body. A coincidence, maybe. She wanted to find out a few things before deciding for sure.

"If you don't mind me asking, what happened?"

Mr. Haigh pinched his lips tightly. "I was attacked from behind outside my office." He folded his arms across his chest and added, "The police I spoke to have no idea why."

"But you do?"

"Indeed, I do, my lady." He hesitated to say more, his sideways glance coinciding with a nurse pushing a cart laden with clean rolled bandages. Stacked into multi-rowed pyramids, they seemed likely to roll and spill out onto the floor at any moment. He waited until the nurse was four beds down before saying, "I'm convinced someone wanted my invitation."

"Your invitation? To the royal reception?" Why would someone want it so much they'd almost killed the man for it?

"Yes. Well." He must've mistaken the disbelief in her voice for recrimination, for he shifted again, shoving back his pillows, nervously. "Not my invitation, exactly, but the one that arrived for Sir Peter, the owner of the Majestic. As he's out of the country at the moment . . ."

"You saw no harm in your attending in his place?" Stella suggested.

"That's it, precisely, my lady." He was all smiles now.

"Why would anyone do something so ruthless just to get an invitation?"

"Not just any invitation, if you'll excuse me for saying so, but an invitation to a private reception with Her Royal Highness, Princess Beatrice, the daughter of Her Majesty, the late Queen Victoria. Even being an American, you should appreciate the magnitude of such an event. It would've been the honor of my life to attend." His passionate enthusiasm put Stella to shame. Stella hadn't even wanted to go. He suddenly busied himself wiping his spectacles with the corner of his bedsheet. "But alas, someone wanted it more than I."

Who could that be? How would they have known about it? Mr. Middleton came to mind.

"Did you see who hit you?"

"Only their shoes."

"What were they wearing?"

He blinked, startled at the question. "I believe they were black, patent leather Oxfords. Similar to the ones I wear." He pointed beneath his bed. Beside a pair of plush chenille embroidered slippers sat the shoes as he described.

"Are you sure?" Stella was the first to admit that men's footwear wasn't her expertise. She rarely noticed what a man wore, but she pictured a brown shoe on Mr. Middleton's foot for some reason.

"I could be wrong, my lady."

"Who would've known about the invitation? That you would have it and not Sir Peter?"

Mr. Haigh puckered his brows and fiddled with the folds of the blanket in his lap. "Members of staff, of course. I might've mentioned it to a few guests I'm friendly with: a couple from Swindon that stay every year, Lady Ottersby, who also planned on attending, that sort of thing. I never mentioned that I intended to use the invitation, mind, just that it had arrived for Sir Peter and how much I'd admired the exquisite stationery."

That didn't narrow it down much. Anyone at the hotel could've overheard the manager bragging about it, Mr. Middleton included.

"Did you attend, my lady?" The wistfulness in his voice confirmed what Stella suspected. He hadn't learned about the bomb yet.

"I did, and I wish I never had." Stella sighed, suddenly exhausted by the ordeal. All she wanted now was Lyndy, a hot bath, and a door to lock the world out.

"Why is that, my lady?"

"Mr. Haigh, someone tried to kill the princesses by setting off a bomb."

The manager's face paled, and he grabbed the edge of his mattress for support. "Please tell me the fiend didn't succeed."

"No, they didn't succeed." She leaned forward. Instinctually Mr. Haigh leaned in too. "And between you and me, I know for certain the princesses are upstairs right now, as we speak. From what I understand, they'll be fine." She knew she wasn't supposed to tell anyone, but didn't the ardent loyalist deserve a little joy?

Mr. Haigh immediately glanced up at the ceiling. After a moment, he glanced back at Stella. He pointed upward. "Up there. Right now?"

Stella nodded. "Would you like me to tell them about you, your injury, and your disappointment in not getting to meet them? Lord Lyndhurst knows Princess Beatrice personally."

"No, no, my lady," Mr. Haigh frantically waved away the suggestion. "That's kind of you, but . . . I couldn't possibly intrude upon Their Royal Highnesses in such a time of distress."

Inexplicably discombobulated, the manager fumbled with his sheets, plucking and pulling at them. When a pillow dropped to the floor, he unthinkingly lunged for it, nearly crashing out of bed. On the opposite side, Stella helplessly watched as he struggled, caught like a fly in a tangled web of sheet. A nurse dashed across the aisle to push him back into his bed, which creaked under the sudden shift in weight. Suppressing the sudden urge to giggle, Stella squatted down to retrieve the pillow from under the bed and handed it to the nurse. After slipping the pillow behind his head, the nurse efficiently tucked her patient tightly back in.

"Are you okay, Mr. Haigh?"

"Thank you, my lady," he said, his breath heavy from his near fall. "I'm as right as rain."

The nurse tsked, her professional opinion obviously differing from her patient's. Mr. Haigh ignored her.

"But I do wonder, did the police catch who did it, who planted the bomb?"

With her hands still tucked beneath the mattress, the nurse's head shot up in alarm. Stella had both the nurse's and patient's attention.

"Not yet, but I'm sorry to say that the one they suspect was a recent guest at your hotel."

Mr. Haigh groaned, collapsing back into his pillows.

CHAPTER 22

What a strange turn of events! Three nights ago, Stella had arrived in York anticipating spending the whole of her honeymoon at the Majestic Hotel. Now, she and Lyndy, at the insistence of his aunt, were on their way back to Hubberholme Park. Taking her cue, Owen had generously offered his estate to the others as well, to recuperate far from the death and danger York seemed to pose. Stella didn't think it was York that was dangerous, but she'd been happy to agree. A change of scenery, particularly one as spacious and breathtaking as the Yorkshire Dales, was always a good idea. She'd be able to relax, ride, step back from it all and think.

Was Mr. Middleton the culprit of everything that had happened: the bomb, the paint on the Kings' Screen, the attack on Mr. Haigh, the stolen formula, Mr. Wingrove's death? Detective Sergeant Glenshaw had arrested Max for the theft, but Stella put little faith in the detective's conclusions. Even he admitted he hadn't found the formula on Max or among his things. Yet it was hard to believe Mr. Middleton, or anyone for that matter, was capable of wreaking such havoc alone. Why would Mr. Middleton leave Mr. Wingrove's invitation on the carpet only to turn around and assault Mr. Haigh to get the invitation from his office? Unless Mr. Haigh's attacker didn't know of Mr. Wingrove's invitation and thus never entered his room. No, there had to be at least two people involved. But if Mr. Middleton was the bomber, as everyone was convinced he was, but not Mr. Wingrove's killer, who was?

Of all the possible suspects, Morgan rose to the top. He had a motive, having inherited the entire confectionery company. He had the opportunity. Staying in the hotel and being the victim's nephew, Morgan could easily have convinced Mr. Wingrove to let his killer in. And Morgan had the means—stuff the pillows up the chimney while the coals burned and let the fumes do all the work. If Mr. Wingrove hadn't already been asleep or sedated by his medicine, even the chambermaid would've been able to overtake the sickly, frail old man.

Yet to be fair to Morgan, anyone with either access to a key or whom Mr. Wingrove found friendly enough to let into his room could've done it. Any member of the hotel staff, any hotel guest, anyone who'd known Mr. Wingrove was staying at the Majestic could've come in the night and killed the chocolatier. As always, the answer lay in a question. Why?

The carriage creaked in protest as it rumbled across a stretch of cobbled street. Exhausted, Stella had welcomed the suggestion to hire a cab to the train station. They'd cut through town, inevitably passing beneath the shadow of York Minster's towers, stopping at the hotel long enough to change and see that Ethel and Finn pack the trunks and follow. Stella would send a telegram to her mother later. She wasn't coming until the day after tomorrow. Maybe Mama could come to Hubberholme as well?

The train station loomed ahead, a squat but sprawling structure of honey-colored stone and glass-fronted archways. In a few minutes, they'd be on a train, clear of the city. In four long, eventful days, they'd unexpectedly come full circle.

That's how Stella felt. Like she was going in circles, her mind swirling with possibilities.

Stella wrapped her hands around Lyndy's arm and rested her back against the padded wall of the carriage. From under half-closed eyelids, she studied Morgan and Miss Evans sitting across from her. Miss Evans, her back as straight as a wrought-iron fence post, stared out the window. With her hands tightly clasped in her lap, she incessantly rubbed her right thumb over her left. Still wearing a thin strip of bandage around his head, Morgan stared into his lap.

Stella had been happily surprised when Aunt Winnie invited Dr. Bell to join them. As the mistress of Hubberholme Park had explained, it was Dr. Bell, after all, who'd selflessly cared for the injured at the Guildhall. He deserved a bit of a country respite. The doctor had been reluctant to accept, offering up excuses of a trip planned to Durham the following day, but no one said no to Lady Rountree. Owen had graciously extended the invitation to Morgan, though the magnanimous gesture didn't fool Stella. How else could Owen ensure that Miss Pegg, whom Owen also invited, came?

He doesn't know when to give up.

But Miss Evans? Why was she coming? The secretary hadn't even been at the unveiling, never experienced the traumatic explosion that bonded the others together. When she'd learned of the bombing, she arrived at the hospital demanding assurances Morgan was all right. When Morgan was released, he assured her that he was fine and didn't need her to stay in York anymore. Without articulating it, he told her to go home to Wolverhampton. Instead, she'd invited herself to Hubberholme Park, insisting she'd prove invaluable in Morgan's recovery. Owen hadn't objected, hope twinkling in his eyes. Did Owen imagine Miss Evans might put a wedge between Morgan and Miss Pegg, giving him a chance to slip in? He must. Why else would he suggest Morgan and Miss Evans ride with Stella and Lyndy, leaving Miss Pegg to ride with him, his mother, and the good doctor? Could Owen be right? Could Miss Evans have a fondness for Morgan beyond the professional? Stella didn't think so. Why the secretary refused to go home was a question she couldn't answer, yet. But no matter how much Owen schemed, Miss Pegg and Morgan were going to be married.

Unless Morgan turned out to be a killer.

The hiss of steam and a high-pitched whistle signaled the departure of a train. The horses snorted in displeasure and stopped abruptly, forcing the carriage to jerk to a halt. Stella lurched upright, tightening her grip on Lyndy's arm for support. They were still in the middle of the road, a few yards from the grand arched entranceway.

"Why have we stopped?" Miss Evans complained.

Stella wondered too. The carriage horses would never be spooked by something they heard all day. She peered out the window to see a man in a herringbone cap scurrying across the street after having crossed dangerously close in front of the carriage. He was limping. With a click of the tongue, the coachman encouraged the horses forward.

"Stop!" Stella yelled as the carriage began to advance.

Lyndy banged his fist on the roof. Not waiting for the wheels to stop turning, Stella flung open the door and leaped out, Lyndy mere breaths behind her.

"Felix Middleton. Over there." She pointed, and Lyndy sought out the herringbone cap as Mr. Middleton weaved himself into the crowd of train passengers.

"Good eye," Lyndy said.

The pair followed him inside the train station, temporarily losing him in a plume of steam spewed from an arriving train that lingered under the building's impressively large, curved, glass and iron roof. When Mr. Middleton reemerged, he was standing on the platform with a small case clutched in his hand, his head turned toward the arriving train. They didn't have a plan as they approached the anarchist, but it proved unnecessary. Without provocation, Mr. Middleton shoved his case into the chest of a passing gentleman who stumbled into Stella and Lyndy's path. He couldn't have spotted them.

Then why was he running?

Mr. Middleton fled down the platform, skirting women in wide-brimmed hats, porters pushing luggage-laden carts, and at least one conductor who tried to grasp his arm to slow him down. Stella's dainty, new high-heeled pumps weren't the best shoes for chasing criminals. She didn't let that stop her. Balling her skirt in her fist, she raced after him. When her hat flew off and floated onto the tracks, she didn't stop. His flight confirmed her suspicions; this was the man who tried to kill innocent people. She was not going to let him get away.

Mr. Middleton slipped through a side archway, pushing past a second conductor checking for tickets, and back out into the street. When Stella and Lyndy emerged from the train station behind him, he was aiming for the nearest access to the medieval city walls, dodging dangerously close to an oncoming wagon transporting travel trunks. Hand in hand, Stella and Lyndy weaved their way more carefully through the traffic. A passing hansom cab with a slow-paced black mare with prominent withers obscured their view for a moment. Then a loud pop, like the backfiring of her Daimler automobile, startled the horse. The mare reared, then landed heavily on her hooves. The horse skittered down the crowded street, pulling the frantic driver and his shouting passenger behind her.

During the commotion, Stella sought the automobile that backfired, but didn't see one. Only carriages and wagons filled the street. "What happened?"

The words died in her throat as she spotted the prone figure sprawled against the first few steps of the stone stairway leading up to the top of the walls. Stella's heart leaped painfully in her chest. *Just like Daddy.* Although this man had fallen up the stairs, not down. With a tight grip on Lyndy's hand, she crossed the last few yards of the road and approached. Stella's gaze combed the area for others who might've seen what happened. Still distracted by the runaway cab, no one else seemed to notice the man. On closer inspection, she recognized the herringbone cap that lay half on his head, half on the step above him, leaving open a grisly view of the dark, ragged-edged circle in his temple. It was Mr. Middleton. When a fly buzzed past and landed on the blood trickling down the dead man's cheek, Stella bent over and retched.

CHAPTER 23

Stella closed her eyes, the chilly breeze rushing against her cheeks, and trusted the horse to know the way down the hilly, treeless pasture. She forced out pent-up breath as she rocked in rhythm with the horse's gait. It was good to be in the saddle again.

It seems she wasn't as used to seeing dead bodies as she'd thought.

Although she'd never erase the image of Mr. Middleton's dead body, her revulsion at seeing the bullet wound had faded, dissolved by the crisp air, the reassuring stability of Roopa, Owen's solid Cleveland Bay beneath her (though how she wished it was Tully), and the subtle, earthy, herbal scent of damp grass and heather kicked up as the horse navigated the brushy moors. The scene in the shadow of the York city walls was a vague memory—the vigil beside the dead man, the arrival of a uniformed policeman, the brief statements she and Lyndy gave him before rejoining the others in the train station. The journey to Hubberholme Park was equally a blur. She'd held Lyndy's hand as the city receded from view until her fingers tingled and turned white. Had they been alone in the first-class compartment? Where were Owen and his mother? What had happened to her hat? She'd stared out at the passing scenery, seeing nothing but the memory of two men, Mr. Middleton and her father, sprawled motionless against stone stairs. Neither was a good man. She could admit that now about her father; Daddy had been a manipulative bully. Mr. Middleton had been a criminal. Both had met violent ends. She'd made peace with her father's death, and she hardly knew Mr. Middleton.

Then why had she felt so haunted?

As if in answer, an image of Mr. Wingrove reposed in bed, a cast of peace on his features, flashed in her mind. Where did his death fit into all of this? He wasn't a bad man, yet he'd met an untimely end too. Where was the justice in that?

Hearing Lyndy's horse whinny behind her, Stella opened her eyes. Hubberholme Park's stone stable was in sight. They slowed to a trot as they entered a stone-lined lane. With his proud head held high, Roopa unhurriedly slapped his tail at a fly.

Minutes after reaching Owen's family estate, Lyndy had proposed a ride while they waited for the servants to arrive and settle them into the cottage, which Aunt Winnie insisted they take. (The dear lady understood their need for privacy.) Until then, Stella gratefully wore a borrowed riding costume that Aunt Winnie claimed she'd never use again. The skirt gaped around her waist, being slightly too big, but what had Stella cared when she and Lyndy had galloped off onto the Dales on borrowed horses?

In the stable yard, Lyndy leaped off his horse, tossing the reins to the waiting groom and reaching for Stella's hand. She didn't need his help, but his eagerness was irresistible, his concern palatable. She leaned down, and Lyndy, reading her intention, stretched up to meet her kiss. They could've died today. They hadn't spoken of it, not once, but it drifted around them like invisible haze.

She jumped down to the paving stones, outlined by yellowing trampled weeds. Still clutching hands, they walked in silence to their small, two-story sandstone cottage, a short distance from the main house. Inside, a fire crackled, warming the chill from her face. When they entered, a maid, who was setting out a small dinner brought down from the manor house, paused to wipe her hands on her starched apron. The food, including root vegetable consommé, roasted chicken, and peas, was still steaming, and its aroma filled the cozy space. Considering the exotic tastes of the food Aunt Winnie preferred, Stella was surprised to find such standard English fare. Yet Stella wasn't hungry. Lyndy promptly dismissed the maid.

"Well, that was an eventful day," Stella sighed when they were alone.

"I believe you are mastering the art of understatement, my love."

She'd tried to ignore the danger they'd been in, the evil they'd seen, the questions that buzzed inside her brain like a pesky mosquito, but in the quiet safety of the cottage, she couldn't keep the tremble of dread out of her voice.

"I could've lost you." Whispered as if speaking to herself, Stella half hoped Lyndy didn't hear.

He had. With all the urgency of a man on fire, Lyndy rushed to embrace her. She met him halfway. Their kisses were urgent, hard, as if each were trying to consume the other, desperate to be inseparable. Lyndy wiggled out of his jacket before yanking off Stella's riding coat without severing the contact between their lips. For a few blissful moments, Stella sought to banish the fear and shock and ugliness of it all by concentrating on the touch and taste of Lyndy.

When they eventually collapsed in a spent heap together into the overstuffed chintz couch near the fire, Lyndy tenderly stroked her cheek. "I won't let anything happen to you. I couldn't bear it." The intensity in his tone threatened to evoke the tears she'd struggled to fend off.

Stella playfully tousled his already messy hair. "And if something were to happen to you? You'd leave me alone, defenseless against your mother."

Lyndy halfheartedly chuckled at her attempt to lighten the mood. "You, defenseless? Mother hadn't a chance the moment you roared up in that motorcar of yours." He turned to stare at the flames of orange and red, gently lapping at the newly stacked pile of wood in the grate. How handsome he was in the firelight. "Not the honeymoon I imagined."

"Me either," she said, turning his chin toward her with her finger. Then she smiled impishly at him. "But it's not over yet. We can start again, can't we?"

His lips slowly spread into a crooked smile. He tucked a loose strand of her hair behind her ear. "Yes, let's." He leaned in.

As his lips sought hers, she added, "Right after we eat. I'm starving."

Lyndy laughed, shaking her as he did. The sweet sound of it, so genuine and rare, swept aside all thoughts of hunger or murder or firelight. As he wriggled aside, giving her room to stand up, Stella hooked her arm around his neck and pulled him back toward her.

Chicken was good cold too, wasn't it?

Owen watched the embers flick and jump in the grate and shot back the last gulp of whiskey. What a hell of a day he'd had. First, the bloody bomb, his mother's battering, some chap gets himself killed steps from Lyndy and Stella, and then Maisie's final rejection. It made a man pause.

What had he been thinking?

It was a last-gasp attempt, and he knew it. He and Maisie had played together as children. Why was he just realizing how much he adored her now?

He'd arranged to have Maisie ride beside him back to Hubberholme Park. Perhaps if he could separate her from Morgan, she'd show where her true affections lay. It was no use. After much convincing, she agreed to be separated. Owen had spent the entire journey hanging on her every word, imagining what her lips tasted like, how it would feel to hold her in his arms; all the while she spoke incessantly about her concern for the chocolatier's nephew. Yet Owen was never one to give up. The moment they'd arrived, he'd asked her to join him in the garden while everyone else got settled inside. He'd led her to a wooden bench set among his mother's collection of exotic rhododendrons, their colorful pink and purple blooms long since shriveled up, and declared himself to her. She'd smiled benevolently at him, almost pitifully, placing the soft palm of her hand against his cheek, touched by his affection. She absolutely adored him, she'd said, as a beloved cousin. How could she not? But alas, her heart belonged to Morgan Amesbury-Jones.

The truth tasted bitter in his mouth, all the more for knowing it beforehand but unwilling to accept it. Owen fancied demanding whether Amesbury-Jones had taken advantage of her the night he'd seen the blighter outside Maisie's room, but knew it would only serve to alienate her. No, he had to accept he'd lost this one.

But wasn't a fellow allowed a little companionly wallowing?

Lyndy, who normally would've happily commiserated while drinking Owen's father's excellent aged whiskey, was holed up in the guest cottage. Owen had only himself to blame. He'd been the one to suggest offering the honeymooning couple the privacy the cottage afforded. Why, tonight of all nights, had he chosen to be so selfless? Not only must he acknowledge his defeat, but he had to forfeit Lyndy's company as well.

Well, at least someone's enjoying himself.

The grandfather clock in the hall chimed twice. It was high time he found his bed. Owen swayed as he rose to his feet.

How many whiskeys had he had? With everyone else long since gone to bed, Owen had elected to drown his sorrows in his study. It wasn't the first time. It was here he'd spent the night his father died. He shoved off the armchair and staggered across the room and out into the hall.

"I say, what are you doing, old chap?" Owen called to Amesbury-Jones, mounting the stairs. "Do you know how bloody late it is?" The object of Maisie's affection gave no reply. "I say, Amesbury-Jones!" Still no reply. "What kind of bloody game are you playing at?"

The rascal ignored him. *He's got some cheek!*

Owen's self-pity grew into anger as he took the stairs two at a time, his hand clutching the thick but highly polished banister railing for support. When he was in range, Owen grabbed the chap by the shoulder. Morgan's body gave no resistance, pivoting with Owen's grip. Amesbury-Jones was suddenly facing him, his jaw slack, his gaze unfocused, as if Owen wasn't there. Unnerved, Owen released his grip. The moment he did, Morgan swung back around and continued on as if nothing had happened.

Bloody hell! What's wrong with him?

With a strange compulsion to see what Morgan was up to, Owen trailed him, a pace or two behind as the man meandered aimlessly through the manor house. Never once acknowledging Owen's presence or muttering a word. When they'd reached the wing with the guest bedchambers, Owen stopped at the one where Dr. Bell had been put up.

"Dr. Bell!" The whiskey having loosened in his tongue, Owen called out far too loudly. He proceeded to bang on the door.

The doctor swung it open almost instantly, as if he'd been waiting for the knock. His hair was matted where it had met the pillow, and he was dressed in rumpled pajamas, but otherwise, he was alert and focused.

"Will I require my bag?" he demanded. Obviously, this wasn't the first time the doctor had been called to help in the early hours of the morning.

"Couldn't say." Owen swayed, the banging disrupting his balance.

Dr. Bell caught him under his arm and leaned him against the wall. "Are you ill?" With one whiff of Owen's breath, Dr. Bell scoffed good-humoredly, "Drunk men don't need doctors, Sir Owen. They need sleep."

"No. It's not me. I can handle my drink. Amesbury-Jones is the one acting peculiar. Follow me."

Owen led the doctor, medical case in hand, down the hall to where Maisie's fiancé had disappeared around the corner. On the way, Owen described Amesbury-Jones's odd behavior. His revelation seemed to ease the doctor's concern.

"Ah, I see," was all he said.

When the men rounded the corner, Amesbury-Jones was nowhere in sight. Then a door slammed. Owen swiveled about to peer out the nearby window. Beneath him, Maisie's preferred lover was haltingly crunching across the gravel drive in bare feet. Dr. Bell joined him at the window and, putting his finger against the glass, pointed to where Amesbury-Jones was heading.

"Where does that path lead?"

"The millpond." The pond, hidden behind the long, bending fronds of a line of weeping willow trees, was over an acre and an excellent place to fish. "And beyond that is the churchyard." From this vantage point, the tip of the ancient stone church's steeple was visible above the trees.

"We need to stop him," Dr. Bell said, already heading back toward the grand staircase.

"This way. I know a quicker way out."

Finding his legs a bit more responsive, Owen hastened to the servants' door at the end of the hall. With his rapid footfalls echoing against the wall, he stumbled down the dark, narrow stairwell, Dr. Bell on his heels, and dashing past the scullery, threw open the servants' entrance to the outside. The cool air smacked him in the face as he spotted Amesbury-Jones ambling straight for the willow trees. As they ran to catch up, the manicured grass, heavy with dew, instantly dampened their feet.

"What's wrong with him?" Owen panted as he batted away the willow branches. One got past his hand and tickled him in the nose.

"He suffers from somnambulism," the doctor pronounced.

"Sleepwalking? I've only heard of such things. I never witnessed it for myself. Is he in any danger?" Owen wasn't as concerned for the man's welfare as much as Maisie's. If anything should happen to him while at Hubberholme Park, she'd never forgive Owen.

"We should steer him inside. We wouldn't want him falling into the millpond or making it into the churchyard and tripping over a tombstone."

They caught up to Amesbury-Jones, and each, with a firm grip on the chap's arms, led him pacifically back into the house. With the sleepwalker safely back in bed, Dr. Bell assured Owen the fellow wouldn't remember a thing.

"It does answer something that's been concerning me," Dr. Bell said as he quietly closed Amesbury-Jones's guest-chamber door.

Owen silently agreed, relieved that the chap, most likely sleepwalking that night Owen spied him near Maisie's door, had more principles than Owen gave him credit.

He still doesn't deserve Maisie, though.

"What concerned you, Dr. Bell?"

"The night Mr. Wingrove died, I saw Mr. Amesbury-Jones near the old gentleman's suite, and the next day when I suggested we both suffered from insomnia, he denied it. He probably has no idea he suffers from somnambulism. I will have to inform him in the morning."

"And I'll tell my mother and Miss Pegg, in case they see him like this. We wouldn't want the ladies thinking Amesbury-Jones is up to no good."

"Quite right, Sir Owen," the doctor agreed lightheartedly. "Better a sleepwalker than a scoundrel, eh?"

The doctor bid Owen good night, his unintended cutting remark ringing in Owen's ears.

CHAPTER 24

Somewhere in the distance, a chorus of sheep bleated. Stella, for less than a second, wondered where she was. Then she reached for Lyndy. He wasn't there. She threw off the bedcovers, snatched her embroidered silk robe up from where it had dropped from the back of the chair, and slipped into it. She glanced over at the elaborately carved oak bed. Already risen above the nearest ridge, the sun streamed through the window, lighting up the crisp white linens like a lantern. What time was it? She sought the small, highly decorative blue, red, green, and gold enamel clock on the bedside table. Another souvenir from Aunt Winnie's travels, no doubt, it provided an unusual but strangely harmonious splash of color among the subtle earth-toned decor of the cottage. The clock read almost nine.

Where was Lyndy?

Stella shivered. She stepped into her slippers and, tying the robe's belt more tightly around her middle, headed for the main room of the cottage. No wonder it was so cold. The fire had gone out. Then she remembered they'd rejected the maid's offer of lighting the fire this morning. Stella was poking at the embers with the wrought-iron fireplace poker, hoping to revive some heat when Lyndy, wearing a greenish-brown tweed cap that matched his suit and tall, almost knee-high boots, strode into the cottage as if returning from a long, brisk walk. He closed the cottage door behind him and picked a dried, rust-colored leaf off his tweed jacket, a telegram clutched in his hand.

Stella's heart skipped a beat. A rush of the past day's events flooded her mind. What could it be now?

"Good morning, my love. Sleep well?" Lyndy's arms welcomed her, wrapping his warmth around her like the blankets she'd rashly thrown aside.

"I can't believe I slept so late."

"Well." Lyndy had the decency to look a bit sheepish. "We did stay up rather late. The maid's brought breakfast if you're hungry." He pointed to a wicker basket covered in a blue and white gingham cloth on the table, set for two.

"I'm famished."

Stella smiled at the memory of their "late night," and before her face turned red, she lifted the cloth from the basket to find boiled eggs, a slab of cold ham, several smoked kippers, toast and marmalade, slices of apple, and a pot of tea wrapped in a quilted cozy. It all smelled heavenly. Still standing, Stella poured Lyndy a cup of the still steaming tea before fixing herself one, dropping several pieces of sugar into the thin, delicate teacup depicting an Asian garden in red, green, and white. She handed Lyndy his cup of tea.

Trying not to let her concern creep into her voice, she said as casually as she could muster, "Who's the telegram from?"

She took a sip of her tea. The warmth, the sweetness, the aroma did wonders to calm her rising concerns.

Lyndy frowned. "I rose early and went up to the house to see how Owen's getting on."

"And?"

"And this was already waiting for me. I never saw Owen and spoke to Aunt Winnie only briefly. I knew you'd want to know." He handed the telegram to Stella.

It was from Detective Sergeant Glenshaw expressing his displeasure that they'd left York without telling him or giving him a formal statement about Mr. Middleton's demise. He requested they return at "their earliest convenience, preferably before the inquest." The inquest into Mr. Wingrove's death was set for tomorrow. As almost an afterthought, he'd tacked on the fact that they'd had to release Max, the hotel porter, for lack of evidence. If he'd stolen the formula, it was long gone by now.

"Looks like we're going back to York tomorrow," Stella said when she'd finished reading. She handed Lyndy back the telegram and took another sip of her tea.

"So much for restarting our honeymoon," he grumbled, tossing the telegram onto the grate. With such little heat in the embers, the paper smoked as it caught, flaring into flame only as the last of it was consumed. "At least we kept our suite at the Majestic."

"At least I won't have to wire Mama. We'll go back early, give our statements, and then spend the day with her."

"That was my thinking," Lyndy said. "I've already arranged for us to ride in with the others in the morning. Of course, Morgan will want to be at the inquest, and according to Aunt Winnie, Dr. Bell received a telegram as well, requesting he give evidence. I thought I might sit in on it while you entertain your mother."

Stella, divvying the breakfast dishes between the two plates, stopped what she was doing to kiss him. "What a terrific idea. Then you can tell me everything they say."

"I suspect you know everything already," Lyndy teased. Still standing, he picked a piece of buttered toast off his plate and took a bite. "If not more. Now, to lighter things. Since the weather is unseasonably warm and splendid—"

"You call this warm?" Stella rubbed her hands up and down her shoulders. She swore she could see her breath.

Lyndy chuckled. "Trust me. This is as good as it gets this time of year. To enjoy it, Aunt Winnie has arranged a picnic luncheon excursion to Bolton Abbey for the whole lot. I'd told her how much you enjoy eating outdoors. It's in a bucolic spot beside the River Wharfe, and there's a pleasant path we can hike. Aunt Winnie will send your lady's maid down at eleven to dress you if that suits?"

Stella's mood darkened. A sense of dread crept in, and was trying to take hold. The last picnic excursion they'd been on had ended in murder. With thoughts of her father's death, yesterday's gruesome encounter sprung to mind. She regarded the breakfast plates, her hand drifting to the cold knot in the pit of her stomach. She wasn't hungry anymore.

Sensing Stella's hesitancy, Lyndy added, "I thought you'd enjoy it, but we don't have to go."

Lyndy was right. Until that awful day, she'd loved picnics. Was she going to let someone else's evil deeds stop her from enjoying her honeymoon?

"No, I'd love to. It sounds like fun." She took a deep breath and mentally shook off her melancholy mood, like a horse ridding itself of pesky flies. "But that's not for a few hours yet. What shall we do before then?"

Lyndy tossed his half-eaten toast onto the plate, his face a mask to his emotions, and in one quick gesture, scooped her up into his arms. She giggled in delight at his impulsiveness.

Unable to hold his composure any longer, Lyndy burst into a smile as he carried her back toward the warmth of the bed. "I think we can think of something, my lady."

The open-topped carriage shifted and swayed beneath Stella, her shoulders bumping lightly against Lyndy's as the sure-footed horses picked their way down the narrow, curving road lined with dry stone walls. Not a cloud marred the vast blue sky as Stella studied the Dales with the attentiveness of someone wanting to commit the highly varied terrain—the lush riverside meadows, the sweeping green valleys, the swaths of leafy woodland, the moor-covered hilltops, and the craggy, gray cliffs—to memory. Stone cottages dotted the valley, some in clusters large enough to be considered a village. She took to the landscape like a native, wanting to explore it more and more.

Their two carriages approached a single-laned stone bridge, arching over a narrow stream, its crystal-clear water riffling over limestone boulders jutting up from the riverbed. A one-horse wagon transporting bales of yellowish-green hay approached from the other side. With not enough room for the vehicles to pass, the coachman of Stella's carriage halted the horses and leaped from his seat. The wagon driver also got down. Aunt Winnie's driver stopped behind them but stayed put. After much quiet discussion, which Stella couldn't hear, the wagon driver grabbed the bridle of his mare, a thick-necked brown and white Shetland pony. The pony swished its lush brown tail rapidly in agitation. Yet with a few clicks of the tongue and a firm grip, her owner persuaded her to back the wagon to a spot wide enough to allow the two carriages to pass.

"Does that happen often?" Stella asked Owen, her body twisted in the seat to watch the hay wagon take its turn to cross up and over the bridge.

"Does what happen?" Owen muttered grumpily.

Stella swiveled back around. For the majority of the trip, Owen had sat across from them with his chin resting on his chest. She would've thought he was asleep, except every bounce of the carriage brought a wince to his slack features. After guessing the cause of his misery, Stella had been reticent to mention it.

"Long night, old chap?" Lyndy said.

Owen glanced up, squinting and shielding his eyes from the sun. "Couldn't sleep."

"Up to all hours drinking too much whiskey, more like," Lyndy ruthlessly teased.

"And all alone, thanks to you." The carriage hit a dip in the road that followed the meandering stream, and Owen groaned.

"Isn't the headache powder I gave you helping, Sir Owen?" Dr. Bell, seated beside him, asked.

"It is, my good doctor. I wouldn't have attempted this journey otherwise. That reminds me." The brightening of his tone pulled Stella's attention away from the flash of blue she'd spotted, a kingfisher flying low and fast along the water. "Did I tell you Amesbury-Jones is a sleepwalker?"

"He is?" Stella said.

When Stella was nine, a groom insisted she'd sleepwalked into the stables late one night, plopping down in the straw of an empty horse stall, clutching a pillowcase. When he'd asked what she was up to, she'd continued to sit, vacantly staring at the wooden wall. Then without warning, she'd stood and, dragging the pillowcase behind her, walked back to the house without saying a word. She'd had to take the groom's word for it; she hadn't remembered a thing.

"Indeed." Owen nodded enthusiastically before wincing in pain again. "I caught him wandering about on my way to bed. He was acting so rather odd, I aroused Dr. Bell, who confirmed it. The chap hadn't an inkling, had he?"

Stella and Lyndy both looked to Dr. Bell for confirmation.

"No, he was rather stunned when I informed him of it this morning, even refuting my diagnosis, but there's no doubt. It's much more common in children, but I've seen cases of it in adults during nightly rounds in hospital."

"I assumed you were in private practice," Owen said, dismayed.

"I am now, but I worked in hospital during my training."

"Oh. For a moment, I thought Mummy strong-armed you into coming, keeping you misguidedly away from your patients."

"No, no. I'm still on holiday. I'd planned to go to Durham today to see the cathedral there when your gracious mother offered this lovely respite in the country. How could I say no?"

"She does rather get her way, doesn't she?" Owen smiled crookedly, revealing more warmth for his mother in that small gesture than Stella had ever seen come from Lyndy.

How sad. Lyndy deserved to feel that way toward Lady Atherly. Stella had always known such affection. She'd been flooded with love for her mother as a child, and again the moment she saw Mama last week.

Mama! Stella's stomach fluttered with excitement. She couldn't wait to see her tomorrow.

"Bolton Abbey is no Durham Cathedral," Owen said, "but hopefully, changing your plans to placate Mummy will be entertaining enough. She did so want to thank you for your kindness."

Stella craned her neck to view the carriage following them. Morgan and Miss Pegg cuddled together while Aunt Winnie shared the seat with Miss Evans. Aunt Winnie's uninjured hand moved as she told a story, her face flush and animated with expression. How different the two sisters were: one welcoming, curious, lively, the other intolerant, unapproachable, and for the past few months bent on preventing Stella from joining the family. Yet Stella had seen a softening in Lady Atherly's hard facade after Daddy's death. And now that Stella was Lyndy's wife, and her inheritance had secured the future of Morrington Hall? It should make all the difference, right? Stella was hopeful that Lyndy would soon think as warmly of his mother as Owen did.

"I'm rather looking forward to seeing Bolton Abbey," Dr. Bell was saying. "From what I've read, the priory church dates to the twelfth century." The doctor's voice rose as he spoke, his enthusiasm growing. "It was stripped of all its assets during the Reformation and the dissolution of the monasteries. Here, as at Waltham, Lanercost, and Bridlington, the nave was saved as a parish church, supposedly the prior at the time negotiating a pact with Cromwell. Half chapel, half ruin. It's a sight worth seeing."

Owen yawned.

"Of course, seeing your mother return to full health," the doctor quickly added, "is reward enough."

Owen nodded appreciatively. "What you say about the priory's true, Doctor, though I can't say I've been inside more than once. I kept to the ruined part, myself, especially as a lad. Lovely, out of the way spot it was too, when accompanied by the local sheep farmer's daughter." Ignoring Lyndy's eye rolling, Owen added, bringing the conversation back to where it started, "So, it seems I was wrong about Amesbury-Jones, after all. He hadn't been to Maisie's room, as I feared. He wasn't even aware he'd been out of bed."

"At least that's something," Lyndy said.

"But there's more, old chap. Tell them what you told me, Doctor."

Dr. Bell shifted his weight under the sudden scrutiny of everyone's full attention.

"What is it, Dr. Bell?" Stella asked impatiently, her curiosity piqued.

"I told Sir Owen that discovering Mr. Amesbury-Jones is a sleepwalker eased my mind about him."

"In what way?" she asked.

Too impatient to let the doctor finish his explanation, Owen blurted, "Dr. Bell saw Amesbury-Jones outside Mr. Wingrove's room late on the night of the murder."

"Really?" Stella said, looking expectantly at Dr. Bell.

Owen started to nod until the pain in his head got the best of him.

"Why were you on the fourth floor?" Lyndy demanded.

"I'm an insomniac, myself," was the doctor's explanation. "It helps to walk around."

"Can you believe the good doctor here has been suspecting

Amesbury-Jones all along?" Owen conspiratorially said as if revealing some long-kept secret. "And I thought I was the only one."

"I've been hesitant to accuse him of anything, just having met the man."

Stella's ears burned with embarrassment. That hadn't ever stopped her before.

"So, you can imagine how learning that he was sleepwalking and not up to something more nefarious was quite the relief," Dr. Bell said.

One of the carriage wheels rolled over a large stone, jerking the passengers forward as it landed back on the road. The sudden motion dampened Owen's enthusiasm, but only slightly.

Owen cradled his forehead in his hand, but laughingly quipped, "I'd say! I don't fancy thinking we'd invited a killer to our house party."

CHAPTER 25

Stretched out on the banks of a wide, shallow, meandering river, with lichen-covered headstones punctuating its ancient churchyard, Bolton Abbey had a haunting quality to it. Like York Minster, it was laid out in a cross formation, yet only the nave was covered with a roof and intact, as if cut in half, the rest discarded and allowed to crumble. Columns rose with no ceiling to support, gaping holes where stained glass should be, framed views of the blue sky. Green stretches of grass grew across its foundation, long since replacing the gray, flagstone floor. Yet the weathered skeletal remains of the choir, the altar, the side chapels, the towering arch of the east window stood, stubborn and proud, to its full height.

As the carriage descended the gentle slope down to the lush green valley and the awaiting church, Stella stared in wonder, pleased she hadn't let bad memories stop her from coming.

"Gosh," the doctor exclaimed, half standing to get a better view. "Didn't I say it would be a sight worth seeing, Lady Lyndhurst?"

Stella heartily agreed.

The carriages halted beside the River Wharfe, upstream from a wooden footbridge and a string of large square stones jutting up a few inches above the rippling water. The stones spanned the river's width in a straight line in regular intervals, about the distance of a man's stride. Stella counted sixty in all. On the opposite bank, a footpath climbed to the top of a gentle, stony bluff crowned with sessile oaks. It was an idyllic spot. Stella, eager to explore, was the first out of the carriage, beating even the footmen who'd accompanied them. When Lyndy caught up, she grabbed his hand and led him to the riverbank nearest the stepping-stones.

"Ready?" she said, a mischievous grin on her face.

"Perhaps I should go first?" Lyndy offered, staring uncertainly at the white-crested ripples colliding against the stones.

"Absolutely not."

Stella lifted her green and black checkered woolen skirt to keep the hem from touching the soiled, sun-bleached surface of the stones (with their honeymoon being in a city, neither Stella nor Ethel had thought to pack a short-hemmed walking costume) and guided her foot toward the first one. The distance between the steps was a comfortable stretch, and she easily strode from one to the next, the rush of water loud in her ears. Lyndy followed less enthusiastically behind her. When she reached midway, she stopped, the stone scarcely large enough to accommodate both feet.

Lyndy, three stones behind, called, "Are you all right?"

She smiled reassuringly over her shoulder at him, catching a glimpse of Aunt Winnie already settled into a chair set out by the footmen and Dr. Bell marching, like a man on a mission, up the path toward the priory church. Above him, the silhouette of a large, long-winged bird soared into view, flying straight through the ruins' largest arched window.

But Stella wasn't all right.

Despite the refreshing crisp breeze kicked up from the water, the sparkling glint of the sun on its surface, the soothing sound of the river flowing by, Stella couldn't shake something gnawing at her. Could it have been Owen's flippant quip about a murderer among them?

Was there a murderer here?

With careful, tiny steps, Stella shuffled around on the stone to face downstream. Several of the others, not adventurous enough to navigate the rocks, watched the river rush beneath them from the footbridge. Morgan and Miss Pegg stood side by side, shoulders touching. She was leaning over the railing, pointing to something in the water. His gaze was not on the water but riveted on her. They'd all discounted Morgan as Mr. Wingrove's killer, but why? Because he was a sleepwalker? What if he was faking it to cover up being seen that night near his uncle's room? Would Owen or Dr. Bell be able to tell? Morgan had the most to gain, but Maisie would equally benefit from Horace Wingrove's demise when she and Morgan married. Could she have been involved? Stella had never considered her before. Her family already owned a successful confectionery business. Was she so ambitious that she wanted Wingrove's Confectionery too? Besides, she had been at Hubberholme Park that night.

Miss Pegg's twinkling laughter carried across the water. No, Stella couldn't believe it was her.

Stella shifted her suspicious gaze to Aunt Winnie on the shore, fidgeting with her arm in the sling, and dismissed any notions of deception from that quarter. Lyndy's aunt didn't know Horace Wingrove and, like Miss Pegg, would've been missed if she'd left Hubberholme Park. Then there was Dr. Bell, who now stood among the ruins, his neck craned back to see something high above his head. A guest at the Majestic, he, by his own confession, admitted being near the Honeymoon Suite late on the night of the murder. He was also the one who examined the body and pronounced Mr. Wingrove dead of gas poisoning. He could've easily interfered with evidence, misdirecting everyone. But what reason did he have? Like Aunt Winnie, weren't Mr. Wingrove and Dr. Bell strangers? Besides, if he did kill Mr. Wingrove, why wouldn't he have declared the old man had died in his sleep? No one would've been the wiser. Perhaps she was being naive, but from what she'd seen, Dr. Bell wanted to help people, not harm them. He was a doctor, after all.

"Shall we keep going?" Lyndy asked from the stone beside her.

She nodded. As she took the next stone, Stella briefly glanced back over to the footbridge at Owen, his back to Stella and the sun. He was dejectedly tossing pebbles he'd picked up, watching them splash one by one. He, too, was supposedly at Hubberholme Park that night. It was simple enough to check. Tonight, Stella would question the butler to confirm that Owen, Aunt Winnie, and the Peggs stayed put. If anyone knew, it would be Newsham. Besides, why would Owen kill the chocolatier? Like his mother, like Dr. Bell, Owen didn't know Horace Wingrove from Adam.

Which brought Stella to someone who knew the dead man well—Miss Evans. With her arms folded but resting on the railing, her ever-present handkerchief clutched in one fist, the secretary was staring upstream into the middle distance. What was she thinking? Miss Evans's head abruptly tilted back as a sneeze came on her. Despite the muffling of her handkerchief, it reverberated off the water and halfway across the valley. Stella still wasn't sure why the secretary had joined the house party. Didn't she have family, work obligations in Wolverhampton? Was it an ill-fated attachment or some need to control Morgan that kept her by his side? Could she have killed her employer? She was staying in the hotel, but how did she benefit from Mr. Wingrove's death? It was Miss Evans who had suspected how ill Mr. Wingrove was. Wouldn't she have just waited for his time to come?

Stella was convinced. Like Owen had said, none of their party killed Horace Wingrove. It was much more likely to be

Mr. Middleton or Max Telford or someone they hadn't suspected yet.

Then why didn't that nagging sense she was in the company of a killer go away?

Reaching the final stepping-stone, Stella leaped the last few feet to the riverbank. Lyndy more cautiously joined her.

"Enjoy that, my love?" He wrapped his arms around her waist.

"I did."

"Whatever were you thinking about when you stopped out there? You seemed miles away."

Before Stella could answer, a shout rang across the water. Aunt Winnie had stood up and was waving her good arm agitatedly, trying to get their attention.

"Lyndy! Stella! My dears, come back!"

Without conferring, the couple dashed toward the footbridge—it was faster. Those on the bridge were already hurriedly making their way back to the other side. Stella couldn't see anything obviously wrong, but Aunt Winnie continued to wave them on, a thick gold-accented bangle around her wrist catching the sunlight. They picked up the pace, stomping across the bridge, their feet thumping loudly against the wooden slats.

"What is it? What's wrong?" Lyndy demanded when they reached the picnic spot.

The footmen had laid out a long folding table to one side and covered it with a lacy white cloth. It was loaded with white china plates, glass tumblers, napkins, forks, spoons, salt, pepper, and serving platters piled with cold beef, cucumber sandwiches, boiled and canned fish, thick slices of brown and white bread with butter, pickled vegetables, fruit (both candied and fresh), cheese, jam tarts, and slices of pound cake. A large glass pitcher of lemonade, lemon rinds floating in it, sat at the end. Beside it, scattered on a simple picnic rug, were cushions encircled by several low-slung folding chairs.

"Nothing is the matter, my dear," Aunt Winnie said, pointing to the table. "I was afraid you'd keep hiking when the food is ready and waiting."

"Then why all the waving and shouting?" Lyndy demanded.

"How else was I to get your attention?"

Lyndy scoffed with annoyance, tugging at the bottom of his tweed jacket. Yet again struck by the contrast between his aunt and his mother, Stella laughed in relief.

With a full plate of food on her lap, Stella bit into her salty, minced ham sandwich. After forgoing much of breakfast, Stella was ravenous. Lyndy dropped a colorful, thick cushion beside her and, deftly balancing his plate, lowered himself down onto it. They ate companionably in silence, listening to the conversations of the others.

"Did anyone happen to notice how the priory had an octagonal chapter house like the one at York Minster?" Dr. Bell asked.

"Can't say that I ever did," Owen said dryly.

"I haven't even been up to the church or ruins yet," Miss Pegg admitted. A chorus of "Neither have I" followed.

"Have any of you read Anthony Trollope's *Lady Anna*?" Aunt Winnie asked. She was greeted only by shaking heads. "You should. There's an excursion in it, and a dramatic incident takes place near this very spot. Not to give anything away, mind." When no one was drawn in, she continued with, "Did you know that the Brontë sisters, who lived at the parsonage in Haworth, are said to have picnicked here in 1833?"

"Oh, I love the Brontë sisters' novels," Miss Pegg said enthusiastically, almost bouncing in her folded chair. "Don't you, Morgan? *Jane Eyre* is my favorite."

Morgan set his fork down, a sardine speared at its end, but said nothing.

"Romantic drivel," Miss Evans muttered. She grasped a handful of grass and ripped the blades from the ground, leaving a small bare patch of dirt behind.

A tense silence continued as no one knew how to respond to the secretary's venomous retort.

"I like romantic stories too," Stella said. "Though I tend to read those of American authors."

"I prefer adventure stories myself," Aunt Winnie offered, counting them off on her fingers. "*King Solomon's Mines,* Stevenson's *Kidnapped,* Kipling's *Kim,* and my favorite, his *The Man Who Would Be King.*"

"Uncle Horace once met Charlotte Brontë," Morgan uttered softly.

"What fun, Morgan," Miss Pegg said. "I didn't know that."

Morgan told how one day in 1853, the quiet, bespectacled author, inspired to add more "real life" to her works, visited the Foundling Hospital for abandoned and orphaned children in London at the same time an adolescent Horace Wingrove was a resident. His uncle, Morgan said, chuckling, liked to tell how he was already taller than Miss Brontë even at eleven. When Morgan finished his tale, he picked up his fork again.

"I had no idea Horace was an orphan," Miss Evans said, clearly stunned.

"Now I see why he liked to say he 'pulled himself up by the bootstraps,'" Miss Pegg said. Morgan nodded, a wistful smile on his lips.

"Speaking of your uncle's successes, Morgan." With Morgan willingly sharing about Mr. Wingrove, Stella couldn't forgo the opportunity to confirm something she'd been wondering about. "He told us that he and your aunt honeymooned in York, the same as Lord Lyndhurst and me. And in the same suite, forty years ago."

It was this idea that had endeared him to her. She and Lyndy were just starting their lives together while Horace Wingrove had been marking the end of his long marriage. In some poetic way, life had come full circle.

Unless he'd made it all up to hide the real reason he was in York.

A bittersweet smile lit Morgan's face. "It's true. They were married in 1865. Aunt Marie had always wanted to visit York. So, as she told the story, Uncle Horace booked the most expensive room in the city—the Honeymoon Suite at the Majestic Hotel."

Stella inwardly smiled, relieved. She'd wanted to believe Mr. Wingrove's story. Morgan's explanation also answered the question of why Lyndy, too, had insisted they reserve that particular suite.

"Aunt Marie often spoke fondly of that enchanted suite, its view, and about how much her honeymoon had touched her life. She forever credited Uncle Horace for ensuring it was the perfect start to their perfect union."

Morgan's voice warmed with the love that had bolstered that long-ago honeymooning couple for decades. She hugged Lyndy's arm, sincerely hoping that they'd find that kind of lasting devotion; their honeymoon certainly hadn't been the stuff dreams were made of.

"In fact," Morgan continued, caught up in his story, "she loved York so much, they took every holiday there. Agnes and I both grew to love it too."

Agnes?

A sharp inhale of breath was all that alerted Stella to someone else's surprise. Who was it? Searching the other's faces, Stella couldn't tell. Whoever it had been had recovered swiftly.

"When Agnes died," Morgan was saying, "her dying wish was to be buried there. I suspect it was so Aunt Marie would have another reason to visit."

A sharp clap of a gunshot rang across the valley. Stella yelped, crouching over her plate in fear. Lyndy placed a comforting hand on her shoulder. Another, more distant shot followed.

"It's only a pheasant hunter, my dear," Aunt Winnie said, her voice soothing. Stella imagined that's how Aunt Winnie spoke to her cat.

What had gotten into her? She was being silly. The shots were too far away to hurt anyone. Still shaking, Stella sat up, her ears burning with embarrassment.

"Still a bit jumpy, I guess," she said, forcing a deprecated smile to her lips. "I'm sorry, Morgan, but who's Agnes?"

"His cousin." Miss Evans answered for him. "Marie and Horace's only child to live to adulthood. She died of a terrible wasting disease while Morgan was at boarding school."

Could that be the cousin Miss Pegg mentioned before?

"I'm so sorry," Stella said.

"They're both buried there now, Agnes and Aunt Marie. . . ." Morgan's voice trailed off.

"In York Cemetery," Miss Pegg finished for him, encircling his arm with her hands and resting her cheek against it. "And soon, they'll all be together again."

Cold comfort. Stella watched a wisp of white cloud float by, thanking heaven above for bringing her mother back to her.

Owen asked, "All together?"

"Morgan learned from his uncle's solicitor when he came to Hubberholme Park," Miss Pegg said, "that when Marie died a few months ago, Horace purchased a plot for both of them, not far from Agnes, so when the time came, he could be buried with them." She chuckled nervously, glancing at Morgan. "Who would've predicted he'd join them so soon?"

Another distant gunshot rang out. This time Stella's heart stayed steady, but she couldn't suppress the shudder Miss Pegg's grim observation provoked.

CHAPTER 26

"My, I almost forgot," Aunt Winnie said, clapping her hands together. "Maisie, my dear, I hope you don't mind, but I brought this along." She motioned for a footman to hand her something.

Stella swallowed convulsively. It was a box of Wingrove's Cream Milk.

The last time Stella had seen one, the innocuous green and gold package lay among gifts on a table that contained a bomb, perhaps even containing the explosives. But this, as evident when Aunt Winnie slid off the gold ribbon, letting it flutter to her lap as she lifted the lid, was just a box of chocolates. She helped herself to three pieces.

"I'm delighted you did." Miss Pegg held out her hand, and Aunt Winnie passed her the box. "You'd think the daughter of a confectionery factory owner would be sick of sweets, but it's rather the opposite, I'm afraid. If chocolate were an elixir, I'd live forever." Miss Pegg laughed as she selected a piece and popped it into her mouth.

She held the box out to Stella, who tentatively took two

pieces, handing one to Lyndy. Stella eyed the package suspiciously, even as she took a bite. The smooth, milky sweet melted on her tongue, her nose filled with its rich aroma. How could she have hesitated? Even if Mr. Middleton had used a box of Wingrove's Cream Milk to hide the bomb, that didn't negate how delicious the chocolate was or how each piece brought joy. Wasn't that why Mr. Wingrove had doled the boxes out as gifts?

When was chocolate anything short of divine?

Stella, having finished her first piece, couldn't resist a second. She popped this one in whole. It was a mouthful of pure bliss. As the chocolate melted, some seeped into the corners of her mouth. Without her asking, Lyndy handed her a clean linen napkin. She dabbed at her lips until he nodded, signaling she'd wiped it all away. Miss Pegg offered the box to Miss Evans.

The secretary vehemently waved it away. "I can't stand the stuff."

Miss Pegg and Stella exchanged looks of surprise. *Who hates chocolate?*

"I didn't know that." Morgan reached past Miss Pegg and took a piece. "You've worked for Uncle Horace for how many years, and you dislike chocolate? Did Uncle Horace know?"

"Of course he did," Miss Evans snipped, flicking away an ant that had crawled onto her skirt. "I had to explain it to him the first time he offered me a box."

"I'm curious," Stella asked. "What is it that you don't like? Is it the flavor, the texture, the aftertaste?" She couldn't imagine why anyone could have a strong objection to such a sweet delicacy.

"It's not that I don't like chocolate. It doesn't like me."

Miss Pegg put the back of her hand up to her mouth, stifling a giggle. The secretary rolled her eyes. Lady Atherly suddenly came to mind.

"Whatever do you mean?" Owen asked.

"When I eat some," the secretary continued, urged on by Owen's sincere curiosity, "my stomach cramps, and my skin erupts with hives." Miss Evans pointed to the ever-emptying box. "Wingrove's Cream Milk is the worst offender of all. It's almost as bad as my reaction to cats." Miss Evans put her handkerchief to her nose and blew.

"Have some pound cake then, my dear. Mrs. Greenwood took such pains to make it for us. I wouldn't want it to go to waste." Although Aunt Winnie lamented that no one had eaten anything but the chocolates, she only had herself to blame. She'd opened the box in the first place.

"As soon as these are gone." Owen took the box and popped the last piece of chocolate on the top tier in his mouth. He removed the crinkly tissue paper that separated the bottom layer of chocolate from the top, eager to start on the next layer. "I say! We've been swindled."

"What are you on about?" Lyndy asked.

"It's empty."

Owen tipped the box upside down to prove his point. Instead of being empty, two small cardboard boxes fell onto the picnic rug, as well as a white square envelope. Miss Pegg laughingly lunged to catch the envelope in the air, but Owen was too quick for her, snatching it first. Stella leaned over to inspect the plain boxes. They were empty.

"Is that something from you, Morgan?" Miss Pegg teased playfully, holding her hand out for Owen to give her the envelope. Owen, with a mischievous smile, held it out of her reach.

Morgan, perplexed, said, "No. I've no idea what that is."

Miss Pegg's face fell, disappointed.

"It says here that it's for you." Owen handed the envelope to Morgan.

When Morgan hesitated, Miss Pegg, recovered from her disappointment, encouraged him. "Well, go on. Open it up."

Morgan glanced around, weighing the eager anticipation on

everyone's face before tearing the folded corner and then running his finger along the edge. As he did, the envelope faced them. Written in a scrawl Stella had seen before was, *For My Dear Boy, Morgan.*

Miss Evans crinkled her forehead, pinching her brows harshly together in annoyance. "That's in Horace's hand," she said, confirming what Stella had suspected.

For a moment, Stella held her breath. A message from Mr. Wingrove from beyond the grave. *What did it say?* He'd placed it inside a gift. How could it not be something that would ease Morgan's grief, that he might cherish for the rest of his life? Stella would've given anything for a loving message from her father, before or after his death. Even a kind word would've been nice. But now she knew her mother's betrayal poisoned any love Daddy might've held for her mother, for Stella, or anyone. Or was it keeping it a secret that had eaten away at him?

The throaty call of a grouse, like a mocking cackle, echoed across the valley from a nearby hillside.

Stella's heart sank. What if this was one of those caustic secrets? One Mr. Wingrove wanted to reveal but couldn't face Morgan when he did? Why else would he disguise the envelope as the second layer of chocolates and set it outside Morgan's guest room door? Was Morgan about to be crushed by yet another weight, another loss? She watched his face for any hint of distress or enlightenment.

Morgan pulled out a sturdy white card, black words and numbers neatly typed on both sides. Someone had scribbled a few, now faded, almost smudged, handwritten notes along one side. Overcome, Morgan's mouth dropped open in shock.

"What is it, Morgan?" Miss Pegg said, gripping his arm in concern. Instead of the card, she stared into his face.

"It's the Cream Milk formula," he whispered, clutching the card between two fists as if a gust of wind or some thief might wrest it from his grip. A relieved smile gradually spread across his lips. A spark of confidence lit his face. "I wasn't a disappointment to him," he said as if speaking to himself. "Uncle Horace trusted me, after all."

Lyndy shook out his legs and got to his feet. The absurdity of it made him restless. He took a glass of lemonade offered to him by the footman.

"And Wingrove just left the box on your hotel room doorstep?" he asked. *Whoever heard of such a foolish thing?*

Lyndy vaguely remembered a conversation about it during that first jaunt to Hubberholme Park, the morning of Mr. Wingrove's death, and not caring one way or another. That was when they thought it was a simple box of chocolates. Lyndy took a sip of his drink. As usual, it was far too sweet for his taste. He set it down in the grass.

"Anyone could've taken it."

"I know." Morgan continued gaping at the formula card like a fellow with a winning ticket on a 50–1 horse, oblivious to the footman waiting patiently beside him with a full tray.

"Why not hand it to you in person?" Owen said, equally baffled by such reckless behavior. Impatient, Owen reached across the picnic blanket, chose a glass from the tray, and gulped down half of its contents. Lyndy noticed that Stella's lemonade, too, was almost gone.

"To be honest, I chalk it up to Uncle Horace's erratic behavior," Morgan said.

Stella whispered something to Dr. Bell, seated on the other side of her. As she waited for his reply, she raised her glass to her lips. Sun, reflecting off the crystal, caught the gold and diamonds on her ring finger and sparkled like a rainbow. With a thoughtful expression, as if contemplating what she'd said, the doctor nodded his head in agreement. Lyndy would have to inquire later what that was about. He tugged at his jacket sleeve and began to pace.

"I'm just relieved, grateful that Uncle Horace entrusted it to me," Morgan was saying. "What with his lies about acquiring the Peggs' company and his attitude upon seeing me in York, I was beginning to have my doubts."

Miss Pegg, mindful of the others, smiled up apologetically to the footman and selected two glasses from the tray, allowing the servant to continue around. She set one aside for Morgan, then took a tentative sip, her gaze landing on the card in Morgan's hands.

"How could you have doubted it?" Miss Pegg rebuked him lovingly. "Do you think he would've named you as the sole beneficiary of his estate and the company if he didn't believe in you?"

"Yes, but—" Morgan began.

"From what you told me, his solicitor said he'd done it a few days ago. He wouldn't have changed his mind so soon."

"True," Morgan conceded.

Unless something had happened in the interim.

Lyndy chuckled to himself. He was beginning to think like Stella.

"I would have to wonder why he took the formula with him to York in the first place," Miss Evans, her arms folded across her chest, said. She refused the lemonade with a stiff shake of the head.

Lyndy immensely disliked the woman, who seemed to enjoy being contrary and disagreeable, much like his mother, but the secretary had a point.

"Which comes back to the reason he was in York," Stella said.

"Which we still don't know," Lyndy added, returning to Stella's side. He placed a hand on her shoulder. "Do we?" As one, he and Stella regarded the others, silently pressuring them to speak up.

"Not a clue," Owen offered unhelpfully, shrugging. The others shook their heads in resignation.

"And why, having brought it with him, did he then hide it?" Stella mused.

"As I said, he'd been acting rather unusual of late," Morgan said.

"Perhaps that's even why he brought it with him in the first place?" the secretary offered. "He wasn't in his right mind."

Even as Lyndy's doubts rolled onto his tongue, Stella was vehemently shaking her head.

"I might believe that if he hadn't done it the night he died. It's too much of a coincidence, don't you think?" she said.

"My word!" Aunt Winnie said. "Owen said you were a smashing detective, Stella, dear. How marvelous to see your mind in action."

Stella smiled sheepishly up at Lyndy.

"We're missing the main point," Miss Pegg said. "Knowing Horace hid it means no one stole it."

"Righto, Maisie." Owen raised his glass to her with an exaggerated gesture before drinking the rest down. His sudden dramatics left Lyndy wondering if Owen's glass had held more than lemonade.

"True," Stella, ignoring Owen, conceded. "But maybe that's why Mr. Wingrove gave it to you in secret."

"I don't follow," Morgan said.

Passing expressions of confusion, frustration, and epiphany flashed across Stella's face as she worked it out in her mind. Lyndy marveled at how little she hid her emotions. Unlike the members of his family. He loved that about her.

"Maybe he suspected someone was trying to steal it?" she said. "And that's why he hid it. He was trying to keep someone, besides Morgan, from getting ahold of it."

She wasn't certain. Lyndy could tell by the slight hesitation in her voice. She may even have been guessing, but her reasoning was as sound as anything anyone else had proposed.

"But who? That hotel porter?" Miss Evans scoffed. "If I didn't know Horace had brought the formula with him, how could a porter?"

"He saw it in his room, perhaps?" Miss Pegg offered.

"What does it matter why Horace brought it or if he thought someone was trying to steal it?" Miss Evans said. "The formula is safe now." She waved her hand in Morgan's direction.

"Do we still assume then that someone killed Mr. Wingrove to get the formula?" Dr. Bell said.

"Not anymore," Lyndy said, catching movement out of the corner of his eye.

The pheasant hunter, his shotgun resting against his shoulder, his springer spaniel trotting before him tongue hanging out, had come down from the hills and was tramping across the footbridge. Several green-headed male pheasants dangled from a rope clutched in his hands.

"Why not?" Morgan asked.

"Because," Stella said, recalling Detective Sergeant Glenshaw's logic, "whoever removed the pillows from the chimney, presumably the killer, could've taken that time to search for the formula. He—"

"Or she," Owen added, his finger pointed skyward to make his point.

"Or she," Stella acknowledged, "would've known it wasn't there and wouldn't have ransacked the room the following day."

"But what about the poisonous gas?" Miss Evans pointed out. "The killer couldn't have spent too much time looking, or they'd get poisoned too. Perhaps they came back after the room cleared?"

"Maybe, but I think Mr. Wingrove's killer knew what they were doing. They would've understood that after ventilating the chimney, the risk to themselves was minimal, even after long exposure." Stella looked to Dr. Bell for confirmation.

"She's correct."

"Are you saying, Lady Lyndhurst, that there are two people

who violated my uncle's suite?" Morgan asked. "One who killed him, and the other who sought to steal from him?"

"I think so, yes."

"One of them must've been that porter fellow," Miss Pegg said. "He had access to the keys. I got it easily enough from him myself."

"He wouldn't have been the only one," Lyndy pointed out, watching the hunter and his dog climb the path that led back toward the village. He suddenly fancied a taste for pheasant.

"Mr. Haigh, the manager, Mr. Coombs, the desk clerk, even the maids all had ready access to the guest rooms, and that includes Mr. Wingrove's rooms," Stella said.

"As we said before, no one knew about the formula," Miss Evans said.

"Unless Mr. Wingrove told one of them about it and then feared they'd try to take it?" Dr. Bell said.

"That could be," Morgan mused. "Doesn't sound like Uncle Horace of old, but of late? I'm not so certain. And even if they knew nothing of the formula, that doesn't preclude them from being his murderer."

"I know guests can be demanding, even downright rude at times," Aunt Winnie chuckled. "But truly? What reason would any of the hotel staff have to murder the poor fellow?"

"They wouldn't," Lyndy said, watching Stella. Silent for some time, she ran her finger absentmindedly along the rim of the empty glass. What was she thinking about?

"But if not for the formula," Miss Pegg asked, chuckling nervously, "then why would anyone have reason to kill Horace?"

Lyndy caught Stella's brief glimpse of Morgan. Did she think the nephew killed Horace?

"I think that anarchist did it," Owen announced, ticking off his reasons on his fingers. "He was a guest at the hotel, could easily have stolen the key, and already had a penchant for violence." He clambered to his feet. "If so, there's swift justice for you. That detective is bound to be disappointed." Owen smiled smugly. He'd never been overly fond of policemen, particularly after spending time in a jail cell days before Lyndy's wedding.

Stella spoke up. "If that's true, Owen, what reason did Mr. Middleton have? Do you suspect Mr. Wingrove somehow learned of the anarchist's plans?"

Owen's smugness dissolved. "Perhaps."

"I don't know," Stella said. "I have to agree with Detective Sergeant Glenshaw. Mr. Middleton wasn't one for subtleties. He would've sooner smothered Mr. Wingrove with a pillow than use pillows to stopper up a chimney. And we still don't know who then killed Mr. Middleton."

Silence ensued. The hunter's spaniel barked in the far distance.

Aunt Winnie restlessly shifted in her chair, the tip of her shoe clinking against Lyndy's full glass, inadvertently kicking it over. The lemonade poured out, puddling beside the cushion at his feet before soaking into the ground.

"Then we're no further in knowing the truth than we were when we started this gruesome parlor game, are we?"

"No, Aunt Winnie," Lyndy said, searching the horizon for the hunter. "I'm afraid not."

The man and his dog were gone.

CHAPTER 27

Lily spotted Morgan ambling into the ruined north transept, alone. At long last. What with that intrusive lord and lady hanging around or Maisie Pegg always clinging to his arm, Morgan was never without someone around. And that picnic, with all the speculation surrounding Horace, seemed to go on forever. Now was her chance.

Lily skirted the gray and moss-covered headstones sticking out of the ground like crooked teeth, their etched words faded and shallow, as Morgan rounded the corner of the outside abbey wall. She dashed through the church's ruined shell in pursuit, ignoring the chill that prickled up her back as she navigated the shadows beneath the towering, skeletal, stone walls. She aimed to catch him before he reached the entrance to the parish church.

She was too late.

The door closed with a soft thud behind her. Inside, the priory church was like many cathedrals Lily had seen, walls and arches built of limestone blocks, columns marking the side aisles lined with high, narrow windows of stained glass. Yet it was stunted, the east wall being nothing more than that—a wall, no captivating window—and the timbered ceiling hung disproportionately low. It was as silent as a tomb. Lily could hear her heart beating.

She was in luck. The parish church was otherwise empty.

Morgan was settling into a middle pew. He bowed his head, oblivious to her presence. She repressed the urge to rush, to get it over with, but the tap of her heels across the flagstones would alert him to her presence. She approached, tiptoeing down a side aisle. She dried her clammy hands on her skirt. Why did it have to come to this? She resented having to resort to such wickedness. Morgan was a shy man, but hints of a stubborn streak hid beneath the surface.

Like his uncle.

A flash of sunlight through a leaded window into Lily's eyes precipitated a tickle in her nose. Despite her best efforts to suppress it, her sneeze reverberated throughout the church. Horace once teased that they could hear her sneeze on the factory floor, above the machines' whirling, two flights down.

Morgan glanced up, turning toward the origin of the sound. "Lily?"

Lily grimaced in greeting as she slid into the pew beside him. "Sorry. I didn't mean to intrude."

He smiled weakly. "After everything that's happened, and with all that conjecture back there," he motioned vaguely behind them, "I popped in for a quiet think. It's quite peaceful here."

"I can't possibly imagine how you find peace knowing that's there." Lily jabbed a finger at his chest.

Morgan glanced down, then slid his hand inside his jacket, feeling for the formula card protruding from the pocket of his waistcoat.

"It wasn't stolen, Lily. I can't say how relieved I am. Aren't you?"

"I'll be relieved when I know that it's properly locked up in the company safe."

"As it will be."

"When?" She gestured to the church around them with outstretched arms. They couldn't be farther from the company offices than they were now. "You couldn't in any way be planning to return to Wolverhampton today, could you?"

"You know I'm not. I'm waiting for the police to release Uncle Horace's body so I can bury him. Then I'll go home."

"And in the meantime?"

"I'll keep it in the safe at the hotel."

"How can you possibly?" she scoffed. "As events have demonstrated, the hotel staff there aren't to be trusted."

"I could keep it at Rountree's."

"You'd give our competition our greatest asset for safekeeping?" She gripped the cap rail of the pew in front of her, the wood's grain worn smooth by the hands of countless others. Her knuckles turned white. "Horace wasn't in his right mind when he left you in charge if you think that's a good idea."

"Then what do you propose?"

She released her grip on the pew and folded her hands in her lap. She studied the weave of her skirt's fabric; not having packed for a picnic in the country, her gray woolen traveling suit had had to do in a pinch. She carefully considered her reply.

"Let me do it. Let me return to Wolverhampton."

"I already suggested you could. Unless you want to attend the funeral, there's no reason for you to stay."

"I had fancied seeing Horace laid to rest, but now . . . We must think of the company's future. I'll take the formula back, and you, in all good conscience, can stay here to see your uncle buried."

She held her breath. She so wanted to leave this place. The inactivity at the hotel and Hubberholme Park, the stillness of the church, the quiet of the countryside made her skin crawl. The social frivolities were driving her mad. She, who hadn't gone on holiday once in all the years she served Wingrove's Confectionery, was ready to return to the city and get on with things.

On the cusp of his answer, Morgan hesitated when the church's side door creaked open and that Lady Lyndhurst stepped inside. Lily promptly faced forward, her back to the American, hoping the woman would have the good sense to leave them alone.

"No," Morgan said, dropping his voice to a whisper. "It was kindly offered, and I appreciate your loyalty, Lily, but the formula is my responsibility. I'll bring it back once I've buried Uncle Horace. I trust Maisie's father to keep it safe. He's a respectable man. He wouldn't steal from me."

He wouldn't need to.

John Pegg would have a copy of their formula in his private safe long before Morgan came to fetch the original, leaving him none the wiser. No shrewd businessman is that trustworthy. Morgan, quaintly but dangerously naive, would learn that sooner or later.

"And while you're here in the Dales?"

"I can't imagine Sir Owen doesn't have a safe."

Lily inwardly sighed. It was anyone's guess how long the company would survive with such a trusting incompetent at its helm. And Lily's guess? Not long. *No matter.* Lily was already making plans for her future, and it didn't involve Wingrove's Confectionery.

"Very well, if that's your decision, I may as well stay for the funeral."

Lily slid from the pew as Lady Lyndhurst approached. She offered the American something between a grimace and a forced smile, too annoyed by Morgan's foolishness to impart anything close to a friendly greeting as she passed.

Over the *click-clacking* of her heels on the stone floor, Lily heard the American in her grating accent ask Morgan, "Everything okay?"

Lily could feel their eyes on her back, but she didn't slow her pace. She had to get out of this mortuary and into the fresh air.

Hushed voices and the faint scent of recently snuffed candles welcomed Stella as she slipped through the heavy wooden door. She closed it gently behind her, not wanting to disturb the stillness that permeated the space. Nonetheless, the motion whisked up a wisp of air, sending dust motes dancing in the ray of sun shining down from the leaded window on the opposite side. She stepped under the nearest archway, and the whole of the church spread out before her.

After the immensity of York Minster, this church, being less than half its original size, felt more like an intimate chapel, cozy and welcoming. Stella took a deep breath, releasing it slowly, feeling her muscles relax. She was glad that she'd decided to explore the church, leaving Lyndy and some of the others to their fishing. She'd enjoyed learning to fly-fish this summer, but the Blackwater Bend incident had tainted the sport. She'd get back up on that horse, just not today. Stella patted the stone arch, like the flank of a friendly horse, before moving on.

Besides her, only two others had ventured inside. Morgan and Miss Evans, deep in conversation, were seated beside each other in one of the middle pews. As usual, the secretary was scrunching her eyebrows together and pinching her lips in annoyance. What was she so angry about? From the moment they'd met, Miss Evans had exuded nothing but irritation and disdain for everyone and everything, Morgan being the one exception. Until now.

"And while you're here in the Dales?" Miss Evans was saying with a sigh of exasperation.

Stella drifted down the side aisle in their direction under the pretext of admiring the intricate, jewel-colored, glass windows. Yet as she studied the thirty-six scenes depicting the life of Jesus, she kept her ears open. Morgan murmured something Stella couldn't make out.

"Very well, if that's your decision, I may as well stay for the funeral."

Compelled by the terse clip to Miss Evans's voice, Stella left her pretext behind and approached. The secretary scowled at her, nearly knocking her aside as she passed and stomped away.

"Everything okay?" Stella asked Morgan.

The slam of the front entrance door echoed long after Miss Evans had left.

"Company business, that's all," Morgan finally said, slipping his hand between his waistcoat and jacket. "If you'll excuse me."

Stella watched him leave by the side door. *What was that all about?*

Once alone, she slipped into the vacated pew and stared vaguely up at the panels of botanical paintings above the altar, allowing her mind to wander. Aunt Winnie was right. So many questions and they hadn't answered anything. They suspected Mr. Middleton planted the bomb, but that's different from knowing he did. They knew Mr. Wingrove and Mr. Middleton were murdered, but had no idea by whom or why. Were the two deaths connected? They knew Mr. Haigh was assaulted and his invitation stolen. Had Mr. Middleton done it to get access to the Guildhall during the reception? Or had he slipped in the side door of the Guildhall as Stella suspected? And where was Mr. Wingrove's missing suite key?

Mr. Wingrove. It all started with him. What was the real purpose of his trip to York? To attend the royal reception, which he never mentioned, or to celebrate his marriage one last time, as he'd said? An image of Lyndy, his head nestled in the pillow beside hers, his face softened by sleep, flashed in her mind, quickening her heartbeat. She loved him more every day, and she'd been married less than a week. Could she imagine how Mr. Wingrove had endured when his beloved wife died after forty years of marriage? No. Not even her father's death was helpful; she never adored him. Yet Stella could understand Mr. Wingrove going to great lengths to stay in the Honeymoon Suite if it meant recapturing a fraction of his wedded bliss. But why bring the company's secret formula with him?

Stella agreed with Lyndy that Mr. Wingrove had taken an enormous risk by leaving the chocolate box with the hidden formula inside on Morgan's doorstep for anyone to take. Could his judgment have been that impaired? Stella had asked Dr. Bell at luncheon. As usual, he'd been unwilling to say for definite, but with a little cajoling, he'd admitted that if Mr. Wingrove did suffer from Huntington's Disease, as the medicines in his suite indicated, it was possible. Which left Stella to wonder: was it the act of an irrational man, or was he trying to keep it safe from someone? The same someone who ransacked his and Morgan's room?

Stella groaned. The muddle in her mind wasn't getting any clearer. She lowered her head to the top of the pew before her, the smooth oak wood cool against her forehead. Peeking out from under the bench was the brim of a dark brown cap. Stella squeezed down between the pews onto her knees. She stretched her arm underneath along the floor, her neck at an awkward angle, and snatched up the cap. She hoisted herself to her feet, wiggling the chinks out of her shoulders.

It was Morgan's. He must've laid it down, not noticing it had fallen to the floor. Covered with the grayish dust from under the pew, it resembled a giant piece of chocolate that had gotten too cold. *How appropriate.* Stella slapped the cap against her skirts, removing the dust off both.

Then it hit her. Stella knew who had ransacked the rooms and why Horace hid the formula. She had to tell Lyndy! Stepping abruptly into the aisle, Stella collided with Miss Pegg.

"Oh! Lady Lyndhurst!" Miss Pegg laughed nervously, taking a step back. "You startled me."

"Miss Pegg!" Stella said, her hand on her chest. "I didn't know you were there. I never heard you come in."

"I'm hoping to find Morgan's hat." She pointed to the cap clutched in Stella's fist. "He returned without it and hadn't the faintest idea where it might be. I'm certain that man would lose his head if it weren't attached." She chuckled self-consciously.

Stella pressed the cap into Miss Pegg's hands as she side-stepped around her, impatient to get away.

"Good thing he has you then," Stella called, rushing toward the parish church door.

CHAPTER 28

The flickering light from the bedside oil lamp against the crisp white pillows created a beacon in the otherwise darkened room. Long, wispy shadows, like ghostly fingers, from the tall, deeply carved oak bedposts crept across the carpet to the paneled wall and the tightly closed curtains on the other side. The fire in the grate was nothing but glowing red embers. It was perfect. The matching solid, oak wardrobe, so massive and heavy Stella could imagine the room being built around it, was almost invisible in the dim light. So too were she and Lyndy, tucked into the wardrobe between Aunt Winnie's late husband's morning suits, dinner jackets, and khaki dress army uniforms. Lyndy had his hand around the edge of the wardrobe door.

"Ready?" Stella whispered loudly.

Morgan, in his striped pajamas and nestled under the bedclothes, reached for the lamp and lowered the wick. The shadows deepened until only a soft glow on the pillows, the bedside table, and Morgan's face was left. Lyndy pulled the wardrobe door closed, leaving a space the width of his fingers to peek through. Inside the wardrobe, the darkness was complete; Stella couldn't see the slippers on her feet. Lyndy couldn't either and stepped on her toe as he shifted around, trying to get comfortable. Stella jerked her foot aside, and the sleeve of something brushed against her, tickling her forehead. She impatiently nudged it way.

"How long do you think it will be?" Lyndy whispered, his face so close Stella could smell the port he'd had after dinner on his breath. Although the wardrobe could've easily accommodated more people, they huddled together.

Stella shook her head and then realized he couldn't see her.

"They'll wait to be sure Morgan's asleep. Who knows how long that will be."

That was the biggest problem with her plan. They had no idea how long they'd have to wait.

Stella had laid it all out to Lyndy and Morgan in the carriage on the way back from Bolton Abbey. She was convinced that if Morgan announced at dinner that he'd be returning to York early the next morning to attend the inquest and put the Cream Milk formula in a safety deposit box in the bank, the thief would try to steal the recipe tonight. Her idea was to catch the culprit red-handed. Lyndy had been skeptical, but Morgan had been adamantly against it—no one at Hubberholme "could possibly" be the would-be thief. After some persuading, Lyndy had agreed to help. Whether he appreciated the plan's merit or knew Stella would proceed with or without him, she couldn't be sure. Morgan eventually sanctioned the trap too, but purely to prove her wrong. Stella knew she wasn't wrong. But when, not if, the thief arrived, was anyone's guess.

The grandfather clock downstairs chimed one o'clock. They'd been hiding for over half an hour. Tired of standing, Lyndy sat with his legs stretched out the length of the wardrobe, his back against the side. He invited Stella to snuggle on his lap. Stella rested her head against Lyndy's shoulder, his cotton nightshirt cool against her cheek. A few minutes later, Morgan's soft snores reached them through the crack in the wardrobe door. The chocolate maker's nephew had fallen asleep.

Stella, wide awake and keenly listening for the anticipated intruder, sensed a tickle on her ear. Lyndy's breath was warm on her neck as he nibbled lightly on her earlobe, then as he kissed the hollow space below her ear.

Stella put her hand over her mouth to stifle a giggle. "I can't stay quiet with you doing that," she whispered, though she didn't mind at all the tingling his kisses sent down her back.

"Can you blame me?" his voice barely audible, his lips tickling her neck. "You insist we hide ourselves in this wardrobe in the dead of night. How else did you expect us to pass the time?"

She couldn't argue and craned her neck to meet his lips with hers. His arms, already wrapped around her waist to allow for the tight fit, hugged her tightly against him. She shifted again, trying to face him more directly, her knee banging into the wardrobe wall instead.

At the sound of the bedroom door creaking, she froze, still half contorted, and stared into the darkness toward the sound. Someone was coming into the room. Stella twisted around, pushing off the sides of the wardrobe, pressing her elbow too hard into Lyndy's shoulder as she scrambled to stand and not make too much noise. Lyndy hoisted himself up once she was clear of him. Stella groped for the opening they'd left in the wardrobe door, hooked her fingers around the edge of the door, and slowly widened the crack. With their vision adjusted to the darkness, it was easy to see beyond the lamp's limited glow to the outlines of the bed, the dressing table, the figure tiptoeing toward the chair where they'd purposely left Morgan's jacket and waistcoat hanging.

What were they going to do? The plan was for Morgan to turn up the wick on the lamp and reveal the intruder's identity. Yet Morgan continued to snore, and the figure was too close to the bedroom door not to flee the moment they realized they weren't alone. Then how would Stella prove who it was?

Stella pushed the wardrobe door open painfully slow, hoisted up the hem of her nightgown, and reached a leg out. The moment the tips of her pointed toes touched the carpet, she leaned forward and silently drew the rest of her body through. Once outside the wardrobe, she stood motionless, holding her breath. The figure was too preoccupied with searching the jacket's pockets to notice. With Morgan's snores growing louder, Stella could feel more than hear Lyndy follow her lead behind her. When he stood beside her, he pointed in opposite directions. With a slight nod, Stella silently agreed with what he purposed they do next. She then padded toward the nightstand lamp while Lyndy crept across the room to block the culprit's escape.

Halfway there, a floorboard creaked beneath Lyndy's weight, and the figure swirled around at the sound. With the element of surprise gone, Stella dashed to the lamp as Lyndy bounded toward the door.

"Maisie?" Morgan, still half asleep, asked as Stella reached for the wick-raising knob and twisted it too rapidly.

The lamp's flames shot up, higher than the glass chimney, throwing light halfway across the room. Morgan threw up his hands to shield his face from the burst of heat inches from his face. Stella twisted the knob back the other way, subduing the flame.

"Morgan, you have a visitor." Stella directed his focus toward the person muttering a curse at Lyndy, blocking their way out. Morgan bolted upright at the sudden, blaring sneeze.

"No, it can't be," he declared as if he couldn't trust his own eyes. He racked his fingers through his unkempt hair. "Lily?"

With her mouth curled in a snarl, Miss Evans stood her ground in defiance as she wiped her nose with her handkerchief and said nothing.

*   *   *

"How could you?" Miss Pegg, hugging herself, asked in disbelief. "Why?" After Stella explained what all the shouting was about, Miss Pegg had been the first to speak.

Miss Evans remained stubbornly silent, watching in apprehension as Boulder, the cat, weaved his way through her legs. In the same brown traveling suit she'd worn the day before, the secretary was the only one fully dressed. Aunt Winnie, Owen, Miss Pegg, and Dr. Bell, woken by Morgan's demands for an explanation, huddled in their dressing gowns with Stella and the others in Morgan's bedroom. Stella, shivering in her light silk robe, eyed Miss Pegg's flannel one enviously. Aunt Winnie had roused a maid to relight the fire, but the room remained chilly. Even Lyndy's arm around her shoulder didn't help.

"Answer her, Miss Evans," Aunt Winnie insisted, her voice weary. In an exotic peach and yellow kimono robe, she limped over to the plush wingback chair set close to the fire. She wasn't wearing her linen sling but held her injured wrist against her waist. Owen, rubbing his bloodshot eyes, making them even redder, waited by the chair to help her in. "I dare say we all want to know."

Glancing up from Boulder's persistent intentions, Miss Evans aimed her piercing stare at Stella, who glared right back. "Because it rightfully belongs to me."

That wasn't the answer Stella expected.

"I say!" Owen muttered in astonishment. "If that doesn't take the biscuit."

"How can that be?" Miss Pegg chuckled nervously, reaching out for Morgan.

"That's decidedly untrue." Morgan took Miss Pegg's hand. "It belonged to Uncle Horace, and now, as the owner of Wingrove's, it belongs to me."

Miss Evans scowled, trying to shoo the cat away with her foot. "I helped formulate it. Horace said he would give me the credit I was due, but when Cream Milk became the company's biggest seller, he changed his mind. He didn't fancy sharing in the glory or the profits."

"But why try to steal the formula?" Lyndy asked. "Why not approach Morgan with your complaint?"

Miss Evans rolled her eyes. "Why should I? For years, I asked, I cajoled, I pleaded for Horace to give me credit or at least compensation, but all I ever got were promises of 'someday.' Why should I debase myself further to any man when I could take what I deserve?"

"It was you who beguiled the porter into giving you the key to the Honeymoon Suite," Stella said. It wasn't a question. "You who ransacked the rooms."

Solely focused on finding the Cream Milk formula, Miss Evans wouldn't have cared about the royal invitation; if checked, her boot would probably match the footprint left on its corner. But when she didn't find the recipe, she'd lashed out, spitefully stomping on the remaining chocolate box in Mr. Wingrove's suitcase. To be sure, Stella put the questions to her.

"So, what if I did?" Miss Evans raised her handkerchief to her nose and sneezed. "Do you mind," she said, addressing no one in particular. "The cat's making me sneeze." Boulder continued to rub against her leg.

Bent to pick Boulder up, Owen paused to peer up at Stella. "Did she kill the old chap too?"

Before Stella could offer her opinion, Miss Evans blurted, "I didn't kill him. All I wanted was to get what was rightfully mine."

"Don't we all, my dear," Aunt Winnie said as Owen dropped the cat in his mother's lap. She began to stroke Boulder's fur. "But we don't go around murdering people."

"I didn't kill him!"

"But you did follow him to York," Stella said.

"We both did," Morgan said. "Because of the supposed acquisition of the Peggs' company."

"By the way, I've been wondering about that. Was it your uncle who told you or someone else?" Lyndy asked.

Morgan's jaw slackened as he confronted Miss Evans. "You! When I caught you going through Uncle Horace's safe." He turned to appeal to the group. "She said she was gathering the paperwork for the Peggs' company acquisition."

"You made up that story, Lily?" Miss Pegg said. "My father was rather put out by the idea of Horace telling everyone he'd planned to take over Rountree's."

"With Mr. Wingrove out of the office, you planned to steal the formula in his absence," Stella said. "I assume you searched his home too. And when you didn't find it, you followed Mr. Wingrove to York."

"How did she know he'd be in York?" Miss Pegg said, including the others with a sweep of her gaze. "None of us knew he'd be there."

"You forget, I read all of Horace's post," the secretary offered snidely. "A letter from his solicitor mentioned the trip."

Mr. Quiney knew? Stella made a mental note to wire the solicitor from York in the morning.

"And all the while you were reassuring and advising me," Morgan said, "you were pretending. You were lying. You never had the company's best interest at heart." Morgan stared aghast at Miss Evans, calculating the many ways the secretary had manipulated him. "You probably think I'm not worthy of heading the company, that I'm not good enough."

Miss Evans examined her fingernails. "You aren't."

"Who are you to judge?" Morgan said, drawing himself up and straightening his shoulders. "You killed Uncle Horace for a piece of paper."

"You horrible, horrible woman!" Without warning, Miss Pegg flung herself at Miss Evans, her hands and arms flailing as she slapped ineffectually at the much taller secretary.

Miss Evans protectively wrapped her arms around her head but stood her ground. "Get her off me!"

"Maisie, stop." Morgan gripped his fiancée's arm and led her gently away.

"Let me go," Miss Pegg cried, but made no effort to pull away. "She's horrible, Morgan. Always belittling you. I know she thinks she's better than me. She killed the one family member you had left."

Morgan cradled her in his arms as she fought off tears with the back of her hand. Unable to watch, Owen shoved his hands into the deep pockets of his velvet dressing gown and kicked at the leg of his mother's armchair. Jarred by the kicking, Boulder bounded off Aunt Winnie's lap and streaked out the open doorway.

"She didn't kill Mr. Wingrove," Stella said soothingly but decisively.

"She didn't?" Sounding doubtful, Miss Pegg dabbed at her watery eyes with the satin edge of her dressing gown sleeve.

"You sound rather sure, my dear." Aunt Winnie poked her son in the ribs to stop him from kicking at her chair again. Owen jerked away, abashed.

"Well, you see—" Stella began.

"I told you I didn't do it," Miss Evans sneered.

"Miss Evans," Lyndy warned, "let's let Lady Lyndhurst have her say, shall we. Stella? Pray continue."

With Lyndy's encouragement, Stella explained. "What I was going to say is that it doesn't make sense for Miss Evans to be the killer. We know Mr. Wingrove's killer had access to the key to his suite. How else could they have removed the pillows after his death? But if Miss Evans already had Mr. Wingrove's key, she wouldn't have had to get the master key from the porter the next day. Nor would she have had to ransack Mr. Wingrove's rooms. She could've searched when she came back to remove the pillows that same night."

"Perhaps Miss Evans didn't find what she was looking for in Mr. Wingrove's suite and got the key the next day from the porter to search Mr. Amesbury-Jones's room?" Dr. Bell said thoughtfully. Although he'd arrived with Owen and Aunt Winnie, he'd seemed content to listen and observe until now.

He had a point. Stella hadn't thought of that.

"No," Miss Evans said, a hint of desperation in her voice. "I admit to trying to steal the formula. I do. I saw it on the desk in Horace's suite when Morgan and I spoke with him. I came back later that night, alone. I didn't know what I was going to do, sneak in, overwhelm him if needs be, but it didn't matter. Horace must've already gone to bed. The door was locked, and he didn't answer my knock."

"He might've already been dead," Dr. Bell said quietly.

Silence ensued as that thought permeated the room. A clump of burnt coal collapsed into the grate with a soft clunk. Miss Evans was the first to shake off the dread.

"Either way, I tried again the next day." She appealed to Stella. "You can ask your lady's maid. She saw me. The door was still locked, and I didn't have a key. That chambermaid wouldn't give me the time of day." She scoffed at the memory. "That's when I remembered seeing Horace bribe the burly desk clerk to stay in the Honeymoon Suite when he was checking in."

"You were here then?" Morgan demanded. "I wondered how I didn't see you on the train. You said you rode third class. Another lie."

Miss Evans ignored Morgan. "So, I tried my luck, though it was that blond fellow this time at the desk. He was more than keen to help a damsel in distress, I can assure you, without me spending a shilling. With the rest of you gadding about the countryside, I had all the time I needed. Little good it did me."

"Because Mr. Wingrove was on to you," Stella said. "Why else would he bring the formula with him? He knew you were hoping to take it, so he hid it in the best place he knew."

"In a chocolate box?" Owen said skeptically. "I do believe we've already established how foolish it was of him to do that. Anyone could've found it."

"Not anyone," Stella insisted. "No, Mr. Wingrove knew what he was doing hiding the formula in with the chocolates."

"Because the one person he could count on not to open the box or eat the chocolates—" Lyndy said.

"Is someone who suffers from an acute reaction to chocolate, resulting in a vexatious rash," Dr. Bell said, finishing Lyndy's sentence.

"Like Miss Evans," Miss Pegg exclaimed.

"Exactly," Stella said triumphantly.

CHAPTER 29

Although Ethel's arrival with breakfast was still an hour or more away, Stella couldn't lay in bed one minute longer.

I get to see Mama today!

Of course, they'd have to give their witness statements to Detective Sergeant Glenshaw about Mr. Middleton, but Stella wanted to think of the happy part of her day and not dwell on the anarchist's death. Filled with nervous anticipation, Stella slipped out of bed, pulling the soft, creamy-white counterpane off and draping it around her shoulders. Lyndy grumbled in his sleep, rolling onto his side. She shoved her feet into her slippers, still damp from last night's foray to the manor house and back, and thinking better of it, kicked them off again. She padded barefoot over to the fireplace. The coals in the grate were cold and gray. Stella fruitlessly poked at them anyway, only stoking up wisps of ash.

Stella's stomach grumbled. She found a large bowl of freshly picked orange-red-colored Cox's Orange Pippin apples (Lyndy's favorite) and a block of cheddar cheese stored under glass on the broad, hand-hewn table. She selected an apple, cut herself a thick slice of cheese, and drifted toward the oversized, well-worn leather armchair set beside the cottage's most prominent window. She plopped into the chair, curling her feet up underneath her, and tucked the blanket around her lap. She gazed out at the thick, white mist hovering above the ground. In the distance, a horse whinnied.

Stella absentmindedly popped the cheese in her mouth, her mind brimming with memories of her childhood before her mother left: baking Kentucky black cake, receiving her first souvenir spoon for Christmas, and every Christmas until Mama "died," being scolded by Mama when Stella teased a maid about wearing a worn-out hat. Stella smiled as each lesson, each embrace, each treasured moment flashed in her memory. How she wanted to know her mother better again. And oh, the questions she had—about Mama's life in Montana, her new husband, and Stella's half brother, about Aunt Ivy, and the children, and whether they'd heard anything more from Uncle Jed. Yet no matter how hard she tried to focus on her mother and the day ahead, thoughts of Daddy intruded, weaving his way through her memory like the snake in the Garden of Eden. When she'd banished him from her mind, images of Miss Evans crept in to take his place. Stella took a bite of her apple, the coarse, thick-skinned crunch loud in the morning silence, squirting juice into her lap.

Was it only a few hours ago that the secretary was sent packing?

Morgan had wanted to call the police, but Aunt Winnie wouldn't have it. With unfortunate glimpses of Lady Atherly (they were sisters, after all), Aunt Winnie had worried what the villagers would think if they saw a police wagon approach Hubberholme Park in the middle of the night. It had been Miss Pegg who'd come up with something that satisfied everyone. Everyone except Miss Evans and Stella. Miss Evans was immediately put out, fired from her position at Wingrove's Confectionery with no reference, with plans for Miss Pegg to contact all the employment agencies in London and throughout the Midlands, warning of the stain on Miss Evans reputation. Miss Pegg's attempt at justice would probably inflict more harm than anything the police could've done. Without references and no job prospects, Miss Evans was unlikely to find anything suitable, anything respectable, without leaving the country.

The punishment was far too severe to Stella, especially if there was any truth to the secretary's claim that she'd helped formulate Cream Milk. (Why else would Mr. Wingrove have hidden the formula from Miss Evans instead of firing her?) Where was the justice for Miss Evans? For years she'd worked loyally for Wingrove's and watched as the company expanded, as the Wingrove family grew more prosperous, all the while being denied the part she'd played in the company's success. Miss Evans had acted shamefully, but Stella understood her frustration. For years, Stella's father had manipulated her with threats of disinheriting her, of a destitute future. Yet despite Stella arguing for leniency, the others had remained unmoved.

Stella had seen Miss Evans to the hansom cab, slipping her five ten-pound notes. "It's not what you deserved for your share of the formula, but I hope it helps," she'd said.

The secretary had been speechless, meekly accepting Stella's kindness before alighting the carriage and disappearing into the early morning fog.

Did I do the right thing?

Stella finished her apple, shook off her melancholy as she did the counterpane, and hopped to her feet. She was ready to start this exciting day. Bounding to the bed, she nudged Lyndy's shoulder.

"Wake up, sleepyhead."

She leaned over and kissed his cheek. She dodged his arms as he reached for her, attempting to pull her back into bed.

"No, no, you don't. We have to get ready to go back to York."

Knowing they'd be leaving early, they'd said their good-byes to Owen and Aunt Winnie last night. Aunt Winnie had made them promise to return for an extended stay sometime soon. Stella had happily complied.

"How is it you're so spritely?" Lyndy groaned. "We barely slept, we have to face that dreadful policeman again, and then there's the inquest."

"I'm seeing my mama today." Stella's face almost hurt she was smiling so wide.

Lyndy rolled onto one elbow and watched as she located her robe and slipped it on. Not knowing what else to do but wring her hands, she sat down at the simple oak dressing table and, untying the ribbon, began to undo her braid.

"I saw what you did last night," he said.

"What do you mean?"

"With Miss Evans."

Stella regarded Lyndy's reflection in the mirror. He was wearing his old, emotionless facade. She never did care for it. She swiveled around on the bench. "Do you object?"

"I wouldn't have done it." He rolled out of bed and rounded the bedpost. "The way the woman always treated you with contempt, she deserved being put down a peg or two."

"What Morgan and Miss Pegg proposed was more than that. It's not as if she killed anyone. She never even got her hands on the formula. She deserved better."

Lyndy knelt behind her, encircling her waist with his arms and resting his chin on her shoulder. He stared intently at her through the mirror for a moment before he spoke.

"How I do love you. You're unpredictable, yet always kind, and flawed, in the noblest of ways."

"Are you saying I'm not perfect, Lord Lyndhurst?" she teased.

"Ah, but you are rather, Lady Lyndhurst, and may I live to a hundred, I will never know what I did to deserve you."

*   *   *

"Let's get this over with, shall we?" Lyndy said, patting Stella's knee as the horses came to a gradual halt.

Stella couldn't agree more. She was tired of thinking about Mr. Middleton, of driving away the grisly images of his violent demise, and wanted nothing more than to have all this behind her. Weren't they on their honeymoon? *And Mama will be here soon.*

They disembarked from the hansom cab. Before them rose the imposing two-story red brick Courts of Justice complex, fronted with stone dressings, domed turrets, and a center three-story pedimented gable complete with a clock tower. Stella could see Clifford's Tower from the steps, all that remained of William the Conqueror's York Castle, on its grassy hill a block away.

Stella gripped Lyndy's hand as they rounded the side of the complex and entered the attached police headquarters halfway down the block. From the outside, it was nothing like the simple station in Lyndhurst, but inside, the lack of decoration, the smell of stale tobacco, the erratic *click-clack* of a distant typewriter were all too familiar. Only the faded early nineteenth-century lithograph of Bootham Bar hanging on the wall distinguished this police station from the other.

After inquiring at the front desk, the desk sergeant led them into a nondescript room with whitewashed walls, no windows, and a plain table with four wooden chairs. *An interrogation room.* Another difference between Lyndhurst and York. Inspector Brown would've invited Stella to speak in his private office. As if he'd been anticipating their arrival, Detective Sergeant Glenshaw strolled in right behind them and asked them to sit. He took the chair opposite them, placed a large notepad on the table before him, flipped it open to a blank page, and scribbled something. When the bell in the clock tower of the main building chimed, unexpectedly loud despite the thick, brick walls, he leaned back in the chair, the pencil nub between his teeth.

"Cup of tea?" he said, over the chimes.

Lyndy plucked at the sleeve of his jacket, waiting until the clock struck the final eighth time. "Shall we get on with it? My wife's mother is due to arrive at the railway station in less than an hour."

Stella smiled at his impatience on her behalf, hoping it would calm her racing heart.

Glenshaw took the pencil out of his mouth, poised to take down notes, and stared at him. "Indeed, Lord Lyndhurst. Explain in your own words what you saw the day Middleton was shot."

Lyndy recounted how they'd seen him at the railway station, how he'd ducked out suddenly, and how they'd found him on the steps leading up to the city walls.

"Have you owt to add, Lady Lyndhurst?" Glenshaw said when Lyndy had finished.

"I heard what I thought was a car backfiring, but—"

The detective cut her off. "The gun going off, I presume. Neither of you saw Middleton shot then. Pity, that. See anyone running away from the scene?"

Glenshaw sighed his displeasure and frustration when they couldn't help him. Lyndy had bounded up the stairs immediately after finding Mr. Middleton but had seen no one suspicious on the walls. Whoever had killed the anarchist knew how to disappear into the crowd.

Glenshaw finished writing something in the notebook before ripping out the page. "In broad daylight, and no one saw a thing," he muttered to himself. "How did the killer even know Middleton would be there?"

"We told all of this to the policeman at the time," Lyndy said, scraping his chair back, preparing to stand. "Will that be all?"

"If you would, Lord Lyndhurst. Please sign this."

He placed the statement in front of Lyndy and produced a

fountain pen from inside his jacket pocket. He tapped the bottom of the paper to encourage Lyndy to sign.

"We found the missing formula," Stella, watching Lyndy scribbling his signature where the detective pointed, said.

The detective placed his large, rough hand on the statement and slid it back toward himself. "You don't say. The nephew misplaced it, I suppose. Should fine him for wasting police time."

"No. Mr. Wingrove had hidden it in one of his chocolate boxes. Miss Lily Evans, Horace Wingrove's secretary, sweet-talked Max into handing off the keys. She ransacked the hotel rooms hoping to steal it."

"And she admitted this, did she? Well, it does fit with what Mr. Telford told us."

"What did Max tell you?"

"At the time, nowt." The detective hesitated, rubbing the back of his neck as if weighing whether to say more.

"But?" Lyndy prodded.

"But he did have summat to say when I was releasing him. Said he'd heard the officers talking about Middleton's death and wanted me to know about an odd exchange he'd witnessed. He thought it might mean summat. Why he'd volunteered the information . . . ?" Glenshaw paused again.

After how you treated him? Stella silently finished his sentence. The bells chimed a quarter past the hour. Time was running out.

"Never mind why. What did Max say?" Stella asked impatiently.

Glenshaw squinted at her curiously but continued. "He was the porter who assisted with the old man's suitcase. Middleton followed them up in the lift and approached the old fella in his suite, insisting he'd overheard Wingrove call himself a "cathedral enthusiast."

"So?" Lyndy said.

"In his world, *cathedral enthusiast* is code for an anti-royalist, anarchist sympathizer. I've come across it a few times before. According to the porter, Wingrove denied knowing much about cathedrals, let alone being an enthusiast. He gave Middleton a box of chocolates to soften the miscommunication and Middleton's disappointment."

Did Wingrove give everyone a box of chocolates?

"And you believe Max?" Stella asked. After the way Glenshaw acted before, Stella found it hard to accept.

Glenshaw's mouth crinkled into a grimace. "I admit I do. He thought he was helping solve Wingrove's case. We're looking into a connection between Wingrove, Middleton, and Telford but so far have found nowt."

"We haven't come across anything either," Stella said regretfully. Which meant two killers were out there: one who murdered Mr. Wingrove and one who killed Mr. Middleton.

"We're working on the assumption Middleton used that particular chocolate box to house the bomb," the detective said. "It wouldn't be a stretch for anyone to learn of Their Royal Highnesses' penchant for Wingrove's Cream Milk. He probably fancied the irony of placing the bomb inside. Luckily for us, Middleton was an idiot. Any bomb small enough to fit inside a box of chocolates isn't going to bring down Guildhall."

"It still hurt people, and it could've been a lot..." Stella's last word died on her tongue as she remembered someone else saying the same thing. She didn't like what she was thinking. "Dr. Bell called himself a *cathedral enthusiast.*"

"Proves my point," Glenshaw said. "Dr. Bertram Bell is a licensed professional as well as a bonafide cathedral admirer. I've checked him out, seeing as he's going to be a key witness at the inquisition today. As far as I can tell, he has no ties to the anti-royalist group that Middleton hails from, and he's known to request tours of cathedral's all over the country."

Stella repressed the desire to sigh. She was fond of the doctor.

She would've been devastated to discover Dr. Bell had anything to do with bombing the royal event. "I'm relieved to hear it."

"Just goes to show what a complete blighter Middleton was. Can't build a proper bomb and can't identify his own kind. My bet is that he became a liability to the cause."

"You think another anti-royalist killed him?"

"Who else? His murder has the mark of a professional, plausibly military-trained given his past: point-blank, instantaneous, little blood, no witnesses."

"So where does that leave the investigation into Horace Wingrove's murder?" Stella asked.

The clock tower chimed the half hour.

Glenshaw slapped his notebook shut, tapped the end of it on the table, and rose. "Didn't you say you had a train to meet?"

He hadn't answered her question.

CHAPTER 30

After dodging the crush of passengers swarming the platform, Stella spotted her mother disembarking from the train. "Mama!"

Had it only been a week? Stella had conjured a specific image of her mother for half her life; in her mind's eye, Stella's mother had never aged. One meeting, the day of her wedding, did little to change that. Mama looked smart in a red, tailored, two-piece travel suit with black trim and matching black toque, but Stella was again taken aback to see graying tresses piled on her mother's head and the slight sag of skin along her jaw and neck. Happily, her eyes, now searching the crowd for Stella, were as Stella remembered, bright, kind, yet pensive at the same time. Stella called again.

Her mother beamed at catching sight of Stella and waved a lacy, white handkerchief above the crowd at her. When Stella got close, her mother dropped her leather travel bag to the concrete platform and stretched out her arms. Ignoring the startled and disapproving glances, Stella threw herself into her mother's welcoming embrace.

So unlike Daddy. The thought flitted across Stella's mind before she banished it, breathing in her mother's delicate yet unfamiliar perfume. This meeting wasn't about her father. This was about Stella starting her new life with her mother in it.

"I like your perfume."

"You like it? It's new," Mrs. Eugene Smith chuckled, raising her wrist to her nose. "Ivy and I went shopping at Harrods yesterday. But here now . . ." She held Stella out at arm's length and studied her daughter from head to foot. "Let me get a good look at you." She sighed and gave Stella a satisfied smile. "Marriage becomes you, sugar."

"I think so too." Stella laughed, snapping up her mother's bag. She slipped her free arm through her mother's to lead her down the platform. "How was the train ride?"

"Just fine. I still can't believe I'm here, with you." She patted Stella's cheek.

"How's Aunt Rachel, Aunt Ivy, and Gertie and Sammy?"

"They're all well. We've really been enjoying our time in London. What a city that is." In a sudden shift, she added, "What's this your Aunt Rachel's been telling me about you getting mixed up with dead men?" She hesitated, lowering her voice to add, "Aside from your father, I mean."

Stella made a face. Leave it to Aunt Rachel to say something. "It's true. The vicar who was supposed to marry us died."

"And there was something about fly-fishing?"

Stella wasn't about to satisfy her mother's curiosity any further on that score. She'd worry too much. Stella changed the subject. "How are Gertie and Sammy holding up without Uncle Jed?"

"We aunties are spoiling them rotten. Besides, I reckon it hasn't been long enough for Gertie and Sam to wonder about their daddy. They seem fine with the idea of living with Ivy after we all get back. Ivy told them Jed had to go away for a while."

"Any news on that front?"

"Ivy and I visited him a few days ago. He had a sour puss and was oh so remorseful for pickpocketing that jockey's gun. Among other things, I bet. Thanks to you, though, your Uncle Jed has the best lawyer money can buy, and he's hopeful he'll be back with his children in Kentucky before Christmas."

Stella hoped so too. Uncle Jed was flawed: lying, stealing, drinking his way through life, but he wasn't a villain, and he loved his children. *And it wasn't all his fault.* Stella hadn't been the only one her father had wronged. Maybe a monthly allowance from Stella's inheritance would help put things right, once Uncle Jed was out of jail? Stella filed the idea away to discuss with Lyndy later.

"How is the honeymoon going so far?" her mother asked, pulling Stella out of her thoughtful reverie. "All that you expected it to be?" Mama cricked her neck and threw Stella a questioning, knowing smirk. "Relations with your husband all you expected them to be?"

"Mama!" Stella's hand flew to her cheek, feeling the heat flaring up on her face. She wasn't about to discuss her "relations" with Lyndy with anyone, let alone her mother. "Lyndy's wonderful if that's what you're asking. As to the honeymoon, no, it's not what I was expecting."

Stella's mother pulled her arm free and flung it across Stella to stop her advancement. Their abrupt stop created a ripple of travelers sidestepping to avoid bumping into them or anyone else. Not everyone was successful. Someone's suitcase poked the back of Stella's leg.

"Pardon me! Do you mind?" A young man, indistinguishable from so many others in his brown suit and derby hat, carried a large leather case in each hand. He lurched impatiently around Stella and her mother, dangerously swinging his cases in the process before stomping away.

Stella's mother stepped in front of her and faced her, placing her hands on Stella's shoulders. "I know we've only been recently reacquainted, but I am, always have been, and always will be your mother. And I don't like the sound of that. What's going on, sugar?"

Stella glanced around at the busy platform, seeking a better place to talk.

Was there ever a good place to discuss murder?

"Not here. Let's get outside."

She hurried along with the flow of the crowd, gratefully emerging into sunshine, though the thickening clouds were a harbinger of wetter weather to come. She led her mother to the gardens surrounding the Majestic Hotel a few blocks away.

"Look at those stone walls. They're what I imagine when I'm reading stories about knights who slay dragons and such." Mama was pointing to the stretch of the city wall that paralleled the park.

"They're almost seven hundred years old. Some parts go back almost two thousand years."

"Amazing."

Stella recognized the awe. Since she'd come to England, she'd encountered ruins and churches and stone formations that were rooted in what seemed like the dawn of time.

"Is that where you're staying?" Mama indicated the hotel with a nod before selecting a nearby marble bench to settle on. She swept off a few dried leaves from the spot beside her before patting it, signaling for Stella to sit down. "Honeymoon Suite as fancy as it sounds?"

Stella remembered that when Mama married Daddy, they weren't rich. Daddy's fortunes came much later. They honeymooned in Niagara Falls. Then Mama married a rancher in Montana. She'd said she was comfortable, but Stella had no notion how wealthy that meant. From the admiration in Mama's voice, Mr. Edward Smith wasn't as well-off as Daddy had been. Or as Stella was now.

Stella was already scheming how she could give Mama some

of her inheritance, along with Uncle Jed and the children, when Mama slapped Stella lightly on the knee.

"I know you, Stella Eleanor Kendrick. You may reckon because I haven't been around and you're a grown woman, I can't tell that you're holding something back from me."

"It's actually Stella Eleanor Kendrick Searlwyn, the Right Honorable Viscountess Lyndhurst now, Mama." Stella chuckled at the tongue twister that was her new title.

"I don't care if they're calling you the Queen of Kentucky. Something's bothering you. Get it out, sugar."

Stella took a deep breath. "First of all, we're not staying in the Honeymoon Suite."

"Well, why not? I thought your husband said he'd booked the best rooms in the city."

"It's a long story."

"I always did like a good long story." Mama peeled off her gloves and laid them crisscrossed in her lap. "And I'm an excellent listener."

This time Mama wasn't going to let Stella evade telling her everything. Was this where Stella got her irrepressible persistence from? Stella suspected her mother also instilled the insatiable curiosity that had gotten Stella into trouble more than once.

Whom better to tell my problems to?

Stella scuffed her feet back and forth along the grass as she related her and Lyndy's entanglement with Mr. Wingrove: about his bribing the desk clerk, about his death, about his missing chocolate formula, and her involvement with the police. She was hesitant to mention the bomb but imagined her mother would hear about it, even if she were here a short time, so Stella left nothing out.

"Bless your heart, Stella. I had no idea. Here your Aunt Rachel, Ivy, the children, and I have been having the time of our lives touring the sights in London, all the while you're finding a dead man in the same bed you were supposed to spend your honeymoon in. And you almost got blown up by a mad man? Thank heaven you're okay. At least you got to meet those princesses. That's something to crow about, right?"

"Mama!" Stella said, frustrated by her mother's flippant response.

Her mother cupped Stella's cheek. "I make light because if I dwell on it too much, I couldn't bear the thought of all you've had to endure. From your daddy, from my absence, and now this brush with death." Her mother closed her eyes briefly as if trying to shut it all out. "A mother wants to keep her child safe, and I've done so little to protect you, sugar."

"You did protect me, by leaving, by allowing me to think you were dead all these years. If you hadn't lived up to your promise to Daddy, he would've disinherited me. I would've been destitute."

"I still reckon I could've done better. Somehow, I should've done better. At least I can protect you now."

Stella tilted her hat farther to one side and laid her head on her mother's shoulder. "I don't need protecting, Mama. As you said, I'm a grown woman. A British aristocratic lady. And even if I did, I've got Lyndy now."

"I know, and I can tell, despite his overbearing kin, he loves you. Doesn't stop a mother from worrying, though."

"I know, but I don't want you to worry. All I want from you is your love."

"And you'll always have it." Mama rested her head against Stella's. The stiff straw of Stella's hat crinkled beneath the extra weight. "It may not have felt that way, especially when you were little, but I never stopped loving you, sugar, and I never will."

They sat silently watching the flags fronting the hotel whip and snap in the brisk wind. Stella relaxed against her mother's shoulder, basking in the love she remembered from early childhood and never thought to get back. Everything seemed right with the world. Then Stella's stomach grumbled. In her excitement, the apple and cheese had been all she'd eaten this morning.

Her mother stirred, sat up, and fussed with the brim of Stella's hat. When it was adequately straightened, she lightly tapped the top of Stella's head.

"I don't know if you still have as hearty an appetite as you did as a child, but I'm so hungry I could eat a horse. Are there any good restaurants in this ancient city of yours?"

"Of course," Stella laughed.

"Then let's find us one and quick. The air feels like rain, and we still have a lot of catching up to do."

After lingering in the Majestic Hotel's coffee room, with its magnificent views of York Minster and the hotel's gardens, waiting out the rain, Stella and her mother strolled through the city, including the obligatory circuit of the medieval walls. All the while, they chatted as if long-lost friends. When they'd reached the stretch near the train station, Mama was regaling Stella with a story of the first time Stella sat a horse and how she cried for hours after they plucked her kicking and screaming out of the saddle. While vaguely listening (she'd been four years old and remembered the incident well), Stella glanced briefly down at the spot where Mr. Middleton was shot, struck by its innocuousness. A small puddle had collected in an indent worn into a stone step by thousands of feet, but no trace of the violence was left.

Again and again, her mother sighed in astonishment at the views of York Minster as they rounded the walls, but given the choice of going inside, she preferred a leisurely luncheon and a stroll through the abbey ruins. They ended their afternoon together with an extended visit to the Antiquities Museum (Mama was more than intrigued by the Roman artifacts). When the light of the day began to wane, they reluctantly made their way to

Mrs. Helliwell's Boardinghouse, a narrow three-story gabled building of mottled brick surrounded by a wrought-iron garden fence, situated in a quiet neighborhood not far from the ruins of St. Mary's Abbey. Despite Stella's doubts about Mr. Coombs's character, his friend's accommodations seemed more than respectable.

She hated to leave her mother here; they'd had such a wonderful time. As they'd rambled around the crooked, narrow city streets, they'd talked about almost everything. *Almost.* In unspoken agreement, they'd steered clear of any mention of Elijah Kendrick, Stella's father. Stella heard long-forgotten stories of her childhood, learned more about Mama's life living on a two-thousand-acre horse and cattle ranch (from her descriptions, Stella couldn't wait to visit), and forgot, for a few hours, that there was evil in the world.

In return, Mama had peppered Stella with questions about Lyndy, his family, and their courtship. Surprisingly, when Stella had complained about her mother-in-law, Lady Atherly, Mama had said softly, "Don't judge, sugar, until you've stepped in her shoes." Whether her mother was thinking of Stella as the future countess or of the decisions she herself had made, Stella couldn't say. And she didn't care. Her mother's kind remonstrations only strengthened their once-severed bond. Stella was enjoying every minute with her mother and didn't want the day to end.

"Welcome, Lady Lyndhurst," Mrs. Helliwell said when Stella introduced herself.

She clapped her hands together and bobbed as if not sure whether to bow. A plump, blond woman in her late thirties, Mrs. Helliwell was quite pretty despite being dressed in black crepe. The friendly smile stretched across her face, and the blush of excitement on her cheeks only enhanced her charm. Did the widow know of Mr. Coombs's dubious sideline? Stella would bet she didn't. Stella had booked her mother's room here before she knew, but the woman's eager graciousness eased Stella's concern that she should've made other arrangements.

"What impeccable timing."

What did Mrs. Helliwell mean by that? There had been no set time for her and her mother to arrive.

"May I say how deeply honored we are to have your mother stay with us. And all the way from America! I hope you don't think it too much of an imposition, but I've made us some tea. If you'll just give me a moment." She indicated for them to sit in her parlor, a room of pink and gold floral wallpaper, over-stuffed furniture accented with fringe, and a small piano against the wall. As Stella and her mother each settled into one of the chairs, she called over her shoulder, "I've telephoned Charlie. As soon as he arrives, I'll get him to take Mrs. Smith's bag to her room."

Charlie Coombs, here? Stella had hoped to avoid the man.

"Cozy, isn't it?" Mama said, smiling appreciatively. Stella forced herself to match her mother's enthusiasm.

"It is."

The widow soon returned with a tray laden with a porcelain tea service hand painted with swirls of red and yellow roses, teacups that matched, and a plate of thick squares of ginger-bread garnished with dollops of clotted cream and stem ginger. It smelled delicious.

"Have you just arrived in York, Mrs. Smith?" Mrs. Helliwell said, pouring the tea.

"I arrived this morning."

"Then you have missed all the excitement. Which, most certainly, Lady Lyndhurst must've told you about." Without waiting for a confirmation, she continued, "I was beside myself getting to meet Their Royal Highnesses, but who would've known such a tragedy could strike here."

She'd met the princesses? How was that possible? Only those invited to the private reception were given an audience. Perhaps she merely meant she saw them from afar. Besides, Stella didn't remember seeing her there. Yet would she? There were so many people she might not have noticed the widow.

Without thinking, Stella blurted, "How do you know the princesses?"

Mrs. Helliwell, placing a hand on her heart, blushed again. "Oh, my no, not me. It was Charlie that took me." She handed Stella a cup of hot tea. "He's always getting perks for working at the Majestic. Everyone adores Charlie there. How can you not?"

Perks? Is that what he told the widow the bribes he took were?

"Seeing that he's the manager now, he was given the invitation to the private royal reception, owing to Sir Peter, the hotel owner, unable to attend."

Staring at the steam rising off the surface of the tea, the hair on the back of Stella's neck prickled. Did Charlie use Sir Peter's invitation? Then it must've been Charlie who whacked the poor manager over the head. Why? To get the invitation? To get promoted? Either way, an uneasiness crept through her. She shifted in her seat.

"Is Charlie your brother?" Mama innocently asked as she accepted her cup of tea.

"Oh, my no," Mrs. Helliwell giggled. "He rents a room upstairs. He and my Johnny were mates in the war. Charlie was the company's sergeant." She swept her hand over her mourning dress. "Johnny never came home, you see. Charlie's been so good and kind; I secretly think he promised Johnny to look after the children and me."

More likely, Mr. Coombs had designs on the widow.

The Boer War had ended three years ago. Why was the widow still dressed in mourning? With more pressing questions to address, Stella suppressed her curiosity to ask.

"I was at the Guildhall as well," Stella said. "I didn't see you there."

"Oh, yes, well." Mrs. Helliwell's face fell as she offered Stella a piece of gingerbread.

Normally the sweet, spicy aroma alone would've enticed her,

but suddenly, Stella had no appetite. She politely waved the plate away. Mama happily selected a piece.

"We'd just had our audience when something urgent came up at the hotel," Mrs. Helliwell said. "I was most bitterly disappointed to have to leave early." Then her expression brightened again. "In the end, I suppose it saved us from that dreadful bomb, though, didn't it?"

Stella involuntarily shivered when a chill ran down her spine, raising goose bumps down her skin. Was it a coincidence that they left before the bomb went off? Or had Charlie known about the bomb all along?

"You wouldn't happen to know if Mr. Coombs is a cathedral enthusiast?" Stella ventured.

She was taking a risk by asking. If this woman wasn't as innocent of Charlie's activities as she appeared, Stella and her mother might be in danger. Mrs. Helliwell, who'd been taking a sip of her tea, squinched her eyebrows in surprise.

"Funny that you should ask. Just the other day, I overheard Charlie say that very phrase to a fellow former soldier, a private someone, who stopped by. I was surprised to hear it, myself. I'd never known Charlie to take much interest in cathedrals before."

Stella's heart thumped hard against her rib cage. "This private, could you describe him?"

Mama shot Stella a questioning look, but Mrs. Helliwell, oblivious to the sudden strain in Stella's voice, described Charlie's friend: a slim young man with a pencil mustache and stubble on his chin who wore a herringbone cap. It was Felix Middleton.

"Taking tea late are we, Mrs. Helliwell?"

Stella fumbled her teacup, spilling some of it into the saucer, when Mr. Coombs, unannounced, strolled into the room. She hastily set it down on the low table in front of her. She tried to catch her mother's eye to suggest she do the same. They had to get out of there. Mama was too focused on the newcomer to notice.

"Charlie. You remember Lady Lyndhurst, and this is her mother, Mrs. Eugene Smith, from America. She'll be staying with us tonight."

"Ladies." Charlie slipped his brown fedora from his head and familiarly tossed it onto the piano.

"Mr. Coombs." Luckily Mama's hearty greeting covered Stella's half-choked mumble.

"I was just telling Lady Lyndhurst about your friend's visit and my surprise to learn about your interest in cathedrals," Mrs. Helliwell said.

Charlie caught Stella's eye, and the menace she saw there pinned her to her chair. She swallowed hard.

"Ah, they don't want to hear about that. But were you aware, Mrs. Helliwell," he said, keeping his cool stare on Stella but bending toward the widow's ear as if passing along a bit of harmless gossip, "that Lady Lyndhurst found two dead bodies this week?" He laughed lightly as Mrs. Helliwell gasped in horror. "Who knows how many more there'll be before her honeymoon's over?"

The veiled threat galvanized Stella. At the same time her muscles stiffened in fear, she sprung from her seat, her shed gloves dropping from her lap to the floor. The other women flinched at her sudden agitation. Mr. Coombs didn't move except to squint suspiciously. She purposely avoided his intense scrutiny as she snatched her mother's teacup out of her hands, her palms sweating. It slipped from her hands, landing on the carpet with a clink as the cup toppled over. Luckily, it was empty.

"Stella, what's gotten into you?" Mama said, retrieving the teacup and saucer and placing them on the table. She then picked up Stella's gloves.

Mrs. Helliwell, her hand on her heart again, said, "Then it's true, m'lady? You did find two dead bodies?"

Stella wanted to shout, "And Charlie killed at least one of them," but instead, said, "I'm so sorry, Mama, but I forgot we were supposed to meet Lord Lyndhurst and Detective Sergeant Glenshaw after the Wingrove inquest for supper."

"I thought you and your husband were planning a quiet late supper alone?" Mama said, obviously perplexed.

"We changed our plans." Stella grabbed her mother's arm and forcefully pulled her mother clumsily to her feet. Concern flashed across her mother's face. Stella regretted the deception, but there was no way to explain their danger. She warded off any more questions by declaring, "We're already running late."

"Oh, dear. I've kept you too long, haven't I, Your Lady-ship," Mrs. Helliwell fretted. "I do apologize."

"No, Mrs. Helliwell, you've been very nice," Stella said, seizing up her mother's overnight bag. If nothing else, she could try to hit Charlie with it if he came after them. "But we really must be going. Come on, Mama." With her head turned away from Charlie, Stella mouthed "Go!" to her mother, who shrugged in confusion, unable to read Stella's lips.

"I'll see you out," Charlie said, his hand straying to his hip as if to reassure himself something hidden was still there.

Was that a bump beneath his hand? Couldn't he easily hide a gun tucked into his waistband? As an afterthought, Stella peeked down at his shoes. They were black, patent leather Ox-fords. Just as Mr. Haigh described.

"No need," Stella said, waving him off as nonchalantly as she could but unable to hide her trembling hand. "We'll see our-selves out."

In a panic, her whole body trembling now, Stella smashed her shin against the low table as she stepped forward, urging her mother ahead of her.

Ow!

"Nonsense," Charlie said. "How impolite would I be if I didn't show you such little courtesy, m'lady?" He spoke the last two words accentuated with sarcasm.

As he stepped toward them, Mrs. Helliwell leaped to her feet. "Oh, dear. How right you are, Charlie, to remind me of my duty. I'll see the ladies out."

"But, Mrs. Helliwell—"

She placed a hand on Charlie's shoulder. "You help yourself to some gingerbread. I'll be right back."

Stella's stomach lurched at the fury and hostility on Charlie's taut, reddened face when Mrs. Helliwell's back was turned.

"When do you think you'll return, Mrs. Smith?" Mrs. Helliwell asked, once in the vestibule. "I don't want to inconvenience you in any way, mind, but I do lock the front door at nine o'clock."

"I don't reckon I know," Mama said, holding Stella's gloves out for her to take. "I do hope before then."

Maddened by their oblivious banter, Stella didn't wait for their hostess to open the door. She grasped the handle like a lifeline and flung the door open. She grabbed her mother's arm, yanking her forward as they stumbled down the stairs and into the street.

"Slow down, sugar! What has gotten into you? You don't even have your gloves on yet."

With her chest tightening in frustration and fear, Stella pushed her mother ahead of her and screamed, "He's got a gun, Mama! Run!"

CHAPTER 31

Lyndy stifled a yawn as the hansom cab rocked back and forth over the uneven street. The inquest had been tedious. There hadn't been any surprises, not even that Miss Pegg, clutching Morgan's arm, had joined the dead man's nephew in attending. Eliza, the chambermaid, had described her discovery of Wingrove's body. Dr. Bell had recounted his medical examination of it, giving his professional opinion on the cause of death—gas poisoning. Glenshaw testified that he'd interviewed all pertinent witnesses and inspected the victim's room, including the chimney, giving into evidence the contents of the dead man's room. He referred to Wingrove's apparent frailty and acknowledged that the missing chocolate formula had cast some initial suspicion on the case. Now, with the formula turning up, he confidently concluded the man's death was an accident. He'd said nothing of the missing pillows or the missing suite key. The detective mentioned the feathers Stella found (without giving her credit, mind) only after Mr. Haigh, newly released from hospital, sprang from his chair to reiterate that the chimney had been cleaned in the last fortnight. Glenshaw suggested that the culprit was a recent blockage due to a bird's nest. With that, the ruling had come quickly—death by accident or misadventure.

Stella won't be pleased or surprised.

Lyndy leaned back against the smooth, black fabric lining the cab, allowing his mind to drift to more pleasant thoughts. Now that all this distasteful business was behind them, he and Stella could at long last resume their honeymoon. They'd planned a quiet dinner in their suite at the hotel, alone. Lyndy couldn't wait.

"Detective! Stop!"

At the sound of his wife's desperate cry, Lyndy bolted upright, craning his neck around the edge of the cab's open front, searching the street.

With her skirt bunched in one fist, Stella was running and waving frantically at a hansom cab driven by a large, bay Yorkshire Coach Horse in the traffic behind his. Red-faced and out of breath, Stella's mother stood partially bent over half a block behind. Lost in his thoughts, Lyndy had missed seeing them. The cab carrying Detective Sergeant Glenshaw navigated around an empty delivery wagon and pulled to the curb. When the inquest had concluded, Lyndy, Glenshaw, Morgan with Miss Pegg, and Dr. Bell had gone their separate ways. Unbeknownst to Lyndy, Detective Sergeant Glenshaw had been heading in the same direction and following not far behind.

Lyndy pounded at the back wall of his cab. "Stop!"

The moment the cab lurched to a halt, Lyndy vaulted from it, his shoes hitting hard against the pavement. He raced toward Stella, who was speaking to the detective still ensconced inside the other cab. She was gesturing in the direction of the hotel.

"Oi!" the driver of Lyndy's cab yelled, afraid he'd not get his fare.

"Stay until I return," Lyndy shouted over his shoulder.

Glenshaw had opened the door to the cab, and Stella was clambering in when Lyndy reached them. "What's this then?"

"Lyndy!" Stella said. "Charlie Coombs killed Felix Middleton, and he knows I know. I thought he was going to come after Mama and me, but I think he might head for the hotel."

"Why go there and not the railway station?" Lyndy asked.

"He's got a locked cabinet at the hotel. I think that might be where he keeps his money."

Lyndy was dubious, but who was he to question his wife. How often had she been right before?

"If she's right, we can't waste our time gossiping in the street," Glenshaw said.

"I've got a cab waiting," Lyndy said after a moment's hesitation. (Why should they even involve themselves in this?) "Stella, I'll go with Glenshaw. You fetch your mother."

Despite his misgivings, he'd had to offer to help. If a dangerous criminal was at large, he had no intention of letting Stella face him alone. Which knowing her, she most certainly would.

Stella wavered, her foot still on the step of the hansom cab. For a moment, Lyndy thought she'd object to the compromise, but then she nodded and ran back to her mother. As it was, with Glenshaw having to stop by the railway station to alert the station officer of Coombs's possible escape attempt, the two cabs arrived at the hotel at the same time, and Stella, taking the steps two at a time, reached the doors before either of the two men. Mrs. Smith wisely stayed safely behind in the cab.

Stella didn't wait for the doorman to let them in. She yanked the door open and dashed inside, the men close on her heels. As they hastened toward the registration desk, an elderly couple in evening dress skittered out of the way. Max Telford glanced up from the registration book laid out on the desk, forewarned of their approach by the rapid tapping of their shoes on the marble floor.

"What can I do for you this evening, Lady—"

"Have you seen Mr. Coombs?" she asked, slightly breathless.

"I have, actually. He just popped in, though it's his day off."

"Where is he?" Glenshaw demanded.

The detective produced his truncheon, brandishing it as if he meant to beat the answer out of the porter. Shrinking back in fear, Max pointed mutely at the door behind him. The detective shoved his way past Stella, pushing her backward as he made his way around the desk. Her shoulder collided with Lyndy's. Before Lyndy could protest the rough treatment, the detective put a finger to his lips to silence them all, then turned and kicked the door open. A loud crack echoed throughout the lobby as the hinges broke. With his club held at ready, Glenshaw charged in. A heavy thud followed a cry of pain. Stella's mouth opened, the worrying question written on her face. Who now lay on the floor, Mr. Coombs or Detective Sergeant Glenshaw? Lyndy maneuvered Stella behind him and waited.

"Will someone bloody get me summat to tie this bugger up with?" Glenshaw shouted. "And call the station! I need backup."

Stella dashed toward the windows and untied the gold-braided ropes that held the drapery back. As Max Telford rang for more police, Lyndy followed Stella into the austere room that reminded him of a diminutive servants' hall lined with lockers. Mr. Coombs lay on his stomach. The detective straddled his back, his knees pinning the clerk's shoulders against the floor. Sprinkled about the linoleum were several one-pound notes, and on the far side of the room, as if flung or kicked, a brown canvas kit bag lay open, the barrel of a gun sticking out. Glenshaw reached for the ties Stella passed him and secured Mr. Coombs's hands behind his back while Lyndy crossed the room, picking up the pound notes as he went. He retrieved the kit bag, which besides containing the gun, held a large bundle of one-, five-, and ten-pound notes tied with a rubber band.

"My, bribery pays, doesn't it?" Lyndy quipped.

"That's mine," Mr. Coombs hissed.

"Couldn't leave York without your stash, eh, Coombs?" Glenshaw said. "Though I do wonder why you kept it here?"

"I'm guessing he didn't want to take the chance that Widow Helliwell accidentally found it," Stella said.

"Get off me, you bloody royal sympathizer," Mr. Coombs said, his face contorted with rage.

With his prisoner immobilized, Glenshaw took the kit bag from Lyndy and peeked in. "Brought that gun back from the war, did you, soldier?"

Mr. Coombs struggled beneath the detective in protest, but he wasn't going anywhere. Despite the clerk's brawn, Glenshaw outmatched him in size.

"Soldier?" Lyndy asked. "Wasn't Middleton in the army?"

Glenshaw nodded, a self-satisfied grin spreading across his lips. "Indeed, he was. Hence the name, 'the Private.' And this gun of Mr. Coombs's was common among officers during the Boer War. Is that why you fancied Their Royal Highnesses dead? Because of some complaint you had against the war?"

"You're bloody right, I have a complaint."

"I served too, Coombs." He pointed first to his drooping eyelid and then raised his palm to reveal the scar there. "So, I don't want to hear it." He slapped Mr. Coombs on the side of his head. "But I appreciate you confessing to being Middleton's accomplice."

Mr. Coombs spat. "Accomplice? That idiot couldn't eat his way out of a chocolate box."

"So, Mr. Middleton did use the box of chocolates Mr. Wingrove gave him to house the bomb," Stella said. "Did either of you kill Mr. Wingrove?"

Mr. Coombs scoffed. "Clearly, Private Middleton couldn't kill a pampered royal. And as to me killing that old businessman, why would I? He earned his wages. Wasn't given a posh life handed to him, was he?" He twisted his head as best he could in his compromised position and smirked up at Stella. "Besides, Wingrove offered me money to vex a pair of aristocratic twats."

"How dare you!" Infuriated by this vulgar, reprehensible insult (and in the presence of his wife!) Lyndy lunged forward, preparing to smash his fist into the clerk's cheek.

"Oi!" Glenshaw shouted, reading Lyndy's intent. It was enough to make Lyndy hesitate. "I need him conscious, Lord Lyndhurst. He's still got some answering to do."

Lyndy took a few steps back, the moment of anger having passed, and tugged at the lapels of his overcoat.

"Now, Coombs," Glenshaw continued, "you were saying?"

"I have nowt to say to you."

"How'd you know Middleton would be at the railway station? Did you follow him? Plan to meet there when the job was done?"

"Job wasn't done, was it?"

"He was trying to abscond, was he, and you were waiting for him?"

Mr. Coombs struggled against his restraints. "Get off me!"

"I'll take that as a yes. I agree Middleton was a mug, but why kill him, Coombs?" When Mr. Coombs sniffed contemptuously in response, Glenshaw dug his knee into the clerk's shoulder until the man beneath him cried out in pain. "Why kill him?"

"Because the bugger was a loose cannon, like his painting of the Kings' Screen. That stunt could've cost us everything. If you bobbies were even a bit clever, you might've figured out what we were up to. Besides, Felix had become unreliable and ineffective. Those bloody princesses are still breathing, ain't they?"

"No thanks to a rotter like you."

Without warning, Glenshaw wrenched Mr. Coombs's tied arms upward with a sudden jerk. After a sickening pop, Coombs screamed.

"Charlie Coombs, I'm arresting you in connection with the murder of Felix Middleton and the attempted murder of Her Royal Highness, Princess Beatrice, and Her Highness, Princess Victoria Eugenie. That's high treason, that. I'll see you hang."

Despite the man's groans of pain, the detective hauled him to his feet and shoved him out the door.

CHAPTER 32

Stella never understood how the sun could shine while some-one was laid to rest. This was England. Shouldn't it be raining or misty, at least? Yet the morning was crisp and clear as she stood next to yet another grave, the strong scent of freshly turned soil in the air. She hardly remembered attending her fa-ther's funeral, but he was at the forefront of her mind as she stared into the gaping hole in the ground at Mr. Wingrove's cof-fin. Beside it was his wife's grave—a slightly sunken plot with moss already spotting the stone with patches of green. A slight breeze rustled the dried leaves on the oak towering above her head.

Two funerals in two weeks.

As if sensing her sorrow, Mama reached out for Stella's hand and squeezed it. Last night, after a second trip to the police sta-tion to make statements, Stella, Lyndy, and her mother had re-turned to the Majestic for a late supper. Mama had still been willing to stay at Mrs. Helliwell's Boardinghouse, but neither Stella nor Lyndy would hear of it. They'd gotten her a room, two floors down, and had slept better knowing she was safe.

Mama let go of Stella's hand when the Anglican priest stopped talking, and only birdsong, the clatter of wooden wagon wheels, and the distant whinny of a horse interrupted the silence. Morgan threw a clump of soil on the coffin. After a few more words from the clergyman, the mourners, made up of Morgan, Miss Pegg and her father, Stella and her mother, and Lyndy turned away as men in thread-worn brown suits with hands like leather snatched up their shovels and began filling in the grave.

"We are going to have a small gathering at our house," Miss Pegg said lightly. "I hope you can come."

"My mother has a train to catch," Stella said, "but we'll be there."

They walked in silence down a tree-lined avenue, each lost in their thoughts. As they passed, Stella, her arm looped around Lyndy's, read the names etched into nearby headstones, green with lichen, jutting up from the ground in rows: Agnes Bell, Joseph Richard Terry, Florence Edith Masterman, Amelia Wrigglesworth, Lawrence Hawkswell. A lone figure emerged when they came to a gray, stone chapel lined with columns, built to resemble a Grecian temple.

Stella froze, halting Lyndy in the process. Her mother, taken by surprise, stepped on Stella's heel.

"Stella?" Lyndy said, glancing over his shoulder to share a concerned look with his mother-in-law. "What is it?"

Stella tightened her grip on his arm. "Lyndy," she whispered in his ear, "I think I know who killed Mr. Wingrove. It was—"

"Dr. Bell," Morgan called, startling Stella into silence. "I wasn't certain we'd see you again to say good-bye."

Dr. Bell descended the few steps of the chapel to join them. "I came to pay my respects."

"How kind of you," Miss Pegg said, "though I'm sorry to say you missed the service."

"Was it nice and proper, then?"

"What else?" Morgan said.

"Mama, this is Dr. Bertram Bell," Stella said. "Dr. Bell, may I introduce my mother, Mrs. Eugene Smith. Dr. Bell is also a guest at the Majestic, and we've all become fast friends."

"Please to meet you, madam," Dr. Bell said, touching the brim of his tan fedora, encircled with a band of black ribbon.

"Likewise, Doctor."

"It was Dr. Bell who saved my fella after the bomb, Mrs. Smith," Miss Pegg said, gazing up at her fiancé. She licked her finger and then rubbed at an imperceptible smudge on his cheek.

"Then I reckon he's a good friend to have around," Mama said. Miss Pegg nodded enthusiastically.

"We're gathering at our house," Mr. Pegg said. "It's the Georgian town house on St. Martin's Lane. You are most welcome to join us, Dr. Bell, after all you've done."

"After all I've done," Dr. Bell mumbled quietly under his breath. "Thank you," he said, addressing the Peggs, "but I'm due in Durham tonight. Another cathedral beckons." He forced a chuckle.

After a round of good-byes, the others ambled toward the gatehouse at the cemetery's entrance; their cabs waited beyond the wrought-iron fence. Holding her ground, Stella watched Dr. Bell stride down the lane in the opposite direction.

"Sugar? Are you coming?" her mother called.

"I'll be back in a minute." She scampered away, pulling out the hat pin and slipping her hat off. It would only slow her down. "And don't worry! We've got plenty of time until your train leaves."

"Now, where's she off to?" she heard Mama say. Too far away to hear him, Stella could imagine Lyndy's unamused retort.

She briskly made her way to Dr. Bell's side, who'd stopped in front of a well-settled grave. Stella had seen this name before. *Agnes Bell.*

"Your wife." It wasn't a question.

An almost imperceptible nod was Dr. Bell's reply.

"For some time, I've suspected Mr. Wingrove wasn't murdered, after all, but took his own life." She spoke quietly, gently, monitoring him out of the corner of her eye. "It would explain why he wanted the suite for one night." When Dr. Bell continued to stare down at the grave in silence, she added, "I also think someone helped him cover it up. Until now I didn't know it was you. I still don't know why."

Dr. Bell sighed. Then he motioned for her to follow him to a nearby bench, set beneath the thick, outstretched branches of an ancient, gnarly oak. Dried leaves littered the ground. Lyndy, with her mother beside him, a restraining hand on his arm, watched her from a distance. Even from here, Stella could see the tightening of her husband's jaw. He wasn't happy. But would Dr. Bell speak freely in front of Lyndy? She couldn't take the chance. She grinned and waved to reassure him before joining Dr. Bell at the bench.

"How did you know it was me?" the doctor asked when they'd sat for several silent moments together.

"The formula. The morning . . . after it happened, you gave Morgan the chocolate box the formula was hidden in."

"He could've found it on his doorstep as everyone assumed."

"After going to such lengths to safeguard the formula from Miss Evans? No. Mr. Wingrove would never have left its discovery to chance. He'd give it to someone he trusted implicitly, ensuring Morgan, and Morgan alone, would receive the hidden formula. You, Dr. Bell."

"I admit Horace entrusted me with the formula, but his death was ruled an accident."

"Officially, yes. Again, it goes back to the formula. Ever since learning Mr. Wingrove hid it purposefully, I've suspected he's been behind everything that's happened. Even his death. His fingerprints are everywhere. He got his affairs in order, very recently, to the point of compelling his solicitor to track down Morgan at Hubberholme Park. He bribed Mr. Coombs to spend his last night in the suite that meant so much to him and his late wife. He arranged for you to deliver the formula into Morgan's hands without Miss Evans knowing about it. He even sent you a letter, didn't he?"

Dr. Bell started. "How could you possibly know?"

"I was there when you got it, remember? It upset you. I took a guess it was from Mr. Wingrove."

Dr. Bell pulled the letter from his breast pocket and handed it to Stella. He'd folded and unfolded it so many times, deep creases lined the paper. It was a brief but sincere note signed *Horace* and written on Majestic Hotel stationery, thanking *his dear Bertram* for easing his mind as he planned to end the suffering of his body. It also contained a certificate of shares in the Wingrove company.

"He promised me he wouldn't give me anything. I don't want a reward for doing this." Dr. Bell threw the certificate of shares into the leaves at their feet.

"If you have no use for it"—Stella leaned down and picked up the certificate—"I know a widow with children who might benefit." Stella could imagine what Mr. Coombs's conviction as a murderer would do to Mrs. Helliwell's reputation and her boardinghouse bookings.

"If it will do some good, you're welcome to it."

"Thank you." Stella dropped the certificate in her handbag and cinched the string. "What I still don't know, Dr. Bell, is why he needed to cover it up."

"Why do you assume he wanted it covered up?"

"Because of the missing pillows. Someone removed them from the chimney and disposed of them after the fact. I assume Mr. Wingrove gave you his key?"

Dr. Bell sighed. He reached into his pants pocket and produced a long, skinny, yellow brass key. He stared at it lying in his palm as he spoke.

"A couple of days before, Horace asked me to join him in York. As I can never visit the Minster too many times, I heartily agreed." He made a fist around the key. "You have to believe I hadn't the faintest idea what he was planning."

"And when you got here, he laid it all out?"

Dr. Bell nodded. "He invited me to his room, handed me this key, and before I realized it"—he snapped his fingers—"he was making me promise to return late enough for the gas to have taken its effects. Helps to be an insomniac, I suppose." He chuckled mirthlessly. "As you suspected, I removed and disposed of the pillows Horace had stuffed up the chimney. I didn't think to look for the broom that he must've sweet-talked a maid into providing him. And then, when his body was found, I was to verify gas poisoning. It was the truth, if not in its entirety."

"But why? Why involve you?"

"It had to be deemed an accident. Otherwise, his suicide would taint his legacy and Morgan's fresh start with the business. Besides, Horace was convinced he wouldn't be given a proper Christian burial if the truth was known. He was haunted by stories of people suspected of suicide, buried at the crossroads with a stake through their bodies. That's since been outlawed, of course, but as it was, Horace was old enough to remember his father's funeral, at night without a Christian service."

His father killed himself too? How horrible.

"So that's where you came in. As a doctor, you couldn't ethically assist in Horace's suicide, but what he asked of you, you could do. You could help him make it appear like an accident and testify at the inquest to that effect."

"Yes."

"I assume his health had something to do with it?"

"As I suggested before, he suffered from chorea, and his prognosis was dire. He had months, not years, to live. He hated the idea of being bedridden and completely dependent on others, robbed of his speech, his ability to swallow, his dignity."

"And that's why you helped him. Because you've seen how devastating his disease can be."

Dr. Bell gazed out across the field of headstones and, seeing something Stella would never know, said nothing.

Stella glanced over toward the grave of Agnes Bell. "Your wife died of the same disease, didn't she?" A single tear dripped down Dr. Bell's cheek. "And this disease runs in families, doesn't it?"

"It does."

"Was your wife Horace Wingrove's daughter?"

"Yes. My darling Agnes."

Still keeping his distance, Lyndy abruptly coughed. Stella held up her palm, asking him to stay put. He forced another cough but didn't interfere. Dr. Bell gave no sign he'd noticed Lyndy's impatience. His arms hung limp at his sides, the key still clenched in his fist, but he continued to stare straight ahead.

"Why doesn't Morgan recognize you?" she said.

"He was at boarding school when Agnes and I were married. By the time he returned, Agnes was dead, and I'd joined a practice in Leeds, so we've never met."

"So, with that terrible bond between you, that grief you shared, when Mr. Wingrove asked for your help, you couldn't say no."

Although terrible, it was a bond Stella almost envied. It was forged out of love. As a child, suffering the loss of her mother, she received no empathy from her father, as he knew his wife was still alive. And now that he was dead, no one else grieved for Elijah Kendrick, least of all his wife.

"That's where you're wrong, Lady Lyndhurst. I could've said no. I should've said no." He raised his clenched fist, his knuckles whitening around the key as he glared at his hand. "I'm a doctor. I've spent my whole life trying to heal people."

Stella laid her hand on his arm. He flinched, but she didn't take it away. "But you couldn't save your wife or Horace, could you?"

"God knows I tried. I read everything about chorea I could find. I even contacted Dr. Huntington, but there's no cure. The medicines ease the symptoms for a while, but the result is the same in the end. It's horrible." The key clattered against the stone bench when he dropped it, burying his face in the palms of his hands.

"So, you decided that if you couldn't relieve his physical suffering," Stella said, "the next best thing was to give an old man some peace of mind."

"And paid for it with my own. Suicide is still a crime, and I helped Horace conceal it." His head jerked up, his muscles beneath her hand tightening. "Are you going to notify the police?"

"About what? Detective Sergeant Glenshaw is more than happy with the coroner's ruling."

"Thank you."

"What will you do now?"

"Go to Durham as I planned. Surrounding myself with the awesome power of God and the ingenuity of man has never failed to soothe."

"Are you going to tell Morgan who you are? I think he'd welcome having a cousin-in-law."

"Maybe someday." He stood, brushed a crushed leaf from his leg, and forced a smile. "Well, I better be off. Good-bye, Lady Lyndhurst. Be well."

"Good-bye, Dr. Bell."

The doctor slipped his hands into his pockets and wandered away, leaving Stella awash with melancholy.

"Stella?" Lyndy had approached while Stella had been fixated on Dr. Bell's departure. He'd come alone. Stella glanced up the lane and saw her mother had joined the others. "Was it him? Did he kill the chocolatier?"

"No, Mr. Wingrove killed himself. He was going to die soon regardless and wanted to go out on his own terms. Dr. Bell merely helped him make it appear like an accident."

"And you let him walk away? I can understand the secretary, but—"

"Dr. Bell was Wingrove's son-in-law, Lyndy. He watched his young, newlywed wife die of the same horrible disease."

When he grasped the parallel between Dr. Bell and himself, denial, horror, empathy flashed across Lyndy's face. To hide his raw reaction, he pulled up the collar of his overcoat against a nonexistent wind. "I can't imagine what he went through."

"No, neither can I." Trying to shake the sadness welling inside, she rose, clutching the brim of her hat in her fist. She wrapped her arm around Lyndy's and leaned her cheek against his shoulder as they slowly strolled toward the entrance gates. "Time to see Mama off?" she said, forcing a gaiety she didn't feel. "After that, we have the rest of our honeymoon to enjoy."

"Indeed!" But Lyndy wasn't fooled. He kissed her hair, his lips lingering a moment or two on her head. "Have I told you how much I adore you today, Lady Lyndhurst?"

That made her smile. "Yes, Lord Lyndhurst, you did, but it bears repeating, don't you think?"

ACKNOWLEDGMENTS

There was a time when I wondered if this book would ever be. Happily, for me, I have a wonderful network of friends, family, and fellow writers who never lost the faith. For them and their undying support, I will always be grateful.

Although I can't name everyone who helped me see this book finished, I'd like to give a special shout out to my fellow Sleuths in Time: Jessica Ellicott, Colleen Gleason, Nancy Herriman, D.E. Ireland, Alyssa Maxwell, Erica Ruth Neubauer, Victoria Thompson, and Ashley Weaver whose encouragement kept me going as well as to Anna Lee Huber for her thoughtful words of advice.

To my agent, John Talbot and the team at Kensington: John Scognamiglio, Larissa Ackerman, Robin Cook and the creative pair behind my amazing cover art, Andrew Davidson and Janice Rossi Schaus, I want to express how grateful I am to still be working with you.

And to my family—Brian for suggesting we spend Christmas in Yorkshire, Mom for reading every word I wrote, multiple times and Maya for her many creative plot twists—I couldn't love y'all more.

Author's Note

A few years ago, I was lucky enough to spend Christmastime in York and the Yorkshire Dales National Park and couldn't imagine a better place for Stella and Lyndy to visit. While there, I learned that not only is horse racing in York celebrated for its ancient pedigree (going back to Emperor Severus in Roman times) but that its racecourse boasts the world's first grandstand. When I discovered that a historical visit by HRH Princess Beatrice and HH Princess Victoria Eugenie "Ena" to York for an unveiling of a statue of HM Queen Victoria lined up with Stella and Lyndy's honeymoon, I knew it must be fate. Since then, I've uncovered a wealth of historical facts that I've either interwoven into the story unchanged or as inspiration for a fictionalized subplot.

York Minster did (and still does) have a specialized constabulary responsible for the cathedral's security. Charlotte Brontë visited the Foundling Hospital in London in 1853 and all three Brontë sisters were known to take excursions to Bolton Abbey, the peculiar half-ruin, half parish church set on the banks of the River Wharfe. The stepping stones, a crossing point for lay workers at the Priory, are still a popular draw for tourists.

Queen Victoria's granddaughter, Princess Ena, was indeed the target of an anarchist bombing plot. However, the historical event took place not in York, as it's portrayed in this book, but in Madrid. Princess Ena married the King of Spain, on the 31st of May 1906. As she and her new royal husband's carriage made its way along the wedding route, lined with hundreds of thousands of well-wishers, a powerful bomb exploded near their carriage. Thirty-seven people were killed, including a footman on the royal carriage and over a hundred people were injured, some of them seriously. Seven of the eight carriage horses were killed as well. Amazingly both King and Queen of Spain escaped serious injury.

York, although famous for its gothic cathedral, its rambling alleys, and its rich, ancient history, is also called "The Chocolate City." And for good reason. In the nineteenth and early twentieth century, York was home to not one but three very successful confectionery companies: Craven's, Terry's, and Rowntree's. Rowntree's (founded 1862), on which "Rountree's" in the book is very loosely-based, is well-known for its Fruit Pastilles, Fruit Gum, and for its inventing both the Kit Kat and Aero. The modern-day company is now run by Nestlé and its York site is one of the largest confectionery factories in the world. In the book, I respelled Rowntree to Rountree to reflect the surname of my fictitious characters, Sir Owen and his mother, Lady Rountree. (Believe it or not, I had named Lyndy's cousin from Yorkshire, Sir Owen Rountree by complete coincidence. So of course, when I discovered Rowntree's of York, I knew I had to incorporate a fictionalized version of the company into the story.) The Pegg family, (again, purely figments of my imagination), weren't based in any way on the actual owners. In contrast to Rountree's, Wingrove Confectionery is a completely fictionalized company. Wingrove's Cream Milk, however, is a direct tribute to Dairy Milk, the Cadbury chocolate that swept England when it was introduced in 1905 allowing Cadbury to pull ahead of its competitors.